COLD SILENCE

ALSO BY DANIELLE GIRARD

Chasing Darkness
Ruthless Game
Savage Art

COLD
SILENCE

Danielle Girard

AN ONYX BOOK

ONYX
Published by New American Library, a division of
Penguin Putnam Inc., 375 Hudson Street,
New York, New York 10014, U.S.A.
Penguin Books Ltd, 80 Strand,
London WC2R 0RL, England
Penguin Books Australia Ltd, Ringwood,
Victoria, Australia
Penguin Books Canada Ltd, 10 Alcorn Avenue,
Toronto, Ontario, Canada M4V 3B2
Penguin Books (N.Z.) Ltd, 182–190 Wairau Road,
Auckland 10, New Zealand

Penguin Books Ltd, Registered Offices:
Harmondsworth, Middlesex, England

ISBN 0-7394-3015-7

Copyright © Danielle Girard, 2002
All rights reserved

REGISTERED TRADEMARK—MARCA REGISTRADA

Printed in the United States of America

PUBLISHER'S NOTE
This is a work of fiction. Names, characters, places, and incidents either are
the product of the author's imagination or are used fictitiously, and any
resemblance to actual persons, living or dead, business establishments,
events, or locales is entirely coincidental.

For Jack,
May life treat you to many years of adventure and
excitement, tamed by the shelter of
good friends and much family.

For Steve,
As you enter this new phase, I hope you keep in
mind how talented and bright you are.
Remember those things and be true to yourself.
Everything else will follow.

For Pat Frovarp, owner of Once Upon a Crime,
To a passionate bookseller who gave this new
writer a chance. Thank you.
And for Ryan.

ACKNOWLEDGMENTS

The words may be familiar but their intent is as genuine as the first time I wrote them. Thank you to: Chris, Claire, Jack, Nicole, Blake, Luke, Mom, Dad, Tom, Steve, Bob, Donna, Sue, Marcie, Sharon, and everyone else who listened to me complain about lack of time and sleep. And especially to those very talented writers who read and reread: Diana Dempsey, Sonia Rossney, Taylor Chase, Lisa Hughey, Malia Martin, and Monica McLean.

And to the agents, officers, linguists, and technofolk who answered all my questions, including but not limited to: Andrew Black, FBI, San Francisco; Frank Bochte, FBI, Chicago; Andrea Wagner, Santa Clara County Coroner's Office; Dr. Steve Heydon, Bohart Museum, Department of Entomology, University of California, Davis; Sonia Rossney, Mei Lau, Tonia Tersigni Ho, and Stephen Vilke.

And finally a very special thank-you to Helen, and to Genny.

Prologue

The acrid taste of ash was gritty on her tongue. Heat trapped her like a burning timber on her chest. The one thing missing was the shriek of the smoke detector. It sat silent above, the unlit light a dull red through the smoke. There would be no alarms, no quick response of fire engines. *They* would have made sure. And yet, despite that, Megan Riggs felt an almost giddy sense of relief. It was over. They had come and now she would test the plan she had mapped out day after day and week after week. The only thing causing the dense thunking in her chest as she rolled off the bed and onto the floor was Ryan. She had to get to Ryan.

She waved at the smoke that clouded her vision. She focused on movement, letting her mind roll over the realities.

She refused to die. For Ryan's sake, for Mark's sake, she wouldn't give up. Sweat already beading on her lip, she swallowed another mouthful of thick, smoky air and pushed forward. She pulled the gun from the spot between the mattress and the old rotting box spring and checked that it was loaded. Then she towed herself along the floor with her moist hands, wiping them on her side as she went. In the distance, she heard the wail of the Devereaux's baby downstairs and the commanding shouts of Jack directing his family out of the lower level of the house. She couldn't go out the main door. That would make it too easy for them.

She quickly tied a discarded T-shirt from the floor over her face to ease her breathing and moved like a choking lizard. She and Ryan needed to be long gone before the fire department got here.

Flames had begun to eat her blue-and-yellow floral wallpaper on the far side of her bedroom, and she scrambled faster to escape the chunks of fiery plaster falling from the ceiling. Heat singed her leg as a flame caught the pant leg of her sweats. She spun around and pounded the fire out with a shoe from the ground, breathless and shaking.

Pressing forward, her fingers found the backpack she'd prepared for such an occasion under her dresser, and she yanked it toward her, continuing across the room on her stomach. Ryan. She had to get Ryan.

Her hands were black from soot and it was already clinging in her throat and nose. The smoke seemed to sink lower with each motion, and she knew it wouldn't be long before it smothered her. She reached for the doorknob and prayed the heat hadn't warped the door.

It was cooler than she'd expected. The fire must have been started in the living room. Tucked in the small bedroom at the back of the house by the bathroom, Ryan would be safe. He would be okay. Losing Mark had been bad enough. She couldn't bear to lose them both.

Curving her fingers along the underside of the

door, she pulled it open. The door stuck and then released as a rush of smoke covered her. She guarded her nose and mouth with the T-shirt, coughing, and pushed herself onward.

Closing the door behind her to slow the spread of fire, she scrambled on her hands and knees down the short hallway. The heat scalded her skin and face.

She couldn't take any risks. She had the training for this sort of situation. It'd been fifteen years since she trained to be an agent—fifteen years since she'd been made to shoot and run and swim and complete the obstacle course, but she had been convinced it would all just come back. And it had.

The smoke's dark clouds were illuminated by the flames, which were beginning to lick the floor beneath the bedroom door behind her. The heat and smoke made it hard to see shapes, so she followed the floor with her palms. The thought of her five-year-old son sitting in his bedroom, terrified, made her almost desperate to scream out to him. But she wouldn't. She wouldn't risk letting someone know that she was alive. "I'm coming, baby," she whispered instead.

She longed to hear him whimpering in the distance, awakened from one of his terrible dreams. His room was too far. She had always hated how the two bedrooms were laid out at opposite ends. But of the apartments she'd seen, this had been the best. Her meager salary didn't afford her much in the way of choice. She'd anticipated this moment, needing to get to him in an emergency. She would do it.

She reached Ryan's room and saw him, facedown on the floor.

"No," she said in a sob, pulling him toward her.

"Ryan." She turned him over and lifted his head onto her lap and felt for the pulse in his throat. It was there, strong and solid. Thank God. He'd fallen from the bed, maybe passed out from the smoke, but he was alive. Now she needed to get them out of here.

She paused, wondering if her plan would work. She caught herself and forced the doubt from her mind. She'd practiced this from start to finish dozens of times. Only she'd never had Ryan with her.

She moved them toward the small balcony that was supposed to be a monument to the French in old New Orleans. She'd warned Ryan never to go out there. She hadn't been sure it would hold them both. Now she knew it was their only chance.

Taking Ryan with one arm, Megan sucked in a deep breath and slid them along the floor to the window. Her eyes closed against the fierce heat and smoke, she moved cautiously until she felt the wall against her outstretched hand. She dropped her face and sucked in a deep breath and then forced air into Ryan's lungs with CPR.

"Hang in there, buddy. We're going to make it." They had to survive.

She found the handle to the old balcony door and pulled off the two-by-four she'd used to block Ryan from climbing out. On the far side of the balcony was a small ledge. Beyond that, there was a narrow stretch of roof that would get them to the building next door. From there, they could traverse to the building farther down where the car was parked.

The window's glass was cool against her fingertips and she could almost feel the fresh air outside. Using the edge of Ryan's blanket, she cranked down the latch and pushed the old window out. The hinges squeaked but released. She stepped out first, testing the balcony before pulling Ryan out with her.

He was heavy and her biceps ached immediately from the weight of him, but there wasn't time to adjust the load. Instead she pushed the window shut again, and, gripping Ryan with one arm and the ledge with the other hand, she made her way across the narrow landing. She could hear the steady rasp of Ryan's breathing in her ear, and it was all she needed to push her onward. Her body pressed to the wall, she crept until she could feel the old ladder to the roof against her shoulder.

From the direction of a window in the building across the street, she heard the rough tones of male voices. She pressed herself against the building, fighting the tremors in her legs and hands.

She knew the harsh Russian accent. She could picture the faces. She'd been waiting for this for two years. And finally, they were here to finish off the business Oskar Kirov had threatened.

You will pay. You and your son will pay for my son's death. I don't care how long it takes.

Forcing herself forward, she lifted Ryan up over her left shoulder and stepped onto the first rung of the fire escape toward the roof. Down below, she could hear the fire engines arrive. She could now see two men standing in a window across the street, pretending to watch the fire. Megan recognized their light hair and angular faces. They were Oskar Kirov's remaining sons. The building cool on her back, she forced a breath. The small balcony outside Ryan's room was hidden from their view, but it wouldn't be long before they realized she wasn't inside her apartment. She only wished the engines had been slower to arrive.

Moving more quickly, she pulled them up the ladder, rung by rung. Her hands were soot-covered and slipped against the old iron. Her arm and back muscles burned, and she tucked her elbow under one of the rungs to leverage her back strength and continue upward. She heard the ladder make a deep moaning sound beneath her and she blinked hard, praying it would hold. It moaned again and she pulled them up another rung. She looked up. Two more. Ryan coughed and she felt his head lift off her shoulder. "Mom?"

Afraid he would look down and yell, Megan hurried to push herself off the last step and sprang for the edge of the roof. She laid Ryan down on the gravel surface of the roof.

His face was covered with soot, but she kissed his cheek and whispered to him, "Come on, buddy."

Ryan opened his eyes and coughed again and Megan helped him sit up. "Are they here to get us, Mom?"

As he opened his mouth to talk, Megan pulled him close and hugged him. "We're going to be fine."

He looked around and rubbed his eyes. "They found us, didn't they?"

She nodded. "We can't talk now, baby. We need to change our clothes and get out of here. Remember the plan we talked about?"

Ryan looked around the roof. "Are they going to kill us like Daddy?"

She shook her head and touched his hair, his beautiful blondish brown hair. "No way, baby. Not us. But we have to be quiet now. Okay?"

The resignation in his face made Megan want to

cry. "Okay, Ryan," she said, pulling a change of clothes from her pack. "Put these on."

Megan took jeans from the backpack for herself and lay on her back, pulling off her sweatpants and replacing them with jeans. She lifted her dirty shirt over her head and dropped it on the roof, pulling on a plain gray sweatshirt and tucking the gun into her pants. She added a Gap ball cap and turned to help Ryan. He was already dressed. He was too grown-up for five. She tied his shoelaces and looked at his dirty face. Using the edge of her sleeve, she cleaned him up as much as possible.

Then, stuffing their nightclothes back in the bag, she took his hand and pulled him across the roof.

She had money tucked away in a safe-deposit box at a bank thirty miles outside of town under a new name, a name that had been chosen for her years before by Mark, just in case. Once she had that, they were leaving Louisiana.

The FBI had hidden Ryan and her, given them new names, a home. James, they'd called Ryan. And she'd been Mary. Mary and James Hall. Friends she'd trained with, worked with, had sworn they'd be safe. Three months had passed before she'd started to feel Kirov—watching her, waiting.

Paranoid, she'd told herself. Delusional. Tired and worn down from the hours of secretarial work at Tulane University, of trying to help her then three-year-old son understand why he couldn't use his real name, why his daddy didn't come home, why he would never come home again.

At the edge of the first building, she lifted Ryan across the two-foot gap. "Don't look down," she told him. With her holding on, he reached the other side and pulled himself over without ever looking down.

She jumped across and quickly scanned the roof for assailants. Finding none, she rushed onward, Ryan in tow.

"Good job, baby. You're doing great."

Ryan looked behind them again and kept moving.

Just then she heard the distant sounds of breaking glass and curses in the familiar language. She thought the sounds came from the balcony of her apartment.

Ryan was shaking, but she put an iron fist to her own fear. "It's okay," she whispered, pushing him ahead.

She led them to the door at the center of the third roof, tucking Ryan to her side to guard him against any attacks. Pulling out her lock-picking tools, she put them in the lock of the door to the roof access and worked them around as she'd done fifty times before in preparation for this night. The lock clicked open with ease. Pulling the door open, she helped Ryan through and locked the door from the inside.

On the ground floor, she entered the main corridor, looking in both directions before stepping out and opening the door to the basement garage. She took the last flight of stairs, knowing the most difficult part started now.

Inside the garage, she found the 1988 Toyota Corolla that she'd bought for a thousand dollars and kept unregistered in this garage. She never drove it except to let the engine run so it wouldn't be dead when they needed it. She ran her hand along the bumper until she felt the small magnetic box that held the key. She opened the back door first and squeezed Ryan's hand. "Remember how we practiced?"

"Are they coming after us, Mommy? The men who killed Daddy?"

Megan blinked. "No, baby. We're going to be fine. You trust me?"

Ryan nodded silently and curled into a ball in the car, pulling the blanket from the floor over himself.

Megan smiled. "Perfect. We're almost done."

From under the front seat, she pulled out a small bag and dumped the contents on the seat beside her. She put on the gray wig and Irish golf hat and pressed the mustache and beard against her mouth as she had in each practice. Then, making sure her own hair was hidden under the wig, she started the engine.

"You okay back there, buddy?"

"Yeah," came the muffled reply. "Good luck, Mommy."

Megan blinked hard. "Here we go. I'll let you know when the coast is clear."

Ryan didn't respond. For some kids, this would have been a fun game. For Ryan, fear had become his existence. He knew this was how he'd lost his father. Enough of that. The FBI had failed her, but Megan would create her own witness protection program. Ryan would never have to go through anything like this again. She would make sure of it.

Chapter 1

Three Years Later

Cody O'Brien pulled herself into her final sit-up. "Two-fifty," she breathed, wiping her forehead with her sleeve. Rolling onto her stomach, she pressed twenty-five push-ups to complete her round.

She heard the familiar ding of E-mail and stood up from the nine-by-nine rug where she worked out, then crossed the room to the computer and desk that were her office. Three years ago, she never would have imagined life could feel good again. Now, working as a programmer and consultant from home for start-ups in Silicon Valley, Cody had everything she could want for herself and Ryan. R.J., she reminded herself, still fighting calling her son something other than his natural name. Cody, on the other hand, had started to grow on her.

Most of her mail, including her paychecks, came addressed to "Mr. Cody O'Brien." And that was perfect for her. She didn't want to be known. Her jobs were booked through a referral service with whom she'd interviewed three years ago. Almost none of her work was done over the phone and none was in person. It was part of her stipulation. It would have sounded bizarre in the traditional business world, but techies were weird and untraditional; everyone knew it.

She touched her mouse and stared at the request for a follow-up on some work she'd done a few months back. She sat down and typed a quick message to indicate her schedule was open for the work and sent it off. Glancing at her watch, she ran through the office door and up the short flight of stairs into R.J.'s room.

"Sleepyhead, it's time to get up."

The denim lump in the bed moaned and then rolled over.

Cody sat on the edge of the bed, prying the covers out of her son's hands and exposing his face. He squinted at the light and rolled over again, burying his nose in his pillow. Watching him struggle with the mornings always made Cody think of his dad. She tickled him, and he bucked and laughed.

"Come on, up and at 'em."

He rubbed his eyes with balled fists, and Cody could still picture him as an infant doing that same thing. "Can I stay home with you today?"

She shook her head. "No way."

"Ah, Mom." He groaned and tried to dig his way back under the covers. "It's too cold to go to school."

"Too cold? This is California. It's warm here."

"Uh-uh. It's freezing."

"Then you'll have to wear a turtleneck and sweater." Cody stood and stripped the bed, so he had nowhere to hide. "Up, soldier. Right now. I'll make pancakes if you promise to be downstairs in ten minutes. Plus, it's Friday."

"It's Friday?" R.J. sat up in bed. "I'm playing with Peter Landon after school today."

"Okay." Peter Landon had become R.J.'s best friend over the past year. She kept hoping the choice would change, but she shouldn't have complained. Most people would be thrilled to have their son play with Travis Landon's son. Landon was an extremely successful entrepreneur. His first company, Web-Mast, had been a small, unlikely start-up ten years ago. Less than five years ago he'd sold the Web browser software to Yahoo!

Landon's more recent start-up, TecLan, was about to put revolutionary new Web page software on the market. Despite one pesky glitch in testing, the TecLan Pro software was supposed to be the best. And Travis Landon himself was probably worth $100 million on a bad day.

She'd done some work for him here and there, and she saw him often enough when he came to pick up Peter in the evenings. One of those nights, he'd asked her out. She'd had a glass of wine after a long day and had let herself enjoy his easy banter. Pretty soon they were laughing, and he'd suggested dinner. A casual enough proposition, but she'd turned him down flat. Men, and especially high-profile men, were not in her future.

And she would have preferred R.J. had chosen a lower-profile friend. There was still at least an article a week on Landon, his dual life as CEO and single parent, although she'd noticed more of them had started to focus on the software glitch, but that was typical media.

Cody crossed the room, glancing at the computer with the bright fish floating across the screen. Beside it was a stack of computer games. She picked up the one on top: Rogue Warrior. "Don't forget to return his game to him when he's here tonight."

"I won't, Mom. We borrow all the time. He even loant—loaned me his Chicago Bulls jacket."

She ran her hands over the jacket on the back of the chair. "It's nice, but be careful not to get anything on it."

"Yeah." R.J. swung his feet onto the floor and rolled his eyes at her warning.

Cody launched herself at her son, knocking him back onto the bed and tickling him until he was howling.

"Uncle, uncle," R.J. screamed.

Cody rolled off and R.J. promptly started to tickle her. She rolled back and forth, pretending to try to escape him until he finally stopped and they were both breathless.

"Mom?"

"Yeah?"

"You've got roots."

Cody sat up and looked at her son's dark hair. They were light-haired naturally, but she and R.J. had been dyeing their hair since they'd left New Orleans. "Guess it's time for a root party."

"Can we have root-beer floats?"

"Of course. And beetroots."

R.J. scrunched his nose. "I didn't like the beetroots. How about root-beer candy?"

"Sounds good. How about we do it tonight?"

R.J. turned his back to her. "Not tonight, Mom."

Cody went around and sat beside him. "Why not?"

"'Cause I want to play with Peter."

Cody shrugged. "I thought we could do it after he

leaves. Or we can do it tomorrow. Did you want Peter to spend the night?"

R.J. stared at his feet. "That's the thing, Mom. I want to go to his house."

Cody flinched. "No way."

R.J. leaped to his feet. "Mom, he's got the new Sony system."

She stood up. "You can play Nintendo Sixty-four instead."

"No."

"Yes." She was through discussing it. She started for the door.

"But he has a pool."

The image made her shudder. She'd had a bad pool accident as a child, and she hated the thought of him in the water almost as much as anything else. "No." She disliked the water herself, but in training as an agent, she'd spent plenty of time in it. Eventually she'd learned to set aside her fears when swimming was necessary, but she hadn't been in water since she left the Bureau.

"I'm a good swimmer, Mom."

It was true. He swam like Mark had, as though he'd been born for the water. But thinking about it, even more than watching it, terrified her.

"I went there last time and it was fine."

"Not overnight, you didn't."

"I'm eight years old, Mom. You can't hide me here forever," Ryan said in a defiant voice.

His words knocked the wind out of her. She turned back. "Ryan, we've talked about that. You know why."

"I know about Dad and everything." He waved his hand. "But no one knows who we are. I've never said a word—ever. I'm really careful, Mom, I swear."

She shook her head.

"Mom, please. I hate always asking kids here. And Peter is really cool. I feel like a dork asking him to always come to my house." Ryan gave her the wide-eyed look that had been his father's. "And you know Mr. Landon—he's real responsible."

Cody sank into Ryan's desk chair, deflated.

"I'm going to have to do it sometime, Mom. How would I go to college?"

She smiled at the image of her eight-year-old in college, but she knew he was right. She couldn't keep him under her wing forever. But she could keep him there longer. "We'll talk when you're ready for college."

"Mom!" Ryan launched himself off the bed toward her. "I want to go tonight. Come on."

She shook her head. With that, she stood and walked out of the room. "I'll see you downstairs in ten minutes for pancakes."

He didn't answer her, but she hadn't expected him to.

As soon as she reached the kitchen, Ryan called down to her, "Mr. Landon wants to talk to you, Mom. He's on the phone." She frowned at the kitchen phone as though it were hosting bacteria.

"This isn't going to work," she called back to him before picking up the receiver. She hated the phone. She didn't have friends, wasn't allowed to communicate with her family, and all her work correspondence was done via E-mail. It had been hard at first. She'd occasionally lifted the receiver and started to dial one of her sisters before realizing she could no longer talk to them.

She remembered the last time she'd spoken to her family on the phone. It had been set up as a safe call from New Orleans, and the thought of that conversation made her ache. They had been such a close family—the house full of the sounds of girls bickering, laughing, and playing. Megan was the second of four girls, only six years between Alison, the oldest, and Nicole, the baby. All of them had stayed in Chicago. But Megan was gone now. There was no Megan—just Cody.

She wondered if they were all still there. How many kids did her sister Alison have? Was Amy married? The last time she'd heard from them Nicole was expecting. They'd all guessed it was a boy. Had it been?

"Mom!" Ryan called. "Phone."

Cody pushed her family from her mind and picked up the phone. "Hello?" she said.

"Mrs. O'Brien, it's Travis Landon." He spoke with the same awkward tone she'd heard since her rejection of his dinner offer.

Cody glared in the general direction of her son's room. "Hello."

"I realized when you were coming to the phone that I don't even know your first name."

"It's Cody, Mr. Landon," Ryan added from the extension upstairs.

"Thanks, R.J."

"Okay, R.J.," Cody said, "you can hang up now."

She waited until she heard the click of the extension. "How can I help you, Mr. Landon?"

He paused. "I understand you don't want R.J. to come over tonight. I promised Peter he could. I told the kids I'd pick them up myself and we'd rent *Terminator*. Are you sure he can't come, Cody? They have such fun together."

Cody shook her head. "I think it's great that they

want to play together. They are welcome to come here if they want to have a sleepover."

"Of course, but you should let me return the favor. You've had Peter spend the night lots of times."

"Thank you, but . . ."

Ryan appeared at the kitchen door, dressed and holding his backpack in one hand and an overnight bag in another. His wide eyes pleaded.

"I promise they'll be fine."

Cody turned her back to her son and blinked hard, forcing back the fear. "You'll be picking them up from school?"

"At three o'clock on the dot."

She pinched the bridge of her nose and shook her head.

"I'll make sure he eats vegetables," Travis added with casual humor. He had no idea what this could mean.

"I'd prefer they not swim unattended. And it's a bit cold out right now. . . ."

"The pool is closed and the gate is locked. They won't even be near it."

She blew her breath out. "Have R.J. call me before bed."

"I will. Peter will be thrilled. And you enjoy the evening alone."

"Thanks," she choked, knowing she would do no such thing. She said good-bye, the fear from her days in New Orleans rising to the surface again.

Cody hung up the phone, thinking about how difficult things had been for them. R.J. was her best friend. She couldn't bear it if something happened to him.

No mother and child she knew had ever been through the kind of ordeal they had. And despite her continuing fears, R.J. had finally started to feel comfortable with his school and with his friends.

Cody knew she couldn't let her own fears stand in the way of letting her son have some semblance of a normal childhood.

She turned to Ryan and saw a mirror image of her husband's eyes and the stubbornness in them. Ryan was just like Mark.

"I'll be fine, Mom. I promise."

She reached out and pulled him to her in a quick hug. "You'd better," she warned. Then, with an aching breath, she said, "Pour yourself some juice and sit down. I don't want you to be late for school."

As Cody mixed the batter for pancakes, she watched Ryan pour his juice and sit down at the table. He pulled open the paper and found the comics and began to read. Every motion reminded her of Mark, and pride filled her in a warm rush. She hoped Mark was watching them to see how incredible their son was.

Cody turned to the skillet and poured batter, feeling the heat on her hands and praying she would someday be able to let go of the fear.

Chapter 2

Before getting out of her car at the café where she was to meet Dmitri, Jennifer Townsend popped open the container with gloved hands and took out two small triangular white pills, washing them down with water. Then she opened her compact and checked the bruise around her eye. She wished it would just be gone already. She hated the looks she got and the constant worried coos people made. It was nothing. A little argument, not that she'd tell them that. It wasn't like he meant to do it. She could have knocked him on his ass if she'd wanted to.

But frankly his anger had startled her. And he had a right to be angry. The pressure from his father about Viktor. She knew it made him feel miserable. Viktor. Even dead he was Oskar Kirov's first thought. Dmitri deserved better. She knew. She'd been the second child her whole life. And that was what Dmitri was. Second. Even to a dead first.

She glanced into the compact one last time. The theater makeup she'd been using did a pretty good job of covering it, but you could still see the bluish tint in strong light. She snapped the mirror closed and tucked it back in her purse. The heater was blowing on her feet and she wiggled her toes in her shoes. She leaned her head back and took in a deep breath before opening the car door. Bundling herself up, she wrapped the scarf around her head and zipped up her jacket. She felt the muscles in her neck start to soften and she strode toward the restaurant, anxious for a drink.

Dmitri was sitting at their table, wearing the gray cashmere sweater she'd bought him and black pants. His long black leather coat hung over the chair behind him. He looked positively edible. She tossed her blond hair over her shoulder as his eyes met hers. He smiled and lifted a cosmopolitan toward her. She took it in her gloved hand, clinked her cosmopolitan against his martini, and together they finished the drinks in one toss.

Sitting, she laughed as he leaned across and kissed her softly on the lips.

"Jenichka," he said. It meant "dear little Jen" in Russian. He spoke to her in Russian, and over the years she'd picked up some of the language. Russian always sounded so sexy to her.

She removed her gloves and laid them on the table beside her.

Dmitri ordered another round of drinks and then took her hands across the table. "You are beautiful, Jenichka."

She grinned. "I know."

He let go of one hand and reached into his pocket. "I brought you something." He pulled out a small red Cartier box with a white ribbon. It was a box every woman in America could appreciate.

He laid it in the palm of his hand, and she noticed how perfectly it fit there. The size of a ring box, maybe slightly larger. No. It couldn't be that. For a moment she was nervous. But she knew Dmitri better. They would be together eventually, but this was not how he would do it.

She laughed at her own ridiculous imagination and reached for the box.

Dmitri snapped his hand shut and she let out a high shriek as he laughed. She laughed again and they repeated the game until the waitress appeared with more drinks. Ruining the moment, the waitress set her cosmopolitan almost under her chin. Dmitri laid the box down and pushed it toward her.

She eyed him with a smile.

"Open it."

She took a sip of her drink and stared at the box.

"Open it," he insisted, pulling her drink from her fingertips and holding it away from her.

She scooped up the red box with a rush of adrenaline and let the silky white bow slip off between her fingers. She lifted the lid and found a small red velvet pouch resting on a cloud of cotton inside.

She raised an eyebrow as Dmitri leaned in to watch her. "What?"

He rolled his hand to move her along. "I want to see what you think. Hurry up."

She pulled open the pouch and let the contents slide onto her palm. Three cabochon rings she'd admired in the window once months ago—one sapphire, one emerald, one ruby. She'd never even mentioned them, but he'd been with her, walking down Michigan Avenue, when she'd seen them. She blinked back tears as she lifted them from her palm. "How did you know?"

He smiled and cocked his chin up in triumph. "I was right."

"I loved them in the window. They're beautiful."

"I saw you. I was so sure." He stroked her arm and laughed again. "Then I got nervous. What if you were looking at the diamond stud pin behind them?" He clapped once. "I'm so glad I was right."

"Of course you were. They're perfect." She started to slide them on when he stopped her. "There's a special order," he explained. He laid them on the pouch and picked up the ruby one first and slid it onto her ring finger. "The red is for blood, so it stays close to your skin. The green is for the earth, so it goes next," he continued, putting the emerald ring on top of the ruby. "Finally, the blue sapphire is for the sky, and it goes on last."

She smiled and leaned forward to meet his lips. She kissed him. He kissed her back in the same soft way that made her stomach dance. She touched his cheek and tucked her head under his chin. He had known. He'd been the only one who had ever known what her tastes were, who cared enough to pay attention to what she would like.

She sat back up and stared at her outstretched hand. "They're truly beautiful, Dmitri."

He waved his hand to dismiss it then lifted his glass and raised it toward hers. They clinked and drank again.

She moved her hand to watch the stones catch the light.

"Things are still bad with Papa," Dmitri said, watching her.

She stilled her hand and focused on him. "I'm sorry."

He finished the drink, then rubbed his eyes.

"Did you sleep last night?"

He shook his head. "I keep trying to think of ways to find her." He looked up at her, his eyes pleading.

Then he dropped his gaze to his hand. "I need to get this over with. It's all he talks about. The plans, the business, it's all going to hell because of Viktor."

She laid her hand on his. It was her fault. Dmitri had never told his father that Jennifer had been the source, but she and Dmitri knew it. He wouldn't mention it, of course, but it was true. She had let the location of the warehouse slip. The drugs were there. It had been a stupid mistake. Megan had never known about Jennifer's affair with Dmitri. She knew better than to admit dating anyone connected to the mob. Dmitri had his own business. He'd been clear about wanting to stay away from his family's mob connections. But then Viktor had been killed and everything had changed. It was getting harder and harder for Dmitri to stay out of it.

But Jennifer had told Megan a story about Viktor Kirov. Viktor was considered quite a playboy in Chicago, and many of his escapades made the society section of the paper despite his questionable business dealings.

When the girls' night out had led to discussions of local bachelors, Jennifer had simply told a story about a friend who had gone to a party at a warehouse with Viktor Kirov. She'd been there too, but she couldn't say that. She was FBI and he was a felon. They'd been drinking, Megan as much as Jennifer, and she'd thought it was all in good fun. Jennifer didn't know Mark Riggs was working a case involving Viktor.

Without even thinking, Jennifer had told Megan all about the warehouse. And Megan had called her husband and used it. Both Mark and Viktor had died that night. Mark's death didn't make Megan's betrayal any easier. And Megan never knew that Viktor's death meant anything to Jennifer. She'd seen Megan only one time after that, at the funeral for Mark. Through it all, Jennifer had held her anger against Megan. It was still there, just under the surface.

At least Dmitri had never been implicated in anything. It was always Viktor. Dmitri ran an importing business—alcohol mostly.

Oskar Kirov wanted Megan Riggs dead.

"I'm working on it."

He looked up. "I know you are. But he's risking everything on this. Why can't he just let it go?"

She squeezed his hand. "I'll get something soon. I promise."

He nodded and ran his thumb across her rings. "You should get back." He pulled a small paper bag from his pocket. "You asked for these."

She took the bag and put it in her purse.

"I'll see you tonight."

"It might be late." She stood and took the box and ribbon and tucked them in her purse, too.

He grabbed her hand. "Not too late, I hope."

She leaned over and kissed his brow. "Not too. In the meantime, go back to the house and get some rest. We'll order something when I get home."

He nodded, lost in thought as she left the bar. She looked at her rings in the fading sunlight. They were gorgeous. And what other man would buy his girlfriend Cartier for no occasion?

Back at her car, she opened the door, put her key in the ignition, blasted the heat, and drove three blocks before stopping the car again. She opened the tin of mints she kept in the glove compartment, chewed three until her mouth burned, and then pulled out the plastic pill container from her purse.

She rolled a pill onto her palm and then thought twice and added another. Popping the two into her mouth, she leaned back against the seat and swallowed them dry.

She lifted the pill container and toasted the air in front of her. "You can't hide forever."

Then she pulled away from the curb and headed to the office. It was late enough in the day now that she hoped to be able to go in without seeing anyone—or at least not anyone important. She hadn't wanted to have to answer questions about her eye. She looked down at her rings and considered again how incredibly thoughtful Dmitri could be. She was lucky to have him.

Chapter 3

They were so close. It had been that way for three weeks. What was he going to tell them?

It was one little glitch, one bug, and yet no one could figure it out. How he would have loved to go and find a bar stool and drink until the bug disappeared into a bad memory. Those had been the days, when he could leave a problem at work and drink it away. Now it was always there. He was the CEO, not some programmer. "It" was his life.

He looked at the clock on the dash and pushed the accelerator down. He was barely going to make it to the school by three. He hated to be late. He wasn't supposed to let that happen. He was a good father. It was practically the only thing he hadn't struggled with. And the one thing the media gave him an ounce of credit for was his ability to raise his son on his own. That was it. He couldn't go screwing that up, too.

He sped off the exit and turned up the small winding road that cut to the back of his son's school.

The day had gone to hell from his first cup of Peet's coffee. He'd managed to spill some of it on his pant leg in the car. Traffic was a nightmare because of the rain. Then Tofigh, who had promised the kinks would be worked out, had called to say they weren't having any luck. His PR people were having a heck of a time with what to tell the media. And his CFO had been by twice about a strategy with the VCs. Because they were going to need the venture capitalists again. The current investors were starting to panic. Not that he blamed them. Of course they were nervous. There had been a lot of rough going in the start-up market, but he believed in this product. If only they'd give him a little more time to sort out the bug. But they had a stake in the company and they'd weaseled some language into the loan agreement that allowed them to do more than just sit by and watch the money drain away. The latest was some PR plan.

They'd hired an outside PR agency and were devising a plan they hoped would shine some positive light on TecLan. That was what they said the company needed. Travis was trying to focus on getting the product out and they were working on some media scam.

But no matter how he sliced it, TecLan needed a cash infusion. It used to be as easy as getting blood at a hospital. VC money had become very hard to obtain, and Travis would need to prove they would launch before he'd get any more.

Legal was still stressed about vendor contract renegotiations, and his head of operations, Carson, was losing sales staff left and right because they weren't able to tell potential clients that the product even worked.

It had to be something simple. But he'd sat with Tofigh; he'd gone through the troubleshooting. He had no idea what he was missing.

Peter was sitting on one of the giant eucalyptus logs that marked the edge of the parking lot. His skinny legs were pale against the brown bark. His small feet kicked alternately, right then left, right then left. The collar of his shirt was tucked under one side of his school sweatshirt. The other side stuck straight up in the air. Though it had stopped raining, he had to be freezing.

Travis honked and Peter looked up, the expression on his face changing from despair to a flash of relief and then a smile. He knew Peter was thinking about his mother. He worried constantly that his dad might disappear the same way his mother had. In hindsight, Travis suspected he'd let Jill keep the cancer a secret too long.

He pulled around the bend and leaned over to open the door of the Mercedes for Peter to hop in.

"Dad, you're late. You promised you'd be on time."

Travis shook his head. "I know, partner. There's no excuse. I'm sorry. Are you really mad?"

Peter hung his head.

"Where's R.J.?"

"He got picked up when you didn't come."

Travis frowned. "I was only ten minutes late." His new PR staff had kept him on the phone about this and that. He never realized how much of running a business would be the damn PR.

"Fifteen, and you promised his mom you'd be right on time."

Travis nodded. "I know. I'm sorry I'm late, Peter. I'm here now. What can I do to make it up to you?"

He pouted. "Nothing."

"Should we go to R.J.'s house and get him?"

Peter shook his head.

Travis thought immediately of R.J.'s overprotective mother. "His mom picked him up?"

Peter shrugged.

Travis put his arm around his son. "Tell me what happened, partner."

"He didn't even tell me hisself. Jamie Underwood told me he got picked up by his dad."

"I didn't know the dad was in the picture," Travis said.

Peter looked at him with a frown. "In what picture?"

"Still around. Where does his dad live?"

Peter shrugged again, disappointed.

Travis looked around the schoolyard. "You're sure he got picked up?"

Peter nodded. "Positive."

"By his dad?"

Peter nodded again.

"Because I was late?"

Peter crossed his arms. "Yes."

"Should we call him?"

"I don't know."

That meant yes. "Do you know R.J.'s number?"

He recited the number from memory.

Travis ruffled his son's hair and then pulled out his cell phone and dialed. "What's his mom's name again?"

"Mrs. O'Brien."

Travis laughed, remembering now that her name was Cody. "Her first name's not Mrs., silly."

Peter broke into a smile.

He listened to the phone ring but no one answered. He dialed again and let it ring again. Still no one. Who in the world didn't have an answering machine these days?

Travis closed the phone and looked at his son. "They're not answering. Should we try later?"

"Forget it. He won't be able to come over now anyway."

Travis let his head fall back and then sat up again. "Okay, Dad's a jerk. I'm a big, fat, terrible jerk, okay?"

Peter cracked another smile. "Okay."

"So what can I do to make it up to you?"

"Can we have McDonald's for dinner?"

Travis thought about the pork chop being cooked for him at home. "Sure."

"And can we still rent *Terminator*?"

"Sure."

"And you'll watch it?" Peter pressed.

"I've seen it twenty times."

Peter frowned. "You asked what you could do to make it up to me."

Travis raised his hands in surrender. "You're right. Okay, we can rent *Terminator* and I'll watch it."

"The whole thing."

Travis crossed two fingers over his heart and then raised them in the Boy Scout pledge. "The whole thing. Do we have a deal?" He reached his hand out to his son.

His son took it, and while they shook, Travis reached over to ruffle Peter's hair again.

Someone knocked on the window and Travis and Peter looked up. It was Wendy Dickson. She was a divorced mother of a little girl in Peter's grade, and she'd been hinting at Travis about a date for the whole year.

Travis rolled his window down. "Hi, Wendy."

Wendy ran one finger across the edge of the car door. "Travis. I saw you sitting here in your car and had to stop by." She looked into the car and waved at Peter. He turned to the window, pretending he didn't see her.

"Did you say hello to Mrs. Dickson?"

Peter waved without looking at her. "Hello, Mrs. Dickson," he mumbled.

"Well, it's good to see you. Don't you two get too crazy, now." She winked.

"Thanks, Wendy. We promise to behave."

She leaned down and whispered in his ear. "If you're looking to misbehave, you can always give me a call."

He laughed and waved good-bye, starting the car and pulling around the drive toward the street without looking back. His phone started to ring and he handed it to Peter. "Want to throw it out the window?"

Peter's eyes lit up and he grinned. "Can't you just turn it off?"

"Absolutely." Travis opened the phone and pointed to one of the buttons. "Push that one there."

Peter turned off the phone and closed it up. Then he looked at his dad. "Would you really have let me throw it out the window?"

Travis rubbed his head. "Probably not."

"I didn't think so."

Travis looked at Peter, who was now staring out the window. Maybe Peter had already forgotten about being mad at him. But Travis wondered how many times he could afford to screw up. He had to be more careful. At least it was the weekend. Nothing about work would get done now. He could concentrate on Peter. Next week he might not have the chance.

"Dad?"

"Hmm?" he said, pushing his company from his mind.

"Can we rent *Terminator II* instead?"

"Sure, partner."

"And can we get bubble-gum ice cream?"

Travis laughed. If only life after forty were as simple as Arnold Schwarzenegger and bubble-gum ice cream.

"Can we, Dad?"

"Absolutely."

Chapter 4

Colonel Walter Turner knew something was wrong. He had known it from the day they moved in. He split the shades wider with two fingers and surveyed the windows. The boy's room was straight across from the window, but tonight it was dark. He'd seen her in and out, but not the kid. Tonight was the first time he'd noticed the kid out at night. It wasn't normal for a kid that age to spend every single night at home. That had been one of his first clues that she was on the run. Not that many would notice, he didn't think. She was attractive—lean and angular like a distance runner. She wore her dark hair down and it had the gentle wave that the women in the shampoo commercials always tried for, but the way she dressed made it clear she didn't put much into it. She wore jeans and flannels most of the year—shorts and tees in the hot months. She had light brown or green eyes; he'd never been quite close enough to tell. And she was relatively tall— five-seven or maybe five-eight, and not more than one-thirty. If he hadn't taken the time to watch her, he would have thought she was simply not interested in knowing her neighbors. But there was more than that.

He'd studied her, and he had some ideas about her, but that was all they were. She'd never let on about her story. But thirty-seven years in the Marine Corps had given him a damn good eye for trouble. She was ex-law of some kind. A street cop, detective, maybe even military, he wasn't sure. It was in the way she pinned her shoulders back when she walked, the way her eyes scanned left and right when she took out the trash or swept the front walk, the way her right hand flirted with the inside of her left jacket whenever anyone approached.

There was no weapon there, but he'd seen the instinct. He watched her pull the blinds apart with her fingers, just as he had, and look out. He dropped his hand, but she'd seen him. She let go of the boy's blinds and the light went on and then, after a minute, off. He lifted the edge of shade and looked back out, wondering again where the boy was.

R.J. was his name. Florence had asked one day when they were outside. The boy had hesitated, then looked at his mother, who had given him a slight nod. It had been his second clue. He was about the same age as Roni's boy. Nine years since he'd seen his daughter.

He made his way out with the trash, thinking about R.J. The kid had just grown on him. Every time he saw him, he thought of Roni. He wondered what her boy was like, what his name was. And even when he tried to ignore R.J., he couldn't. The kid was too damn smart.

Colonel Turner had made the mistake of telling R.J. that he collected bugs as a hobby. It was something he'd done as a kid. He'd had them pinned in a shoebox inside his closet because his mama had put her foot down when he'd started to pin them up on his bulletin board.

Most people looked at him like he was just plain weird when he told them he was a bug collector. But R.J. seemed to think it was just about the neatest thing ever. The boy had promptly returned to tell the colonel that his mother said he couldn't start his own bug collection.

"That's okay, son," he had told R.J. "You can come see mine anytime." And damn if the colonel wasn't surprised when the kid had shown up. And the boy had learned the names. He'd come around from time to time with a new bug and ask what it was. The colonel had taken to saving the new ones for R.J., and they spent an average of an hour or so together a week. He enjoyed that time as much as any other. That kid was special.

He knew the mother didn't like it, but R.J. never said anything about her. Or his father. In fact, just about the only thing they ever talked about was bugs.

Just then he heard the O'Brien woman behind him.

She seemed startled when she saw him, so he tried to smile. "Where's the little guy tonight?"

She gave him a glare.

"Just noticed he wasn't home."

"He's out," she said, throwing her bag into the trash can and turning back to the house without another word.

The colonel shook his head and turned back toward his own house, telling himself to mind his own business. He'd never managed to get that much right. Why should he worry about anyone else?

He kept to himself as a rule, and he didn't mind others who did, but in the same right, he liked to know who his neighbors were. His Florence had always been the friendly one, his social butterfly. Now on a good day she knew her name and his. On a bad day she thought she was a butterfly and she ran from him in fear as though he might try to capture her with some giant, invisible net. He watched her mind melt before his eyes, day after day, month after month. And there was not a goddamn thing he could do about it.

First the cancer. Then Roni's drug-dealer boyfriend and the pregnancy. She'd been stealing for him and gotten caught. His daughter in jail. The colonel bailed her out, but when that no-good son-of-a-bitch ex-con came back for her, he and the colonel had had it out. The colonel had hit him, knocked him down, and told him to get lost.

But Roni had chosen him, had sworn they'd make a life together. The colonel had never believed it. He'd warned her off him, told her not to make that kind of mistake, told her how guys like him turned out. And when push came to shove, Roni had chosen Doug over her father. She'd walked out and sworn never to come back.

And she never had. It had been too much for Florence. She had fought off the cancer, but the heartache had been too strong. And he knew that was when she had started to shut herself out. She felt too much. He didn't feel enough and she felt too much. She'd always told him that. Forty-three years they'd been married, thirty-seven of it in the marines. And now his girls were gone. Roni was living with an ex-con and their son, and Florence spent most of her days like Alice in Wonderland.

He rubbed at the empty feeling in his stomach. Heartburn, he told himself, though he hadn't eaten in hours. He pushed it aside and went up to look in on Florence. She was snoring slightly, one balled fist stretched out as if she were reaching for something with all her might.

Tucking the comforter to her chin, he leaned down and kissed her wrinkled black forehead. Her skin was cool and moist, as though she might have been working in her dream, but her expression was calm. He ran his knuckles over his cheeks as he stood again, then marched to his study. He had been reading a new book on the history of slavery in the South. He wondered if Roni kept up with her heritage. Someday he hoped he'd get to tell his grandson the stories his grandpa had told him about growing up. Someday.

Chapter 5

Cody had read the same paragraph of the article about the progress of the expansion of the San Francisco airport six times. She folded the paper and set it down on top of the stack of mail. The clock said nine-fifty. What time was bedtime? Why hadn't Ryan called? R.J., she reminded herself. Why hadn't R.J. called?

She lifted the phone and turned it on, checked the dial tone and turned it off again. The phone was working. She'd looked over the caller ID box, but the two numbers had been unavailable, probably telemarketers. She knew Peter's number had shown up in the past. So he hadn't called. She didn't want to embarrass him, but this was ridiculous. She glanced at the school directory that had been open for the past three hours and dialed the number she had memorized nearly that long ago. She cleared her throat and waited for an answer. After one ring, she heard Travis Landon's voice announce that no one was able to answer and would they leave a message. Cody cleared her throat again and waited for the tone.

"It's R.J.'s mom. Just have him give me a quick

call when you get this. Thanks." She tried to sound relaxed and breezy, which was anything but what she felt. She looked at the clock again. Nine fifty-two.

Getting up from the couch, she took the stack of freshly folded laundry upstairs, put it away in R.J.'s drawers, and sat on the bed she'd made an hour before. She lifted the chambray pillow and brought it to her nose. She loved the smell of him. He still had the slightest remainder of sweet baby smell combined with the scent of ground-in dirt.

Behind that was the pineapple scent of the shampoo she insisted he use twice a week, and the banana suntan lotion she'd put on him before his T-ball game the night before. His games always reminded her of playing softball as a girl. Her mother was very athletic, and she and Megan's father had always encouraged the girls in sports. Her sister Nicole had played soccer at Stanford on a scholarship, but Megan had always loved softball. On Memorial Day they played a family game: Mom and the two oldest girls, Dad and the two youngest. The rivalry had continued up until the last Memorial Day that Mark was alive. She wondered if they still played.

She returned the pillow to its spot and forced herself off the bed. She went into her room and picked up the extension there, dialing the Landons' number again. No one answered.

To hell with it, she cursed to herself, grabbing the car keys off her bureau and heading downstairs. She put on her coat and armed the house as she did even to walk to the small market down the street. She left the house through the back door and jogged to the green Jeep Cherokee that made her look like every other parent in California. She revved the engine, blasted the heat, and drove toward the Landons' house.

She shouldn't be going there, she told herself. She should trust R.J. He would call her before bed. Maybe Peter went to bed later. She knew his mother wasn't around. Maybe Landon let Peter stay up all night. Or maybe Landon had reminded R.J. and he'd just forgotten. But it wasn't like R.J. to forget. He remembered how important it was that they always be able to reach each other. He remembered that night in New Orleans.

The rain started up again and she tightened her grip on the steering wheel as she turned between the large stone pillars that marked the entrance into the exclusive community where Landon lived. The in-law attachments here were bigger than the house she and R.J. shared. She didn't care. Her life wasn't about money or power or any of those things. It never would be, and the thought brought neither disappointment nor envy.

She pulled the Jeep into the circular drive in front of Landon's house and killed the engine. Maybe R.J. had already called her at home and she'd simply missed it. She picked up her cell phone and punched four to dial her home voice mail. The electronic voice told her she had no messages.

Ending the call, she set the phone on the passenger seat and opened her door. She crossed the small grassy yard and took a deep breath before ringing the white bell beside an oak door that looked like it belonged on a king's castle. The sound echoed through what she imagined was an enormous entryway, and she waited to hear the sounds of footsteps. Landon had said the boys would be renting a movie, and she hoped he hadn't decided to take them out instead.

She turned around and looked back at the street as the misty rain turned to drizzle. She didn't see any cars on the street, but the garage was closed. Where the hell was Landon? Where was her son? She turned back and rang the bell again, feeling the fear saturate her blood like alcohol.

"I'm coming, I'm coming," came the scratchy voice.

There was the click of a lock, and the giant oak door opened with a resounding moan.

Travis Landon stood behind it in a pair of pajama pants and nothing else. She diverted her eyes from his tanned chest. He looked tired, but he was handsome the same way Mark had been. He had straight, medium-brown hair that appeared thick and slightly untamed. The whole effect was rugged, and she could imagine he looked slightly out of place in a suit, just like Mark. Travis frowned and ran his hand through his hair.

Cody kept her eyes on his face as she stepped into the foyer and tried not to wipe her wet feet on the beautiful, expensive-looking Oriental rug. The house was bigger than she'd thought, with a marble floor and the kind of grandiose style that felt gauche and overdone. "R.J. never called. I just wanted to talk to him for a second. I tried calling, but it went straight to voice mail."

Travis stood motionless with the door in his hand.

Cody shivered against the cool night air.

Travis blinked and looked outside and then closed the door. "R.J.'s—"

"It's okay. If he's asleep, I'll just go and talk to him for a second. I promise not to wake up Peter." She heard a squeak from the top of the stairs and looked up. Her heart danced at the form of a small boy standing at the top of the stairs, but she quickly realized it wasn't R.J.

"What's going on, Dad?"

"I'm not sure." Travis looked back at Cody and shook his head. "R.J.'s not here."

Cody turned to him, looking for the smile, the joke. No one was laughing.

Travis reached out to touch her, but she pulled away. "What do you mean, he's not here?"

Travis looked up at Peter and then back to Cody. "I called you twice on our way home, but no one answered." He raked a hand through his hair. "Jesus, he got picked up."

"Where is he? Where's my son?"

"His father picked him up. Peter, isn't that right?"

Cody nearly choked. She shook her head as her hand covered the gasp that escaped her lips. His father couldn't have picked him up. Ryan's father was dead.

Peter started down the stairs, his figure like a tiny ghost of her own child.

"Peter?"

Peter was nodding slowly, and in his eyes Cody saw R.J. as he had been that morning: his chin up, his eyes narrow as he demanded to spend the night at his friend's house. She'd deferred to his stubbornness, let him out of her protective shield. And now he was gone.

"Jamie told me he left with a man," the child whispered, now standing beside his father.

She blinked hard, forcing R.J.'s features off his face.

"Earlier you told me R.J. left with his dad. Was it a man or his dad?" Travis asked.

The words were like shots to her ears. "No one should have picked him up but me." She looked at Travis. "Where were you?"

"I was there, just a few minutes after three."

"You were late," she said flatly, turning her back on him. "Peter, who picked R.J. up? Can you remember, sweetie?"

The boy's wide eyes moved slowly between Cody and his father. "I don't remember."

Travis stepped closer. "You don't remember what Jamie said? This is serious, son."

He shook his head quickly.

Travis spun toward her. "Is he in danger? Is his father dangerous?"

She stepped backward and hit the solid oak of the closed door. She was moving her mouth, trying to get the air to speak. She saw Oskar Kirov as he had been in the courtroom the day he was sentenced to seven to ten years on a laundry list of convictions, including fraud, drug trafficking charges, and tax evasion. That day in the courtroom was the one time she'd seen him after her husband and his son had died in a shootout.

He had looked at her with glaring gray eyes and in a raspy accented voice had said, "You will pay. You and your son will pay for my son's death. I don't care how long it takes."

First Mark, then Ryan. What better way to make her pay for Viktor Kirov's death? It was Kirov—it had to be. She'd never even sensed they were close. She had no idea how they'd found her. But they had. Kirov had found her. The Russian mob had Ryan.

She clasped her hands together, wrestling her

emotions. She wanted to scream and kick and also to collapse. Instead she ran her hands over her jeans and drew in a deep breath. Ryan. She kept her eyes closed and exhaled. Please, not Ryan. She smoothed the hair back from her face.

Travis's insistent voice invaded her desperation. "Is he dangerous?"

He grabbed her shoulders and turned her toward him. She felt the heat of his hands through the thin shirt. The reality of his touch shook her back.

"Are you okay?"

She nodded, the coldness starting to set in. She could do this. She'd been through it before. She'd get him back and they would move on. By God, if Oskar Kirov hurt her child, she would tear his eyes out.

"Cody."

She looked up at Landon. Focus on getting him back. Kirov wanted her to suffer. That was what this was about. They wouldn't kill Ryan. Not immediately, at least. But how long did she have? The thought made her panic again.

"Jesus Christ, say something," Travis said. "Is R.J.'s father dangerous?"

"His father's dead," she said, expelling the words as if they were her last breath. It was exactly how she felt. She was dying. Ryan was gone. No, she refused to accept that Ryan was gone. Mark was gone. She'd seen his body. Held his cold hand in hers.

"Oh, Jesus," Travis whispered.

But not Ryan. He was vibrant, alive. He was his father's son. He would fight. And she would find him.

Travis was kneeling beside his child, holding his shoulders. "Did you see who picked up R.J.?"

Peter shook his head.

Cody drove the panic from her chest. Focus on the details. Work it like a case, like any other case. She remembered when she first heard of Mark's death, the way it had consumed her like a fever, unsettling her entirely. She felt the same heated chill now. Forcing herself to move, she passed Travis and took Peter's hand. "Can you sit down for a minute? I need to ask you a few questions."

She could feel the pressure of Travis's gaze on her, but she ignored him. She sat Peter on the edge of the stair and turned him to face her. His eyes were wide, his jaw slack.

"It's going to be okay," she said.

Travis started toward them. She put her hand out to stop him.

Travis halted as Peter looked over his shoulder.

Travis looked from him to her and back again. "It's okay, partner," he said, casting her a glance that asked a dozen questions she would never answer. "Answer Mrs. O'Brien's questions." He looked at Cody. "I'll go call the police."

She stood so quickly that Peter flinched. Police in a kidnapping case meant FBI, and FBI wasn't an option. She put her hand on Peter's shoulder to reassure him. "No," she said, drilling her gaze into Travis. "Don't do anything yet."

His eyes narrowed. "We have to call the police."

"Not until I know what I'm dealing with."

"Who the he—" He halted and reached for his son.

"I just want to ask a few questions first."

Travis didn't respond.

Peter nodded.

Cody watched the boy, wishing his father would disappear. "Maybe your dad will make us something to drink after we're done, like you and R.J. do when you're at our house." Images of their last overnight were sharp in her mind, each smile and laugh like a dagger now. She looked over at Travis.

Travis didn't budge.

"Can we have hot chocolate?" Peter asked.

Travis nodded slowly. "You want to come with me, partner?"

Peter shook his head. "I can stay and tell Mrs. O'Brien about what happened."

Travis stood in his spot.

"We'll be right here."

His gaze swept across her face. "What are you doing?"

"I'm trying to find my son."

"That's not what I mean. What's really going on here? Why wouldn't we call the police immediately?"

From the corner of her eye, she saw Peter look at her. She wished she could make Landon stop. He was only making it tougher. Stay calm, she told herself. Stay calm. "I'm just working the best way I know how."

Landon didn't bite. "By not involving the police?"

She nodded. "That's right. Not until I know who the captor might be and what he might want."

"The captor?"

"The person who took my son."

There was a pregnant pause and Cody remained silent. She didn't know what to tell him. Certainly not the truth: that she was an ex-FBI agent, that the Russian mob had killed her husband and wanted to kill her and her son, that she had been in witness protection and they had found her even there. That her son might be with the Russian mob as they spoke, that the time he was wasting might cost her the only thing in the world that mattered at all. She wouldn't trust anyone with the truth. Not after the betrayal in New Orleans.

No, the truth was hers alone. The mob wanted her and her son dead because Mark had killed Viktor Kirov. But Mark was dead, too. Hadn't she paid enough with her husband?

"It's okay, Dad. I'll tell her about it," Peter said.

Cody smiled. "Thank you, Peter. I promise it'll only take a couple minutes."

Travis stepped between them. "Go on and watch TV for a few minutes while I talk to Mrs. O'Brien."

Cody felt the wind rush from her lungs. Every moment felt like R.J. was being pulled farther away. She blinked to battle the tears that lined her lashes.

Peter looked between her and his dad. "But R.J.'s my friend—"

"I know. And we're going to find him."

Peter stood up and padded across the floor toward the back of the house. From behind, he could have been R.J. The thin frame, the lazy slapping feet, the red pajamas. She closed her eyes, holding the image of his motion, praying that she would watch her own son again.

Travis grabbed her arm. "Who would take your son?" He sounded panicked.

She shook her head without saying more.

"If it wasn't his dad, who was it?"

She started to turn. "I don't need to answer your questions."

He held tight to her arm. "You do if you want to talk to my child."

Cody felt her chest heave beneath the weight of his threat as she pulled herself free. She needed

Peter's help. She calculated her response. "Fine." She forced her shoulders down in defeat, though it was nothing like what she felt. She ran her hands through her hair and leaned against the banister. "His father's not dead," she whispered, her voice cracking with emotion. She now lied with an ease that had once frightened her. "He's crazy." She shook her head, keeping her face down. She worried her expression would give her away. Her voice she could control; the determination in her eyes, she wasn't so sure about. "I took R.J. away to save him—to save us both."

"Why did you say he was dead?"

She clenched her jaw. "Because I don't like to talk about him."

His voice was soft and she felt it like breath on her neck. "You're sure it was him?"

She nodded, frowning. "As sure as I can be."

Travis expelled a breath and sank onto the stairs, dropping his head in his hands. "Jesus." He sat in silence and then said, "Well, at least we know who did it. Where is this guy?"

She stepped away, sitting on the far side of the stairs from where Travis was. She pulled her chin up, imagining the resources available to Oskar Kirov. Seven hours had passed. Ryan could be anywhere by now. "I don't know. I haven't known since we left."

"You think he would do this?" he probed again.

She thought about Oskar Kirov. "I know he would. I just need to ask a few questions, get as much information as possible before I decide how to approach it."

"Why wouldn't we call the police? If he's dangerous, they can help us."

She shook her head. "Please let me do this my own way. I know what I'm dealing with here, and you really have no idea. I just need to ask Peter a few questions and then I'll go."

Travis looked at her and nodded. Turning his back, he crossed the hall to get Peter.

Cody leaned against the banister, the air spilling from her lungs in relief. A million thoughts entered her mind. Where was he right now? Were they hurting him? Was he cold? Was he hungry? It was too much to bear. It piled on her until she could feel her knees shake under its weight.

She walked along the edge of the living room off the entryway. A small table sat in between two upholstered chairs, and she scanned the pictures: Peter and his dad in front of a lodge in the snow, Peter getting dropped off at camp, Travis and him in front of a reddish brown stone fireplace with a high oak mantel. Next to those was one of Peter and his mother. Cody leaned down to study it. She was a beautiful woman with long, curly auburn hair and dark eyes lit with happiness.

The door opened and Peter shuffled across the floor, followed by Travis. "I'll help you, Mrs. O'Brien."

Turning back, she watched his wide green eyes and forced herself to smile. "Thanks, Peter. That means a lot to me." She glanced up at Travis, who nodded.

"You guys sit down and I'll go make that hot chocolate."

Cody sat on the stair beside Peter and crossed her hands in her lap. Her every hope was vested in the wide-eyed eight-year-old sitting across from her.

God help Ryan.

Chapter 6

It was late on Friday night when Mei Ling answered her line at the Bureau. "Computer Intrusion Squad, this is Mei Ling."

"Such a mean name," her mother said to her in Cantonese. She meant the name of her squad at the Bureau. Mei couldn't remember a time when her mother called without starting with that same comment. It had been even worse when she'd been in the special Virus Squad. In Chinese custom, speaking about illness was like asking it to strike.

"Hello, Mother," she responded in English.

"Why do you talk to your mother that way?"

Her mother meant in English. "Just busy." She wasn't sure how or why the ritual had started, but with her family she always tried to speak English as much as possible. Each of them spoke some English. Her father spoke the most because he had been an alderman representing their district in the local Chicago government. But they all refused to speak English to her.

Also, it was awkward to speak Cantonese in the office, especially around Jennifer. Coworkers had told her more than once that it was unnerving when she spoke Cantonese, because it seemed like she was talking about them so they couldn't understand. At least they had told her. Jennifer just complained to their manager every time it happened.

Her mother was sullen and silent, and Mei knew she could sit on the other end this way forever. It was a no-win situation.

"How is Baba?" she asked about her father.

"*Mah mai dei la,*" her mother answered in Cantonese, meaning "so-so."

Her father would be "so-so" if he were planning to run a marathon the next day. Mei wasn't sure how she'd ever know if they were really sick, the way her mother exaggerated.

"Is it worse?"

"Always bad. Always very bad," her mother lamented.

"Can I bring him something?"

Her mother harrumphed as though Mei had insulted her ability to care for her husband. "You come to red egg and ginger party for Lai Ching. We're having it this Sunday. Two o'clock."

It wasn't the first time Mei's mother was throwing a red egg and ginger party, the traditional party for a new mother with a one-month-old baby. Mei could appreciate the party despite the fact that it originally had been celebrated only for boys. The smooth, round shape of the egg represented tranquility and was a symbol of fertility. The ginger, representing yang, warded off evil spirits and complemented the yin of the new mother. Red-tinted hard-boiled eggs and sliced sweet pickled ginger were served at the celebration as symbols of rebirth, good luck, and happiness.

The party was supposed to mark the first time the mother and child left the home since coming back from the hospital. Lai Ching had wanted to keep with the tradition and had refused to take the baby to her doctor appointments. So Mei had to drag her sister and the baby to her three-day and two-week appointments.

Like many of the Chinese traditions, keeping a baby at home for a full month struck Mei as ridiculous when it could jeopardize the baby's health.

"You coming?" Her mother's tone told her this was not a point of negotiation.

"I plan to come. As long as I don't have a work emergency."

"You always work. You have no life. You need to stop work and find a good man before it's too late." There was a brief pause, but Mei knew better than to think her mother was finished. "You at work now, you work middle of the night," she added in broken English, as though that might somehow get through to her daughter. "This is your family. Your niece. You must come."

"*Hou a.* I'll do my best," she whispered in Cantonese with her hand carefully cupped over the receiver.

"Perfect. I'll make your favorite—*ham yu yok bing.*"

Mei wrinkled her nose. The traditional Cantonese dish of minced pork and salted fish had never been her favorite, but that of her father and sisters. "I can't wait," she said.

Her mother clicked her tongue as she did when she was particularly pleased and rang off.

She was used to this push and pull. Her life had always been a complex draw between two very different worlds. Hers was a traditional Chinese family, despite the fact that they had been in the States for more than three decades. Her two sisters, one older, one younger, both led traditional lives. They were married, each had produced a son, and now Lai Ching had a daughter and Man Yee was pregnant again.

As a child, Mei had been the rebellious one by Chinese standards. Especially for a girl. After school, she used to sneak to a seedy little theater on the edge of Chinatown that played American action-adventure movies.

She'd grown up with *Star Wars* and *Jaws* and three different James Bonds. In the evenings, she would go into the small bathroom in her family's flat, the only room where she could ever be alone, and practice her defense moves until someone dragged her out.

She had always wanted to be an FBI agent. Even after ten years, her parents still asked her when she planned to move home and get married. There was no man. Dating, like everything else, felt like a pull between two drastically different realities. She didn't want the life her parents and sisters had, and yet the American culture and its dating rituals seemed completely foreign as well.

Mei made a note in the calendar, although there was little risk that the plans would interfere with anything other than her job. Her life was almost all work. In her free time, she still devoured the same movies she had always loved.

Just then, Jennifer Townsend entered the office they shared and closed the door behind her. Mei thought it was a little late to be showing up for work, but she said nothing. Jennifer hung her coat and scarf and pulled off her gloves. Her back turned, she didn't even look at Mei, let alone say hello. It had been like this off and on the entire time Mei had worked with her. Ten years already. They had been young when they'd started working together: Jennifer twenty-six or -seven and Mei only twenty-four. Despite the relatively narrow age gap, Jennifer had always treated Mei as an unwelcome stranger. Things had been getting worse for years, but the last twelve months had been almost unbearable. And Mei knew there were a lot of things Jennifer didn't talk about. The case they were working right now wasn't helping matters. They'd had more late nights and weekends than either cared to discuss. The problem was, criminals didn't keep bankers' hours. And Mei's mother had learned that the later she called, the more likely Mei was to be at the office and actually answer her live.

Jennifer sat at her desk and unlocked her top right drawer. Mei heard the familiar rattle of a pill bottle before the drawer closed and locked again. It was the same sound she heard a half-dozen times a day. Mei wondered if anyone else had heard it, too.

There were eight other agents in the Computer Intrusion Squad, but the groups tended to work on cases in pairs, and for convenience, Mei was almost always paired with Jennifer. They were also the only two women. There had been a third—Megan Riggs—ages ago, but she was long gone. Every once in a while, Mei thought about how Megan and her son were doing, if they were still alive. She'd been in the Federal Witness Protection Program for a couple of years, but supposedly a leak had led to the Russian mob tracking her down. From what Mei had heard, the leak had come from the Office of Professional Responsibility and Megan had gotten away. Mei could only imagine where she was now.

Mei thought it was about the same time that Megan escaped the Russian mob that things with Jennifer started to go downhill. Jennifer and Megan had been close. Jennifer had looked up to Megan, almost like an older sister. And despite their insistence that Mei was a welcome member of the team, Mei had always felt like an outsider.

She had never mentioned Megan to Jennifer. Occasionally Jennifer would bring it up, worrying out loud about how Megan was coping, but only then did Mei ask if she'd heard anything. Jennifer never had.

Typical Chinese not to get involved in someone else's business, Mei scolded herself. But it wasn't just Jennifer's business. The constant pill popping, the long lunches that ended in her return in a cloud of alcohol fumes, made it hard for Mei to get Jennifer's input when she needed it. And yet none of it seemed to affect Jennifer's work. She was as detailed as always, as diligent and as respected. She was always the lead agent on every case, and Mei ended up doing more of the grunt work. She didn't mind it, but Jennifer remained as detached as she could, and Mei had felt as though they had stopped working as a team months ago. And worse, Mei didn't know who to talk to.

Their supervisor, Dennis Eaton, was not someone Mei could relate to. He traveled to meet with local law enforcement on projects while the agents worked from the extensive computer system at the Bureau. And he and Jennifer were much closer than he and Mei would ever be. She had broached the subject with him more than once, but with Jennifer's performance as good as it was, he'd been skeptical at best. Maybe the problem was with Mei.

Jennifer slammed something down and Mei tried her best to ignore it. They were working on a case that involved the disruption by hackers of service to several of the biggest Internet service providers. Mei had spent the day sending information about the attacks back and forth with the companies' systems people, who seemed to work best at midnight Pacific time. Jennifer seemed unconcerned about the progress on the case, but Mei needed some assistance, so she brought it up anyway.

"We finished the filter process on case 282-CG-114230," Mei said, referring to their DDoS case, the Distributed Denial of Service that had targeted the highest-profile Internet service providers. "We're still running the search on the trigger machine." The process the Bureau used to locate the actual hacker was done with a specialized filtering software that removed any normal message traffic and allowed the agents to focus on the suspicious traffic. Still, even when suspicious traffic was located, the process of trailing it back to one machine was like searching for a needle in a Chicago-size field of hay.

Jennifer didn't respond.

Mei waited patiently. She wasn't known to lose her temper—had done it only a very few times and never in her work. But Jennifer was pushing her toward the edge. "I assumed you'd have an opinion on this."

Jennifer shook her head. "Not really. You can handle it." Jennifer was hunched over something on her desk.

Mei crossed the room and stood beside Jennifer's desk. "What is wrong?"

"What do you mean?" Jennifer said, her voice slow and deliberate. Her face was hidden beneath the strands of blond hair. Mei could see a small patch of makeup on her neck. She stared and felt her irritation boil into anger. It looked like a hickey. They were swamped with cases and Jennifer didn't show up to work until evening because she was with some man.

"You missed the meeting with Eaton this morning. He asked where you were but I had to tell him I didn't know, that I hadn't seen you since yesterday." She blew out a flustered breath. "I think you need to tell me when you're going to be gone for so long. I feel stupid when I can't explain where my partner is."

Jennifer didn't look up, didn't respond.

"I'm trying to understand."

Jennifer's head dropped lower and Mei thought maybe she was coming around. "Fuck you," she finally whispered.

Anger traveled like a shock through her until she reached out and grabbed the notebook from in front of Jennifer and yanked it off the desk. The page was blank.

"What are you doing?" Mei demanded.

Jennifer shifted her head slightly, but still refused to face Mei. "Thinking."

Exasperated, Mei turned Jennifer's chair to face her. "Tell me what is going on."

Jennifer waved her hand at Mei and tried to turn back, but Mei held on to the chair. Though her face was heavily made up, Mei could see the bluish tint beneath her left eye.

"Oh, my God, Jennifer. What happened?"

"I fell coming out of my apartment last night—all the damn ice." She touched it gingerly. "That's why I wasn't in earlier." She waved it off. "It's so embarrassing." She scanned Mei's gaze and then focused on the far wall. "I should've called, though. I'm sorry."

Mei knew instantly that Jennifer was lying. If she weren't, she would have told Mei to bug off by now.

Instead of anger, Mei was struck by the heavy hand of guilt. They were partners; Mei should have known what was going on with her. "Who did this to you?" She looked at Jennifer's eye and saw a sprinkling of tiny red cuts around the bruise. "Was it about a case? Were you attacked?"

"No," she said, holding her collar shut in response to Mei's stare. "I said I fell. I'm fine."

Mei was tired of the bullshit. "You fell coming out of your place? What did you hit—someone's hand? Don't lie, Jennifer. You need help. I can help you. We should call Eaton."

Jennifer scoffed. "I don't need help, Mei." She pulled a compact from her purse and looked at herself in the mirror without the slightest bit of reaction. With a small circular sponge, she applied makeup under one eye.

Mei refused to back down. "You didn't fall, Jennifer. You were hit. Someone hit you. Whoever he is, we can call Lieutenant Vilke and have him picked up."

Jennifer shook her head.

"He'll do it. I know he will. I've worked with him before."

"Stay away from me."

"It can't go on like this," Mei said, both frustrated

for herself and scared for Jennifer. "You're not yourself; you're not acting as a team."

"I am too. Don't tell me how to do my job."

"You're never here. I've been making joint decisions on my own and I can't keep doing it."

Jennifer's eyes narrowed. "Don't you try it, you
bitch."

"Try what?"

"To steal my job. I know all about you and your
perfect family and your perfect record." She motioned back to herself. "I'm the senior agent here,
not you."

"I don't want your job, Jennifer. But if you don't
get your act together, I'm going to talk to Kemper."
She threw out Kemper's name, hoping it would
cause a reaction. Eaton might be a pushover, but his
boss, Assistant Special Agent in Charge Alan Kemper, was a shark. Not that Mei would ever have the
guts to go to the ASAC.

Jennifer jumped up from her desk. "Tell whoever
you want. No one here trusts you anyway, you
Chink bitch."

Mei watched as the door slammed; then Jennifer
was gone. Jennifer's comments were meant to hurt,
she reminded herself, though she couldn't deny
that they had worked. Mei *was* trustworthy. If she
told Eaton what had just happened, he would believe her. She paused and looked across the room,
shaking her shoulders as though she could rid herself of Jennifer's anger as quickly. Mei wasn't going
to let this go on.

Mei opened the office door and looked in both directions. The hall was empty. Closing the door again,
she turned the inside lock and crossed the room to
Jennifer's desk. She'd been wanting to try to figure

out what was going on with Jennifer, but she'd felt guilty at the idea of looking through Jennifer's things. Now she was too angry to feel guilty. If Jennifer was going to treat her like crap, Mei at least deserved to know why.

She pulled on the top desk drawer, suspecting it was locked. It was. She picked up the container of pens and lifted the contents out of it. The bottom held two safety pins and a paper clip. She returned the pens and set the container back down. The only decoration on the desk was a picture of a beach at sunset in a small wooden frame.

She picked up the frame and opened the back, looking for anything hidden there. There was another picture behind it, one of a beautiful couple with a small girl. None of them was Jennifer, but from the appearance Mei guessed the woman might have been Jennifer's sister. Mei realized she'd never heard Jennifer speak of her family. Mei avoided conversation about her own family for many reasons, but what were Jennifer's?

Mei sat down in Jennifer's chair and stared at the thin black blotter that covered the surface of the metal desk. Piles of case files and documents covered the two right corners. The far left was occupied with her computer monitor, propped up on a 1998 Chicago yellow pages. Mei ran her fingers over the corner of the blotter. Feeling a small bump, she lifted the blotter and pulled out a key.

She stared at the key and then at the desk. She unlocked the door and checked the hall again. It was still empty. Gathering her courage, she went back to the desk and pushed the single gold key into the lock and turned it left. The lock clicked and the drawer loosened. Mei pulled the drawer open and saw the almost empty pill bottle in the front. The small triangular pills were unfamiliar. She read the prescription: Ativan. She'd never heard of it.

She pushed through the contents of the drawer, looking for something that would explain Jennifer's condition today. There were a few unlabeled disks, a Rolodex, and several loose business cards, nothing that looked significant. She flipped through the Rolodex and saw a listing for Megan Riggs and stared at it. Beside Megan's name was a series of little doodles in different colors. The entries were clearly outdated.

Lifting the Rolodex, she searched beneath it for anything that she might have overlooked, but the rest of the drawer was empty. Whatever Jennifer's problems were, Mei couldn't find any evidence that they were related to the job.

Mei relocked Jennifer's drawer and returned the key to its spot beneath the blotter. She scanned the desk to make sure nothing was out of place, unlocked the door, and headed back to her desk as the phone was ringing. It was after midnight. When would her mother leave her alone?

Frustrated, she snatched the phone and said in Cantonese, "This is my workplace. You cannot keep calling me here."

"Ling Mei?" a male voice said with a Cantonese accent. He spoke her name in the traditional Chinese format, surname first.

"This is Ling Mei," she responded in Cantonese.

"I am surprised to find you here at this hour of the night."

"*Bin go a?*" she asked. *Who is this?*

"My name is Lieutenant Andy Chang of the Office of Professional Responsibility," he introduced himself in English. "I was going to leave you a message. I thought maybe I could come by sometime so we could talk. Are you going to be in tomorrow? Or when is a good time?"

Her face flushing, she looked at Jennifer's desk and wondered if somehow she'd been caught on tape. "I was just working late this evening on a case in California. I am usually gone by now. I should be in about nine tomorrow, though," she said, wishing immediately that the call had been her sister to yell at her about red eggs and ginger.

Chapter 7

Oskar Kirov's breathing grew louder and louder as he watched his sons eat dinner at the long, narrow table. His fingers itched to rub at the pain in his gut, but he didn't move. He knew it was getting worse. He had less time without the pain, and when it came, it was steely cold, like death itself. Plus, he was sick all the time—nauseous and hunched over—and even the medication didn't help. He'd grown thin and he felt weaker. He focused on his boys, pulling his thoughts from the symptoms of his own mortality.

They were eating a late dinner. Dmitri shoveled food in deep, sweeping motions, loading butter onto his plate in thick chunks like it was bread. His tongue smacked against the roof of his mouth. Feliks sat across from him, eating in tiny bites like a frail bird as his fork clanked on the porcelain. He knew Feliks went the wrong way. There were words for it. *Goluboy* in Russian, and American words—gay, homo. None of them made it better or worse. Feliks wasn't manly. How had this happened to him? He was a strong father, not the type to have a *goluboy*. It was his mother's fault. She had been *slabi*, weak.

Feliks, at least, had his intelligence. He did the numbers for the business, reported them weekly. Oskar had never had the patience for numbers. He always checked Feliks's, though. One could never be too careful, and Oskar wanted it to be very clear that he was in charge. There had always been someone else to do the grunt work. That was how it should be. It had been Oskar's brother before he had died. Then Viktor, now Feliks.

Dmitri, on the other hand, had his mother's brain. He was better at the people side. People trusted him, confided in him. He couldn't add two and two, but he was good with people and he obeyed the rules. He kept the family name clean. Smarts wasn't something everyone could have. But right versus wrong, at least Dmitri knew that.

Only Viktor had had both; only he had been worthy of the empire Oskar had created. And Viktor was gone.

"We should go over the books," he told Feliks.

Feliks glanced up at him. "Of course. Whenever you'd like."

Oskar nodded. "Not tonight." He was too tired. He was always too damn tired. He watched them eat and felt even worse.

"*Menya goshnit*," he snapped at them. They made him sick.

His sons sat up and dropped their forks. "Papa?" Feliks said.

"You eat like a woman." He looked from Feliks to Dmitri. "And you like a pig."

The two boys exchanged insolent glances and shrugged. "*Gdye tei*," he called to their houseboy, Andrei. "Take these plates off the table."

The houseboy removed the boys' plates and then stood there. Oskar waved him away.

Feliks was still, his shoulders slouched, his head dropped. He picked at a piece of skin on one finger.

Dmitri stood up, his chair scraping against the tile floor.

"I didn't tell you to get up," Oskar thundered. Porcelain and silverware rattled as his fist slammed onto the table.

Dmitri walked away. Walked away from him.

He deserved better than this. Viktor had been his true son, the firstborn. Dmitri was weaker, more like his mother, Sophya, had been. And Feliks. He shook his head and carved the pork in a long, smooth motion. Feliks *was* Sophya.

At least she wasn't there to further influence them. She hadn't been strong enough. Her heart, was what the autopsy had said. It hadn't been her heart he'd broken, but it was good enough. Good enough to tell her sons. Only Viktor had handled the news with the appropriate male response. Dmitri and Feliks had wailed like babies. And Viktor was the one he lost. He paused and chewed his food with a low growl, stuffing in another bite and chewing harder.

He felt the burn in his gut again. He kept himself from rubbing it. He wasn't about to show his sons any sign of weakness. It had been difficult to do. He'd been ill in front of them on a few occasions, unable to hold off the nausea. But he'd told them it was food poisoning, and while he sensed they knew something was wrong, they certainly didn't discuss it. He would not share his problems with them. He had to be strong, in charge.

And he was even more careful in public. He'd told his business associates that he'd lost the weight on his doctor's recommendation. They had no idea that he was simply wasting away. Or if they did, he didn't know about it. Business was going to hell, and any sign of weakness would let others step in. He wasn't going to have that. He longed for a Zantac to ease the ache. The doctor was always warning him about salt. Goddamn doctors. He liked salt. He'd earned it, and he'd eat as much of it as he pleased.

Andrei returned and filled his glass with Grey Goose, straight from the freezer.

Feliks nodded the boy over, but Oskar shook his head. "None for him," he snapped in Russian.

Feliks made no move to stand up for himself. Oskar glanced down at the salty pork on his plate and narrowed his eyes. The meals were always salty now. Did they know?

He swept his arm across the table and shoved the plate to the floor. It shattered in a wonderful crash. Two maids came flying from the kitchen.

"Sweep this up," he demanded. "And then get back to the kitchen. There will be no women in my dining room."

The houseboy let them clean without helping. Oskar nodded to him. Someone who understood the pecking order.

Feliks met his gaze and Oskar waved him off. "Go, *nyezhenka*," he said, using the Russian word for "sissy."

Feliks didn't argue. He just scurried out of the room like a mouse.

"He'll not eat here again," he said to Andrei. There would be no women in his dining room, even in men's clothing.

The phone rang and Andrei brought it to him.

He answered without a sound.

"Krov, please," the man said, pronouncing Kirov's name like the Russian word for blood.

His jaw tensed. *"Eta Kirov,"* he answered in Russian.

"I've done it."

"You've been successful?"

"I have him."

Viktor eased himself back into the ornate mahogany chair.

"You are pleased?"

He smiled—the first smile in months. "I am pleased."

"I am glad."

He waved the houseboy from the room and dropped his voice to a gravelly whisper. "You'll tell no one of this. You deal only with me."

The man on the other end was easy. "What do you want me to do?"

"Nothing yet. I'll be in touch."

He hung up the phone and settled back into the chair, draining his glass. The vodka was smooth against his lips, the cold moving down his chest and easing his pain. Grey Goose was tonight's medicine of choice, although he preferred Ketel One. He debated calling for Andrei but decided against it. It was his turn to enjoy the solitude. He pulled the pills from his pocket and let two roll onto his palm. He took them with the final dribble of vodka and began to rub a small circle on his chest with the ball of his thumb.

He leaned back and closed his eyes, pushing until the push hurt more than the pain. Damn the pain. This wasn't supposed to be how Oskar Kirov died. He thought of his Sophya and Viktor, waiting for him. At least there would be Viktor.

The pain settled deeper and he could no longer reach it with his thumb.

"Andrei," he roared.

The boy came running and Oskar pointed to the vodka on the table in front of him. "My glass is empty."

The boy filled it and stood beside him as he drank in silence. A third glass, then a fourth, until the bottle grew empty and the pain grew soft.

Chapter 8

"Are you going to find him?" Peter asked.

Cody forced herself to nod. She would find him . . . even if it killed her. "Can I ask you about school today?"

Peter glanced over his shoulder, looking for the comfort of his father.

"He'll be right back. He's just making us hot chocolate, remember?"

Peter nodded.

Cody smoothed her hands across her jeans and slid down to the stair below Peter so they were eye-to-eye. "Can you start with this morning? When was the first time you saw R.J.?"

"We have math first, with Dr. Teller," Peter said, rolling his eyes the way only children do about teachers.

"Did you see him before class?"

He shook his head. "I was real late. Dad got an important phone call before we left."

Cody nodded, thinking again what a fool she'd been to trust Travis to pick up her son. "And after that?"

"We go to different homerooms, but we always meet up for lunch."

"What did you guys talk about?"

Peter shrugged. "The normal stuff." He paused and his face brightened. "And about tonight. What games we were going to play, what to get on our pizza."

"And then?"

"Then more school."

"And you didn't see him?"

Peter shook his head. "Not till P.E. with Mr. Crowley."

"And everything was normal in P.E.?"

Peter nodded.

"And after that?"

"After that, we went back inside to get our stuff, but then R.J. ran back."

Cody felt her breath still. This was it, the most important information. "Why did he go back?"

Peter looked over his shoulder again. "Don't tell Dad, but he left my jacket out by the playground. Dad made me swear not to let anyone borrow it, but R.J. really liked it. I knew he wouldn't hurt it."

Cody swallowed the thickness in her throat and nodded. "I'm sure he didn't mean to leave it on the playground."

"No. He wouldn't do that. He's real 'sponsible, Mrs. O'Brien."

She blinked hard and Peter patted her hand.

"I'm sure he'll come back soon."

She forced a smile. "Thank you." She inhaled and willed her body to process the air, to keep moving. "What happened then?"

"That's all I know, 'cause when I got back from

getting my stuff, Jamie Underwood told me R.J. had left with his dad."

"So you didn't see him leave?"

"No."

Cody's chest tightened. "Did you see the car?"

Peter shook his head.

Travis reappeared, carrying a tray with three mugs. "The one with marshmallows is yours," he told Peter. He set the tray down on the step beside Peter and then sat across from her, one step below his son.

He lifted one mug to Peter. "Be careful, it's hot."

Cody could picture Ryan's small, soft features against Mark's strong ones. How unfair that they'd never really had the opportunity to be father and son. She was more jealous of Travis in that moment than she'd been of anyone in a long time. Travis lifted a mug and passed it toward her. She held it tight in her hands, soaking in the heat until it was uncomfortable. At least it was a real sensation. "What exactly did Jamie Underwood say?"

Peter shrugged. "Just that R.J.'s dad had come to get him."

Cody looked at Travis. "Do you know the Underwoods?"

He shook his head. "Not well. He's a lawyer, travels a lot. She's at home."

"Where do they live?"

"A couple miles from here." He paused.

"Do you have the address?"

He gave her a reluctant nod. "Maybe I can help, go with you or something."

She shook her head. She thought about how much she wanted to call her family. Her sisters would know what to do: Ali had always been the problem solver, and Nicole always knew exactly the right thing to say. But Cody couldn't call them. She couldn't call anyone, not without risking Ryan's safety.

She was in this alone. She couldn't take anyone's help, and especially not Travis's. Plus, she still had to think about what she could say. She wasn't sure it would be the same thing she told Travis. She didn't want to start rumors about Ryan's father that he would have to deal with when he was back. She ached. Of course he would be back. She shook herself mentally. She would go there, tell them whatever she had to in order to get help.

Travis left to get the address, and she set the untouched mug back on the tray. It was then that she realized Travis had made coffee for her, not hot chocolate. She put her hand on Peter's shoulder. "Thanks for your help."

"You're welcome. Will you call when you find him? And tell him I'd really like him to come spend the night sometime."

She smiled and nodded. "I promise to call."

"Don't worry, Mrs. O'Brien. I'm sure R.J.'s dad is taking care of him."

The image of Mark watching over Ryan brought tears trickling down her cheeks. She smiled through them. She prayed he was right.

She passed an antique wooden coat rack that she'd missed coming in. Bright-colored baseball caps hung off a few of the limbs like fruit off a tree. She stopped and pushed aside a heavy leather jacket. Behind it was the small red jacket that she'd sent Ryan to school in the day before. She turned back to Peter.

"He gave it to me when he took my jacket," Peter said. "I was going to give it back when he gave me mine." He paused.

She ran her hand over the smooth, satin-like fabric, forcing herself to refrain from leaning forward to smell it. She felt a large lump in the jacket pocket. She pulled out Ryan's handheld Gameboy and shook her head. He knew he wasn't supposed to take it to school. But the thought of her baby tucking it away in his pocket and sneaking it off to school made her smile. He had grown up. He was growing up, she corrected herself. Dear God. She prayed he was still.

"That's R.J.'s, too," Peter confirmed.

Travis walked back into the room, holding a slip of paper. He frowned when he saw her holding the jacket.

She put the Gameboy back in the pocket. "I'll just leave it here."

Travis looked confused.

"It was in his jacket pocket," Peter explained.

Travis raised his eyebrows at his son. "You borrowing each other's toys?"

"We always share stuff."

"It was nice of you to loan R.J. your jacket, Peter. When R.J. comes home, I promise not to let him borrow it again. And I appreciate your help."

"Sure, Mrs. O'Brien. Tell R.J. to call me when he gets home, okay?"

Cody didn't answer him. She couldn't bear to.

Travis walked her to the door. "Please let us know if there's anything we can do to help."

Cody held the mobile phone in a trembling hand. She had to call. To find Oskar Kirov, she'd have to rely on someone. She thought about Mark's old colleagues, but she'd never known any of them well enough. The one man Mark had trusted without question had died the same day he did. She'd been through the people from her own past.

She needed help: information on Kirov and his most recent associates.

She paced across the basement floor again. She'd gone over the names in her head and there was only one person who could potentially help her. One person whom Cody still thought she could trust. Jennifer Townsend. They had been close when she was at the Bureau.

Cody stared at the phone, the memory of that morning in New Orleans flashing back at her, the heat almost blinding even now. She had never discovered the source of the leak, but she was sure it had come from the Office of Professional Responsibility, the Bureau's version of Internal Affairs. They were the only ones who had access to her whereabouts.

No, Cody had to trust someone, and Jennifer Townsend was her best bet. That was what this was now—a gamble. If she didn't make the call, she knew she'd never see Ryan again. And that was not an option. With a deep breath, she opened the phone, powered it on, and dialed the number from memory.

It was one o'clock in the morning there. She would just leave a message with what she needed and let Jennifer know she'd call back.

The phone rang twice and then someone picked up. "Computer Intrusion Squad," a woman's voice answered.

Cody hesitated. "Jennifer?"

"No, this is Mei. Can I help you?"

Cody shook her head and then forced herself to speak. "Is Jennifer in?"

"No, she's . . ." Mei paused and Cody felt herself holding her breath. "She's gone. Can I leave her a message?"

"No. This is her sister. I'll just call back." Cody hung up before Mei could say anything else. Damn it. Since when did agents answer each other's phones? Would Mei have recognized her voice? She gripped the phone in her fist and hoped Jennifer was still on speaking terms with her sister. They'd never been close.

Furious with herself, Cody punched in the number for Jennifer's old pager, and when the recording started, she dialed the code that they had established to mean the other one needed help: 911, then a 0, then the last four numbers of her badge number from the Bureau. At least Jennifer would know who called. And, she hoped, Mei wouldn't. With that finished, she returned the phone to its spot under the storage cabinet in the cold basement, grabbed a shovel, and headed outside in the dark.

Cody worked with an efficiency she hadn't felt since right after Mark's death. Shovel in hand, she followed the path out back to the small plot she'd dug when they had moved into the house. She began to dig. The rain had stopped, and though the air was still cool, sweat trickled down the back of her neck and her back. She ignored it.

Her heart pounded, throbbed even as the earth crunched beneath her shovel. Her throat burned. *Crunch.* Dump. *Crunch.* Dump. She moved in perfect strokes without slowing or stopping. Anything to avoid thinking about Ryan. It would do her no good to think about him. She had to work. And the night was the best time to do it.

Gather the equipment, her files, clear the house of

their presence in case someone came, and find out as much about Kirov as she could. Figure out what would be next. Why would he bother taking her son if he knew where she was? Why not follow them home and take care of them both at once? A child was high maintenance—even if all you intended to do was kill him.

The thought ripped through her like an electric shock and brought her straight to her knees. "Oh, God." She tried to pull herself up but noiseless sobs racked her. Be strong, she told herself. Be strong for Ryan. She wiped her face with her hands, feeling the granules of dirt scratch her skin.

In the years since Mark's death, she had always been strong for Ryan. But if something happened to him—if he was— She couldn't even think it. It couldn't be true.

"You need help?"

Cody spun around on her knees, gripping the shovel like a weapon in front of her. It was almost eleven at night, and the last thing she'd expected was another voice.

Colonel Walter Turner hung his upper body over his side of the fence and stared down at her, rubbing his hands together against the cold air. Her neighbor was retired military, and everything about him made Cody uneasy. In one of the three or four times she'd been forced to share dialogue with him, she'd made the mistake of calling him an ex-marine.

"Once a marine, always a marine," he'd quipped in response. "It's like being black—you can't take it out of me. Right down to the grave."

Colonel Turner was everything Cody sought to avoid—aware, observant, suspicious, nosy, and highly intelligent. And the combination was one she wanted to stay as far from as possible.

"Just doing yard work," she lied. She'd chosen this hiding spot before she'd met Colonel Turner, but in hindsight, she should have picked a spot as far from his side of the fence as possible.

"Looks like some serious work to be doing by yourself in the middle of the night. You need help?"

"No. Thanks."

"Didn't see the boy come home tonight."

Cody stood and started to move the dirt she'd dug up into small piles. Without looking at him, she said, "He's staying at a friend's."

"Glad to hear it. I hope they were playing outside some today. He spends too much time on that computer, if you want my opinion. Kids these days, communicating through machines, blowing things up right and left. Real blood, those games show. Don't learn anything about people—don't learn to respect life and death. That's why we got all these kids walking into school with guns. It's like some damn game."

Cody didn't answer. Instead she shuffled the dirt in small circles, waiting for the colonel to leave.

"You in trouble, girl?"

The paternal tone of his voice caught Cody by surprise and she looked up.

His eyes caught hers, holding their stare with his own. His dark brow furrowed, the vertical lines between his eyes like exclamation points as he watched her.

Tearing her gaze away, she shook her head. "Just trying to get some work done before"—she paused to put her mouth around her son's name—"before R.J. gets home tomorrow." Pressing the end of the shovel to her chest, she let it dig in until it was painful. The sensation was almost a relief.

"I know trouble, and I can smell it on you sure as that dirt you're working in."

Cody felt the anger wash over her, pushing aside the fear and the hurt. "I'm very busy, Colonel. Perhaps you could leave me alone."

"Okay, Miss Cody, but I know something's up. I didn't spend thirty-seven years in the armed forces—"

"Go away, Colonel," Cody said, letting the frustration slip off her tongue. "Please," she added.

He turned his back and walked away, uttering something she couldn't make out.

Cody turned back and moved faster, digging through the dirt in the dark until she heard the clink of her shovel against the buried box.

Chapter 9

Travis watched Peter sleep long after he had read him another chapter of the latest Harry Potter novel and tucked him in. He had blue and pink stains around the collar of his red flannel pajamas from the bubble-gum ice cream. Travis, too, felt slightly ill from the McDonald's cheeseburger and french fries he'd eaten in record speed. And Mrs. Patriarcchi, or Mrs. Pat as they called her, was ready to crucify them for passing on the pork chops she'd prepared. He'd promised they'd eat them tomorrow.

He watched Peter lick his lips in his sleep and wondered if he was imagining more bubble-gum ice cream or some of the magical treats from the Harry Potter story. He knew he should get to work, and yet he just couldn't get himself to leave the room.

Running a start-up meant crazy hours. And because of the flexibility he needed with Peter, the extra time usually came in the middle of the night. Still, he wouldn't change what he had for the world. It was thrilling, even if it had its stressful moments. They would fix the program glitch. He knew they would. He only hoped they could find some money to tide them over until then.

Trimming the fat was the first necessity. They were hiring four new programmers to work full-time on the glitch. Once they got through the initial troubleshooting phase, they wouldn't need so many technical people. He hoped that would hold things for a while. He was also pushing his designers to move on a new version before things got stale in the marketplace. New innovations, new features, they needed to push forward as quickly as possible.

Though everything seemed strong to him, the company's valuation was dropping with every failed dot-com, and he was starting to see critics of the software get more print space. He reminded himself that it was the industry, but he knew the employees were taking it hard. When so much of their compensation was tied to what the initial public offering stock price might be, it was tough to see valuations fall. That was if the stock even went public. It would.

He leaned forward in the chair, resting his elbows on his knees and watching the gentle wave of Peter's chest as he breathed. And despite all the company concerns, his mind still shifted constantly to R.J. O'Brien.

Cody O'Brien had made it perfectly clear she didn't want his help. But damn if he could just step aside like that. He tried to picture the man taking R.J. Had the danger been that close to his own son? He wiped his palm across his knee and shook his head. He didn't know what he'd do.

He watched Peter and let his mind work on the puzzle of R.J.'s mother. There was something about her, something more than what she said. He pictured her wiry frame, the snaking tendons in her fingers and hands. She was strong, exceptionally strong. He had seen the outline of her muscles beneath the shirt she'd worn.

She was thin, too. He'd seen a lot of thin women. Most of the ones he met these days were straight and flat from birdlike eating and whatever ridiculous aerobic ritual they suffered. But the O'Brien woman was different. She wasn't thin. She was lithe, strung like a cat and ready to pounce. Her dark hair and light eyes were stunning, and yet she seemed to do everything possible to make herself unattractive.

Maybe it all came back to the husband. He knew it was possible that it was just as she said. Women were abused. He didn't doubt it. And he'd heard the statistics.

It could happen to anyone. When he'd been building his business, he'd had an employee who'd seemed to have it all. And yet he'd discovered that her husband had been abusing her. He'd been shocked. He'd even met the husband and never thought for a moment that it was possible. He was being naive. Just because R.J.'s mom came across stronger didn't mean she wasn't exactly like his employee had been.

He pulled himself up from the chair and set the Harry Potter book on the bedside table. Then, wiping the moist hair off Peter's forehead, Travis kissed his sweaty brow. Peter licked his lips and rolled his head away from his father.

Travis padded down the hall in his bare feet, the cool hardwood floors moaning as he went. He passed his bedroom but couldn't imagine sleeping. He entered the small, dark room next to it. He had a full den downstairs, but he used this room to do some of his quieter work.

Leaning back, he settled into the chair and rubbed

his eyes. He pictured Peter waiting for him outside the school. What if Peter had gone missing? What if his damn job cost him *his* child? Jesus, was it worth it? He had to do something to help Cody.

She'd told him not to help, but he couldn't just sit by. Hell, he felt responsible to start with. He wrestled with that for a moment, wondering if he really could have done anything about it. Maybe R.J.'s dad was just going to show up there anyway. Maybe a few minutes wouldn't have made a difference.

He grabbed on to the moment of relief that thought brought but couldn't sustain it.

He forced himself out of the chair. What was he thinking? This was her child. He was all she had. He left the room and walked down the curved staircase to the cold marble floor of the foyer and on to his den. It was too late now, but in the morning he'd have to help. For now, he should focus on how to make his company's money last until they could get more, if they could get more.

He sat himself down at his desk and pulled the brass cord to turn on the lamp. The light created a green hue in the dark room and branded bright spots into his vision. He leaned forward on the desk, staring down at the budget numbers. *Marketing expenses,* he started. They'd have to cut back there immediately. He made a red mark next to that.

He kept reading down the list until the numbers grew stale and their meaning was lost on him and his eyes pulled themselves closed like shades being drawn down by heavy hands.

Chapter 10

Cody pulled the last picture from its frame and sealed them all in a gallon-size Ziploc bag. The four pictures of Mark she had saved were already safely there: one of them on their wedding day; one of the three of them only minutes after Ryan was born, Cody with dark black circles under her eyes and a sweaty brow; and the third of Ryan and Mark roughhousing. It was the last picture she'd ever taken of Mark.

There was also one photo of her entire family as they had been that last Christmas. She studied their faces, the smiles, the bright colors, all the kids. She and Mark had been pinched in the center, Ryan in Mark's arms. There had been fifteen of them that day, and they'd barely all squeezed into the picture. She refused to even consider how her family had grown in her absence.

Pushing herself onward, she tossed the plastic bag in the pile of things that would go—tax records, social security cards, two Zip disks of all her system backup that she'd mail to a post office box she had in Austin, Texas, and a small sack of clothes for herself and Ryan. She erased the rest of the files on the computer and checked for prescription medications in the medicine cabinet. There was only one, cough syrup with codeine, from the time Ryan had been sick last winter. She tore the label off and put it in a bag of papers to be disposed of.

She checked her medical supply kit and then added it to their bag of clothes. The house was clear. It could as easily have been a corporate apartment or a hotel room as anyone's home. She had been sure to systematically destroy records with their names: old bills and checks were always destroyed. Cody had only one Visa card and it drew money directly from a bank account at a Northeastern bank. The bank statements were accessed only via a password on the Web. She could do that anywhere.

She took a last look through Ryan's room, lifting his favorite teddy bear, Nicky, off the bed and pressing it to her nose. The bear was named after a puppy they had had before Mark had died. The scent of Ryan pushed her to move on. She tucked the bear under her arm. He would be thrilled to see it when she found him.

She went through the rest of the rooms with the bear in one arm and checked and rechecked for any evidence of her existence. Only her fingerprints would be left. And only for a few hours. It was the last thing she needed to do in the house. But first she needed to take care of the documents.

If the Russians showed up before then, they might or might not check for her prints. There was nothing she could do about that. She'd always known there would be something left. She took out the postal card that noted the change of address to her second P.O. box in Savage, Minnesota, and set it out to make sure it got mailed first thing. There were other P.O.

boxes, all routed and rerouted to each other in a circle that only she understood. She would use them as they were needed, open new ones and close them as they moved.

She carried the last things downstairs to the basement. Then she took a final look around the house and wondered what someone would think when they entered. It had never had much in terms of personal charm. But it felt cold and foreign now, even to her. She turned away from it before the thought struck her too deeply, and set to work in the basement.

She shredded the papers to be disposed of and packed the bag of clothes, medical supplies, and Ryan's Nicky into a large plastic container in the back of the car. The container was always in it, usually empty. But it was important to her that the car looked as it always did, even if she was on the move.

When the car was packed, she set the bag of pictures on the seat beside her. Those had to be hidden separately, but she needed to take care of something else first.

She pulled the car out of the garage and down the street in the darkness. Once she'd turned right onto the next street, she flipped the lights on and drove for fifteen minutes through the Oakland hills until she was certain no one was following. She took two turns and got onto Highway 24 and headed for Jack London Square.

When she'd first arrived three years before, they had been starting to rebuild the Jack London Square area. A theater had been added; Yoshi's Sushi had moved from Claremont to the square. There were a few big shops: a Beverages and More Cody had never been in, a Cost Plus where she always bought chocolates for Ryan's stocking at Christmas and cola-bottle gummies for herself. She wished her trip there today were for something so sweet.

She passed the central area and followed the street three blocks to a much quieter area. The large produce markets she passed were closed up, even the early-morning trucks nowhere in sight. A few people milled about in front of Yoshi's, probably discussing the late show that had ended an hour before. It was the quietest part of the night now.

In a few hours, huge trucks would arrive to unload goods for the day. Cody would be long gone by then.

When she and Ryan had just arrived, Cody had sought out a safe place in one of the buildings to use for a hiding spot. She'd had to move her stuff because of one building after another being torn down until she'd discovered the loft where she went now. It was the only building in the area that still had not been updated.

She'd actually found the spot through an article in the paper. The eccentric owner had been written up for refusing to either sell or update his building. He said he'd sell it when the price hit $100 million but he was at least a decade away. In the meantime, he lived in the top loft and the bottom sat filled with junk from the home he'd had. His home had been bought by some construction company that was building condos. He'd been ripped off, he'd said, so keeping the run-down, vacant warehouse was his way of getting back.

Cody had staked the place out a million times. Despite the article, the guy seemed pretty normal to her. She sympathized with getting screwed by the system. Glen Kunka was probably in his late fifties, early sixties, and drove a gray diesel Mercedes that he pulled into the bottom part of the loft at night. He worked at a small bookstore in Berkeley, one of those that had barely hung on after the big chains had taken over. Cody had been in once and bought something. He'd been friendly and helpful, but not intrusive. She'd liked him. Unfortunately, she knew she couldn't go more than once at the risk of being remembered.

Mr. Kunka always had a stack of books under his arm when he entered his home. He turned off the main light sharply at nine, and a small light usually shone until almost midnight. She always wondered what he was reading but had never been close enough to tell.

He left every morning at nine and returned home at seven in the evening. Even the days he didn't work, he went out—usually to the streets near the bookstore where he worked. He did some shopping, or sat in the park and read. He led a quiet life, and for that Cody envied him.

She drove past the building and turned the corner before parking. She shut her lights off and waited. Ten minutes passed before she moved again. There were no lights, no motion but the cars speeding along the freeway in the distance.

Unlatching the car door slowly, Cody moved with quiet purpose, taking only her gloves and a small dustpan and broom. She shut the door behind her until she heard the lock click and headed around the back of the building, pulling on the gloves as she walked.

She entered through the same tight, square window at the back of the downstairs space where she always did. The small back lot was surrounded by a tall, rotting fence that protected her from being seen by the tenants next door.

Stepping up onto an old spigot on the back of the place, she climbed onto the windowsill and opened the window toward her. It moved a few inches, then locked in place. She reached inside, lifted the ancient fastening mechanism, and the window opened with a slow, low moan.

With the dustpan and broom tucked in the back of her jacket, she moved through the window on her belly. Her eyes closed, she lowered herself toward the floor until she could feel a file cabinet teeter beneath her foot.

She eased herself down onto the corner of the cabinet and then to a crate and finally to the floor. A heavy film of dust coated everything like paint, and she was careful to disturb only a small edge of it on the cabinet to avoid being detected. A small cloud of dust rose as she passed, and she covered her nose and mouth to avoid sneezing. Nothing had been moved in the space since she had started to come here over a year ago, but she never knew when it might happen.

Crossing to the far corner, she slid the two boxes away from the wall and edged open the door that had originally held the central electricity for the building. It was the ancient knob-and-tube electricity, and neither that nor the space had been in use for years. She reached her arm in and loosened the heavy flame-resistant pouch from its spot behind the wall. She opened the small lock on the bag using Mark's birthday as the code. Then, sitting on the floor, she took stock of the contents. Her current passport, reading Cody O'Brien, and R.J.'s. Those she took out, along with six thousand dollars in hundred-dollar bills. That would be enough to get them out of the country, and from there she would have access to funds from a Swiss account. But that was a last resort. She would never be able to work abroad, and she feared for how they would survive.

She took her second passport, the one that read Emily Page. She might need another one down the road. There was no matching passport for Ryan. She would worry about that later. She could find a social security number for Ryan easily enough with the obituaries and a little research.

She wondered if he would ever get to be Ryan James Riggs again. On his tombstone. The words sneaked up and slapped her. She didn't let herself even imagine it. It would do her no good now, and her energy had to be expended on the belief that he was still okay.

She found one last picture she had stored in the plastic bag and stared at Mark and Ryan. She focused on Ryan's tiny body in Mark's arms and pulled her breath in as though Oskar Kirov held it in his hands. She forced the photos from her white knuckles and locked the pouch before tucking it into her jacket to be mailed to one of her P.O. boxes tomorrow. With the money and their passports zipped into a money pouch inside her shirt, she pushed the boxes back against the wall. Pulling out the small dust broom she'd brought with her, she smoothed the dust on the floor so the path of the boxes was no longer visible and headed back to the window.

As she hit the ground outside, she looked at her watch. In and out in five minutes. She was slowing down. Too much thinking, not enough action. She was tired. The fear was slowing her down. That was exactly what Kirov would have wanted.

Jogging back to the car, she told herself she would not allow that to happen. No matter what, Kirov would not win. She took a few minutes to watch for anyone nearby and started the car to head home. She had always made these trips with Ryan safe at home. He always knew she was going but never where. She set the silent alarm downstairs, and they each had cell phones that they talked on when she was in the car. She held her phone in her hands now, willing it to ring and knowing it wouldn't. Ryan's was already packed into the trunk.

Only determination fueled her drive home. She was going to find Ryan if it killed her. And she knew quite well that it might.

Chapter 11

Jennifer Townsend woke up Saturday morning looking horrible. Seated in front of the mirror, she spread Preparation H around her eyes and then dotted it along the corners of her mouth where the swelling was still bad. Whenever she saw the Preparation H tube, it reminded her of her sister. Her perfect sister. Tiffany Townsend Sheffield. Married to a ninth-district judge, with two beautiful girls. President of the Junior League, on the board of the country club, she was her parents' dream. One child, her father had told her mother. You can have one child. His own pending judgeship meant his wife had a lot of duties to take care of, and one child would be plenty burden on his schedule.

But Tiffany had been so easy that Emily Townsend had convinced her husband to have one more. Jennifer had been a difficult pregnancy. Emily had been sick during one of the judge's most trying times. Then Jennifer had been colicky and a miserable, unattractive child. Nothing she'd done had ever been good enough for Judge Townsend. Not quite good enough grades, never fast enough in track, never pretty enough or polite enough or funny enough. Never Tiffany enough.

So after college, Jennifer had done the least Tiffany-ish thing: She'd sought a career in law enforcement. Not just law enforcement, but the most distinguished branch, in the eyes of her father: She'd joined the FBI. And they'd accepted her. And she'd loved it from day one. The people were sharp and no-nonsense. They didn't care about hair or makeup. They wanted results. And results were something Jennifer could deliver.

But even Jennifer's success with the Bureau was deemed too pedestrian by the esteemed judge. It had taken that to make her realize nothing would ever be good enough. It still didn't take away the hurt.

But she had more than Tiffany did now. She didn't envy her sister anymore. The last thing Jennifer wanted was to be a soccer mom in worn pink sweats. That was Tiffany. Jennifer had a high-powered job in which she was an expert in her field. And she was sexy. Dmitri made her feel sexy—sexier than she ever had before him. She knew there was something naughty about his family that made it a little more exciting, but Dmitri was legit. He had his own importing business, separate from his father, and he did quite well. And yet he was still rough and edgy. That was what had kept her with him. It was never dull, never what was expected, like her life growing up.

She looked back at the spots where the Preparation H had soaked into her skin. It was a trick her sister had taught her. Of course, Tiffany and her perfect husband had never had a real argument, Jennifer was sure. In fact, she'd be amazed if they ever really talked. Her husband had about as much passion as their father—zilch. Tiffany had used Preparation H in high school for those mornings when she woke up with puffy eyes from crying over some cute boy.

This was one of the first times Jennifer had used it. She looked down at the makeup bottles that covered the vanity of the second bathroom for something that would do the trick, but even the theater makeup didn't completely cover the bruise. She looked back in the mirror and leaned against the sink.

Catching one of the bruises on her thigh, she jumped back and let the side of her robe fall open, biting back a cry. She had a welt from where he'd grabbed her that was just now reaching premium tenderness.

She looked at her eye and debated ways to hide the bruise from her nosy colleagues at work. But none came to mind. It was Saturday, but the office would still be full of people. She probably should just work from home.

Dmitri was still dead asleep in bed. Too much Ketel One vodka. She had a headache herself. They'd gone to a late-night club after she left work and then had come back and gone straight to bed to conclude the making-up process. She hadn't gotten much sleep, but she was tired and sore in the way that reminded her of how incredible Dmitri was.

Normally she would have taken a hot shower and dragged herself to work, but the bruise by her eye was still too obvious. It had been impossible to even get by Mei for a couple of hours, so she couldn't risk a full day.

She twisted the cabochon rings on her finger and considered the ramifications of not going in to work. Mei could struggle through this case without her.

Screw it, she decided. She'd call in and then get
back into bed with Dmitri. If he didn't have any appointments this morning, they could even make
breakfast. Dmitri made a wonderful western omelet.
It was the first thing he had ever cooked for her, and
she still thought it was ironic that the best western
omelet she'd ever had was made by a native Russian.

She picked the cordless phone off the sink where
she'd left it last night, and cleared her throat before
dialing Mei's number.

Mei answered on the second ring. The tiny
choppy accent in her soft voice made it sound like
she was on a bumpy elevator ride.

Jennifer shrugged off the irritation she always felt
when she heard it. "It's Jennifer," she croaked, taking a few big breaths through her mouth to dry her
throat out and make her sound worse.

"Hi," Mei answered coolly. Anyone else and Jennifer would have taken offense, but Mei always
sounded like that. Until the night before, Jennifer
had never seen Mei upset enough to raise her voice.
The downcast eyes and soft features, her low voice,
it all reminded Jennifer of Tiffany. Perfect Tiffany.

"I'm a little sick."

"Okay," Mei said, and Jennifer could feel the
anger in her tone. Whatever. She didn't have to explain anything to Mei.

There was an awkward silence.

"You want me to take care of anything for you?"
Mei asked, her tone softening.

"No, thanks. I'll check my messages and all from
here. I'm just a little under the weather—like the flu
or something," she lied. "Back and neck are sore,
throat hurts, that kind of thing. I know we were sup-

posed to work on case 297 this weekend, but I just need to rest up."

"No, you definitely shouldn't come in. Take a hot bath. Put some green tea in the bath and grated ginger; they're good for healing."

Jennifer shook her head and cleared the tears from her throat. "Green tea and ginger," Jennifer repeated.

"Yeah. It sounds funny, like you're making yourself into tea. But it works. Must be an old Chinese thing. You can drink them, too. Also, if you can get your hands on any Cucurbitaceae fruit—a lot of herbal places call it the magic herb. Chinese call it the longevity fruit. It's good too, very sweet, and will help with the pain and recovery. Come to think of it, I think I know where to get some extract. I'll send it over later. Is there anything else you need?"

The way Mei sounded, Jennifer was beginning to think she was really concerned. "No. I'll be fine. I'm here if you need anything, and I'll be checking E-mail. And I may try to come in later," she added, mostly for show.

"Okay. Feel better."

Jennifer felt relieved. Mei worked all the time, anyway. She could cover for Jennifer over the weekend. She didn't seem to have anything else but work, after all. Maybe she just liked working all the time. Jennifer didn't care.

Jennifer had started to hang up when she heard Mei's voice.

"Hello?" Jennifer said into the receiver. She traced eights across and around the bruise on her thigh, testing its sensitivity and imagining herself in a bath with grated ginger.

"Yeah, I forgot to tell you that your sister called

late last night. I picked up your extension because it was so late and I thought it might be an emergency."

Jennifer halted, her finger pressed into the bruise's sorest spot. Her sister, Tiffany, would never call. Even if one of her parents were dead, surely it would be Tiffany's husband who would deliver the news. Tiffany would be too distraught, and probably too caught up in the details of the funeral.

My sister, Jennifer repeated silently.

"Did you hear me?" Mei asked.

She lifted her finger off her leg. "Yeah. Sorry. I thought I heard the doorbell. Did she leave a message?"

"No. Just that she'd try you again later."

"Okay," Jennifer said casually, the thoughts now racing in her head. That definitely didn't sound like Tiffany. Tiffany would have left a long-winded message, screeching and cooing in all the right spots and sighing when the note taker didn't write fast enough. Or was she wrong? Could it have been Tiffany?

She hung up and stared at the phone. She had no idea what her sister's number was. She crossed through the bedroom and looked at Dmitri's tanned chest, eager to get back in bed beside him. Curiosity pulled her to the small spare bedroom she used as an office. She found her briefcase and reached in for her PalmPilot when she felt her beeper go off on vibrate mode.

She lifted the pager and scanned the screen. Three new pages. She scanned the first two, which were Bureau business from yesterday, then got to the third: *91105453*.

"Jesus," she whispered, cupping her hand over her mouth as soon as she'd spoken. Only one person would know that code. How could it be? She'd been gone for years.

The eight numbers burned into her mind until she could see them imprinted when she blinked. Was this some sort of joke?

The 911 for emergency, the 0 for a break, and the last four digits of her badge number. It had to be her. Megan Riggs had paged her.

Jennifer hit the two buttons to erase the message as she felt her shoulders droop. She fingered her rings and thought about what an incredible surprise Megan Riggs would be for Dmitri. He would be thrilled. Finally the guilt would be gone. They could appease his father and put it to rest.

She turned back and nearly ran into Dmitri.

She gasped and laughed as she touched his chest. "You scared the shit out of me. I called in so I don't have to go to work today. I was just coming back to get into bed with you."

"It sounded like you were sneaking around," he replied, his face set in a frown.

She ran her fingertip down his chest. "Look who's cranky today." She raised the beeper in her hand. "Just checking my messages."

Still frowning, he took the beeper from her hand and put it back in her briefcase. Then he took her hand. "Come back to bed. It's too early."

"I'm coming," she told him in Russian. She thought about mentioning Megan Riggs and decided to wait. She didn't want to get his hopes up, but if the message really was from Megan, things were definitely looking up.

He sank onto the bed and pulled her into his lap with a heavy thrust. The bruise on her leg knocked against his knee and she let out a groan. Dmitri took it for excitement and rolled her onto her back, spreading the robe with strong hands and cupping her breasts. She let her head fall back as she arched toward him.

When she looked up again, he had shed the white cotton Calvin Klein boxers and was coming toward her.

She grinned at his body, his passion protruding.

He reached down and grabbed her buttocks and lifted himself onto her, thrusting himself inside in a deft motion that took her breath away.

For the moment, she pushed her pathetic sister and Megan Riggs from her mind and let Dmitri fill it as he was filling her body.

She and Dmitri were meant to be. All they needed to do was help his father and Dmitri swore they would be free of it. Jennifer had no problems with that. Megan Riggs deserved what she had coming. She never should have betrayed Jennifer's trust.

Yes, she and Dmitri would be together, and getting Megan Riggs would merely be icing on their wedding cake.

Chapter 12

Cody watched the next morning as her neighbors the Dawsons pulled out of the garage and headed off for their Saturday activities. The house was completely clean, prints included. And to keep from messing it up, she'd spent the night in the garage on a cot, though she wouldn't have called it sleeping. She'd been waiting for someone to arrive for her. If Kirov had Ryan, surely he would come for her, too. Or perhaps the torture of not knowing was his way of making her pay. It was too subtle, she decided. Subtlety wasn't like Kirov. Oskar Kirov had something bigger in store.

She watched the neighbors' car until it had disappeared around the corner and then waited another three minutes. They had breakfast and played Saturday-morning bridge at some friends' house, Mrs. Dawson had told her once. It didn't matter where they were going. Just that it was the same place as every week and that they wouldn't be back for at least three hours.

Dressed in sweats and running shoes, Cody headed out her back door. She crossed the sidewalk and entered the Dawsons' side yard. Moving swiftly, she followed the slippery brick path around the side of the house to the fence, then reached up and unhooked the latch. The door came loose and Cody opened it slowly, waiting for the dog to appear. The Dawsons' dog, Jerri, was a German shepherd–collie mix that they had once asked Cody to take care of when they'd had a family emergency. This morning she was taking Jerri out for her own purposes.

Jerri bounded across the yard as Cody found his leash on a small hook on the outside of the house. He pawed and licked at her as she tried to maneuver the clip onto his collar, and she immediately thought of how funny Ryan had thought it was to watch her go through the same thing. He'd lain on the grass, roaring, while she had struggled with the dog that weighed almost as much as she did.

When she finally got the leash attached, Jerri bounded around in a circle, and she knew he was missing Ryan, too. "It's going to be okay, Jerri. We're going to go get him."

She led the dog out of the yard and closed the gate behind her. She opened the back of the Jeep and pulled the dog in before closing the hatch and getting into the driver's seat. The Underwoods' house was exactly where she'd expected it to be, a few blocks from Landon's in an equally wealthy neighborhood where people had 2.4 children and 2.9 cars and 1.5 dogs that they walked on a Saturday morning. She drove past as slowly as she could without being conspicuous. The light was on in the kitchen, but she didn't see any signs of activity. There was one car, a gray GMC Suburban, in the driveway, and the garage was closed.

She continued on a couple more blocks and parked her car near a corner so it would be hard to tell exactly where she was headed. She was anxious to get to the Underwoods', but it was early still. Little boys were rarely outside before nine or so. So instead of heading toward the Underwoods' house, she started to run with Jerri in the opposite direction.

She and Jerri made a three-mile loop, passing the Underwoods' house twice in the process. It was still quiet the second time she came by, so she continued to run. Her breathing measured, she was more relaxed than she'd been since the time Ryan had been picked up from school. In the past hours, she had wondered a thousand times what she was doing or thinking the moment Ryan was stolen. Had she felt his pain? It was not something she let herself dwell on now. She focused on the pattern of her breathing, on the steady *whoosh-whoosh* of the air as she pushed it out her mouth. Her feet went *plat-plat* on the moist concrete while Jerri's chain *tink*ed beside her.

Jerri was keeping up, although she knew he wasn't used to so much exercise. She would make sure he got plenty of water afterward. She made a smaller loop and started up the Underwoods' street in time to catch the gray Suburban backing out of the drive. She ran faster, waving to stop them despite the fact that she couldn't possibly explain why she would be asking questions about who had picked R.J. up from school unless something was desperately wrong.

She waved anyway. Something would come to her.

The driver of the truck was about her age, maybe a few years older. His hair was salty on the edges and he appeared to be balding. He looked short behind the wheel, and as she reached the car, he stopped and rolled down the window.

She stopped running and shook her head to give herself time to suck in a deep breath. Beside him in the passenger seat sat a young boy. He wore a navy-and-white game shirt. She hoped he wasn't Jamie because the chances of getting to talk to this boy alone didn't look good.

"I just had a question about today's soccer game," she said, noting the shin guards the boy had in his lap and praying she'd guessed the right sport.

"Claremont or St. Stephens?" he asked.

St. Stephens was where Ryan went. "St. Stephens," she answered, feeling the words come out in a croak.

He smiled. "Inside. I'm on Claremont today. Lisa can help."

"Great."

He waved and started off, the diesel Suburban a rattling roar on the quiet street.

She waited until he was out of sight to turn to the house again. It was still quiet and she didn't want to ring the bell and have to explain to Peggy that she needed to talk to Jamie. She found a spot of sidewalk that was blocked by a hedge and sat down to stretch. If anyone asked, she'd just say she pulled something. Everyone in their forties could appreciate that.

Jerri formed a furry ball against the cool cement, lying on his face and dropping his chin on his front paws as he panted to cool off. She wished she'd brought some water with her, but they'd both have to wait. She looked repeatedly at her watch. The Dawsons were never gone more than about three and a half hours, and she needed to get the dog home before they returned.

Almost a half hour had passed before she finally

got to her feet and started to think of excuses to ring the bell. As she started in a slow stroll toward the house, a kid on a scooter zipped by and dropped the scooter at the bottom of the Underwoods' stairs before bolting up them and pulling his helmet off.

He rang the bell once, waited not quite ten seconds, and then rang it two more times.

Standing in front of the neighbor's yard, she heard someone yell from inside.

The door opened and a boy R.J.'s age came out to join the second kid, a scooter in hand.

She watched the two of them talk, wondering how to intercept them before they took off. Looking down at Jerri, she had an idea. She unhooked his leash and bent down to rub his head. "Okay, Jerri. Be a good boy. Now go."

Giving him a little shove from the backside, she watched him take off down the street. Just like a dog. She gave him a healthy head start and then started after him. "Madison, come back. Maddie!" she yelled, afraid that calling him by his real name would simply bring him back. She passed the boys and stopped, pretending to be out of breath.

She bent over her knees and dropped her head. "Darn it all."

The boys were laughing.

She looked up and gave them a tired smile. "I'll give you guys ten dollars if you can catch that dog."

They exchanged an excited look. "Heck, yeah," Jamie Underwood said, strapping his helmet on.

The two of them took off down the street and Cody followed close behind.

Jerri had gone only half a block before stopping to rest. The boys halted within a few feet and clapped their hands. Jerri bounded over and Jamie caught hold of his collar.

"You owe us ten bucks," the other kid said.

Cody nodded. "I know. I can't thank you guys enough. He really takes off sometimes. I don't know how his leash came off."

"No biggie," Jamie said, beaming.

She took hold of Jerri's collar and made work of reattaching the leash. She knew the boys weren't going anywhere now. Not without the ten bucks she owed them. "You're Jamie Underwood, aren't you?"

He looked at her exactly the way she'd trained Ryan to look at strangers who spoke to him.

"I'm R.J. O'Brien's mom."

He nodded slowly.

She put her hand through Jerri's leash and reached into her pocket. "Let me find that money." She figured it was now or never. "He got picked up by his dad on Friday. I heard you were there."

Jamie frowned. "Yeah."

"His dad is up in Tahoe and the phone lines are down, so I'm trying to figure out how to reach him."

Jamie Underwood's face softened just slightly. The other kid looked bored.

"I'll know where they were going by what car they had."

"What car?" Jamie asked.

The other kid shrugged. "My dad does that. He's got an old truck he only drives up at his ranch in Mendocino. He never takes his Merc up there."

Merc? She nodded agreement.

Jamie frowned. "I guess it was like a van."

"A van? Do you remember what color?"

"He's got two vans?" the second kid asked.

She ignored the kid and focused on Jamie, who didn't seem to mind the question.

Jamie frowned again, watching her hand and waiting for the money to appear. "I don't really remember."

"Shoot," she said, pulling out her wad of cash. "It really would help me."

Jamie stared at the money. "I don't know, maybe it was blue." He paused. "Or gray."

"Blue or gray," she repeated.

"I think."

"Can we have the money now?" the other kid asked.

She nodded, unable to find another question to get at what she needed. But without something from Jamie, she was at another dead end. She handed the money to Jamie. "Thanks again for helping me with the dog."

"Sure."

The other kid reached for the money from Jamie, but it was already in his pocket. "I caught the dog," Jamie reminded him.

The other kid gave him a silent glare.

They turned to go and Cody just watched. Her skin tingled with desperation to reach out and grab Jamie, to sit him down and hound him for information. But she stood still, Jerri heaving and panting on the ground beside her feet.

Jamie got on his scooter and then turned back. "I think the van was white."

"White?" she repeated.

He smiled, proud that he'd remembered. "I'm pretty sure."

A white van. What could be more difficult to find? She dropped her head and turned back toward the

Underwoods' house and the direction of her car. She'd find another option. There would be another clue. Kirov would contact her. Something had to happen, she reminded herself. She would make it happen.

As she focused on the street before her, a navy blue Porsche pulled to the curb. Cody passed, anxious to get home and figure out what to do next.

She walked another ten feet before she heard a voice.

"Hi there!"

She turned back to see Travis Landon standing beside the car.

"I'm glad I caught you." He crossed behind the car in a pair of worn Levi's and a faded navy T-shirt that made him look like a model for a summer vacation spot in the mountains. "I've been thinking about this all night, and I know you don't want to call the police, so I've got an investigator we can talk to. His name's Dusty McCue. He's done some employee background work for me. He's got a lot of ties with the police, but he's not a cop." He held his hand up as though to interrupt her if she started to argue, which she didn't. "And he's very discreet. I've already called him and he's available."

She exhaled and wished she could disappear. She forced her shoulders back and weighed Travis's offer. Nothing sounded better to her ears than the help of someone professional. But what would McCue do? First he'd want to know who would take Ryan. It was a question she couldn't answer—not without risking too much. He'd want to talk to Jamie about the man he'd seen. That meant involving Jamie's parents and the school. Media. It would all lead to media. And increased media attention meant increased pressure on Kirov. That was the last thing she wanted. She needed to stay calm, stay quiet, and work this from the inside. Just her and whatever FBI help she could get in silence.

"Cody?" Travis said, drawing her from her thoughts.

"Oh, sorry," she said, feeling her lips tremble as she forced them into a smile. "I was just thinking about the crazy night we had. R.J.'s home. He came home this morning."

Travis frowned, his gaze traveling over their surroundings as though questioning why R.J. wasn't right there. It would have been a good question. When she found Ryan, she wasn't going to let him out of her sight again—ever. He motioned to Jamie's house. "I was just coming to talk to Jim and Lisa Underwood, see what Jamie remembers about who picked up R.J."

"No need. R.J.'s fine, came home right after I left your house," she lied, forcing a smile.

"Really. Where was he?"

"His uncle picked him up. R.J. was supposed to tell me about it but he forgot."

"And he had plans with Peter," Travis said.

She nodded, letting her gaze go to the dog circling her legs so that she didn't have to look at Travis. "I know. I'm sorry about that. I promise we'll set things straight with Peter."

She glanced up as Travis's eyes narrowed. "He's back," he said, looking skeptical.

"Yep. I need to get back to him now," she said, backing away from Travis.

Travis watched her. "His uncle brought him back?"

She nodded. "Just went to dinner and a movie."

"I wish you had called. I was worried."

She tripped on a piece of cracked sidewalk and stumbled. "I apologize. It was so late." She shrugged as lightly as she could manage, every muscle in her body quivering. "I really should go. We'll talk soon. Maybe Peter can come over next weekend or something."

Travis raked his hair. "Yeah, sure." He paused and put a hand out as if to add something when she waved and turned her back. She started jogging down the street again, the tears streaming down her face. She hoped the sobs that racked her just looked like normal running, because she couldn't stop them now.

Chapter 13

Travis slammed the door to his Porsche and revved the engine high. He peeled off the street, letting the engine roar though he kept the car in first gear. He needed to drive off this steam. What the hell was wrong with him? He had other things he could do if Cody O'Brien didn't want his help. So she lied. He shouldn't care. He should keep his nose out of her business.

He crawled through the small town, itching to put the pedal to the floor. People crossed in front of him: a woman with two dogs, a man with a jog stroller. He needed open road. He wound through the streets and over the hill down toward the freeway. He hit the on-ramp at sixty in fourth gear and was doing eighty-five by the time he'd shifted into fifth.

The car hummed beneath him like a tank, and for a second with the radio turned off, he could almost imagine that he was on top of the world again. He passed two exits and pulled off to turn around. He knew exactly where he was heading. He couldn't shake it. No. Go home, he told himself.

He hit ninety on the way back, zipped off the freeway in time to make the light, and was on his block in less than two minutes. He stopped at the end of his block and reversed into a small spot between two trucks. From behind the wheel, he watched the street, unmoving.

He smacked the steering wheel. He deserved to have some answers, didn't he? After all, he was the one feeling responsible that R.J. had been picked up under his watch.

He stared out his windshield. "What the hell?" he muttered, revving the engine and pulling onto the street again. He drove to the O'Briens' house, parked and got out of the car.

He'd just make sure everything was okay and then he'd go home and get Peter. He'd give the nanny, Mrs. Pat, the day off, and he and Peter could do something fun. Maybe even go throw the ball around at Golden Gate Park, get some hot dogs. They hadn't done that in forever. That was it. He'd take two minutes to put his mind at ease and then it was off to the park.

Travis shut the door and walked up the small incline to the house where he'd dropped Peter no fewer than ten times. He'd never been invited in. Cody O'Brien barely even opened the door enough for him to look at the foyer. He didn't care. Really, he didn't.

Maybe she just didn't trust men. No surprise there, if what she said about her ex was true. This wasn't about her, he reminded himself. It was simply about his kid's best friend.

He started up the steps. At the door he rang the bell two times quickly and then stepped back and waited.

For a full minute he watched the house silently. He saw her Jeep on the street. Where the hell was she? He rang it again and waited. Okay, so she was in the shower, but then where was the kid?

He moved around the far side of the house in search of a clear window to look through. A gate locked off the back of the house, and he tried to find a way to reach the latch but couldn't. He circled back and rang the doorbell again. Still no answer. If she was like some of the women he'd dated, she could probably spend an hour in the shower. Or maybe she had the hair dryer going. That could take an extra hour. He shook his head. She didn't seem like the hair-dryer type. In fact, she didn't really even seem like the long-shower type.

He followed the small path around the other side of the house and noticed that each window was completely covered. Levolor blinds and shades covered every single angle, even in the middle of the day. He frowned. She seemed awfully paranoid, but maybe it was all just as she said it was.

"Can I help you with something, fellow?"

Travis turned around to see an older black man starting up the O'Briens' path. He pointed to the house. "I was trying to reach Mrs. O'Brien."

"Seems she doesn't want to be reached, don't it?"

Travis smiled. "I suppose it does. Have you seen her today?" He thought about the boy. "Actually, I was trying to talk to her son, R.J. Have you seen him around?"

The man's eyes gave nothing away as he nodded. "Haven't seen a thing, but maybe you ought to just come back later."

Travis stepped forward and offered his hand. "I'm Travis Landon. My son, Peter, is a good friend of R.J.'s."

"Walter Turner," the man said, returning a shake that was definitely U.S. government trained.

Just then, a window on the upstairs level cracked. "Colonel, what are you doing?"

"Just talking to your friend here. He's looking to talk to little man R.J."

Cody O'Brien's scowl shifted from Travis to Walter Turner. "Colonel, please go home. And you, too, Mr. Landon. Home." She pointed like he was a stray puppy.

Travis turned his back on the colonel. "I need to talk to you."

"Yeah, Cody, come on down. I've got a couple questions, too," the colonel added.

There was a short pause and the front door opened just as Travis reached the doormat. Cody pushed him backward and stepped outside, pulling the door shut behind her. She wore a pair of men's boxer shorts and a black Nike T-shirt. Her legs were everything he'd expected: thin and long, with muscle definition that made it clear she'd be a match for himself and most men. He forced himself to move his gaze.

The colonel kept his distance. "Where is R.J.? I thought I'd show him my new ant farm."

"He's sleeping. He had a late night. I'll have him call you later."

The colonel watched her and then nodded. "I'll look forward to it."

Cody watched him go and then turned the same appraising look on Travis.

Travis found it made him want to smile. "Quite a neighborly relationship you've got there."

Her expression lacked even the slightest flicker of a smile. "What the hell do you want?"

"You surprised me this morning, R.J. being home and all. I thought you would have called."

"I told you, it was late, Mr. Landon. I was tired and so was he."

"Travis. You can call me—"

"Thank you for worrying. I do apologize for not calling." She turned back to the house. "I really need to go back inside."

He found his eyes shifting across her backside.

She turned around swiftly and he swung his gaze to the front of the house. "Sure. I wanted to see R.J., check and make sure he was okay." He watched her scan the street behind him.

He turned back to look, but he couldn't see what she'd been watching. When he looked up, her gaze was back on him.

"He's fine, but we're all a bit tired. I can have him call Peter later, if that's okay."

"I think Peter would love it if R.J. could come over tonight."

"Oh, I'm sorry. I don't think tonight would be a good idea. He's just gotten home. I'm sure you can understand." She turned to open the door. "Thanks for coming by, though." A car drove past and she studied it as the driver craned her head out the window as though looking at the street numbers.

"Are you okay?"

"Fine," she said without taking her eyes off the car. "There's the phone. I've got to go." With that, she disappeared inside and he heard the clunk of locks turning.

He hadn't heard the phone ring. He watched the closed door for a minute, waiting for her to open the door and laugh. But her strange behavior was no joke. The woman was paranoid. He shook his head and wondered if she'd hidden R.J. herself so she could put on her little show.

He drove home and set it out of his mind. Sure, the kid had tough breaks, but lots of people grew up with weird parents. He knew all about that first-hand.

By the time Travis got home, it was after ten and Peter had gone out riding bikes with a couple of the neighborhood kids. Though he had wanted to spend the whole day with Peter, Travis was relieved to have a couple hours to sort out things at work. Plus, he and Peter had made plans for the evening.

Mrs. Pat was making meatloaf for dinner, which he knew would get no points from Peter. The pork chops would have been better, but she'd said they'd be no good today and she'd had to toss them out. But she'd also made Peter's favorite peanut-butter cookies to go with the movie they'd rented for the night—something with Adam Sandler that he knew would make them both hysterical. That was one thing he and Peter had in common—taste in movies. He knew a lot of people would comment on that, but hey, what good was life if you couldn't be a little silly sometimes?

It was about an hour later when he heard Peter tearing down the hall. Travis stood and stretched, ready for some fun.

Peter burst into his office. "Dad, you got to see this!" His shorts were pulled down around his hips in the current fad and he wore a long-sleeved blue shirt beneath a red short-sleeved one.

Travis smiled. "What do I have to see?"

"This Web site. It's got R.J. on it."

The sound of that name made him frown. Not that

again. What he needed to do was find his son a new friend. R.J.'s mom was so overprotective. "R.J. has a Web site?"

"It's not his Web site. It's just his picture, but the Web site's got my name. It's so cool. Come on, Dad. You've got to see it." Peter turned and ran back down the hall and up the stairs.

Travis followed more slowly. The Web site had Peter's name? He shook his head. Peter wasn't making sense, that was all. Maybe R.J. had posted something about the day's events.

Kids these days had Web sites and instant messaging, and if Travis hadn't gotten cable Internet access set up, he didn't think he'd ever be able to use the phone line in his own house.

When Travis reached Peter's room, his son was sitting at his computer desk, typing something. "You messaging with R.J.?"

He shook his head. "I tried, but he's not on-line." His son closed the pop-up box and displayed the dark screen behind it. "See," he said, pointing to the picture on the screen. "That's R.J."

Travis leaned forward and stared at the picture. Just the darkness of it made his gut sink. He leaned in and squinted. It was a boy standing against a white wall with his hands by his pockets. He looked pale and sickly . . . and very frightened. Travis scanned the top of the screen for the url. He read it and blinked, sure his eyes were playing tricks on him. But even when he refocused, what he saw was still the same: www.ivegotpeter.com. Peter? "'I've got Peter,'" he said out loud. "How did you get this?"

"The link came to our E-mail address," Peter answered.

"Our E-mail?"

"Our 'PeternTravis' one. It's the one in the school directory and stuff."

A million thoughts came to him at once, but at the center of it was an icy current of guilt. Her child for his. An accident. An error.

But R.J. wasn't missing anymore. Cody had said so herself.

He shook his head. It felt all wrong. "What the hell?"

"I know—isn't it weird, Dad? He's got my jacket on." He pointed to the brown satin Bulls jacket.

Travis's stomach tightened.

"And he was wearing that shirt at school yesterday," Peter said, pointing at the black T-shirt with the Quicksilver logo that showed under the unbuttoned jacket. "I know 'cause it's the one I want. Remember, I showed you in the store?"

Travis stared at the picture as chills washed over him. His hands moved to his son's shoulders. Peter. I've got Peter. He knew the two kids even looked alike. Mrs. Pat mentioned it constantly. *Twins separated at birth,* she always teased them as she handed them each a small bag of snacks and said she couldn't tell them apart. Mrs. Pat joked for their benefit mostly. They weren't that similar, but the coloring . . . the dark hair and light eyes, their size . . . Oh, Jesus.

"What's R.J.'s number at home, Peter?"

Peter repeated the number out loud and Travis dialed.

"Hello?" came Cody's tentative voice.

"It's Travis Landon. I—"

The phone clicked dead. He looked at the phone to confirm she had indeed hung up on him. Jesus

Christ. He held back swearing in front of his son, but a string of not-so-nice words came to mind for Cody O'Brien.

He punched redial and heard the phone ring again. There was no answer, and after four rings, then five, then six, he hung up. What home didn't have an answering machine? Jesus, he was going to have to go back over there. Son of a bitch. "Uh," he groaned, livid.

"Maybe they're not home."

Travis nodded, refusing to draw his child into Cody O'Brien's petty game. "Print that page out, will you?"

Peter's tiny fingers flew across the keyboard as he hit the Ctrl-P function.

Over his son's shoulder, Travis searched the site for links or text, anything that might offer more information, but it was blank but for the picture.

He ran his mouse over the page, searching for a hidden link or text.

"There's nothing but the picture, Dad. I already checked."

Travis blinked and looked at Peter, nodding, but his gaze was instantly drawn back to the frightened expression on R.J.'s face. Someone had been very careful to make sure all they showed was the boy. The boy who should have been his child.

"Where's the E-mail?"

Peter shifted the mouse. "Right here."

Travis read the return E-mail address. It was a Hotmail account, and the name was a series of numbers. He memorized them and realized it was today's date. He knew they'd learn nothing from that. The E-mail had come in early that morning.

"Someone can come try some cookies," Mrs. Pat called from downstairs.

"You're sure R.J. was wearing this yesterday?" Travis asked.

"Positive," Peter said, staring back at the picture.

"Cookies," Mrs. Pat called again.

Travis ignored her, too many thoughts battling for space. "Oh, God."

R.J. *was* gone. For some reason he didn't understand, Cody was lying. Her son was missing, but he hadn't been the target. Peter was the target. Someone had meant to kidnap Peter and had gotten R.J. instead. He knew what that meant: It meant R.J. was actually missing. R.J. and not Peter.

"Something's wrong, isn't it, Dad? Something with R.J.?"

Travis gripped his son's shoulder and pulled him close, trying to figure out what to do. Instead he ran his hands through his son's hair. "Yeah, partner. Something's wrong."

Chapter 14

Sitting on the cold, hard cement, Cody heaved the Browning Rimfire Grade 1 rifle onto her lap and broke the gun open to clean it. She'd done the same for the three other guns, and her hands were black from the gun oil she used to wipe out the barrel and lubricate the parts before putting each one back together.

The phone sat beside her on the floor and she stared at it between moves, silently cursing Oskar Kirov. When she felt herself close to breakdown, she gritted her teeth and polished and scrubbed the gun's surface harder, not allowing herself to slow for the ache in her forearms or the echoing emptiness of her gut. Food would wait. She needed to be prepared when he came.

And he would come. She had to believe that this was just the beginning of his game. She heard the creak of the porch stairs and set the gun silently down on the cement floor. Lifting the Glock, the gun the Bureau had taught her to shoot with, she clicked the release and slid the magazine into her opposite hand. It was full. Replacing it, she took a deep breath and held the gun straight down at her right side, her finger off the trigger, before slowly moving toward the door to the basement.

The footsteps continued slowly across the porch, and Cody strained to hear others. They wouldn't all come to the door. She wondered how many there were and where they were positioned. Lifting her pant leg, she tucked a second gun, a derringer, into the holster under her sock and straightened her cuff. She heard the bell ring and waited. The footsteps were silent.

Cody moved slowly up the inside stairs until she could see the hallway. Sitting down on the step, gun in front of her, she tucked her head around the corner and stared at the shape behind the curtain on her front door. The bell rang again and she jumped slightly, wondering if Kirov's men would ring three times before breaking the door down. The shadow turned back to the street, and then she saw a male face flash beneath the raised blinds on the side window. He cupped a hand over the window and looked around. As he did, Cody measured his features. It wasn't Kirov. Damn it. It was Travis Landon again. Why wouldn't he go the hell away?

The bell rang again and Cody tried to ignore it. When it rang for the fourth time, she went to the door.

"Damn it all," she muttered, tucking the Glock in her belt and walking up the rest of the stairs. She crossed the foyer quickly and pulled the door open.

Travis looked up and stared at her, blinking.

"I told you to go away, Mr. Landon. How much clearer do I have to be?"

He pointed to her face. "You're . . . you've got a smudge—"

She realized she was covered in gun oil and dirt. "I was cleaning." She didn't say what.

He nodded, still frowning. "I need to talk to you. May I come in? Just for a minute."

"No. You may not. I don't know what your problem is, but I'm very busy. You have to leave."

"We really need to talk. It's about—"

"I don't have time." She started to close the door.

"It's about R.J.," he said. "I know he's gone."

Cody stopped and looked at him. His face made her insides freeze. She glanced down to see that the street was quiet. Colonel Turner must have retreated into his house, and she didn't want him to hear this. Waving Travis inside, she quickly closed the door and pointed to the small sitting room she used as a reading room. Travis perched on the edge of one chair while Cody stood at the door without touching anything.

She watched Travis look around, clearly curious about the house. Every moment he did tried her patience more. "This needs to be quick, Mr. Landon."

He pulled open his jacket and removed a white envelope from the pocket.

"What do you know about R.J.?" she asked.

"I know he's been kidnapped."

Cody pressed her hands into her jeans, glancing down at her blackened nails and nodding. "And?"

Travis looked around at the house as though something were seriously amiss. "I think I know why."

Cody stared at him. How could he possibly know? Travis Landon couldn't have a connection to Oskar Kirov. It was too outlandish. "Please tell me, then."

"I wasn't sure you'd answer the door, so I put it in an envelope."

"What is it?"

"It came in an E-mail." Travis handed her the envelope. "Peter downloaded it earlier this morning. There's a Web site listed."

Cody took the envelope, watching how the black on her hands smudged against the envelope. Her prints, as surely as though she'd been arrested and printed with black ink, showed up on the surface. She didn't want those ending up in the wrong hands. She pulled out a folded paper and opened it up, tucking the envelope under her arm. The E-mail said only, *Go to www.ivegotpeter.com.*

The thoughts bombarded her mind like bullets. The return address was a series of numbers at a free E-mail provider, not easily traceable. But Peter. Peter was at home. Ryan was the one missing. A wave of coldness crashed over her and she looked up at Travis, shivering. "Peter?"

He nodded, reaching for the envelope, but Cody didn't offer it back.

"I don't have time for computer games. Is this about Ryan? Is that what this is about?"

"Ryan?" Travis repeated.

Cody blinked back anger at herself for misspeaking. What was wrong with her? "R.J. Is this about R.J.?"

"Yes." Travis tugged at his hair in a gesture Cody read as guilt and pain. "He's on that Web site—a picture of him in Peter's jacket."

A heavy whooshing filled Cody's head. The jacket. Oh, Jesus. The jacket that Ryan had left on the playground and gone back to get when someone took him. "The Bulls jacket?"

Travis nodded. "Peter said R.J. is wearing the same shirt he had on at school. Here, I've got the—"

Without letting him finish, Cody turned her back on Landon and sprinted back to her office. Slamming herself into her desk chair, she turned her Gateway on and waited while the PC started up. It was hardly thirty seconds but it felt like forever. Oh, God. What was going on? A Web site, a picture of Ryan . . . it felt all wrong.

She double-clicked her Microsoft Explorer icon, typed in the url, and hit enter. She could hear Travis crossing the floor behind her, but she didn't care. She felt the gun press into her back and realized he would have seen it when she turned. It didn't matter. She didn't care. None of it mattered—only Ryan.

The page loaded slowly, the image coming in thin strips from the top. First she saw a white wall and the top of a dark head and then finally a forehead. Slowly the face filled in, and when the image reached R.J.'s chin, she gasped and touched the screen, her hands smudging black over R.J.'s cheek. "Oh, baby."

Travis came into the room. "I've got a printout of it here." He waved a piece of paper at her, but she ignored him.

Her heart was racing.

"I'm so sorry," he offered, and she wished he'd shut up. "I can't imagine what this must be like. If it was Peter . . . but if the Web site is ivegotpeter.com, then it should have been Peter." From the corner of her eye, she watched him pace a small circle. "I can't think who would do this, but the Bulls jacket that R.J. had borrowed . . . Peter wore it everywhere. People knew him by that jacket. Maybe someone thought Ryan was Peter; maybe the kid in the picture should be my son and not yours."

She listened to him. Someone had kidnapped

Ryan. It was Oskar Kirov, wasn't it? She thought over the past eighteen hours. Why hadn't Kirov shown up? Why would he take Ryan and not make another move?

Her stomach tightened with dread. She felt feverish and she wanted to be sick, but she couldn't move. Instead she stared at her son, the lines of his tearstained cheeks jagged on the screen. She ran her finger along the outfit she'd seen him come down the stairs in yesterday morning.

She ran her mouse around the Web site and looked for a link to show up. She couldn't imagine Oskar Kirov setting up a Web site, taking a picture, and loading it on the site. It felt too subtle. He would have just taken them out, sneaked into the house in the night, shot him, then her, and been done with it. Kidnapping a child and holding him without contacting her was all wrong.

She cupped her hand and looked back at Travis, who was staring at her. Oskar Kirov didn't have Ryan. Oh, thank God. Thank God that monster didn't have her son.

She blinked and looked back at her son—at the image of him God knew where. But if Oskar Kirov didn't have him, who did? Could it be someone worse than Kirov? She looked back at the Web page. "'I've got Peter.' Who is this? Who's doing this?"

Travis grabbed her chair in a tight fist. "I wish I could tell you. I can't believe this could happen. And it's my fault. Peter shouldn't have loaned his jacket out. I shouldn't have been late. Jesus, if I'd been there right on time, maybe he wouldn't be gone."

Travis looked breathless when he finished, unsteady on his feet.

Cody stood and motioned Travis to a chair before he fell over. "Sit."

He did, his face showing he was still wallowing in guilt and self-pity.

"Who could have done this?" she asked.

"I—I don't know," he answered, looking away.

She grabbed his shirtsleeve. "Think, Landon. Who? Your ex-wife?"

He shook his head. "No. My wife's dead."

Cody stopped, thinking instantly of Mark. "I'm sorry. What about an old girlfriend . . . ?" Cody stared back at the picture and shook her head. This wasn't a woman's crime. The electronic setup, the impersonal way of communicating the kidnap-ping—it felt male. She looked at Travis Landon, thought about his business. "Someone who knows what you're worth. Have you received anything about ransom?"

"No, nothing."

"You've checked the E-mail again?"

"Jesus, no. I didn't even think."

"Do it again as soon as you get home. He'll proba-bly contact you soon for money. How are you for cash?"

Travis shook his head. "Jesus."

Cody felt herself panic. "They'll ask for a lot— we can expect to need ten to twenty percent what you're worth in cash to meet the ransom. You can leverage your house and your business, I'm sure. What are you worth?"

He looked up at her blankly.

"What are you worth? What do the papers say is your worth? About $100 million, right? It might give us an idea of what they'll ask, so we can start getting things ready."

Travis shook his head. "I haven't even received a ransom note yet."

"I want to start thinking about all the angles. I want to be ready when they ask." She thought about Travis's words. Why wouldn't the kidnapper have asked for money yet? Was he just making him sweat? She tried to remember back to her colleagues at the Bureau. After years of relying on her own resources, Cody was wired to work alone. And as long as she'd had Ryan, she'd been okay. She didn't want someone's help. She wanted Ryan back. She didn't think she'd survive without him.

She focused on the problem. The MO brought her back to Landon's business. His company developed software to build Web pages. Whoever had kidnapped Ryan was somewhat techno-savvy. Not unlike someone who might work for Landon. Or might have worked for him. An ex-employee?

She hesitated, looking back at the picture of R.J., not wanting to move it from the screen for fear that it might be gone when she went back. That was ridiculous, she told herself. Still, she hit Ctrl-P and heard her printer click on as the image began to materialize on the page.

"What are you doing?" he asked.

"Checking something."

She chose File, Save as, and chose Text as the document type. She typed the file name *Kidnap* and felt her own insides stiffen. When the file was saved, she launched Microsoft Word and opened Kidnap. At the top, it clearly said PageMaker. Not TecLan Pro. She exhaled, deflated.

"What?"

"PageMaker. I was thinking it might have been—"

"TecLan Pro? You were thinking it was someone from my company?"

She cracked a knuckle, ignoring the strange glance she got from Landon. "We have to think. Assuming this person was after Peter, why? Who would want to hurt you like that?"

"Jesus, this is nuts."

"It's most likely personal. Statistically speaking, these crimes usually are."

He looked up at her. "You a crime buff?"

She didn't answer him. Instead she tried to think through who might want to make Travis Landon's life a living hell. There was the competition, but she couldn't see LandStar or TelMart taking their business this far. Those companies weren't suffering because of Landon's business. This wasn't Microsoft and Apple; this was normal business competition. She dismissed another company and continued to think.

"Maybe they're after money?" Travis added, his voice still stunned.

She thought about his theory. "Maybe. We have to wait for a ransom note. In the meantime, we should consider other possibilities."

She found herself coming back to the idea that it was personal. She knew Landon was right—money was a good motive. Someone could have heard about his money, heard about his dead wife and found out where his kid went to school. But Cody didn't want to believe it was a random kidnapping. If it wasn't personal on some level, the chances of finding the kidnapper dwindled to almost nil. And that meant the chances of finding Ryan alive were that low as well. And that, she refused to think about.

"What about an ex-employee? Someone who quit."
It might even make more sense that they hadn't used
TecLan Pro. Wouldn't that be too obvious?

Travis looked at the screen and shook his head.
"Maybe. There've been people who've left . . ."

Cody jumped on his pause. "Not just someone
who left. Was there anyone you fired or forced to
leave? Someone who is unbalanced, angry. Someone
who felt cheated. I know it's not the only possibility,
but it's one we can manage." She had to keep it
manageable.

Travis put his elbows on his knees and dropped
his head in his hands. "It's possible. I can think of a
couple people who swore they'd get back at me. But
kidnapping?"

"Can we get files for those people? I want to know
who they are and where they live and where they
grew up and went to school."

He nodded weakly. "I'll get the files and we'll call
Dusty McCue."

She paused, thinking of McCue again. The situation had changed. She could no longer count on help
from the Bureau. The kidnapper was no longer a
known entity. It was like trying to grasp onto a
handful of sand and it kept slipping through her fingers.

"He's the best bet if we want to keep the police
out of it. And Peter's in danger here. If someone re-
alizes that they got the wrong child, they may come
after him. I need to protect him. I can't just stand by
and do nothing."

She forced herself to nod. "Okay."

Cody put her hand out and stopped Landon from
taking another step. "Okay, we'll use McCue, but
that's it. No one else, and he needs to keep this com-

pletely quiet. No one else." She studied his reaction. "There can be no police. You need to understand that it's a matter of life and death."

Landon looked puzzled but he nodded. "No police. I swear. Plus, it's probably in our best interests to keep it quiet, especially if that someone still thinks he's got Peter."

The thought frightened her. She hoped Ryan just played along with whatever the kidnapper said.

"Can you tell me what you have against the police? Is it something you did?"

She watched him, knowing the question was coming. She had to answer it. Not because he deserved an answer. He didn't deserve anything. But she knew he would be curious and he might start digging around. And she didn't want to risk that he might find anything. Even discovering that Cody O'Brien had no credit history beyond three years ago was too much. "His father is on the police force. Ryan was abused," she said. "We were both abused."

He sank low into the chair.

It appeared to be working so Cody continued. "Badly abused by R.J.'s father. We got away, but it hasn't been easy. We've been living here for a few years and I don't think . . ." She paused, inventing as she spoke. "I don't think Carl knows where we are. But he still works in law enforcement in California. When R.J.'s picture got out—if it got out—he'd find us. He'd find me. And if I found R.J., we'd end up back there. It wouldn't be as easy next time."

"Your husband was a cop and he abused you? That's terrible."

She nodded slowly. "It happens more than you think."

Landon eyed her head to toe as though summing up the kind of woman who was abused by a cop husband. "Weren't there legal channels you could follow to get away?"

She looked away, continuing the charade. She could do this. She could lie until kingdom come, if she had to. "I tried the legal channels. We had restraining orders and trials and doctor's reports showing the breaks and bruises. Everyone was vigilant for a while—the local police, the neighbors. But if someone wants to get at you, the truth is, a piece of paper won't stop them."

Landon laid a hand on her shoulder. "You won't risk that Carl finds out."

She nodded, relieved both that he remembered the name and that he seemed to understand.

He nodded in return and lifted his hand. "Okay. We'll use McCue, then."

"You should make sure he gets access to a full list of ex-employees or contractors of TecLan. That's probably the best place to start. That and . . . does he have any experience with cyber crimes?"

Travis wore a blank expression. "Cyber crimes?"

"This Web site is criminal. There are ways to track the activity using specialized software to where the signals to the site are coming from."

She paused at his expression. "It was on an episode of *Justice Files*," she offered.

He nodded. "I've seen that show." He looked at the computer and then shook his head. "I don't know. I'll find out, though." He grabbed a piece of paper from the printer and started to make notes. "I'll see when McCue can meet us. He swears complete discretion, but I can understand if you don't want to meet him. You don't have to. And I can warn him about your ex, if you think that's smart."

Did she want to meet McCue? Not particularly, but it seemed hard to imagine losing control over the investigation. Maybe there was more she could do on her own. Maybe there were ways for her to track down the owner of the Web site on her own.

"I'll call him as soon as I get home." She thought about what pieces she'd put into play. It didn't matter that she'd packed up the house and wiped away all the prints. She'd shredded documents, though nothing that was really important. But what if Jennifer had answered the phone last night? She'd almost made contact with the Bureau again. She'd paged Jennifer without leaving a return number. At least she hadn't given anything away. It would be a mistake to contact them. No FBI. No law enforcement.

"All right," she said, still thinking about how close she'd come to unleashing the past. What if she had? Would Jennifer have insisted on getting the Bureau involved? Would her situation have leaked out?

Landon took a step closer. "I know you're scared," he said and she frowned, wondering what he'd seen in her face. Whatever it was, he had no idea why she was scared or about what. "Your husband was a bastard, Cody."

She flinched at the reference to Mark. He was referring to her fictional husband, she knew, but it reminded her of the loss all the same.

"But that doesn't mean everyone is." He set his hand on her shoulder.

Landon's fingers tightened on her shoulder, and for a moment the pressure was almost a relief. She stood and moved across the room. "Go ahead and contact McCue."

"I'll call right away. He's been standing by until I talk to you. What time works for you?"

"I'll be there when he's ready. The sooner, the better. Maybe I can find something in the meantime." Cody went to whosit.com and typed in the Web site address. She watched the information come up. The site was supposedly registered to a John Doe of Portland, Maine. The P.O. box was 12345. Definitely a fake. "Damn."

Travis watched over her shoulder. "Not listed."

There were other ways to do it, but she didn't want Landon to see what she knew how to do.

There was nothing more to say, so she turned her back to Landon and clicked back to the url with Ryan's picture.

She heard the front door open and click shut and she went to the door and checked that Landon was gone. Back in the chair, she spent the next thirty minutes trying all the tricks she knew for tracing a site without special Bureau resources. None of them worked. Whoever had set up this site knew how to avoid a trace.

Her stomach heavy, she ran her finger along her baby's face and found herself with so many prayers, she didn't even know where to begin. She prayed the kidnapper didn't realize his mistake too soon. If he realized he didn't have Travis Landon's child, she didn't know how he would react.

She wondered if she was right not to involve the police. What if they could find him faster? Or the Bureau? At least there she had contacts. Maybe Jennifer's team could track the Web site within hours.

The biggest risk was still the newspapers. She'd

seen them freak out kidnappers and make them dispose of children where they claimed they wouldn't have otherwise. And she'd also seen times when the press helped locate someone who knew something. She tried to remember what she knew about hostage negotiation. What did they do when there was no ransom? No demands yet.

Each time she thought she was better off without the police, she tipped back the other way and wondered if they would discover some clue to finding him faster. "Oh, baby," she whispered.

Using all available resources was worth the risk that Kirov found her if it meant she found Ryan first. But what if somehow Kirov got to him? She'd been so used to a private life, to lying to everyone, that she couldn't imagine dialing 911 and telling them her story. And yet, she knew she alone would have to live with the risks of not calling.

What if she made a mistake? What if her decisions cost her Ryan?

She right-clicked her mouse on the picture and saved it to the computer's wallpaper, then copied it into her picture software to expand it. Just the motion of doing something made her feel better.

She enlarged the picture to 130 percent until Ryan filled her computer screen. She toggled up and down, studying the background, his clothing, his hands, face, ears, hair, every detail in search of a clue. Just like a crime scene she told herself. A photo of one. Every few minutes her eye caught his and she felt as though the breath were being sucked from her. She forced her gaze away, then noticed the index finger on his left hand was curved back toward him as though pointing. At first, it looked like his hand might have been tucked in his pocket, but she could see all four fingers and his thumb. What was he doing?

She followed the line of his finger until she saw a small shadow on the edge of one of the folds of his shirt.

Her heart jolted. What did he have? She enlarged the picture again to 180 percent and focused on the small detail. At first it looked like a tear in his shirt, and she wondered what he was trying to tell her. But as she squinted she realized it wasn't a tear at all.

She let out a stilted laugh. Thank God. Thank God for Ryan. He'd sent her a gift. And in that moment, it was the most amazing gift in the world. On a small fold of his dark shirt sat a big, ugly bug. Damn if Ryan wasn't the smartest kid in the world.

Now the question was how to find out what it was. She knew one person who might know. And right now, she'd do anything to find out.

Ryan was fighting and so she would, too. He was going to make it. She had to believe it. He was smart and he was fighting. She was more proud of him then than she ever had been before.

"Way to go, buddy. Mommy's going to find you. I swear, she is."

Chapter 15

The colonel was standing at the side of his house, peering into the hutch that held his ant farm, when he saw Cody O'Brien come around the corner toward his house. She looked behind her carefully and then ran up the twelve steps to his door.

"Don't ring that bell," he cried out, hurrying around the corner.

Cody leaped back, looking startled.

"You'll wake up Florence. She's napping." The colonel waved her toward him. "Quieter back here, anyway."

She descended the stairs and came partially around the side of the house.

He paused and looked at the white page she held in her hand. "What you got there?"

She hesitated and then stepped closer and held her hand out. "It's a bug." She shook her head. "Or a picture of a bug, I should say." She looked up and held his gaze. "I was hoping you would recognize it."

He squinted at the poor photo. It had been cut from something larger so it was barely the size of a silver dollar. "I can't hardly even see the thing. Where the hell is it?"

She took the page and turned it toward the light. "It's there. It's sort of like a red fuzzy fly."

He stared at it, squinting and turning the page until he thought maybe he could make out the shape. "It's got wings?"

"Yeah, they're black." She pointed to the top of the bug where the background was black.

He shook his head. "I can't tell anything from this picture." He looked up at her and raised his eyebrows. He'd never seen her look the least bit feminine until that moment. Her bottom lip was tucked into her mouth and her eyes were wide, her brows straight. She looked smaller, and he realized then how upset she was. He touched her arm. "Can we get a better picture? I'm sure I'll be able to tell with a better picture."

She stared at it and shook her head, the softness disappearing from her face as she did. "I don't have a better one. This is all I have."

"This about the boy?"

Her eyes snapped up to his and they were both silent.

She cleared her throat. "I appreciate your help, Colonel. Sorry to have bothered you for nothing." She took two steps away before he had a chance to speak.

"Why was that Mr. Landon over here looking for R.J.? I haven't seen the boy since yesterday morning. Why is that?"

She didn't turn for a moment, and when she did her brow and her mouth were perfect parallels. "I would just like you to identify a bug. Can you do that?"

He shrugged. "I'd like to help if I can."

She didn't move.

"I know you need help."

She shook her head. "I don't need help. I need you to ID a bug, Colonel. But if it's that much trouble, forget it."

He found himself smiling. "Damn if you aren't stubborn."

"I've got too much to do to waste my time with you." She started away again.

"Maybe you'll let me tell you what I know," he called after her.

She turned back, her gaze showing just a speck of hope. "What do you know?"

"I know your kid is gone."

She started to speak but he stuck his palm out to stop her.

"I know you used to work in law enforcement."

Her mouth fell slightly, but she stayed quiet.

"I know you're on the run from somebody."

She snapped her jaw closed and started to shake her head.

He grabbed her arm. "I don't care. I don't care if you've done something bad or if someone has done something bad to you. I can help you. I can help you find Ryan."

He watched her face. The use of the boy's name, his offer for help. He watched her double over as though she'd been hit. Damn his big mouth—he'd gone and made it worse.

She held her hand to her mouth and shook her head. "No," she whispered, the word more of a gasp.

"Yes. You could let me help. I swear it would be

okay." He looked up at the heavens. "I swear to God it would."

He took a step toward her, but she backed away. "Don't," she pleaded, turning her back and wiping her face. "Please don't. I can't." She straightened and turned to face him. "You don't know anything about this. I don't know how you found out his name..." She paused and covered her mouth to hold back her emotion.

He could see her fighting to hold it back. He knew how it felt. He'd felt that same way when he'd watched his best friend get shot up in Vietnam. He remembered the pain of watching Henry die like it was yesterday. He pressed his hand to his chest.

"He let it slip one time, made me promise I wouldn't tell you."

She shook her head.

"It was an honest accident. He's just a kid. But I knew then that you all were on the run. What right-minded folks would name a kid Ryan O'Brien?"

She half laughed, half sobbed. "Oh, God. I can't. I can't do this. I have to go." He couldn't tell if she was going to run or collapse, so he continued carefully.

He caught her arm, then, for fear she'd run off and he'd never get to explain. "I'm not helping just for you, Cody. I never intended to go liking your child, but damn if he didn't grow on me. I got a grandson that age." He motioned to her. "A daughter your age, too, and I never met him." He shook his head. "Never met my own grandson. Little Ryan's the closest I've got."

She surveyed the street. "Please don't call him that."

He nodded. "Never again. But let me help you find him."

Cody collapsed into herself then, curling her arms across her chest and her hands over her face as she leaned down to sob. She was fighting it, but he knew she'd think clearer once it was all out. He'd been that way, too, after his friend Henry's death.

He took a step forward and put one arm around her, patting her back. "Don't you worry. He's one hell of a smart kid. Any kid can get out of this, R.J. can."

Just then, the sobs hit harder and she leaned into him. He let her, using whatever soft words he could find in an attempt to calm her. For a moment he imagined it was Roni he had in his arms. One day he hoped he'd get to hold his own daughter. Boy, he'd screwed that up. He pushed it aside and focused on Cody.

When she was done, she stood back and wiped her face. "I'm sorry," she said, as though some alien being had possessed her body for the past few minutes.

He shook his head. "Don't you apologize. Sometimes getting it out's the best thing."

She wiped her face again and nodded.

He put his hand on her arm and motioned toward the street. "Now let's go take a better look at this bug."

Chapter 16

Mei turned her wrist and glanced at her watch for the tenth time in twenty minutes. Maybe the eleventh. Since she'd told him she was going to be in the office on Saturday anyway, Andy Chang from the Office of Professional Responsibility wanted to see her at 3:30 P.M. off premises. He had called late last night on her way out and it had been all she could think about since. Then he'd left her a message this morning asking her to meet him at a local coffee shop. He had even described what he was wearing so she'd be able to pick him out.

There was little discussion around the Bureau about the protocol of firings. Terminations were few and far between, and seldom discussed. In the ten years since Mei had started, people had left, but Megan Riggs was the only person Mei had known to go into the Federal Witness Protection program.

Megan had crossed Mei's mind three or four times in only a few days, and Mei began to wonder why she'd come back into her thoughts. Mei's mother had always said that people crept into your mind for a reason. Mei wasn't sure if that was Chinese superstition talking or something her mother had picked up all on her own. If Chinese were considered superstitious, Mei's mother was superstitious even by their standards. Every time Mei had to go to a job, her mother would appear with a sack of things Mei needed to pack to make for a safe journey. She'd explained to her mother that her job wasn't dangerous. It was computer crimes, not drug enforcement. But her mother would hear nothing of it. "It pays to be cautious."

Mei thought maybe Megan had been on her mind because of Jennifer's increasingly strange behavior. At least Megan would be someone Mei could confide in. The rest of their group was male and mostly single, making them a difficult bunch to relate to unless you were willing to hang at Tommy's Pub and shoot pool. Mei had gone once and beat most of them, and that had been her last invitation to Tommy's.

Mei missed the times when there had been easy banter in the office and even a bit of camaraderie between her and Jennifer. She didn't remember much of either since Megan had left. Megan had a raw, smoky voice, similar, she realized, to the way Jennifer's sister had sounded on the phone. She'd sounded upset, desperate to reach her—and oddly not like the cool debutante sister Mei had imagined from the photo she'd seen.

Mei looked back at her watch. She still had time before she was due to meet Chang at the little coffee and sweet shop, Baccione, around the corner.

Jennifer had called in sick, and though her absence saved Mei some stress, the fact that she was gone also made Mei wonder if Jennifer didn't have something to do with the mysterious meeting with

Chang. Jennifer was capable of a lot of manipulation, and Mei wondered if she hadn't convinced someone that Mei, rather than herself, was the weak link.

Mei had asked Jennifer if she knew Chang, and she'd answered that she had no idea who he was.

Mei had also spent more time thinking about Jennifer's bruise. In hindsight, she thought maybe she'd seen suspicious marks before. Purplish green shapes around the cuffs of her shirts, turtleneck sweaters a couple times in the summer in Chicago—even once when there had been a power outage and the air-conditioning wasn't working in the building. There had been one occasion when they'd met for a case in Philadelphia and Jennifer had a bluish black mark under one eye that she'd sworn was from some stupid beginner in her tae kwon do class.

As much as Mei had seen and done as a child compared to her sisters, she'd always been gullible and she chastised herself for not picking up more. She knew Jennifer didn't trust her. Once she'd even implicated Mei in leaking Megan Riggs's whereabouts to the Russian mob who had come after her in New Orleans. Mei had been dumbfounded.

She'd heard Jennifer refer to her as a Chink on several occasions. Mei had met a lot of people who felt that way, more as she grew older. But Mei was American-born Chinese and for her, America was home and China was more mythical land than reality.

She always wondered how people could so easily forget that America was really a country of immigrants, the melting pot and all that. Jennifer discussed her English heritage as though her parents were right off the *Mayflower* but the fresh-off-the-boat Chinese in America were somehow a source of shame.

Mei glanced at her watch again and jumped up. Three minutes until her meeting with Chang.

She grabbed her coat and made sure she had a few dollars in her pocket. If this guy was going to fire her, she certainly wasn't going to appease his guilt by letting him pay for her coffee. Checking her waistband for her ID card, she scanned her office as though it might be the last time she saw it, and headed down the hall.

Red-and-blue tie. That was how she was supposed to recognize Andy Chang. Too stunned to think, she'd agreed. But as soon as she'd hung up, she realized a red-and-blue tie was about the most common tie combination that existed. On the way down in the elevator, she spotted one just red and blue and one that was mostly red and blue but had a bit of green and yellow, too. Would that one count? She glanced at the face of that man, then turned immediately away again. He was all wrong. Chang was Chinese, spoke Cantonese.

She reached for the building's door when someone pulled it open from behind her. She looked up at the smiling Chinese face. She smiled awkwardly and looked away, pushing herself out the door.

The man followed right behind her, so she found it impossible to look at his tie without turning around and staring. Instead she walked briskly to the corner and then stopped as though she were going to cross the street. The Chinese man passed her and walked directly into the café where she was supposed to meet Andy Chang. Had that been him? At least he'd been ugly. The Andy Chang on the phone had been charming, and the last thing she wanted was to be fired by a charming, attractive man. Better he was charming and ugly, she thought.

The man she'd seen had a large forehead and eyes just slightly too far apart. His nose was flat and thick and he was shorter than she'd hoped. Mei was tall for a Chinese woman, almost five-seven. Her sisters were only five-three and -four, and her additional inches added to her feeling of isolation from them. Being taller made her more American and less Chinese.

So at least he wasn't attractive. She should have known better than to expect Chow Yun-Fat. It had been his voice on the phone. It was so masculine, so American. And the way he'd jumped back and forth from English to Cantonese . . . She shook her head. She'd found it sexy.

Feeling foolish, she waited a few moments until he was safely out of sight. Then, before allowing herself to think any more, she headed to the café. The man was standing at the counter placing an order, so she found a table at the back and waited.

She sat with her back facing the front and waited until he'd gotten his coffee. She glanced around the center of the room, noticing a couple leaning over, talking together. She watched them for a moment, studying how their fingers played between their coffees. She wondered about them, the way she always wondered about strangers in relationships. Her job was often about trying to learn what people were thinking, what made them tick.

Computer crimes were the least understood in terms of criminal behavior. What would motivate someone to start a computer virus or to block accessibility to a site like Yahoo!? She'd attended a series of courses at Quantico on criminal behavior, but it hadn't included cyber-crimes. Her hope was to someday be part of the team to develop a profiling system for cyber-criminals. For now, the science was in its infancy. She *had* hoped to be involved, she thought, as she looked back up for the man in line.

She frowned. He was gone. She started to stand when someone spoke to her. "Ling Mei?"

She looked up at a strange face. Not the man in line at all. This was an attractive man with large hazel-brown eyes that glinted with a hint of mischief. She nodded dumbly.

"Chang Andy," he said, maintaining the traditional Chinese order of their names. "Is this seat taken?" he asked in Cantonese.

She shook her head, disappointed at how good-looking he was.

He sat down and put a cup of coffee in front of her. "Nonfat latte, one sugar."

She looked at the cup and frowned. "How did you know?"

He smiled broadly, exposing a line of straight, white teeth that had clearly had the benefits of American dentistry. "I work for the FBI."

She laughed and thought it was an odd way to begin a conversation with someone you were about to fire. Then why had he called her here? She sipped the drink while taking in his appearance out of the corner of her eye. He had thick hair cut short except for in the front, where it was longer and flat over his forehead. It was like George Clooney's. She caught her ridiculous thought and pushed it away.

For the first time she looked at his tie. He wasn't wearing one. "Where's your tie?"

"I took it off. I thought it would be fun to watch

you look for me. I didn't realize there would be another Chinese man in here at the same time. When you saw he was gone, I wanted to catch you before you ran out."

He smiled as he spoke, as though they had been set up on a blind date, but she fiddled awkwardly. She kept her shoulders back and tried to look relaxed.

"That's it? No more small talk?"

She felt her cheeks blush. "Uh . . ."

Andy touched her arm. "I was just kidding, really."

She forced a smile. "I guess your call made me nervous."

"Really?"

"A call from the Office of Professional Responsibility?" The sentence came out in a voice that was more a squeak than anything else. She lowered her voice again. "Doesn't everyone get a little nervous when you call?"

He raised both hands over his head and with wide eyes said, "Whoa. No bad news here, I promise. Everyone raves about you."

She relaxed for a moment and then realized that the couple playing fingers were now staring at her. "Then why did you call?"

"Actually, I'm sort of returning your call."

"My call?"

He smiled. "You talked to Dennis Eaton about some issues with Jennifer Townsend."

She nodded. Eaton had spoken to the Office of Professional Responsibility?

"Well, the information made its way to me, and I think maybe we can help each other."

"I didn't expect Eaton to talk to you guys."

"It wasn't anything official. Word just sort of got to me."

She looked down at her latte, wishing this were over.

"Can you stay for a minute? I promise it's not poisonous."

She bit the inside of her lip and nodded.

Andy shook his head. "I'm going to have to kick Tony's butt."

She frowned. "Tony?"

"Tony Lew said you'd appreciate the whole tie joke. Something about a blind date in college."

Mei blinked and then smiled, stifling a laugh. Tony Lew had been the biggest jokester she'd ever met. He'd spent four years of college torturing everyone into doing stupid stunts because he swore people would find them amusing. He was notorious among U. Penn alumni. "Tony Lew put you up to this?"

He nodded, his expression slightly hurt, as though he were being left out of the joke.

"Never believe anything he tells you."

"That's why he's a public defender?"

She laughed. "Exactly."

He paused and studied her for a minute. "I wonder what else he lied about."

"Probably everything," she said, taking a sip of her coffee.

"So you're happily married with two-point-five children?"

She felt her face blush and she detested the sensation. She shook her head and laughed as though she got asked that every day. "God, no. Not married and no kids."

Andy smiled and lifted his coffee cup. "To Tony Lew and his bad jokes."

She raised her cup, watching him. Was this some sort of joke? It would be like Tony, but it would also be cruel. She'd kill Tony if he was messing with her. She touched her cup to Andy's and said, "But I can't believe you called me here as a joke to Tony or anyone else."

He took a sip of black coffee and shook his head. "Actually, I do need to talk to you about Jennifer."

That was what she had been afraid of. Mei set her cup down. "Okay."

"We know she's been involved with a Russian for almost seven years." He pulled a picture from his breast pocket and slid it across the table toward her, the way she'd seen people do in spy movies.

The man in the photo was standing on the street, his face turned sideways. The angle gave her a clear view of a very crooked nose. He was attractive in a hockey player sort of way—wide, bushy brow, and a thick neck. He had a set of deep blue eyes the color of pool water. He looked innocent enough in the photo, but Mei instantly imagined he could have been the man who'd given Jennifer the bruise on her eye.

"You've seen him?"

She shook her head. "I don't think so."

He took the picture back and put it away. "They're pretty discreet and we don't have enough on him to pursue it, but his father is high up in the local Russian mob."

"Why did you call me?"

"Well, Eaton talked to someone in my office about the issues between you and Agent Townsend."

"Eaton talked to your office about it?"

Chang raised his hand. "Like I said, nothing official. He said he would handle things himself." He paused. "Which I'm guessing he didn't do."

She shook her head.

"Things with Agent Townsend have been rough?"

She didn't answer. She didn't know how much to tell him.

"Okay. Let me tell you my part first. Then you can decide what you want to say. When I heard there were some issues with Townsend and her partner, I thought maybe they were related."

"Related to her dating a Russian mobster?"

"Maybe."

"Why would Jennifer date someone like that?" Mei asked.

Andy shook his head.

"She makes good money, is smart, intelligent."

He gave her a sad smile. "Who knows?"

Abuse was less rare than she wanted to think, but Jennifer came from a good family, was an FBI agent. She didn't fit the victim profile. "Is there a specific reason you're interested in the fact that Jennifer's with this guy?"

Andy raised an eyebrow and smiled.

She shook her head. "I mean, besides the fact that she's FBI and he's mob." She sounded like an idiot. "That didn't come out right."

"No. It's a fair question. Obviously we don't track the dating patterns of all of our agents." His gaze stuck on her a moment too long, and she looked down at her coffee and then took a sip to avoid making eye contact again.

"This has to be in the strictest of confidence."

She looked back up and nodded. "Of course."

He eyed her for a moment and then nodded as

though he had decided to believe she could be trusted. "In this case, we have some specific concerns about what Jennifer might be able to provide him."

She thought about their work. "He's interested in computer crimes or something?"

He shook his head.

She watched him, puzzled. "What, then?"

"We think her boyfriend, Dmitri Kirov, is trying to help his father locate Megan Riggs."

Mei was surprised by the mention of both Megan's name and Kirov's. But it was the fact that Megan had entered her own mind so recently that surprised her most. "Kirov," she thought out loud. "His brother was the one—"

Andy nodded. "Viktor Kirov was the one Mark Riggs killed. His father, Oskar, vowed revenge. We think that's what happened to Megan down in New Orleans, but we've never had the chance to tell her."

"I heard the leak came from your office," she said slowly.

"My office? You mean, Professional Responsibility?" His expression showed his surprise.

She nodded.

"We confirmed the leak was from Megan's group." He paused and started to nod. "I bet I can guess from whom you heard that the leak was from our office."

"Jennifer."

"Exactly what I guessed."

Mei shook her head. "Why would Jennifer help this guy find Megan? Those two were like sisters."

"The Russian mob can be very convincing."

Mei thought about Jennifer. "Oh, God."

"Megan Riggs is in danger again. Unfortunately,

we don't know where she is any more than the Russians do. And when they find out, we need to be there."

"What makes you think they'll find her after all this time?"

Andy shook his head. "I saw the last person who wronged the Kirov family. He was in hiding for eleven years before they got to him. His own wife didn't recognize him. Megan Riggs is next on the hit list."

Chapter 17

Cody paced the floor of the small covered patio at the back of Colonel Turner's house. The boards rattled beneath her in tempo as she moved. *Squeak, squeak* then a long *moan, step, step*; then the whole sequence repeated as she started the circle again.

The colonel finally looked up, peering at her from over his bifocals. "Are you going to stop that?"

"It's driving me crazy to just sit here."

"Then help me. I think this could be the legionary ant, but I'm not sure. This is a lousy picture."

"It's the best I could do."

The colonel nodded. "I just can't tell if the thing has a pedicel."

Cody stopped pacing. "A what?"

The colonel motioned her over. "A pedicel—a waist. Look at this and tell me if you think the thorax and abdomen are broadly jointed or if they taper at the waist."

Impatient, Cody pulled the paper from his grasp and tilted it under the light. She turned it forward and back. "I don't know. I can't tell."

He pulled his glasses off and rubbed his nose in a gesture that looked like he was holding off his agitation. "Well, you need to look more closely. It makes a big difference. If it's got a pedicel, then it's definitely in the wasp or bee family, or maybe the legionary ant. If it doesn't, it could be a sawfly." He leaned over to look at the page again. "Can you tell if it has clubbed antennae?"

She squinted. "You mean little balls on top?"

"Right. They widen toward the ends."

She nodded slowly. "I think they do." She paused and looked again. "Definitely. Clubbed antennae on this thing, and I don't think it has a waist." She looked over at him. "What does that mean?"

He gave her a little smile. "It means it could be a sawfly." He pointed up at the shelves. "Pull down a few of those and look for any references to sawflies." He kept his nose in his book without responding.

"Where are sawflies found?"

The colonel looked up and shook his head. "It'll depend on the type. They've got some in Canada and New England and some out here. I can't say until we've found it." He looked back down. "You're just going to have to be a little more patient."

The breath froze in her chest. "Canada or out here? Like mountainous regions? The Sierras or the Canadian Rockies?"

He shrugged. "Don't know yet. I've got to find the right one."

"The Sierras or the Rockies?" she repeated.

"I said I don't know yet."

"What about the Himalayas or the Alps?"

He raised an eyebrow. "Yeah, maybe there, too."

Dread paralyzed her. This wasn't the answer. She needed to do something else. But what? She felt completely powerless. She had been able to find out who hosted the www.ivegotpeter Web site, but that

was as far as she'd gotten. She'd called the Web site
hosting company, but they had refused her any additional information. When she'd tried to escalate
the issue, the supervisor had said he could shut
down the site for displaying a minor, but that was
the last thing she wanted them to do. She wished
she knew someone who worked there. But she knew
almost no one, period.

Travis was even asking his employees if anyone
had a contact at the Web hosting service, Align.com,
but so far no luck.

In the meantime, Cody was going positively crazy.

He pointed to the books. "You found the sawfly
yet?"

She stared at the books. Impatience itched her skin
like poison oak.

"Get to it," he said, and then focused on the book
in front of him.

He was right. She had to follow this through. Find
the damn bug. She pulled one off the shelf and
opened it, blinking off the headache that had descended like a vise on her temples.

She flipped through three books before she found
a listing of the sawfly. When she flipped to the page,
she found a photo of the *Tenthredo originalis*. "I found
it." She exhaled, defeated. "And it doesn't look anything like the one Ryan has."

The colonel knelt beside her and smiled. "That's
the Northeastern sawfly. Not the one we've got." He
flipped the page. "Ours is this guy, I'm pretty sure."

She looked down at the picture. "The rusty willow
sawfly?"

"Yep, the *Cimbex rubida*."

"Where's it found?"

He scanned the page with one finger. "Says river

margins and lowland woods from coastal California to the Sierra Nevada mountains."

She exhaled. "So he's still in California."

He frowned without speaking.

"What? What is it?"

"There's another sawfly called the Western willow sawfly, or *Cimbex pacifica*."

"What about it?"

"It's almost impossible to tell the two apart."

Cody heard her voice rise as she spoke. "And where's that one found?"

He blew out his breath and pointed to the page.

She lifted the book from his fingers and brought it up to read. "In Colorado or from California to Washington." She dropped it into her lap. She moaned. "This isn't working. It's not exact enough. I need something else."

"We knew it wasn't going to be exact enough with one bug to find him."

She stood. "That may be all we get. How do we know we'll get another?"

The colonel stood as well, though the process took him longer. "Because he's your son. He'll find a way."

She shook her head. Waiting on Ryan wasn't enough. "I can't just sit here and hope he gets another chance."

"You need to have more faith."

"Faith has never paid off for me, Colonel. Action is what pays off for me."

He nodded. "Okay, you can act and I'll work with faith and these books. You be sure and let me know when the next picture is up."

She dropped the books onto the hardwood floor with a thunk. "He could be anywhere. This is just a waste of time." She started to move toward the door, but the colonel stopped her.

He laid his hand on her shoulder to keep her from going anywhere. When he let go, he lifted the glasses off his nose and rubbed the bridge slowly. "We're not going to get a street address from one bug, Cody. You're going to have to be more patient than that."

"I can't be patient. This is my son. I need answers now." She walked back across the floor twice more and then sat back down on the floor with a thud. "You have no idea what this is like."

The colonel didn't respond. He sat back down and opened his book.

"This is my son," she said softly. "He's all I have. All I have and I've lost him." Her voice hit a high note and cracked and she tried to pull it together, but she felt the fury boil over as she clenched her fists and held herself from kicking something. "Damn it, Colonel. I have to find him before it's too late. I have to!"

"I understand," he said, his head still down.

"You do not understand," she snapped. "So please do not patronize me." She shook her head. "This is my whole family. This is all I have. I've lost everything. You have no idea what that is like."

He held her gaze for a long time before breaking it and returning to his book. "You're going to have to keep it down. Or else go home and I'll call you when I know something."

Cody glanced at the door, torn between giving up and trying something else or holding on to the slim chance that this might work, that Ryan might have picked a bug they could identify and track.

She wanted to trust her son. God, she wanted to.

She wished she knew what to do. Another half hour. She'd give it another half hour. She picked up a book, feeling the weight of the colonel's stare and ignoring him as she opened the next book in the pile and turned to the index at the back.

"Oh, look who's here," a woman's voice said.

Cody jumped, startled, as an older black woman walked into the room. Cody had seen Mrs. Turner only a handful of times since she'd lived next door.

She wore pink sweatpants and a lilac-and-pink sweatshirt with fluffy white slippers. Her hair was matted in the back and on one side, and she kept teasing it as though she sensed it wasn't quite right. "I kept wondering who was denting in the floor down here."

Cody smiled politely, unsure what, if anything, the colonel had explained to his wife about her presence. "I'm sorry. I was . . . I am . . ." She swallowed. "We were just talking."

Mrs. Turner came up and rubbed her cheek. "That's my Roni." Taking Cody's hand, she pulled her onto the small, worn couch and sat beside her. "Isn't she beautiful, Walter?" She slowly rubbed Cody's arm as Cody looked at the colonel, puzzled.

The colonel stood up. "Florence, you should go upstairs."

Cody's first reaction was to move, but she could feel the colonel's discomfort. "It's okay," she said without taking her eyes off Mrs. Turner. "It's very nice to see you."

The woman beamed. "And how is that baby boy of yours?"

She smiled despite the pain in her chest. "He's fine. Getting smarter every day." She had to believe that. She did.

"I'll bet he is. I hear he's a little bug collector, just like his grandpa."

Cody glanced at the colonel, whose gaze was fixed on his wife. The woman thought Cody was her daughter. She'd never experienced someone with Alzheimer's—didn't realize that a black woman could mistake even a white woman for her child. She didn't know what to say, so she just nodded and spoke the truth about Ryan. "He is. The colonel has taught him a ton. I certainly appreciate it."

The woman laughed easily, and it was clear what the colonel must have seen in her. Even now she was beautiful, with smooth dark skin and fine features. She winked at the colonel. "Listen to your daughter call you the colonel." She shook her head. "He almost had me doing it once. I said, no way. I'm not one of your men. I'm your wife. But you . . . you always called him Colonel. Even when you were just a wee thing. A big word like that. Daddy would've been a heck of a lot easier." She laughed again and touched Cody's shoulder. "It sure is good to have you home again, Roni. Just like old times. I've been telling Walter to patch things up. It's been too long. We're too old to be angry anymore. Haven't I been telling you that?"

"Yes," the colonel said, clearing the emotion from his throat. "Yes, you have." He stood then and crossed the room to his wife. Taking her by the arm, he led her toward the door. "Can I make you some tea, Florence?"

"Oh, no. It's too late for tea." She frowned and looked around. "Isn't it almost dinnertime? When's dinner?"

It was barely even two in the afternoon.

"Are you hungry?" the colonel asked.

Florence shook her head. "No. Not yet. I'll come down and thaw out that meatloaf I made last Sunday in a little bit. I'm going up to rest again." She waved to Cody. "You staying for dinner, honey?"

Cody watched the colonel nod behind his wife.

"Of course. I'll be right here."

Mrs. Turner smiled again and blew Cody a kiss. "What a sweet child we have, Walter. What a sweet, sweet child. You let her stay away way too long." She shook her finger at the colonel and then kissed it and laid it to Walter's lips. "And I can't wait to see that grandchild of mine as soon as he's home from school." She rubbed her hands together. "He's just the sweetest thing, that child—like a big, ripe peach."

The colonel watched as his wife disappeared around the corner toward the stairs.

Cody could see the exhaustion in his expression. She had sensed that Mrs. Turner was sick because of how infrequently she was outside. But she had no idea that the woman had Alzheimer's.

The colonel came back into the room and sat down. He didn't say a word about his wife.

Cody watched him return to exactly where he'd been before his wife had entered the room. She watched him for a minute until he finally looked up and raised an eyebrow. "You're distracting me. Either spit it out or get back to work."

Cody couldn't help but give the colonel a quick salute. But then she did as she was told and turned herself back to the book. Maybe she had been wrong. Maybe the colonel did understand what it was like to lose someone.

"Maybe you ought to go check to see if there are

any new pictures on that site," the colonel suggested.

Cody agreed. She stood and set the books on the table.

"You let me know as soon as you see. If I don't hear from you in ten minutes, I'm coming over."

She saluted again, and as his eyes swept to the door, she moved toward it.

The street was quiet as she crossed between the two houses and opened her back door with the key. As she entered the kitchen, she noticed the dishes were put away, the counters clean. She was struck by the odd emptiness of it. It lacked Ryan, but it also lacked all the personal belongings that she had so hastily packed up when she'd thought she was running from Oskar Kirov again.

It was never like that when they were both there. Although they didn't have their true identities, she and Ryan had made a home. They would again. She had to believe it.

Ignoring her surroundings, she locked and bolted the door and went straight to her office and found the site again. The same picture was still loaded, and Cody stared again at the strong, scared face of her child. Faith. She rubbed her eyes, trying to ease the burning. It seemed like a stretch to trust anything other than her own hands and mind. But she had to. To find Ryan, she would have to rely on things outside herself: Colonel Turner, Travis Landon, and perhaps even some faith.

Chapter 18

"Dad, you have to come now."

Travis shook his head and covered the mouth of the phone. "Not now, Peter. I'll be off in a few minutes."

"I can't possibly do that today, Travis," Susan told him on the phone. "We're swamped."

At the door, Peter straightened his arms to his sides in a gesture of impatience. "It's important, Dad."

Travis waved Peter out his office door as he gripped the phone tight in his fist. "I need them now, Susan."

"Travis, we're doing it as fast as we can. We're in the middle of a financial audit. We've got a team of accountants that we're servicing. I don't have the people to handle this, and if you push any harder, you're going to lose your whole damn HR department." She exhaled and he could hear her tapping a nail on her desk, the way she did when she was irritated.

Peter waved from the door to get his attention and Travis shook his head and turned his back. Peter would have to wait. "I'm sorry, Susan. I know you're under a lot of pressure. I just need this to come first. It's important, okay?"

"More important than getting financing?"

He thought about R.J. O'Brien, about Peter's Bulls jacket, about the absolute mess of his life. "More important, Susan."

She whistled. "Wow. More important than the next round of funding—is someone dying?"

"No," he answered quickly and with confidence, knowing his HR director was about as good with a secret as the six-o'clock news. "It's a personal matter. I need to get in contact with someone."

"Well, someone is not a problem. Just tell me who. I can find one, for God's sake. It's putting together eight years of someones that I don't have time for."

"I need them all, Susan. Just do it. I'll be down there later to pick it up."

"All of it . . . Travis, you're talking—"

"Susan, all of it. Tell the staff we'll make it up in bonuses. I promise." He hung up before she could ask more questions or offer more complaints. Leaning his elbows on the desk, he rubbed his temples.

The phone rang again and he snatched it up. "Landon."

"It's Janice. We've got a good media op with CNN."

"When?"

"Today. Anytime before five-thirty."

"Live on a Saturday?"

"Taped. They're going to run it Monday morning—at least twice."

"Okay." He could do taped.

"You want a spokesperson?"

"Janice."

"I know, but it's Saturday. I thought maybe you'd want to be at home."

"I'll do it. Where do I need to go?"

"They have studios in the city or Mountain View. City's probably easier."

"Mountain View is fine. Closer to you anyway."

"I don't mind coming up."

"Let's do it at four-thirty today. E-mail me directions."

"Will do."

"Anything else I need to know?"

"It's the standard stuff. I've got some Q-and-A drafted, so nothing there. We can review it before they tape."

"Include all that in the E-mail. And your cell number. I'll see you at four-thirty."

"One more thing, Travis."

"Yeah."

"Wear the gray suit with the blue-and-yellow tie."

He frowned. "A suit?"

"It's a conservative broadcast; our consultants are saying the more conservative the better, especially until we get the funding."

"A suit," he repeated.

"Just for an hour."

"Right."

He set his hand on the phone and thought about the priority of items he needed to handle. The first thing he needed to do was prepare for the meeting with McCue. Finding R.J. came first.

Before he turned his attention to that, he pulled himself out of the chair and crossed the room. The hallway was quiet. "Peter," he called out.

No one answered. He moved to the base of the stairs and yelled up, "Peter."

He heard the sound of footsteps behind him and turned around. Mrs. Pat walked into the hallway, wiping her hands on a dishtowel. "He was wound up like a top. I told him to take his bike out for a ride around a bit, cool off. He's just in the cul de sac by Tommy's house. His mom was sitting outside watching them."

Travis nodded, feeling uncomfortable that his son was anywhere but under his own roof. "It's my fault he's agitated. He was trying to talk to me about something. I was on the phone."

She nodded and tossed the rag over her shoulder. "He'll be back soon. I'm sure he'll have forgotten what it was by then."

He watched her walk back into the kitchen and wondered if Peter had told her about R.J. Travis had mentioned that they needed to keep it quiet, but he didn't want to tell his son he couldn't talk to anyone about it. It was a lot of pressure for a kid.

Hell, it was a lot of pressure for an adult. Walking to the front hall, he put on his coat and went around the corner to look for Peter.

He was there, riding in circles with two other boys, and Travis stood against a tree and watched them until Peter was ready to go home. They didn't talk on the way back, and Travis respected his son's silence. He hoped he'd talk when he was ready.

As they walked in the door, his business phone rang, and Travis returned to the desk to answer it. He spent the next hour on the phone with business development, and then answered three calls from the head of his sales staff, trying to resolve some issue with the solution to the programming glitch.

When he finally finished, it was three o'clock. He spent the next hour focused on preparing for his meeting with McCue. And by then it was time to get ready for the media opportunity.

He stood from his desk just as the door creaked open.

From the two inches, Travis could see a thin slice of his son's face. "Hey, buddy. You have a good day?"

Peter opened the door and shrugged.

"Sorry about this morning."

He kicked his foot against the doorjamb. "It's okay. Can we do something tonight?"

Travis ran his hand over his face. "I've got to run down to work tonight."

Peter's eyes widened. "Again? But you worked all day."

Travis approached his son. "I know, buddy. I'm sorry. I'm trying to help find R.J. and I need to go to work to do it."

"Why work? R.J.'s not there."

Travis patted his son's back. "I'm meeting someone who I hope will help me find him."

Peter looked up. "Can I come?"

"Not tonight, bud."

"Come on, Dad. Please. I promise not to get in the way or anything. I'll be real quiet."

Travis hoisted his son into his arms. "I know you would. You'd be perfect. But not tonight."

Peter wiggled until Travis set him down. "He's my best friend. I should get to help."

"Not this time."

Peter turned his back. "I never get to do anything fun," he shouted, stampeding down the hall. The sound of his feet disappeared into soft thuds on the carpet as he made his way to his room.

Travis exhaled, meeting Mrs. Pat's gaze. She started to say something, but he shook his head and went to his room to get ready to leave.

Chapter 19

The ride to the warehouse was quiet. Oskar liked it that way. Feliks sat on the far edge of the seat in the back of the limousine, staring out the window. Oskar knew he was anticipating what was to come. There had been very few times when Oskar had had to go to this extreme to make a point. But Feliks had been careless with his affairs. It was one thing to know his son was a *goluboy*, but for others to know was not acceptable. Being gay was a weakness. Not just Feliks's weakness—because people knew he was weak. His being gay also made Oskar look weak. And that, he would not accept. Oskar Kirov was never *slabi*.

He fisted his palm and thumped it against his leg, feeling the strain in his gut as he did. He glanced over at Feliks, still staring out the window, before taking the pills from his inner coat pocket. He twisted the cap off, rolled one into his fist, and threw it down his throat in one smooth motion. The pain was worsening, and the nausea was almost unbearable at times. He'd been sick half the night. At least that was a bit better now.

Feliks looked over at him, an eyebrow raised. "Are you all right?" he asked.

Oskar took the handkerchief from his pocket and dabbed his forehead. He gave his son a twisted smile. "Perfect."

Feliks shook his head as though disgusted.

Oskar would teach him about disgusting. The car pulled into the warehouse district and Oskar could see the hair on his son's neck rising. They had been there twice before. Once when Feliks had gotten caught cheating on a test in the third grade, and once when he had argued to his father's face in front of his business colleagues. Neither time had Feliks lost even a drop of blood. But neither time would he ever forget.

Feliks looked at him, trying to mask his fear. "Why are we here?"

"I have something I want to show you."

"I've done nothing."

Oskar nodded. "Then you have nothing to fear."

The car stopped and the driver circled around and opened Oskar's door.

"I'm staying here."

Oskar shook his head. "There's someone here who would like to see you."

Feliks didn't move.

"Fine." He lifted an arm as he stepped from the car. "You don't wish to see Gary. I'll tell him."

Feliks knew better than to shout, but Oskar knew by the motion behind him that Feliks was following. "Why would he be here?" Feliks asked, trying to sound casual.

"He's been stealing."

That was too much for Feliks. "He has not, Father. He's never stolen. I'm responsible for that department. I would know if he had." He calmed a bit before saying, "Who told you this?"

"Mary Anne," he lied.

"Mary Anne?" He shook his head. "She's wrong. Or mistaken."

Feliks turned toward the warehouse. "I will clear this up. There is some mistake." He started forward but one of Oskar's security men, Sasha, stepped forward to block his path.

"Excuse me."

Sasha simply shook his head.

Oskar watched his son's expression grow from annoyance to panic. Sasha merely stood in his way. Sasha was good that way. Though Americans thought Sasha was a girl's name, it was anything but. And this Sasha was the antithesis of female. He was huge—six-foot-seven and almost three hundred pounds, all muscle. He could only follow single-syllable speech, even in his native language.

Feliks was growing agitated. Finally he turned to his father. "What is this about?"

"It's about your weakness." Oskar spoke in English so that Sasha couldn't understand.

"What?" Feliks said, looking around as though for a way out. "What weakness?"

"You know." None of the others knew the real reason that Gary was there. They had all been told he was a thief. Oskar refused to let anyone else know that Gary and his son had been lovers. The thought was like wet worms sucking on his skin.

Perhaps they suspected, but if they didn't, it would stay that way. Oskar would look a fool if someone knew his son had been screwing his top male accountant. And Oskar Kirov was no fool. He had worked too hard for his position. When he went, it would be quickly and like a man. There would be no loss of face.

Feliks's face went white and he gripped the railing outside the warehouse door for support. "Oh, God. What have you done to him?"

"Nothing less than I'd have done to you if you weren't my son."

Feliks launched himself at Oskar, taking him by surprise. He grabbed his collar, and Oskar was knocked backward before Sasha could step forward. His son clawing at his chest, he hit the ground with a hard thud, which knocked the wind from his lungs. The anger in his son's face was familiar. He saw himself as a young man as he never had before.

For a moment he felt a bond with his son. But then he remembered why they were there. Gary and Feliks. He shook his head. It was too much to think about.

Sasha pulled Feliks off, but he was unable to help Oskar because Feliks was still fighting him. Oskar pulled himself up and commanded Sasha to release him.

Feliks stumbled back and righted his suit jacket. He turned his gaze to his father. "You should never have stepped where it isn't your business."

"I'm your father. This is my business."

Disgust muddied Feliks's expression. "Not anymore, it isn't." He turned his back and entered the warehouse.

Sasha looked to Oskar, but Oskar shook his head. "Let him go," he said.

Slowly Oskar followed. He was still outside the door when he heard his son's anguished cry. Oskar suppressed a smile. Now Feliks would learn to control his urges, to handle them more discreetly.

As he crossed into the shadowed warehouse, he blinked to adjust his eyes to the darkness. In a far corner of the warehouse, Gary was strung up like they always were. From his limp, pale body, Oskar knew it had been rough for him. He'd been weak to begin with, though. That could not be helped.

"Let him down now, Sasha."

There were a series of hushed whispers as Sasha and two of his other guards, Ivan and Mikhail, swarmed Gary like bees. No one touched him.

Oskar halted. "What? What is it?"

Feliks collapsed to the ground, wailing.

Oskar waved to them as he started crossing the room. "Jesus, get him up."

Sasha and Mikhail lifted Feliks to his feet and held him, his feet dangling like a prisoner being hung.

Oskar waved Ivan to Gary. "Bring him down, I said."

Ivan looked confused.

Feliks stood up, his face tearstained.

"Wipe your face, man," Oskar said.

Feliks pushed away from the men and stepped toward Oskar. "*On umer*," Feliks spit at his father. "*Tei yevo ubival.*" *He's dead. You've killed him.*

"Nonsense," Oskar said, waving his hand. "He'll be fine." He looked at his son. "Don't be so soft, Feliks." Oskar stopped in front of Mikhail and looked up at the dangling body of Gary. It wasn't hard to see why Feliks thought he was dead. "Bring him down," he ordered Mikhail in Russian.

Mikhail struggled to loosen the ropes, and as the body was lowered, Oskar could see the wounds on his arms and hands from the pliers. He glanced at his fingers. He still had those. Oskar had told them explicitly not to kill Gary—at least not until he arrived. If Feliks refused to obey his rules, Oskar intended to kill Gary himself.

A few of the toes on Gary's left foot looked bloody and broken, and Oskar guessed that, too, had been the pliers. They'd been thorough. Oskar had known they would be. Thievery from within was a serious offense. He could have punished him another way, but he wanted to be sure Gary disappeared from his son's life. Surely he wouldn't stick around after this lesson.

Oskar stepped forward and smacked Gary's cheek. The head bobbed to one side and then fell forward again. As the head turned, Oskar noticed a line of blood running from one ear.

He grabbed Gary's arm and felt for his pulse.

"He's dead, I told you," Feliks repeated in English. "He's dead and you've killed him."

Oskar looked from Mikhail to Ivan to Sasha. They glanced at each other and then to the ground. He *was* dead.

Oskar shrugged and then turned to his son. He nodded. "He is dead."

Feliks threw his arms up and yelled toward the ceiling. The others stepped back from him, but Oskar did not move. He would allow his son this tirade. Then it would be over.

Feliks spun around and screamed, "You monster. You dirty bastard. You killed your own wife. You killed her like she was a peasant woman." He pressed his splayed hands across his chest, tears rolling down his cheeks. "My mother. Murdered her!" He let out another howl and bent over and sobbed into his knees. He was quiet for a moment, and Oskar thought he was winding down.

"Wait for me outside," he commanded the others.

They obeyed immediately without looking back at Feliks. But they had taken only a few steps when Feliks rose again, holding a weapon someone had left by the body.

"Nobody move!" he screamed, then repeated himself in Russian. Feliks pointed the 9mm at his father. Oskar didn't move. He knew Feliks would never kill him. The men behind him started to go for their own weapons, but Feliks turned and shot. Oskar heard a short moan and then a shuffle as Mikhail dropped to the floor, dead. The others remained silent and still.

Feliks turned his weapon toward his father. "*Menya goshnit,*" he said to him. "You make me sick." He pointed to himself. "I am not the one who is *slabi*. You . . . you are weak."

Oskar didn't respond. A wave of nausea struck him and he swallowed it back. Not now. He needed to be strong, firm. He had to teach Feliks a lesson. Oskar would wait until his son had let out this anger before he scolded him. Mikhail had been one of his best men.

"You are also poor," Feliks said, wild-eyed. "Gary *had* been helping me steal from you. Donations, actually. Huge corporate donations. You looked at the books every week, but you never understood them. I knew it from the start. Your money has gone to protect and counsel abused women. Almost seven million dollars so far." Feliks smiled. "For Mama."

Oskar felt his tongue slide to the back of his mouth and he coughed. "What nonsense are you talking?"

"You're poor. You're ruined. We were almost done. You were almost tapped out. The house is mortgaged to the hilt; we've borrowed against all your assets." He waved his hand around. "Even your little torture chamber. You won't make it another month."

"That's ridiculous. How would you live?"

Feliks looked at Gary and shook his head. "Gary and I had a little nest egg of our own tucked away in the Bahamas."

"You stole from me?" Oskar stepped forward, but Feliks kept the gun on him.

"I stole from you and I'm proud. I hope you rot in hell."

Oskar pushed his chest out. "Well, now that your Gary is gone, you'll just have to return the money. Go and get it back."

Feliks smiled just like a child then. "Go to hell, Father."

Oskar stood facing his son. Feliks raised the gun to Oskar's face and Oskar found he couldn't keep his eyes open. He shut them, waiting for the blow. Killed by his own son.

The gun went off and he jumped. When he opened his eyes, his son Feliks was lying on the floor in front of him in a growing pool of his own blood, the gun still in his mouth.

The pain in Oskar's gut sharpened and he caught himself from falling back. Feliks had killed himself. He was nauseous from the iron smell of the blood. Sophya, then Viktor and Feliks. He staggered back and gripped his stomach.

Sasha took his arm, but Oskar pushed him off. He struggled for his breath and then turned his back on the sight of his dead son. Another dead son. He took another breath and then started for the warehouse door. His throat was closed as he tried to form words.

He thought about the money. What if Feliks had told the truth? What if it was all gone? How would he live?

Money had always been his security net if his health and his family didn't hold strong. And they couldn't have been weaker. *Slabi,* he realized. He was *slabi*—weak and also very old. Too old to start again.

Only one son left. Would he soon be alone and poor? He staggered into the street, bracing himself on the side of the building. Even outside, he could see an image of Feliks's shattered head when he blinked. "Dear God," he whispered. What had he done?

Chapter 20

Cody had spent the rest of the day at home. The colonel was still researching the bugs, Travis had made no progress on his end, and she couldn't get herself to move out of the chair. The dark gray sky and heavy rain outside exactly mirrored her disposition.

Travis had called to tell her the meeting with McCue was set up for seven P.M. at his office in San Jose. He'd chosen the evening hour because there would be fewer people in the office and they would have more privacy. Though the last thing she wanted to do was drive fifty miles in the dark and rain, she would be there.

She wouldn't have much to offer to the meeting anyway, since it was Landon's life they would be looking into. She should have been relieved, but though her own life was terrifying, the thought of what hidden evils were in Landon's was equally so. What sort of past employees had left, vengeful?

Cody had no new information from the Web site. That hadn't kept her from working with it, though. She'd magnified the photo and divided it into twenty-two two-inch quadrants. She'd then magnified each of those by 200 percent and then printed them on the high-resolution color printer she used for her jobs. She'd studied each photo individually and then set up a large puzzle with the pieces on the floor. All in search of one clue as to where they were.

Behind Ryan was mostly white wall. It looked like clean paint, no prints that she could see. It was smooth, like new construction, and the two electrical outlets she saw were grounded, so the room had either been redone or was newer. The floor was a neutral Berber carpet. It looked like a bedroom. She saw the edge of something navy. She guessed it was a comforter or bedsheet, but it was impossible to be certain.

There was a single nail in the wall, and from her best guess, something had been hanging there recently. So whoever had taken the picture was being cautious not to give anything away. She was not especially impressed with the precaution. It didn't take a rocket scientist to realize showing a picture would be dumb.

Besides that, she saw something that looked like an average twig on the floor by Ryan's foot. No needles, no leaves, no fruit. Nothing to learn from it except that it was deciduous and therefore Ryan was somewhere where trees lost leaves. But it was the fall and that could have been most anywhere in the northern hemisphere.

The twig was about two inches long, but that was all she had, so she couldn't even begin to guess what type of tree it had come from. If the sawfly was any clue, it was probably something from the mountains.

Then there was the corner of a wooden table or ledge in one corner. It could have been anything, but it struck her as a rich wood, not something that had been bought for $19.99 and home-assembled. The corner of it was not enough to gain any clue as to how to track it down or even to judge what it was.

When the doorbell rang at shortly after five, Cody knew it was the colonel again. He'd been by twice earlier since she'd left his house, once to bring her an article on the two sawflies he'd matched to Ryan's photo, the *Cimbex rubida* and the *Cimbex pacifica*. The article listed the various known locations of the bugs. There were too many to even count. The second time he'd been by to check on her.

After peering out the peephole, she opened the door and waved him in out of the rain. She could see her breath in the evening air, a rare occurrence in the Bay Area, and she shivered as she imagined where Ryan was at that moment.

The colonel held a large Tupperware container in his hands.

"I'm not real hungry, Colonel."

He nodded and stepped by her. "You will be. This is my special stew. It'll shake off the chill."

"Nothing would shake off this chill except Ryan."

"Well, it's good for the brain. You want to eat by that danged machine?"

He meant the computer. He'd been calling it that since the beginning of their bug search. She nodded.

"Go get a bowl and some napkins and we'll take it up."

Normally she would have told a stranger to go to hell if he spoke to her that way. But she had to appreciate the colonel's gesture. And she'd had about all she could take of being alone staring at the computer.

She got a bowl from the kitchen cabinet. For a

while she'd continued to be cautious about getting her prints on things. Why go to all the trouble of cleaning things off just to dirty them again? But it had quickly become too cumbersome to constantly watch where she set her hands. She wished she had another photo of Ryan or Mark nearby, but the only ones she had were on their way to a P.O. box in Austin, Texas.

Cody led the way to her office, the colonel following behind with the Tupperware container. She sat down at the computer and took the stacks of print-outs, collated them, and set them aside.

The colonel set the Tupperware container down and pulled a chair from the corner of the room. He opened the container and poured stew into a bowl, then handed it to Cody.

The smell reminded her of something her mother had loved to make. There was a hint of ginger or maybe cinnamon. She pushed the thought away.

Nodding to the pile of pictures, he said, "What you got going over there?"

She stirred the spoon in the stew, letting the smell of beef and onion hit her nose. She was hungry. She took a bite and swallowed, her mouth burning from the heat.

"It's hot; watch it."

She set it down to cool a bit. "It's good, though. Thank you."

He nodded. "Told you it would be." He stood and picked up the pictures. "You find anything else?"

She shook her head. "Nothing I can do without some professional help."

The colonel pulled his chair to the table and picked up the first picture, showing the upper left corner of the photo. He ran his hand over what looked like the very corner of a brass wall light.

"Looks expensive, right?" She took a bite of the stew. It was damn good.

The colonel gazed at the photo. "I was just thinking something like that."

"The carpet's clean, the walls look freshly painted," she continued, taking another bite of stew before setting the bowl down.

She lifted the rest of the pictures and flipped to the one that showed the corner of what she had guessed was a table. She offered it to the colonel. "And see this one?"

He pulled a pair of bifocals from his breast pocket and set them on his nose. He whistled.

"You think it's a table?"

"I think it's a nice table." He turned the picture sideways. "Hard to say, but it looks like it could be carved."

She nodded, staring at the way the corner sloped back on itself as it disappeared from the edge of the photo. "I wasn't sure about whether that was just an edge or if it was something more elaborate."

"Not enough to say except that it looks nice to me. I've got an old friend who collects wood pieces. We can ask."

She looked back at the photo, hesitating at the idea of showing it to someone else. She'd already run the keywords "Peter Landon" and "I've got Peter" through the biggest search engines and come up with nothing. Her hope was that the maker of the site was trying to keep it as low-profile as she was. But the fact that they were still without a ransom note had started to make her wonder.

"Maybe we'd best wait until we see what this guy does next."

She nodded. She hoped it would be soon. She ate more of the stew while the colonel looked through the rest of the photos. "You saw the twig?"

He found the picture and studied it.

"Can you make anything of it?"

He shook his head. "The sawfly tells us more."

"So you think it's the sawfly?"

"Yes."

"But it doesn't give us a narrow enough region to start looking."

He set down the picture. "Afraid not."

"That's what I figured." She set the empty bowl down, feeling less nauseated than she had in more than twenty-four hours. She couldn't believe how much had happened in such a short time.

"You should eat more."

"I don't think I could, Colonel." She turned her arm wrist-up and glanced at her watch. It was already five-thirty and she'd have to leave in less than a half hour. "Besides, I've got to get going."

"Where to?"

She explained briefly about Landon's investigator.

"McCue? I knew a McCue once. He in the forces?"

"I don't know anything about him yet."

"You want me to come with?"

She turned back to him and smiled. "I think I'll be okay."

He splayed his hands on his knees. "No doubt about that, but will they?"

"I'm not worried about them." She picked the bowl up off the table and turned toward the door.

The colonel was still sitting beside the computer. "Should I shut this thing off?"

She glanced over her shoulder. "No. I leave it on."

"Holy mother of Jesus," the colonel swore. "Will you look at that."

Cody looked back. "It doesn't hurt it—" She looked up at the screen. She made a small sound like a grunt as the bowl slipped from her fingers.

She heard it crash to the floor before she could get her feet to move beneath her.

Chapter 21

Jennifer Townsend stomped into the front hall, unwrapped the heavy scarf, and dumped her winter boots and jacket by the door. She rubbed her hands together, adjusted the heat, and then headed up the stairs.

In the office, she flopped into her chair and tossed a couple of case files down onto the wooden desk with a thunk. She had spent the afternoon in a quiet conference room at the Bureau, making phone calls and trying to stir up help. And she'd been remarkably successful. Though a lot of the Bureau staff worked Monday to Friday, there were always resources on hand. And today, she'd contacted a few of them, including the department who could access information on calls coming into the Bureau and the research group. She was making headway on finding Megan Riggs and she hadn't felt so good in months.

From the clock on the wall, she knew she had to hurry. She had less than two hours to get through the files and make some calls before Dmitri showed up to take her to a late dinner. They were going to one of their favorites: Gene & Georgetti's. G&G's

was an institution in Chicago and had been especially popular with the Italian mob for a long time. Recently she had seen more Russian mob than Italian, but she enjoyed the food and Dmitri loved the atmosphere. She always dressed in her sexiest outfits so Dmitri could show her off. And they always had wild, wonderful sex after a dinner at G&G's.

She really should have stayed home to work, but he was insistent on taking her out. It was their seven-year anniversary of dating the next week, and he thought he might have to go on a quick trip to Europe. He'd tried to convince her to come, but she couldn't possibly get away from work.

She set aside her thoughts and picked up the phone to check her work messages. She had one from early that morning.

"It's Eddie de la Cruz calling. We were able to track that incoming call. It came from a cell phone."

She grabbed a pen and threw her notebook open. She scrawled the number down as he spoke it and then backed the message up and checked her notes. She had it. She'd found Megan Riggs. She threw her head back and laughed out loud and then rewound Eddie's message and, grinning like a Kodak ad, she listened to it again.

"It's a Michigan number, but it bills to a P.O. box in South Carolina. I had the P.O. box tracked, but now we're working with the postal service, so it's going to take a subpoena and all that. I'm still working on the location of the call's origin, and we're getting closer. It wouldn't have worked with one call, but because there were two—the one to your phone line and the one to your pager number—I think we can pinpoint the location pretty well. It'll depend on the phone's tracking system. If it's got a built-in GPS receiver, we'll be able to get it down to between sixty and two hundred twenty-five feet or so. If it was good, we could have a block or less. They've got systems now that use DGPS and you can pinpoint someone to about three feet."

Eddie continued his technobabble.

"No promises, though. And remember, if the phone doesn't have the GPS receiver, all you'll get is what city the roaming was in—could be as big as an area code. I hope to have an answer by tomorrow or Monday at the latest."

She saved the message and hung up the phone. Megan Riggs's call had triggered a spark of the possibility of freedom from Oskar Kirov, and Jennifer was desperate to fan the spark and make fire. Even if the best Eddie could do was an area code, she was still very close to finding Megan Riggs.

Now if he'd just hurry up. Even a day would seem like forever to wait to find Megan.

There was still work to do. Even if Eddie found a specific street location for the call's origin, Jennifer still needed to find Megan. And the media was her best bet.

She heard a creak below and strained to hear if Dmitri had come early. She wasn't quite ready to surprise him with the news yet. Ideally, she'd hand him Megan's address and tell him to go get it over with. She could just see his reaction. He'd be thrilled. Maybe things would even settle down a bit. If she could just get Dmitri some distance from his father, maybe they could live in peace for a while.

She opened to the first in a stack of news articles that had been culled for her. If Megan had called Jennifer's pager, it meant there was trouble. Since Jennifer would have known if Oskar had found her because she was helping Dmitri, she assumed the trouble was something else. And Ryan was the only thing she could come up with. So as soon as she'd arrived at work, Jennifer had ordered news scans for any cases related to a child between the ages of seven and thirteen. Though Ryan was eight, Jennifer knew it was possible that Megan had altered the records of his age in their move.

Jennifer read each story, watching for clues that would indicate it could be Megan. A single son. An unmarried mother. The woman would be not well known in the neighborhood. She'd do something like contracting work or maybe computers, something with little people interaction. Each was an assumption to some degree, but Jennifer had known Megan long enough to make solid guesses. She couldn't imagine Megan married again; couldn't imagine her in a job that had any kind of profile. She was too cautious, too meticulous.

The stories were mostly atrocities. That was what made the news. The boy who'd been discovered dead in his home after being chained to a bed and left by his mother who went off with a new boyfriend. Drive-by shootings, rapes, fires. They were depressing, but none of them seemed right. What was she looking for? Kids taken hostage in a school or a kidnapping. She paused. What else would make Megan risk calling the FBI?

Perhaps some sort of medical emergency. She looked back down at the articles. A medical emergency wasn't going to make news. But why wouldn't Megan have called again? Had she solved the problem? It seemed unlikely. After what had happened in New Orleans, the Bureau would have been Megan's last resort.

Jennifer picked up the phone and dialed the cell phone number for her data contact at the Bureau.

"Steve," he said, his voice echoing as though she was on a speakerphone. Steve was tall and thin, with thick blondish brown hair and olive skin that looked tan no matter what time of year it was. He had brown eyes like a teddy bear and he was the nicest person she knew. He could literally find a source for anything, and he'd bailed her out of more tough spots in her career than she cared to think about.

"Where are you?"

"At home. Working on a drawing. I've got you plugged in so I'm hands-free. Sorry if it echoes."

"It's fine. Sorry to call on the weekend." She wondered what picture he was working on, but decided to mind her own business. She knew he was incredibly creative. One time they'd had coffee and he'd borrowed a five from her. The five-dollar bill he'd given back had been painted and colored so incredibly, she'd been unable to spend it. She used it as a bookmark now. He said he was an artist in his spare time, and when she thought about him, she occasionally wished she were someone totally different. Someone Steve might have been interested in.

"No worries. Those articles help?"

"They did."

"But you're looking for something else?"

She glanced over her shoulder, suddenly concerned Dmitri would appear and ruin the surprise. He had a way of sneaking up on her that was unnerving. "I am. I'm hoping to find a waiting list for organ recipients. Same age group."

"Hold on. Let me write this down." There was the

shuffle of paper in the background. "You're talking medical records?"

"Right. Anyone waiting to receive a donor organ."

She could hear his pen moving across the page. It stopped. "Any idea what organ?"

She sighed. "No."

"No worries. I think I can handle this."

"I really appreciate it."

"No problem. You're talking same ages, seven to thirteen?"

"Right."

"Ethnicity?"

"Caucasian."

"Sex?"

"Male."

He scratched some more. "Same case number?"

"Yep," she lied.

"I'll call you as soon as I hear anything."

"I owe you, Steve."

"Someday I'm going to collect on that, Jennifer."

"You got it."

He laughed and hung up and she stared at the phone, smiling at the sound of his laugh and his pen scratching against the surface of the page. He was so cute, she thought with a bit of guilt.

Just then, the downstairs door slammed and she heard the sound of something crashing to the floor. She glanced at the empty hallway and stood from her chair. She walked to the door, hesitating to call out.

"Jennifer," Dmitri yelled as something else fell to the floor.

"Dmitri?" she called, coming to the top of the stairs.

He stood, rocking on his feet as though trying to

keep balance on a boat. His face was pale and shiny. He'd been drinking.

"Are you sick?" She hurried down the stairs, waiting for a response.

He staggered a few feet and then swung back around. He muttered something else, but she only caught the word "father."

"What is it, Dmitri? What's happened?"

He turned toward her, one arm swinging out. "Goddamn asshole," he snarled. "He killed him. He fucking killed him." As he swore, he swung his arm again and the back of his hand connected with her cheek with a sharp sting.

"Ow." She flinched and stepped back.

"Oh, Jesus." He opened his arms and approached her. "I'm so sorry, Jenichka. I'm so, so sorry." He rested his elbows on her shoulders and leaned into her. He was heavy and she struggled to support him.

She pushed him back and took his arm, leading him to the living room. "Who killed who, Dmitri? Who's dead?" She found herself praying it was Oskar. Please let Oskar be dead. What problems that would solve.

Dmitri moaned, his head lolling and his feet stumbling as together they staggered into the living room, he from the alcohol and she from the weight. She lifted his arm off her shoulder and pushed him onto the couch. His head fell back and he let out a loud noise like he was snoring. Then he jolted upright. "I saw him. He didn't want me to, but I did. I had to look." He dropped his head in his hands. "He looked terrible, Jenichka. Terrible."

Jennifer sat beside him on the couch and tucked

her feet beneath her. "You're not making any sense. Please tell me what you saw."

His eyes focused on her and he cupped her chin in his palm. "Thank God for you, Jenichka. Thank God for my little *anghel*," he said, using the Russian pronunciation of "angel."

Jennifer touched his cheek. "I'm here. What happened?"

He shook his head. "It's so terrible. He's a monster. He's a monster and he wants me to be one, too."

She thought he meant his father, but she wasn't getting any clear answers. "Should I start some coffee?"

He grabbed her wrist and pulled her back. "No. Please don't go. I can't stay long. They can't know I'm here, but I needed to see you."

"What? Who can't know? What are you talking about?" She shook her head. "Dmitri, you're not making any sense."

"I'll tell you. He shot himself. In the head."

"Oskar?" She held her breath for the answer.

"Feliks."

The wind rushed from her lungs, leaving her breathless and suddenly cold.

"Papa killed Gary."

Feliks's lover. She closed her eyes. She adored Feliks and Gary. "Killed him?" she asked almost in a whisper.

"Had it done."

She blinked away the violent image that played in her mind. She'd never heard details of Oskar's work from the family, but she'd read enough of the case files to know it was not the way she wanted to go. She rubbed the shivers off her arms. "Why?"

"As an example."

She choked on the next question. "An example of what?"

"Papa says he betrayed the family."

Each breath made her throat feel smaller. She shook her head, saving the little breath she had.

"It wasn't like you."

She gasped. "Like me?" She sat back, knowing he was referring to the fact that Viktor's location had come from her. "I didn't betray you. It was a mistake—"

"I didn't mean it like that." He put his palms out. "I meant that Gary was stealing. Papa says they were both stealing."

"Feliks was stealing?"

"Papa says he was." He shook his head. "I don't know what to believe. Papa says he didn't kill Feliks. He swears he didn't." Dmitri's expression was fearful and Jennifer felt it was fear for her and not him. She wanted to ask what his father had said about her, but knew it wasn't that easy. Dmitri wouldn't tell her, and it might put him on the defensive. Would he really hurt her? The answer that came to her mind was a resounding *yes*.

"Papa said Feliks saw Gary and turned the gun on himself."

She shuddered. She could picture that. Feliks had been deeply in love with Gary and horribly torn about his father's views of his sexuality.

Dmitri rubbed his forehead with both hands, his shoulders shaking.

She leaned against him, unable to find anything to say. It was too terrible. And yet she could think of it only selfishly. How much more Oskar would expect of Dmitri. At least when there were two of them, it alleviated some of the pressure on Dmitri. Now it was only him.

"He's finishing up."

She sat up and pushed the hair off her face. "Finishing up what?"

"He wants it to look like he's in control before he's too sick."

She shook her head. "Sick? What do you mean sick?"

"He's got something."

Jennifer felt her chest expand. It was the evil sense of wishing something bad on someone. She didn't try to stop it. "What does he have?"

"I don't know."

"Then how do you know he's sick?" she pressed, hoping he wasn't wrong.

"I see him sneaking the pills sometimes when he thinks I'm not watching."

"What do you think it is?"

"I don't know. I can't tell, but it's getting worse." He focused on the far wall for a moment and then shook his head. "He holds his stomach and I can see that he's in pain." Dmitri dipped his head. "He's getting ready, though. He's very focused on the end, on finishing it."

The panic swelled in her chest. "Finishing what?"

Dmitri blinked and looked at her from the corner of his eye.

It seemed to happen in slow motion, and the look cooled her to the spine. All the moisture seemed to evaporate from the air and it was as though she were sucking on dry ice when she spoke. "What?"

"Viktor."

She blinked and rubbed her hands together. She wondered for a moment if Dmitri had turned the heat down. He did that sometimes. "Viktor?" She paused. The thought of what had happened, of her part in it, still left her cold. If Oskar knew . . . She shivered. "Finding Megan Riggs, you mean?"

"In part."

"I found something on Megan."

He looked back and his eyes widened, suddenly more hopeful.

She went to her office and opened the drawer. Pulling the phone records out, she returned to him and handed them over. "I was waiting to get confirmation, but I think they're in California."

He scanned the numbers. "You found them."

She exhaled. "Yes. I'm waiting for someone to call me back with more information. I hope to have it tonight or tomorrow."

He looked away, the tears, the affection, suddenly gone.

She watched him, trying to gauge his thoughts, his reactions. She'd thought he'd be thrilled. "What's wrong?"

He shook his head. "This is good. It will help with Viktor."

She touched his arm and felt the stiffness of his muscles under her fingers. "What else is there?"

When he didn't answer her, she stood, wrapping her arms against the chill in the room. "Is it Feliks?"

Dmitri focused on the far wall. "That's done now."

She tried to turn the conversation, to bring it back in her control. "I'm sorry about Feliks, Dmitri. I really cared for him. Can I help with the service arrangements or anything?"

"I think it will be a family affair," he said.

She frowned at him, though he was not looking at her. Giving him the opportunity to have some time alone, she started for the door. "I can order us some food for takeout if you'd rather stay in tonight. . . ."

He stood, too. "I should go." He walked to her and took her hands. Then he scanned her, head to toe, as though she were something he'd never seen before. Or might never see again.

"Good-bye, Jenichka." He gave her a light kiss on the cheek and walked to the door without turning back.

She stood watching him. He seemed cold and strangely vacant. Somehow she felt he was saying good-bye for good. But instead of feeling lonely or sad, she was filled with the icy awareness of fear.

Chapter 22

Travis pulled his Porsche in front of the green Jeep he knew was Cody's. It was only nine-thirty at night, but from the look of the house, Cody could have been asleep. He knew, of course, that she wasn't.

He wanted to warn her about the news. He'd had no idea what was coming, no idea how they'd found out about the kidnapping. The interviewer had said there was a "rumor" about an abduction. Travis had denied the rumor and confirmed that Peter was home safely in bed. Would the network edit it out when they ran the taped interview tomorrow?

He rapped three times on the door. He heard shoes on the stairs, but when the door opened, it wasn't Cody.

Travis looked over the colonel's shoulder. "Is Cody here?"

"She's a bit busy, Mr. Landon."

Travis smiled. "You playing butler?" he teased, but realized his offense as soon as the words were out.

The colonel raised an eyebrow.

"Sorry. I was just surprised to see anyone answering her door." He tapped his watch. "Especially at this hour."

"I suppose she's probably surprised to be getting visitors at this hour, too."

Travis stepped back and raised his arms. He didn't want to say anything in front of the colonel. Maybe it could wait. "Right. Just tell her I was surprised she didn't make it to the meeting tonight. I was coming to brief her on it."

Just then, he heard the low moan of the stairs.

The colonel turned back, too.

Cody made her way down the stairs. Her dark hair was down, long over her shoulders, and Travis touched his tie awkwardly. It was the first time he'd noticed how well all that hair framed her face, and he realized that besides being lithe and strong, she was really quite beautiful.

She had very narrow, almost catlike light blue eyes with high cheeks and an angular jaw and chin. Her nose was slender with an even upslope, which broke up the sharp edges elsewhere. She ran her hand over her hair as she approached the door as though she knew he was evaluating her features. He forced his gaze back to the colonel, who was giving him a reproachful stare.

"Have you seen the site?"

Travis felt his stomach flutter. "No. What is it?"

The colonel watched him, his eyes narrow, and Travis felt as though he were under some sort of magnifying glass. Every motion, every reaction was being measured. He did his best to ignore the colonel. "What is it?"

"Another picture."

He looked from Cody to the colonel. "Is he . . ." He couldn't bring himself to ask the question.

"He's fine," the colonel answered.

Cody nodded, crossing her arms. "From the picture, he appears fine."

Travis put his hand out. "I'm so glad. Are there any clues? Can you tell anything about where he might be?"

No one touched his hand, so he quickly drew it back.

"I'm not sure yet."

"Do you have the picture here? Can I see it?"

"It's upstairs," the colonel said flatly.

"Well, I'm sorry to come by so late," he said, still feeling as though he was missing some vital piece of information. "I was surprised to see the colonel here," he added.

"How did it go with McCue?" Cody asked, redirecting.

Travis wondered what the colonel's part in this had become, but he focused on Cody's question instead. "Okay, I think. No leads yet, obviously."

"He has access to the employee records?" the colonel asked.

Travis blinked at him and then looked at Cody. Had she told him everything? Did he know about her ex-husband? Wouldn't he be a risk?

"You gave McCue the records, right?" Cody pressed.

"He's reviewing them at the office now. With someone, of course."

The colonel nodded. "He's profiled the kidnapper?"

Travis avoided the colonel's gaze. He searched Cody's face for a response as to his presence, but she made no move to explain it. "He expects to get through the files by tomorrow."

"He'll be discreet?"

Travis nodded. "Absolutely."

"No press whatsoever."

He tried to find a way to tell her about his interview, but nothing came to him. He didn't want to upset her any more than necessary. "Whatever you say," Travis agreed.

"What's his tactic, then?" Cody asked.

"Narrow it down, contact some people, check current addresses and activities on some of the suspicious ones." He rattled the items off, trying to sound confident despite his own discomfort.

Cody nodded to the colonel, who stepped away from the door.

He gripped his hand in a fist and forced himself to talk. He had to tell her. "I met with—"

"I apologize for missing the meeting," she interrupted. "The new picture came up just as I was planning to leave."

Travis studied her face. Her expression was genuine. He even saw the slightest glimmer of trust, but he wasn't sure it was in him. "He didn't promise much. He's got everything I have and he'll do the best he can do."

She nodded and her lips made the smallest outline of a smile. "I'm sure he'll find something."

He smiled, too, but what he felt was mostly puzzlement. What had happened to the Cody O'Brien he'd seen earlier? He shook his head and forced his mind back to the news. "I also wanted—"

"We're still working on the new picture. Why don't you call me when you hear from him," she said, starting to close the door.

He stepped back so it didn't catch his toe. He raised his hand to say good-bye, but the door was al-

ready closed. He hadn't told her about the interview.
It would probably just blow over. And the interviewer hadn't mentioned any kid other than Peter.

As he turned his back, he wondered about the
new picture. He jogged back to the car, and got into
the Porsche, anxious to get to his home computer.

Chapter 23

Cody raced from the front door to her office, then slowed to an even pace and started circling the room again. She thought about Travis Landon. He'd looked genuinely concerned, but why hadn't he called instead? Was he just on his way back from San Jose now? She considered McCue and sat down at her computer and typed in his name into an Internet search engine. She came up with a few listings for McCue: a dean's list for Eastworth College, a listing of personnel for the United States Department of Arms Control and Disarmament, and a list of kidney donors. None of them was a Dusty McCue. She tried Dustin McCue instead.

She watched the colonel, immersed in his bug book, until he finally looked up. "What?"

"I was just thinking."

"Spill it."

She nodded. She'd wanted to share it and appreciated his no-nonsense attitude. "If you were a private investigator, would you try to keep yourself low-profile?"

He narrowed his eyes in thought and then

straightened his glasses on his nose. "I guess it depends on the clientele I wanted."

"So if you dealt with movie stars and stuff, probably? They'd want someone lower-profile?"

"Right."

She looked back at the screen. "Makes sense."

"You wondering about McCue?"

She nodded without turning around.

"You know anything about him?"

"Nothing."

"Might not be a bad idea to find something out."

She glanced at the phone and decided to call Travis Landon. She dialed his number from memory and waited until the answering machine clicked on. She didn't leave a message. She stood and moved slowly to the office door and glanced into the kitchen at Ryan's favorite Spider-Man cup, fighting off the panic.

She returned to the computer and brought up the Web site again, scutinizing its detail for the thousandth time. They'd spotted the bug immediately. Ryan was in front of another white wall, sitting this time. In the very corner of the picture, she saw a glass. It looked like it had water in it. His hands were crossed over one another and on the back of one, right at the edge of his sleeve, was the moth.

She studied him again. He still looked frightened, but he looked clean. Though he wore the same clothes, she guessed from his hair that he had showered. She was relieved to see the water, too. It was in a jelly-jar glass, the same as they had at home. It wasn't fancy, but it was stylish and definitely not drugstore cheap. Though there were a hundred explanations for how someone dirt-poor could have such a glass, the more she thought about it, she was

convinced the kidnapper had to be someone Landon
had worked with. It just didn't seem like he'd been
kidnapped by someone random.

The phone rang and she stood to look at the ID
box. Still unlisted.

"You going to answer that?"

She shook her head.

"Why the hell not?"

"Because there's no one I want to talk to."

The colonel's jaw dropped. "What about the kidnapper?"

"He'd be calling Landon." She'd thought this
through. No one knew she was there. No one knew
it was her child who had been kidnapped. No one
but Landon, and this wasn't his number. She recognized his numbers now.

The colonel looked over her shoulder at the caller
ID box. "I think you should answer."

"Are you any closer?" she asked, changing the
subject.

He raised a finger like he was about to make a
declaration.

"What?"

"I think this is it."

"Think?"

He nodded. "I'm almost positive that this is a
Hyalophora gloveri."

"In English please."

"It's a moth found in the Sierras."

Her breath rushed from her chest. "The Sierras,"
she repeated.

"But there's a related species, *Hyalophora euryalus,*
which occurs in the Great Basin."

"Turner," she warned.

"Hang on there and listen to what I'm saying."

"I am listening, but I don't understand a word of it."

"I'm saying that there are these two species of moth that come together in one small area of Lake Tahoe and form distinct hybrids."

"How small an area?"

"I'd have to look it up."

She looked at the picture of Ryan. "You think that's the hybrid?"

He nodded.

She wrapped her fingers into a tight fist. "A small area of Lake Tahoe. That's where you think this bug is found?"

He broke a smile. "That's right."

She jumped up and threw her arms around the colonel.

He laughed and pushed her back. "Hold on, there. I want to be positive."

"Jesus, how can you be positive?"

"I need one more book."

"Another one?" She stopped dancing and started to pace again. "It's driving me crazy. Is it the right damn bug or not?"

The colonel stood and took his glasses off, folding them at a pace so slow she knew it was meant to remind her that good research couldn't be rushed. But it could. She knew it could. She'd seen it done a hundred times at the Bureau. And with Mark's job. That was all they'd ever done: rush, rush, rush. They'd talked about having another child after Ryan. They'd both wanted a big family. Especially her. She'd imagined family barbeques, having her sisters over. All the kids running around a huge backyard, playing. But she and Mark had been so busy. Things had been put on hold. And then Mark was gone.

And it was too late. All that rushing around, she hadn't remembered how it felt.

For three years Cody had actually stopped rushing. But now the adrenaline was back and she couldn't slow it. She wouldn't. She needed it. "Colonel. I swear, I'm going to break those glasses into a thousand pieces."

Her gave her a piercing stare meant to warn her.

"This is my son we're talking about."

"Fine. Then run your butt over to my house and get the thick blue reference book on the floor. It was too heavy to carry over."

"What about Mrs. Turner?"

"She's turned in by now." When she hesitated, he shrugged. "I'm happy to go get it, but it'll take longer."

The front doorbell rang as she was heading toward the door.

"Who's that?" the colonel called.

She walked back and shook her head. "Landon, probably. Don't answer it."

Just then the phone started ringing. She shook her head.

As she headed out of the office, she heard the colonel turn on the office television.

The doorbell rang again, but she sneaked out the back door and through the Turners' backyard. She'd never been thankful for the back route before now. She curved around the Turners' yard and entered through the back door. The house was quiet, but it had the sense of being occupied. It gave Cody the creeps, and she moved quickly through the dark kitchen and into the den. She pulled the heavy book into her arms and traced her path back, shielding it from the drizzling rain.

As she came around the corner of the Turners' house, she ran smack into the colonel.

"Jesus, you almost gave me a heart attack."

He looked over his shoulder and took her arm. "Let's go."

She wrenched herself free and looked around. "What are you doing?"

"I'll show you. Just get inside."

She shook her head. "No. Tell me now." She heard the sound of engines on the quiet street; a set of headlights passed them. Then another.

"You're going to have to trust me."

"Who—"

The colonel grabbed her arm and shook it to gain her attention. His brow was closed down over his eyes in a shadow of bad news. "Trust me," he repeated, his voice urgent.

A third car turned down their street, and Cody thought it was a van. She nodded quickly and turned back toward the colonel's house with him close behind.

He shut the door behind them and locked it without turning on the light, then ushered her into the den.

She shuddered and realized she wore only a long-sleeved T-shirt and shorts. The colonel motioned to the couch and she sat without argument. He pulled a wool afghan over her legs and she noted that the itchiness of the wool that usually bothered her was now distant and warm.

"What's going on?"

He nodded and put his glasses on quickly. Then, finding the remote control, he flipped the television on. She shook her head, turning her back to it. She gripped the colonel's sleeve. "Is it Ryan? Just tell me. I don't want to see."

Before he could answer, she heard the voice of Travis Landon.

"I have no comment. Please. This is a personal matter. For the sake of us all, leave us alone."

Cody focused on the image of Travis, in a gray suit, the top button of his shirt undone, his tie pulled loose, standing in front of his house. He was dressed exactly as he had been when he'd left her house less than a half hour before.

"You did an interview for CNN earlier. Isn't that right, Mr. Landon?" one reporter shouted.

He nodded and looked awkwardly at the camera.

"But you didn't tell them about the kidnapping."

"There was no—" Landon started.

"We have confirmation that a classmate of your son's has been kidnapped."

"Is it true that the boy's disappearance is linked to a Web site with your son's name?" another asked.

It looked as though the press had been waiting for him at his house when he arrived.

He raked his hand through his hair like a man who'd never dealt with the exasperation of the media's barrage. Yet he spoke to them.

"No," Cody whispered. "Don't."

"Mr. Landon, can you confirm that your son's classmate, R.J. O'Brien, was kidnapped from the private school he attends?"

Travis halted. It was like he was frozen.

"Move," Cody said. "Just leave."

The voices continued, a cacophony that seemed to surround Landon until he finally spoke. "Yes."

"Damn it." She could have killed him. He'd blown

their silence. He'd sworn he'd be quiet, and he'd betrayed her.

In one corner of the screen, the banner read *LIVE, 10:00 o'clock news*. She focused on Travis's face as it disappeared into the background and a petite Asian woman appeared center screen.

"There has been no update on the case of the mistaken kidnapping of eight-year-old R.J. O'Brien from his exclusive private boys' school on Friday. Correspondent Grace Thompson reports from the home of the boy's mother, Cody O'Brien."

Cody flinched as she saw the image switch to the front of her own home. "Oh, God." She heard the bustle through the colonel's window, the same noises she heard on the TV as several reporters crowded around her front door.

"There appears to be no one currently available to comment at the home of Cody O'Brien, mother of the eight-year-old kidnapped accidentally in place of the son of Travis Landon, president and CEO of TecLan in Silicon Valley."

She watched an image appear in the corner of the screen. It sucked her breath away. As the picture grew, Cody felt herself shrivel. Inside the small, white-rimmed box was her driver's-license photo. "Jesus."

The colonel took her hand like a father and patted it without a word.

"According to sources, the kidnapper set up a Web site to announce his ransom. Details on what he's demanded are not yet available. Local police, however, have not offered any insight into the mistaken kidnapper's identity or the ransom he is requesting. They have been trying to reach Mrs. O'Brien, but according to the head officer, they have

not been successful. This is Grace Thompson reporting." She gave a wide, toothy smile. "Back to you in
the studio, Kyle."

Kyle's mouth moved, but Cody could no longer
focus on the words. All she saw was her image in the
corner of the screen like an hourglass counting down
the seconds until Oskar Kirov arrived at the door.
Cody thought about her phone ringing off the hook
all day. Had it been the police wanting to talk to her?

She stared at the familiar features. They would
know. Anyone would know. The hair color was different; she'd worn glasses and contacts to make her
eyes look brown. She wore heavier makeup, her hair
frizzy and curled, and she'd framed it around her
face. All in an effort to hide her identity.

But it was there. It was all there. Maybe even more
clearly than it would have been if she'd just left herself plain. The bad hair, the makeup, the glasses,
they only drew extra attention to her. And beneath
all of that fake exterior, Cody saw the very clear
image of one petrified Megan Riggs.

She blinked hard, feeling the tears well up. She let
them stream down her face. Her mind flashed back
and forth from her own child to the image of his kidnapper as she tried to picture the man who had
Ryan.

"We should call the police now," the colonel said.

She shook her head.

"It's all out now. They can help."

She thought about the kidnapper. He was orga-
nized. He'd shown no signs of panic. There was a
decent chance that he'd release Ryan when he realized that he wasn't the one he wanted.

She shifted. But if there was police involvement

now, media, he might panic. He might not release him.

What did he want? If he wanted ransom, he might still be able to get it with Ryan. If he wanted revenge, he wouldn't need Ryan. He'd let him go or he'd dispose of him. It was too clean, too cold to be an angry crime. Wasn't it? Too clinical.

"No police." She'd be better off taking a chance to reason with him herself.

She saw the photo of Ryan on the clean carpet with the clean wall. The glass in the corner, his clean hair. He'd washed, been fed. He wasn't being abused. She tried to focus on the details, but her mind kept slipping to another image.

A man standing red-faced in a court of law, threatening her life for his son's. Oskar Kirov would find out where she was and he would hunt her down.

She focused on the friendly face who reported the news of her son's disappearance.

She wondered if he had any idea how close he was to reporting the news of their deaths.

Chapter 24

Mei Ling was pretending to focus on the computer reports that were stacked in front of her. It was well after midnight and Jennifer had come into the office just minutes ago. Mei was surprised she'd come in at all, and it was the first time they'd seen each other since their fight and her talk with Andy Chang. Jennifer had not mentioned the event, so Mei kept her mouth shut. After she told Andy about the incident, he'd told her to disregard it. He wanted her to pretend that she knew nothing and act as she would normally. And that was what she would have done normally. She'd never bring up something like that, especially not to Jennifer.

But with the events of the last two days, Mei noticed more than ever how ill at ease Jennifer seemed in the office. Tonight even her clothes were disheveled, and there was a dull flatness to her hair that Mei had never seen before. She wore navy socks beneath her black pants and she carried a brown Coach bag despite her black shoes. It was as though she'd dressed in a terrible hurry or maybe in the dark.

Andy had told her that the medication in Jennifer's desk, Ativan, was prescribed for anxiety disorders, but Jennifer seemed more anxious than ever.

The phone rang and Jennifer answered it. Mei leaned into her report as she heard Jennifer's voice get momentarily louder. She could feel the other woman's gaze on her back, so she lifted her pencil and made a small mark on the page as though she were completely focused. Jennifer's voice lowered; then she was quiet.

Mei wanted to turn around, but instead she made another note, opened her drawer, pulled out a small paper flag, stuck it on the edge of the page, made a sound like she'd discovered something, and then turned to the next page.

She listened, but behind her Jennifer was absolutely silent. Mei had an eerie feeling that Jennifer was right behind her. Her stomach leaped, but when she turned around Jennifer was still on the phone, her back to Mei.

Mei scolded herself. Calm down. Just work. For a moment she'd imagined herself some sort of Lucy Liu, an Asian Charlie's Angel, and she was struck with how childishly she was behaving. She was giddy. She knew it was partly Andy. He even made her laugh. But the situation with Jennifer wasn't a joke or a game. And she was no Charlie's Angel. She was a desk agent, and clearly she wasn't cut out for much more.

"You're the best, you know," Jennifer said. A pause. "No, I'm on my way to get it now. Thanks for coming in so late to help."

Jennifer's chair scraped against the floor as she stood, and Mei flinched.

Mei looked up at her. The bruises on her left eye had started to fade to a pale green, and in the corner of her eye she could still see the color despite her makeup. Her eyes were accented with deep circles that were colored in a slightly different tone of neutral than the rest of her face. Still, despite a look of general exhaustion, Jennifer seemed genuinely relieved.

Mei shook her head and glanced at Jennifer's phone as though it might explain her partner's expression. "I was just working on these reports from the 282-CG case."

Jennifer nodded. "I've got a stack of those, too." She pointed to her desk although the surface was clean. "I just need to run to pick up a report. I'll be right back."

Mei nodded and turned back to her work as Jennifer left the room. Mei stood and waited ten seconds, then walked into the hallway and turned toward the ladies' room. When she was sure the hallway was clear, she turned back into the office and locked the door.

Jennifer's desk was clear except for a stack of old case files on a previous hacker they'd been tracking. Mei knew exactly what they were because she'd been using them while Jennifer was gone, and she'd been the one to put them back on her desk. The only other thing on the surface was a letter-size spiral notebook that was open. Jennifer's clean, block writing filled the page with notes from the case they were working on. But the date on them was almost two months ago. Mei scanned the page quickly and saw nothing of interest.

She crossed the room back to her own desk and lifted the phone to dial Andy's extension. He would be gone, of course, so she left a voice mail that simply said to call her. Then she opened the office door

again and sat back at her desk. When her phone
rang less than a minute later, she snatched it up.

"Mei Ling," she said, smiling. She felt foolish, but
she hadn't spoken with Andy since their meeting the
day before, and yet found herself walking through
the halls with one eye out for him.

"Ling Mei," her mother's voice said in Cantonese.

Trying to mask her disappointment, she greeted
her mother. "It's so late."

"Can't sleep. Your father, he snores."

Mei lifted her pencil to continue scanning the
computer records while they talked. Her mother
lamented over the price of pork at the market she
went to, and how she could never make it as well as
her aunt.

Mei made all the right conciliatory noises though
she didn't say anything. That was usually how it
was when her mother called. And her sisters, too, for
that matter. Mei seemed to be the only one available
to listen. Only right now, Mei wasn't available. She
had a mountain of work to do.

Her other line rang through.

Her mother was telling her how a boy of one of
her friends had cancer.

"I'm very sorry," Mei said. "I have to take another
call."

"You're so busy, you can't talk to your own
mother? Even at this hour?"

The line continued to blink. "Can you hang on just
a minute?"

Her mother sighed. "*Hou a.*" *It's fine,* she said, but
Mei knew it wasn't.

Mei punched the hold button, then the second
line, but the call was already gone. "Damn it," she

muttered. She returned to her mother. "I'm sorry about Evie's baby boy," she said.

"Oh, you're back," her mother said in Cantonese. "I can't believe you put your own mother on hold. What important case are you working on? Somebody hatching in and stealing money from some bank?" She asked, saying the word *hatching* in English.

"Hacking, Mom."

"Whatever. What people put their money on the Intanet? Dumb. It's their own fault, I say."

Internet, she thought without bothering to correct her again. She also didn't remind her mom that the small branch of their bank in Chinatown was also undoubtedly connected to the Internet.

"So what is this special case?"

"It's not special, Mom. It's more of the same, but I need to go."

"Fine, I'll see you tomorrow. We can talk then."

Mei almost asked what tomorrow was.

"Red egg and ginger," her mother snapped.

"I know. I'll be there."

Her mother hung up, muttering something Mei couldn't understand.

Mei listened to the message from Andy Chang twice, then hit seven to delete it so she wouldn't do it again. What was wrong with her? He'd said he got her message and would try her again in a half hour or so. There was nothing else to his message, no hidden flirtations. This was business.

Just then, Allen Stiller appeared at her door. "Jennifer around?"

Mei shook her head. "She got a call and went to pick something up."

Allen nodded. "That was me. I have these cell

phone records for her. She came by and I was on the phone. She was waiting in my office; then Steve Edwards came by and the two of them disappeared."

Mei frowned. "Cell phone records for what?"

"Case number's right on them." He handed the stack to her. Allen scratched behind one of his large ears. It jiggled as he did.

She studied the case number. "You sure the case number is right?"

"It's what she gave me."

Mei stood and opened the file drawer behind her. In it she had their cases by number. She found the one with the same number and opened the file. The case involved a hacker who had gotten into some DMV files, but it had been closed in July of 2001. Why would Jennifer be looking at it now? She turned back to Allen. "You said she ran into Steve Edwards and took off?"

He nodded.

"Did you see Steve?"

"Sure. He's in his office."

"Thanks, Allen. I'll make sure she gets these."

Allen nodded and turned around, scratching his ear again as he moved down the hall.

Mei snatched up the phone and dialed Steve's extension. "It's Mei," she said when he answered.

"Yeah, Mei." He laughed. "I don't know what I said to your partner, but I sure made her happy."

"That's what I heard. I'd love to see what you gave her. Do you have a copy?"

"Sure. I'll print one now."

"I'll be by in five to get it."

Mei put the phone down and went back to Jennifer's desk. She scanned the open notebook page again for anything she might have missed the last time. What was Jennifer up to? There was nothing there. She flipped the page and found a phone number. It was a 734 area code. A new Michigan area code, Mei thought. She had a friend at medical school in Ann Arbor and that was her area code. Mei transcribed the number onto a Post-it note and considered whether or not to dial it. She went back to her desk and looked at the records Allen had brought. They were for the same phone number. It wasn't in Michigan, though. The phone had been traced to somewhere near Oakland, California.

After what Andy had told her, she immediately wondered if the number had anything to do with Megan Riggs. Snatching her badge, Mei tucked the phone report in a bottom drawer, locked it, and pocketed the key. Then, leaving the office, she headed to see Steve Edwards.

Steve was standing at the printer as she entered the pod that made up his data group. "It's almost done." He pulled a bunch of pages off the printer. "Here's the first part."

"Thanks." Mei flipped through what appeared to be a bunch of newspaper articles. The first was about a fire in Minnesota that had claimed two victims, one an eight-year-old boy. The next was about a drunken driver who killed a whole busload of kids in Atlanta, then one about a missing child from a neighborhood park in New Mexico. She shook her head. What was Jennifer looking for?

"But here's the one Jennifer flipped out over."

The paper was barely in her hands before Mei realized what Jennifer had discovered. "Holy shit."

"Must be good. I've never heard you swear before."

Mei blushed. "Sorry."

"No. I'm glad to bring out such strong emotion." He laughed as she blushed harder.

Mei focused on the features of Megan Riggs's face. She was older, her hair darker, more makeup—a lot more—but it was definitely Megan.

"Who is that?"

"Someone who's in a shitload of trouble."

"Yee-haw. Nail her to the wall."

Mei thought someone was already trying to. She thanked Steve and hurried back to her office as fast as she could without running. She put a call in to Andy, letting him know what Jennifer knew, and then she paged him to call her back. This couldn't wait.

After a moment of looking around the room in desperation for what to do next, she found the phone number Jennifer had written down and dialed it.

It rang four times, and then a computerized voice told her to leave a message. With a deep breath, Mei prayed she was not making a terrible mistake. Then she began to speak.

"Hi. It's Agent Mei Ling with the Chicago field office of the FBI. It's been a long time and I hope you're okay.

"I want to warn you that you may be in danger. An article in the paper may have given away your location, and they may be moving in. I hope I'm wrong and this isn't you, but if it is, call me directly and I'll get you some help out there. Don't talk to anyone else." She paused, feeling like she was quoting some bad police movie. "Please let me help, okay? I'm worried." She left her cell numbers and her pager and urged Megan not to call the office for fear she'd get Jennifer directly.

She opened her directory to the San Francisco field office and called the special agent in charge out there. She left a message on his voice mail and hoped Andy called back before the California agent did. She wanted to get those agents moving, but she didn't have the authority to do it on her own.

Sinking into her chair, Mei pulled her knees to her chest, and crossed her arms around them. Dread pooling in her veins, she waited for something to happen.

Chapter 25

The colonel lifted the last things into the back of the Jeep and closed the hatch. It had stopped raining an hour ago and he hoped the weather held up for the drive. He hated the way folks drove in the rain.

He started the engine and reversed the car into his driveway, and then went to make his phone call and get Florence. He still hadn't heard from his old buddy at the ranger station up there, but he'd left Cody's cell phone number and he hoped he'd call back soon. No reason to stick around and wait.

The colonel had packed a couple days' stuff for himself and Florence. If all went well, that was the most they would need. And he had his books. Cody would have her cell phone and laptop, so they could watch for new additions to the site. But they had the location. Ryan was somewhere in the Sierra mountains. Now they just had to find out where. Damn if that was the hard part. But it wasn't. The phone call was. The one he'd been putting off for nine years.

He had the number memorized. He'd always tracked her, made sure she was safe, that the asshole she'd married hadn't run out on her. But he hadn't. They had a nice little house. She worked at the local library. He worked for the Ford dealership about thirty miles away. All this time he'd seen them, but he'd never called to tell her he was thinking about them. Or to apologize. Damn, apologizing was the worst. And he had a hell of a lot of apologizing to do.

He lifted the cordless phone, and the weight of it made him sit down. He balanced it between his hands and punched the familiar number with his thumbs.

"Hello," his daughter's voice answered, and he could see her with those big brown eyes, her wide smile, and beautiful straight teeth. She looked just like a kid. His thumb moved to hang up the phone. This was when he always hung up.

"Hello," she repeated.

"I'm here," he choked out.

There was silence on the other end. And he thought he heard the sound of a chair moving. Maybe she'd had to sit down, too.

"It's your father calling, Roni. Or do you go by Veronica now?"

She didn't answer, and he wondered what the expression on her face was. Was she angry? Or hurt? Did she even care?

He heard the sniffling sound of someone crying and then realized it was coming from him. "I'll be damned," he said, letting out a coughing sob. "I've turned into a blubbering old fool and I didn't even know it."

He thought he could see her smile on the other end and he prayed he was right. "I need your help, Roni."

"What's wrong? Where's Mom?"

"She's here, Roni. She's still here. This isn't about

us, and I can't explain much. I need to come up there, stay with you. Maybe just your mom, maybe both of us and one other. I can explain a lot more when we're there." He paused and pinched his brow as he waited for her response.

"I need to talk to Doug. I can't just make that decision on my own. We don't do that."

He nodded and stared up at the ceiling, blinking hard. "I know it. You're a good kid, Roni. And that kid of yours is a real looker. Mean on the basketball court, too. Guess he got his daddy's height, eh?"

She gasped, and he searched back for the mistake he'd made. "I'm sorry. I didn't mean to startle you."

Her voice was quiet, almost a whisper, and it sounded more full of awe than anger or fear. "You've seen him? When did you see him?"

"I've been up from time to time, Roni. I didn't think you'd want to see me, but I had to be sure you guys were okay."

"Why didn't you come? Why call now, after all this time?"

"Damn it. I don't know. I was hurt back then and scared. You'd done some rough stuff, but I didn't want you bringing a baby into that world you were in. It was tough for me. I was scared for you because you weren't scared."

"I was scared, Daddy."

"I'm sure you were. And I was no father to you."

She didn't respond to that and he knew she agreed. He'd cut her loose. And now what did he expect? "I'm sorry to be asking something of you now. But it's important. It isn't for me, and it's important."

"I'll ask Doug and I'll call you. You guys have the same number?"

He smiled. "Same number, same old house." Then he read her Cody's cell phone number off a Post-it note.

"Okay."

"Listen, Roni. Tell Doug this isn't about me. There's a boy who's your son's age." He scratched his unshaven chin. "I don't even know your boy's name."

Roni didn't offer it.

"This boy's not nearly as big but the same age. He's gone missing. And I'm going to help his mom find him. That's why we need to stay."

"He's up here?"

"We think he's in the Sierras."

There was no response.

"I called because I want us to talk, too, Roni. I want to apologize for what I did back then, how I reacted."

"But you need help for this other woman's child."

The colonel felt that last one like an electric volt. "Yes, I do."

"I'll call you back."

"Either way, Roni. I'll call you soon. Maybe we can see each other."

"Okay." With that, the phone went dead. The colonel held it, faceup, in his lap until the computerized voice informed him that if he'd like to make a call, he needed to hang up and try the number again.

The colonel helped Florence into the backseat of the car. She sat in the center, as she insisted, saying it gave her a better view of both sides. He and Cody didn't argue. She didn't seem at all concerned about where they were headed. "It's a beautiful day for a drive," she said.

It was almost pitch-black, and the light she pointed to was merely a streetlight that reflected off of the windshield of another car.

"Remember the old model-T Dad had?" She beamed. "That thing never ran right, drove him plain nuts. But, boy, did we kids love it. Didn't we, Daryl?"

"I'll bet it was something, Mrs. Turner."

"Oh, it was." After a momentary pause, her smile broke and disappeared in a flash. "I'm tired, Luanne. I'm going to rest back here. You let me know when we're there."

With that, she closed her eyes and started to snore.

The colonel rubbed at his chest with the heel of his left hand. His right still grasped the phone. It hadn't rung in the last hour. She wasn't calling back. "I'm going to lock up the house and we'll go."

Cody glanced at the phone but didn't say anything, and he was thankful. He didn't want to discuss it. He'd been sure she would call. Maybe she'd say no; he deserved no, but at least he thought his Roni would call back.

He clambered up the stairs, as old as he'd ever felt, and set the phone down in its cradle. He left the den light on and shut the others out and locked the door as he left. He crossed the porch slowly, giving the phone a last chance to ring. It didn't.

At the bottom of the stairs, he looked at Cody, sitting behind the driver's seat, waiting for him, and he wondered what he could possibly do for her. He'd located the region of Lake Tahoe where Ryan's bug was found. But it was still easily one hundred acres to cover. And that wasn't something an old man like him could help with.

He met her gaze as she gave him a reassuring

smile. He saw her excitement, her hopefulness. When had he lost that? Was it because of Roni, or maybe Florence? He moved around the car to the passenger side and opened the door.

"You got everything?"

She tightened her fists on the steering wheel and stared out the windshield as she nodded.

The colonel climbed in and shut the door. As he pulled the seat belt across his chest, he pictured Ryan's face and felt that same well of hope. "Let's go get him."

Cody's gaze flashed to him, and he felt her presence as though she'd physically touched him. Her eyes were wide and her emotion bare, and for a moment he saw young Roni, needing him in those eyes. Damn it all, what a fool he'd been. Well, he wasn't going to be a fool twice. "Let's go."

With that, Cody put the car in gear and they started for Lake Tahoe, Florence snoring in the backseat.

Chapter 26

Cody saw the headlights turn down the street just as she pulled from the curb. She would have liked to ignore them, especially after all the media in and out. But the driver was waving a hand out of the window and flashing the headlights. When the small car zipped toward her and then swerved to the curb, she knew it was Landon.

"Oh, Lord," the colonel said. "Drives like Mario Andretti."

Landon leaped from the car and crossed to her, glancing down the empty street as though to avoid getting hit.

Cody rolled the window down.

Travis looked at the interior of the car and frowned. "Where are you going?"

She shook her head. "Don't start with a question. Answer one first. What were you thinking, answering those questions? And how the hell did the story leak?"

He shook his head, his gaze firm on hers. "I don't know how it got out. I swear I don't."

"Why didn't you tell me you had an interview, and the kidnapping came up?"

"I tried, but the colonel was there and—"

"He knows everything," she interrupted.

"Well, I didn't know that, and you were in such a rush to get me out of there. But I checked the E-mail. We got a ransom note."

"How much?"

"Two million in cash."

Cody flinched. "Jesus." She looked at the colonel.

"You ought to work to put that money together," the colonel told Travis. "We have to go check out a different lead. Maybe it's time to call the police in," he added, turning to Cody.

She thought about it and nodded.

"What lead are you following up on?"

Cody's cell phone rang. She handed it to the colonel. She couldn't answer it, didn't want to.

"Hello," the colonel answered in a booming voice. He looked at her and nodded. "Thanks for calling me back, Marshall."

He turned his head and she watched him frown.

Travis started to talk again, but she waved him off, focusing on the colonel's conversation.

"Do you know how long he's been there?"

Cody gasped.

The colonel shook his head and she found herself grabbing hold of his shirtsleeve.

"We'd like to come meet your men up there."

There was a pause and Cody held her breath.

"I know where it is."

He motioned for a pen and Cody scrambled for one from the glove box. The colonel wrote on the back of one of the pictures from the Web site. "We can be there in less than four hours." He paused and nodded. "Thank you again."

He hung up and looked over at Cody. Then he glanced at Travis.

"What is it?" she begged, the expression on his face making her want to cry.

"They've found a body."

The air escaped her lungs in such a rush it was as though she'd been punched. She couldn't find the words.

"Who?" Travis asked.

"The rangers in a small town up past Placerville."

Cody stared at the colonel. "Placerville. Is that . . . ?"

The colonel looked at his hands, his lower lip running over his top teeth as he gave a short nod. "It's up there."

Cody gripped the wheel until there were sharp pains in her hands. In a tight surge, her muscles cramped and she was forced to release her grip. She wished for the pain back, anything that was sharp and real instead of the terrible ache that was growing like a balloon in her chest.

"We don't know yet," the colonel said.

"I want to go. I need to see."

"I don't know if you'll be able to."

"Why not?" she snapped.

"My contact up there wasn't sure of the state of the remains."

She almost choked for breath. "I have to go there."

The colonel nodded. "I have directions and he said he'll send someone up to meet us, but I need to warn you: There's been some animal damage. I don't know how much."

Travis swore softly.

Cody blinked hard and moved her gaze around the inside of the car in an effort to clear her vision.

She swallowed to dislodge the block in her throat. She pictured her baby struggling against a pack of wolves. No, it wouldn't have been like that. She forced the thought away. It wasn't Ryan. It wasn't. But she had to know for sure. "I'm going."

"We could do it with a photo or video, Cody," Travis offered. "You don't have to be there."

Cody slammed her palms against the steering wheel. She turned to the colonel. "I said we're going."

The colonel remained silent, but she knew he would. He would understand.

"Why don't you let me drive, then?"

Cody shook her head.

"We don't need two cars," Travis said. "Why don't you let me drive?"

"You don't need to come. You should be working on getting that money."

"I'll work on it on the way up. I need to be there."

Cody looked at the colonel, too many thoughts in her mind to make a decision on Travis.

"Then you can follow us," the colonel said.

Travis opened his mouth to argue again, but Cody just stared. Without another word, Travis turned his back, got in his car, and slammed the door. He revved the engine unnecessarily high and made a tight U-turn in the street. As he passed, he rolled down the window. "You have enough gas?"

She nodded.

Cody let her foot off the brake. The car rolled forward, but she felt detached. She didn't feel she was moving at all.

As she focused on the dull red lights of the cars in front of her, she remembered the knock at the door the day Mark had died. It was a muffled sound, a series of thuds. Mark's partner, Geoff James, never knocked that way. His knocks were big and loud, thunder that seemed to shake the house, with a bit of rhythm and attitude tied in. Quite simply, they were just like Geoff.

When Cody opened the door to that dull knock and saw Geoff standing alone, she knew Mark was gone. She hadn't even focused on Geoff's face. Just his presence had told her.

She made a turn at the colonel's direction, only vaguely aware of where they were. Just drive. Focus on the road. She trained her eyes on the bumper in front of her, and forced herself not to let her mind even consider that the body the rangers had found was Ryan James Riggs.

By the time they had passed through Sacramento and were nearing Placerville, the rain had turned to sleet. That meant there would be heavy snow farther up in the mountains. Traffic had slowed to a crawl, and what was normally a four-hour trip looked like it was going to take closer to six. Travis thought about that, about how things were getting more complicated by the minute.

He'd called his attorney, Miles Hoch, and gotten him out of bed to start working on putting assets together to meet the ransom. Miles was also going to talk with the police and get them up to speed. Travis had given him the log-in information for the E-mail account, and the police could access it from any computer.

He had mixed reactions about it all blowing up in the news. In some ways, maybe it made the whole thing easier to have it out in the open. In the half hour he'd been home, he'd gotten more than two dozen phone calls from media and concerned parties. The concern made him feel relieved because now there were others, but he still wondered how the news had gotten out.

He'd stared at that second picture for an hour. There was just something about the surroundings that didn't sit right, and he had no idea what to do about it. That was why he'd had to come with them.

He wasn't going to get a moment's peace about his son or Cody's until R.J. was safely back with his mother. He would do everything he could to make that happen. Even if Cody O'Brien gave him nothing but hell for it. Travis didn't have a clue about her. It didn't matter, he told himself. He would do what he'd come to do. Two million dollars cash was going to take a lot of scraping, and he was glad he wasn't going to be there when Miles tried to figure out where it would come from. Miles was creative, but this was going to require a lot of creativity. Cody had offered her savings, but he would put the money together. He felt it was the least he could do, considering the intended target was Peter.

At least now the authorities were involved. He should have felt some relief about that. But everything Cody had said about her husband left him cold. Back and forth, he'd been wavering like that since he'd pulled into his driveway and seen the first news van.

He'd spent the entire drive up on the phone. He'd called the Placerville police himself, talked to two detectives and the medical examiner. He'd pulled his biggest investor from bed to let him know what was going on and put him in touch with Miles. Miles would break the news that company assets might be needed to reach the ransom total. Everyone seemed to rally. Even Mrs. Pat had taken the news that Peter had barely escaped being kidnapped with amazing togetherness. Now, as they approached Placerville, he just had to wait. The balls were rolling, and a lot of it was out of his control.

With that thought in his head, he followed Cody off the exit to Placerville. As they parked in a small clearing beside a thickly wooded area, the rain had just started up again, and he ignored the frozen mist on his face as he got out of the car.

Cody emerged from her car and he studied her face through the dark haze of the rain. The thin line of her lips, the even steadiness of her gaze—he didn't think he'd ever seen a woman look so determined.

As she set her fierce gaze on him, he found himself taking a step backward, and he couldn't help wondering what man would have the strength to beat that intensity.

Chapter 27

Jennifer lay awake in bed. She should have felt better than she had in months. Steve had found Megan
and her son. He'd been kidnapped in the place of
some tech guy's kid, and there was supposedly a
Web site up with pictures. She hadn't gone to look at
it. Of course, she'd had to tell Steve that it wasn't the
right article, but when he'd read off the headline,
she'd known that it was.

Less than five minutes on the Internet had gotten
her the full scoop, and there was even a photo of
Megan Riggs. She'd left all the information on
Dmitri's voice mail, and she should have felt like a
million bucks. Instead, she'd had a series of horrifying dreams.

In one, she was a wolf snared in a heavy metal
trap. She was desperate to chew one limb off and
gain her freedom, but she couldn't find the paw that
was attached. With each turn, the thick metal jaw
seemed to engulf more of her. Even increasing her
dose of the anxiety medication wasn't helping.

She found herself wondering if Dmitri hadn't
somehow switched the pills. Had he given her
anxiety-causing medication instead? But they had

worked before. On Friday, when he'd given her the beautiful Cartier rings, she'd felt fine.

Either way, she'd taken care of the pills that night. She had flushed them, and left a message begging the receptionist at her doctor's office to fit her in first thing Monday morning. Then she'd taken a long, hot shower. She'd even painted her nails, something Dmitri hated because of the smell. She'd tried to rest, but sleep just didn't come.

Lying in bed, she heard the door open and slam closed.

She sat up in bed, startled.

"Jenichka," Dmitri's voice called.

He was back. She heard his heavy feet in the foyer and jumped from bed and hurried down the stairs. The smell of nail polish was stronger in the bedroom, and somehow she felt more at ease closer to the front door.

"There you are," he said, entering the foyer. He wrapped his arms around her. "I'm so sorry about earlier."

She turned to face him, tucking her hands to her sides in hopes that he wouldn't notice the smell. She rested her head against his chest, relieved he was there. "I didn't realize you were coming tonight. I thought you'd be busy—with Megan Riggs."

He waved it off. "It's not my business anymore. He told me I'm out of it. He found the kid. I got the article you called about, but he'd already found him through someone he knows in Las Vegas."

"How?"

"They got the name of the kidnapper. He owes people money—people my father knows. He's been promising he'd pay them back, that he had a deal that would net him two million in cash. Someone pushed a little and he told them what the deal was. When the news hit, they contacted my father. Everyone knows."

Jennifer felt her throat tighten. "Where is he now?"

He shook his head. "Doesn't matter. Father talked him into a deal." He laughed but it was a raspy, bitter laugh, and Jennifer shuddered.

"All this time, Megan Riggs was out of our reach. And now they have her. They have the kid and she'll come." He clapped his hands in front of her face. "Just like that."

She jumped and he laughed again. "Six hundred thousand he spent on it," he added in Russian.

"Six hundred thousand?" she repeated. He wasn't making sense. His eyes were dull and distant and she knew he'd been drinking.

"Never mind. My father's only concern is Viktor." He paused and she watched his expression change.

"Let's sit down," she said, trying to distract him from thoughts of his father's affection for Viktor. It always made him angry.

But it was too late. He pulled away from her and sputtered a bunch of Russian obscenities, only a few of which Jennifer could translate. "He's wasted the rest of the money finding that kid."

"Ryan Riggs?"

"Six hundred thousand it cost him," he said, shaking his head as he pushed the door closed. He looked around. "I need to get my snow boots. He needs them."

"They're in the closet." She pointed and her hand neared his face.

He sniffed and frowned, and she felt the room cloud with the smoke of his anger.

She lifted her hands to show him. "I painted my nails. I know how the smell bothers you, but I didn't expect you to come back tonight." She stepped back.

He grabbed her hand, pulling her away from the door. "Go clean it off."

He didn't let go of her arm, and she felt the pressure of his grip biting into her wrist. Before Dmitri, she'd always considered herself physically strong. Now it was though each limb were a twig that she just waited for him to snap.

"Why don't I get dressed and we can go out?" she suggested. "We can talk over a drink or something."

He shook his head. "We will stay here."

Staying here meant trouble. She glanced across the room at the doorjamb, dented from a metal bowl Dmitri had thrown at her.

"Okay." Gently pulling her arm from his grip, she smiled at him. "Can I make you something? Some tea or coffee?"

"A drink."

She headed for a small bar she kept on the far end of the dining room. She pulled down two glasses, went into the kitchen to take the Absolut from the freezer, and splashed a little in one and filled the other halfway. She noticed the bottle was lower than she remembered it had been.

"What a waste," Dmitri said.

She knew he was talking about the money again, but she wasn't sure what it had been spent on. "Your father hired someone to kill Megan?"

He waved his hand and she refilled the drink. "Not her, the boy. The wrong kidnapped boy."

"Doesn't the kidnapper still have him?"

"He's about to get six hundred thousand dollars."

He swallowed the liquid without flinching. "And my father will finally get his revenge."

Jennifer tried to follow without probing.

"My father is the idiot. A kid, he wants. He's throwing away six hundred thousand on a kid. He's going to a standard camp in California for a kid."

"Standard camp?" she repeated.

He waved her off.

The words swam around her head. She never imagined it would be the boy. God, he was only eight. "I thought he was going to kill Megan," she said, swishing the drink back and letting it burn its way down her throat. Liquid courage, she thought. She would need it.

Dmitri swayed toward the table and then batted out at her. "Who cares?" He sniffed and frowned. "Go take that *dermo* off," he said, using the Russian word for "shit."

She showed him her nails. "But see how nice they look."

He downed his vodka in one swig, then set the glass in front of her to refill. "They smell."

She refilled the glass quickly. "You're right. I'll go clean them off." She handed him his glass, poured herself another dollop, and swigged it before heading up the stairs to the bedroom. "I'll be right back."

In her room, she moved fast. She shed her pajamas in favor of a pair of jeans, a fleece top with deep pockets, and her running shoes. She headed back out with her wallet and keys in her pocket. Her Bureau gun was in the hall closet, and there was no way to get to it without his seeing her. She had another one put away in the office, but that, too, was impossible to reach without arousing suspicion.

Just get out, she told herself. Get out.

When she came back down, Dmitri was still standing by the bar, finishing another drink. By the look of the bottle, this was easily his fifth since she'd been home. He lifted the bottle again and she watched the clear liquid slosh over the edge of his glass as he poured.

She knew this mood. She crossed the entryway as quietly as she could, and reached the door before speaking. "I'm out of polish remover," she lied, opening the door. "I'm running to that all-night corner store to get some. I'll be right back."

She was at the top of the outside stairs when the door flew back open. Fear rushing over her, she took the first few steps fast and slipped. She fell to her butt, and tried to recover, but Dmitri was on her before she could get anywhere.

He grabbed a fistful of her hair and yanked her back up the stairs. "Inside."

She tried to reach for her wallet, but he only pulled harder. She let out a shriek as he wrenched her back toward the door.

He turned her toward him, his left fist tight in her hair. Then, holding her head at a distance, he punched her squarely in the mouth with his right hand. "Shut up," he said.

She shook her head. "No," she whispered, pleading. She couldn't let him get inside. She had to get away.

He cupped his huge hand across her chest and under her arm, then pulled her toward the door. She tried to loosen his grip, to break free, but he was too strong.

She saw the floor of her apartment and shot her hands out to claw at the doorjamb. Terrified, she kicked at him, used her nails to scratch, even tried to bite. She heard the click of the door shut as though it were a guillotine blade dropping.

Dmitri threw her on the floor of the apartment and she landed facedown, hitting her forehead.

"You can't leave, Jenichka," he said. "We're not done here."

Tears blurred her vision and she rolled onto her back and pushed herself upright. As she wiped her face, she caught the sight of her hands and had the ridiculous thought that he'd broken one of her nails. It made her sob. She wasn't free. She would never be free. "I found Megan Riggs. I came up with the article. I found her." She gasped, sobbing. "I thought that's what you wanted."

"This isn't about me," he said. "It's about what my father wants." He went back to the dining room and poured himself another drink. "His dying wish, Jenichka. You have to understand."

She looked at the door, but just as she did, he glanced back at her.

"Don't make this hard on me, Jenichka." He swallowed his drink and wiped his hairy hand over his mouth. He gave her an eerie smile, baring his teeth.

She shook her head, crying harder. "Don't."

He frowned. "You do not understand. This isn't about you. It's about family, about loyalty."

"Seven years we've been together, Dmitri. Aren't I family, too?" she whispered.

His expression settled, and for an instant Jennifer thought things were going to be all right. Then he lifted his hand.

Jennifer covered her head just as Dmitri threw his glass at her.

He rushed over to her before she could get up. "You, my family? You cunt, you whore."

She trembled, covering her face.

"You killed my brother," he screamed, pounding his chest.

She moved away, trying to distance herself from his fury. Bits of splintered glass cut into her palms and knees as she crawled backward. She lifted her hands, looking at the spots of red on her skin. She started to wipe away the pieces, feeling a deep one catch on her flesh. She shuddered and dug it out, studying Dmitri from the corner of her eye.

Dmitri paced like a lion, moving in a slow semicircle around her, still roaring.

She got the big pieces out and wiped her hands on her jeans. She waited, not wanting to move, unsure whether Dmitri's anger was defusing or still building.

He stopped when her attention was back on him. His eyes narrowed and he moved toward her, hunched over, his hands raised outward. "You're just a whore, Jenichka. A cheap, stupid whore."

He lunged and she rolled back, narrowly missing his attack. He slipped and caught the knee of his pants on a piece of glass. "God damn you!"

Jennifer leaped up and ran across the room for the door.

She fumbled with the old brass knob, her fingers shaky and hot as she tried to get them to mold around the cool metal. She turned it in her palm but she got the door open only a few inches before Dmitri slammed it shut. He took her hair in one fist and wrenched her around so her back was pressed to the door.

She watched the anger narrow his eyes. "No," she whispered. "You love me. We belong together. Your father is sick. He doesn't know. Only we know."

He leaned the forearm of his free arm across her neck until she could feel her air cut off. She grabbed his arm with both hands, struggling to release her neck. The room began to swim. She tried to scream. Tears streamed down her face, but soon all she could do was shake her head and plead with her eyes. Please, no.

"You did this. If you hadn't found that damn Riggs woman, he would have forgotten about avenging Viktor's death. Eventually he would have forgotten."

There were bright spots in her vision, and she closed her eyes. The pressure was too much. She was going to faint. Instead she let her body go limp.

"*Zhopa,*" he swore in Russian as he let her fall to the floor.

She lay facedown, wanting to pant, adrenaline still coursing through her, and she felt somewhere between death and catharsis. Clenching her stomach tight, she moved as little as possible. Her lungs burned for air. Dmitri was still for a moment, and she had no idea if he was watching her for signs of life or simply wondering how to finish her off and where to hide the body. He'd never come that close. She had to get away.

She moved her tongue between her teeth and pressed it into them, trying to distract the panic.

Dmitri's shoes scuffed along the floor as he retreated to the dining room. She heard another glass, the bottle. He was still drinking. She waited until she heard the bottle again and then dragged herself up.

As she lifted herself off the floor, she heard him growl.

She swung her head to the dining room in time to see him lunge for her again.

Letting out a trapped sob, she ran for the stairs to her bedroom. He dropped his glass and was right behind her. He caught her ankle halfway up and she kicked him back. He stumbled down a few stairs, but it was only a couple of seconds before she could hear him coming again.

She reached the top of the stairs just as he did. He snatched her ankle and yanked her off her feet. She hit her chin on the top stair and fell onto her back against the hard wood.

As he reached out to grab her other foot, Jennifer lifted it and kicked him in the chest as hard as she could.

She watched the stunned expression on his face as he fell backwards and rolled down the stairs. He landed with a loud thud on the floor below, and Jennifer slowly pulled herself to her feet.

From the top of the landing, she looked down.

He didn't move.

Her heart pounding, she crept down three or four stairs until she could see his face. A small stream of blood oozed from one corner of his mouth.

"Oh, Jesus." She looked around at the broken glass and at the blood on her hands and on her pants. Oh, God. What if he was dead? A part of her prayed he was. He would have killed her. But if she had killed him, Oskar Kirov would kill her.

Just then she heard him moan.

She shrieked and jumped to her feet. She ran to the office and locked herself inside. She was shaking as she found the key to her file cabinet under the desk pad and unlocked the bottom drawer.

She pulled out her 9mm Berretta and the magazine. She grabbed the box of rounds, her hands shaking.

The floorboards on the stairs creaked and she dropped the clip. He was coming. Scrambling to pick it up, she told herself to keep it together. She emptied the box of rounds on the floor and fumbled to load them into the magazine. Her thumb slipped and the spring fought her. For every one she got in, she dropped at least three. "Come on."

Her mind flipped through the possible problems. It had been forever since she'd even used the gun. What if it didn't work? What if she couldn't shoot?

She heard Dmitri in the hall. He spoke in a low, savage tone that sent a barrage of shivers over her.

"Go home," she shouted as she pushed the magazine with the four rounds into the gun. It made a solid click and she felt a bit better. He would go away. He would go away and she would get help. Someone could help her. She didn't need to let him kill her. She wouldn't.

"We're not done yet."

"Go home." She released the slide and held the gun pointed straight at the door. It was heavier than she remembered and the gun quivered in her grasp. She pulled it to her belly to rest her arms, leaving it aimed.

"*Tei bila plakhaya dyevushka.*" He told her she was a bad girl and then continued in Russian. He said that she had to be punished. "You should know better than to treat me like that, Jenichka." His voice reached the edge of the door.

Trembling, she lifted the gun with both hands and waited for him to force the door open.

It sprang back and slammed against the far wall. Her finger slipped off the trigger and the gun swayed sideways as she jumped. She wedged herself against an old school desk in the far corner.

"What do you have there?" he slurred in Russian. "My Jenichka is going to shoot me?"

"I'll use it," she said, her voice cracking.

He laughed.

She kept the gun aimed, waiting for him to attack.

He widened his eyes and switched back to English. "You would not shoot me."

"You need to leave, Dmitri." Her voice felt stronger. "You're not making sense now. We're finished talking."

Dmitri marched closer and threw his hand out at her. "I will tell you when we are finished."

As he moved, she jerked the gun, trying to keep it pointed at the center of his body.

"I don't care about Viktor. Fuck him. He's dead. Worry about me." He pressed the palms of both hands to his chest.

"Not anymore. We're done."

He stared at her and then at the gun. Finally he raised his hands in surrender. "Okay. Fine. We're done." He nodded. "It makes me sad, Jenichka, but you're right. You did what we asked." He headed back to the door. "Come walk me out."

She shook her head. "Just go."

"Come on. Just come say good-bye. Some of our times were good. It wasn't all bad, right?"

She saw the image of the man she'd fallen in love with then. She started to tear. Not now. "Just go."

"You don't love me at all anymore? Is it all gone?"

"You need to leave," she said, blinking to clear her vision.

"Please, Jenichka. Just a good-bye. Then I'm gone forever."

She shook her head again.

Dmitri looked hurt, but he finally turned his back. As he left the room, she took the sleeve of her sweatshirt and wiped her eyes.

As she opened them again, she saw Dmitri coming at her.

"You cunt," he yelled.

Before she could think, she lifted the gun and pulled the trigger twice. The first shot hit him in the side of the gut, but he took the second square in the chest.

She watched as he fell backward, his arms waving through the air.

His head hit the ground hard, and she stood with the gun pointed at him for what felt like an hour.

Finally she moved slowly across the room, the gun still pointed at him. She should have been terrified, but suddenly her legs felt steady. She stared with an odd indifference at the blood that seeped from his chest.

She stepped over to him, then pushed on his body with the toe of her shoe. His chest didn't rise and fall. His eyes, still wide open, didn't blink. She watched them for almost a minute before she was sure he was dead.

Just like that. He'd made almost no sound. There was no pleading for help, no begging for forgiveness. And when she finally sank into the chair at her desk, the first thought that came to mind was how disappointed her father would be. She started to cry.

She thought about whom to call and wondered how she was going to explain this. She'd killed a man. She'd killed a man she'd once loved.

In the distance, she could hear the *tick-tock* of her grandmother's old clock. The one Jennifer had gotten because Tiffany hadn't wanted it. With each click, she wondered how long it would be before Oskar Kirov realized his third son was dead. How long before he came to avenge Dmitri's death? In a strange way, she was jealous that Dmitri had a father who would even care.

With her own father in mind, Jennifer lifted the loaded gun to her temple.

She felt the pressure build under the pad of her finger. She thought about who might be affected by her death. Only one person came to mind. Setting the gun down, she stepped over Dmitri's lifeless body to try to undo what she'd already done.

Chapter 28

It was pitch-black when they finally reached the body's location. The wind whistled and the cold stabbed right through her layers of clothing, reminding Cody of Chicago winters. The colonel and Florence waited in the car, but Cody had needed to walk. Landon had joined her for a while, trying to make conversation, but she had almost completely ignored him. She was thinking, planning. She needed to prepare herself, not be distracted.

"I'll leave you alone," he'd finally said.

"Thank you," she'd replied.

He'd quickly retreated to the warmth of the Porsche, which had slid and skidded its way to this spot. She didn't worry about how he would get it out. There was only one thing on her mind as she paced along the edge of the woods, desperate to go in and find the crime scene. The snow made loud crunching noises beneath her tennis shoes and she stepped in rhythms of eight, counting each step.

This was not Ryan, she kept telling herself. It was not. She repeated the mantra as though somehow her belief might control whatever reality was waiting for her.

The wind picked up and sliced through her fleece, goose bumps covering her skin. Her eyes watered, more from the memories the cold brought than from the cold itself. She saw Mark and baby Ryan playing in the snow in the small rectangular backyard of their Skokie home.

Without a hill of any kind within miles, Mark would pull Ryan in circles on a bright red saucer. Even when the snow had turned to slush and the ground showed the dull green grass, Ryan would run to his dad and yell, "Sausa, Daddy. Sausa." Saucer.

One day when they'd had a lot of snow, Mark had even built a small ramp for Ryan to sled down. Cody had told him it was dangerous, but Mark couldn't be deterred and Ryan was too excited. Sure enough, Ryan had fallen off one side and broken his left arm. They'd spent most of that Sunday in the emergency room. But the very next weekend, cast and all, Ryan was standing at the window, chanting "Sausa, Daddy. Sausa."

Ryan hadn't seen snow since he was three. They had discussed the idea of skiing once or twice. She and Mark had loved to ski. They'd honeymooned in Whistler, and she remembered the broad expanse of the mountains and the thorny, patched texture of the huge pines, the crisp smell of snow. But somehow she hadn't been able to bring herself to take Ryan. Now, as she looked around at the lightly dusted mountains and white-peaked trees, she wished she had.

After almost forty minutes a ranger's car joined the pack of police cruisers and SUVs parked in the small clearing. For Cody, it felt like an eternity. But the instructions had been clear: If they came into the area without a police escort, they would not be allowed access to the body. Someone had to take them through a very specific path to avoid destroying the crime scene. Cody hoped to God that this was their escort.

A car door opened and out came a burly, gray-haired man with a thick Santa Claus–like beard and the round belly to match. As he straightened himself, he laid a hat just like Smokey's on top of his head.

The colonel and Landon got out of their cars.

Cody moved in first. The ranger's tan uniform fit like the skin on an apple, and a small brass-colored pin identified him as Sam Uldrich.

"Sorry to keep you waiting, folks. We're a bit short-staffed." He motioned toward the woods. "Don't get this kind of action much in these parts, and we don't have the men to handle it. They're getting ready to bring the body out now."

"We can go in?" Landon said, blowing hot air into his hands.

"If you still want to." Ranger Uldrich studied Cody. "Were it my kid, I wouldn't want to see him." He rolled a shoulder toward the woods. "Not like that." His body twitched as he shuddered.

Cody didn't respond.

"We'd like to go in," Landon said.

The ranger eyed Cody, then Landon. He leaned toward Travis and spoke in a half whisper, but his deep voice made the words as clear as anything else he'd said so far. "Animals got to it," he said. "One of my rangers found it. Couldn't tell if it was a boy or girl. You sure you want her in there?"

Landon's gaze didn't flicker. "We're ready to go in, please."

Cody inhaled and felt the colonel's hand on her arm.

"You want me to come with you?" he asked.

She shook her head and didn't meet his eyes. "Stay with Florence. We won't be long."

He tugged on her fleece until her gaze met his. "You sure?"

She nodded, not trusting her voice.

"I'll come," Landon said. His gaze focused on the woods as he spoke, and she could tell from the crease in his brow that he was dreading it.

She didn't stop him. She actually wanted him there. She didn't try to identify the reasons. Instead she nodded at Travis.

"We're ready," he said for her.

The colonel patted her back. "We'll be right here, waiting."

"Okay, we're right this way." The ranger pulled a heavy lambskin coat from the car, wrestled into it, and zipped it up. He took a flashlight from the holster on his waist and flipped it into his palm and snapped it on. Then, as though they were setting off on a guided walk instead of preparing to see a dead body, he led the way.

She and Travis didn't speak on the way out. Instead Cody tried to think innocuous thoughts. She focused on the smell of fresh snow and pine, the bite of the frozen air on her cheeks, and the *whoosh* of snow slipping off the trees above.

Ranger Uldrich kept pausing and looking back. He was breathing heavily, but Cody didn't give him a chance to catch his breath. She needed to see.

They came around a turn in the path and large lights shone at them from the distance. The reflection on the snow felt like direct sun, but she cupped her hand across her eyes and continued.

In front of the lights, Cody counted four people working on the body. There was one woman dressed in snow pants and a parka who was moving around the body, directing a man wearing jeans and a bright North Face coat.

The ranger took them only another ten feet. He paused five feet from the edge of the circle.

"Sheriff," he called out.

The man who turned around was about Cody's age, late thirties, with dark hair and blue eyes. There was something about him that reminded her of Mark: the angular jaw and prominent nose, perhaps. He reached a gloved hand out for her to shake. She pulled her own bare hand out of her pocket and offered it back.

"Drew Hunter."

"Cody O'Brien," she said.

Landon shook his hand, but Hunter focused on Cody as he spoke. "The crime-scene group is done and the medical examiner's preparing to take possession of the body now."

Her gaze flew over his shoulder.

"Before we go, I'd like to tell you what the medical examiner knows. Maybe we can confirm right now that this isn't your child."

Cody clenched her jaw and nodded tightly.

"The victim is a boy between the ages of eight and ten."

She waited.

"He has all his teeth except wisdoms and there doesn't appear to be any damage to the teeth—no chips or replacements that we can see. No braces."

Ryan had all his teeth.

"No silver fillings or anything."

"Right."

"They don't use those much anymore," the sheriff added as though to make her feel better. "Some of the skin is preserved. Are there any markings or scars that you can think of that might identify your son?"

Ryan didn't have any large freckles or moles. In fact, unlike her, he and Mark had very few freckles at all. She thought about the broad expanse of Mark's strong back, his smooth tanned skin.

"Ma'am?"

Cody shook her head. "No."

She thought about the one clue that she had. "I'll know him," she said.

The sheriff gave Landon a skeptical look. Landon, at least, didn't respond.

"Our medical examiner did find one broken bone," the sheriff said. "It appears healed, but from a physical exam of the remains, she believes the victim broke the ulna bone in his left arm."

Cody felt her legs give way. Landon reached out and caught her. She straightened herself, though nothing inside felt right. "My son cracked a bone in that arm; I don't remember which one."

The sheriff frowned.

She started to push past them. "I need to see him."

The sheriff caught her arm. "He's going to need to be identified from dental records. You're not going to be able to identify him." He turned to Landon as though he might be able to talk her out of it. "This is a bad idea. It's only going to upset her."

Cody pulled her arm free. "I was told I could see the body. Now, is that true or not?"

The sheriff let go and waved to the scene. "Be my guest."

As Cody tramped toward the body, those standing at the scene moved back. She focused on the ground in front of her until she knew she was within a foot of the remains. When she looked up, the woman in the ski pants and parka was kneeling in the snow, beside a heavy zipped bag like the ones fancy clothes came from the store in. This one held the remains of a small boy.

"They told you about the shape the body is in?" she asked with more compassion than Cody would have expected from someone who dealt with dead bodies for a living.

Cody nodded and dropped to her knees in the snow.

"If I thought it could be my kid, I'd be doing the same thing."

Cody met her gaze. With a deep breath, she focused on the body bag and nodded.

The medical examiner unzipped the black bag and the sight of the body crushed the air from Cody's lungs. She instantly turned her head. "Oh, God," she whispered, covering her hands with her mouth. She felt her stomach convulse but she closed her eyes and forced herself to calm down.

The men talked in loud voices behind her, but she ignored them. Fighting the alternating waves of panic and nausea, she opened her eyes and looked back at the body. Then, just as quickly, she looked at the medical examiner again.

"Animals," the doctor said.

Cody nodded. The face of the boy had been nearly eaten away. Only traces of frostbitten bloody flesh remained on the upper cheeks and ears. The nose had been hollowed out, the lips were gone and the teeth exposed. The sight was horrifying, but the presence of the large adult teeth and a tiny nose made it all the more devastating. She stared at the teeth, trying to picture the exact spacing and shape of Ryan's. He had his father's teeth—very square and tightly fit. But without a face to fit them to, she couldn't possibly match any memory to the teeth she saw now.

"It can happen that fast? In a day or so?"

The doctor nodded. "Depends on a lot of factors, like food sources and the cold, but yes."

Cody forced her gaze off the remains of the face. But she knew it didn't matter. The image would be forever marked in her mind. The bag the boy was in covered the top of the skull, and she knew her answer would be there. "Can I look at the hair?"

The doctor moved around her, closer to the top of the boy's head. "He's lost a lot of it. Are you ready?"

Cody nodded. But she wasn't. When the doctor moved the body bag to unveil the skull, Cody saw that huge chunks of hair were missing. Underneath were bloodied divots in the scalp. "Oh, God."

"It's the animals. They use the hair for their nests."

The knowledge didn't make the sight any easier. She focused on the task. "Can you shine the light on the hair?"

The doctor frowned, but did as Cody asked. She turned the flashlight to expose the hair.

At the sight of the solid dark strands, Cody felt her chest contract until her breath was forced out. Before she told the doctor what she was thinking, she asked a question. "Does hair change in the death process?"

"Hair is one of the last things on a human body to

decay. Texture does not change for years, as I understand. Dyed hair may fade with time and it may
look darker, depending on whether it ends up wet or
not." She pointed to the middle of the scalp where
there was still a thick tuft. "We've dried this hair
here to take a sample for DNA in case we need it."

The cold had soaked through her pants and the
surface of her skin was entirely numb. If she was
right, this was worth it. "That hair is as it would
look in life?"

The doctor nodded. "More or less. But remember,
it's very hard to tell by color. The darkness is deceiving. Unless your son is very blond, you shouldn't
rely on color."

Cody turned the flashlight and pointed it into the
scalp. She saw no signs that this was Ryan's hair.
Putting her hands on her knees, she lifted herself up.
"This is not my son."

Travis Landon and the sheriff appeared by her
side. "How do you know?"

The M.E. stood, too. "What makes you so sure?"

Cody pushed her hands in her pockets and looked
down at the remains of someone's child. The relief
she felt that it wasn't Ryan was partly overwhelmed
by the grief that someone else was going through
what she was.

"Cody?" Landon looked at her intently.

She took her eyes off the body. "Does anyone have
a pocketknife?"

No one moved.

"A knife. Someone must have a knife."

"You can't touch the body," the medical examiner
said, one hand hovering over the corpse protectively.

"It isn't for him."

The sheriff drew a knife from his pocket.

Cody reached for it and he handed it to her tentatively.

She opened the blade and reached for her own head.

Travis caught her hand. "Let me help."

She met his gaze. "Cut a chunk of the hair from the scalp."

He paused.

"I don't care what it looks like. Just do it."

She felt the tug and heard the gnashing sound of the blade slicing through hair.

Travis handed her the lock. She held it in her hand and told the examiner to shine the light on it. "My son and I have the same color hair."

The men exchanged confused glances and leaned in.

"But yours is colored," the M.E. said.

"So is his. The same color. And it was done the same time as mine. Both of us are naturally light-haired."

The M.E.'s expression was puzzled, but she didn't ask. Instead she flipped open a small toolbox and pulled out a small paper bag and a sealed plastic bag containing scissors. She handed the paper bag to Cody and told her to hold it open.

Breaking open the plastic sack, she withdrew a pair of sterilized scissors and proceeded to cut a small chunk of hair off the victim. Laying it in the palm of her hand, she motioned to the sheriff to turn the light on it. He did and all four of them studied the strands.

Cody waited until the examiner confirmed what she saw. There were no blond roots. Whoever the boy was, he was not her Ryan.

The medical examiner nodded the light away,

took the bag from Cody's hand, and gently swept the boy's hair into it. She tied the bag closed, removed a pen from the same tool kit, and marked a series of numbers and words on the bag. Cody couldn't see.

When she was done, she stood and put the bag of hair alongside a bunch of other bags. "We can pack the body up," she told the two men who had been standing back. "The parents are going to have to meet it in the morgue." With that she turned to Cody. "I'm glad this was a waste of your time."

"Me, too."

Cody's gaze was drawn to the dead boy one last time. Her mind created an image of what his little features might have looked like. She mourned for the child's mother, guilty for the relief she felt. And as relieved as she was, she knew her baby was still out there somewhere.

The colonel was pacing in front of the car when she reached the clearing again.

"It's not him," she said.

His brow lifted slightly. "Thank God. I've been sick about it." His fist was cupped around something, his expression still tense.

"What is it?"

He opened his fingers and showed her a cell phone. "It's yours. It's been ringing off the hook."

She stared at it until the colonel pushed it into her hand. "Two new voice mails." She punched the code to retrieve her messages and hit the number one to start the messages.

The first was from Mei Ling at the Bureau, warning her that she might be in trouble. Cody listened to the message and then waited for the second one to begin.

"Megan, oh, God." Even with those three words, Cody knew exactly who was calling. And she knew what it meant. She pulled her arms to her chest and pressed the phone harder to her ear. She was wrong. She had to be wrong.

Jennifer Townsend wasn't about to tell her that her baby was dead.

"I hope you get this." She was sobbing, and Cody felt her patience explode. "I've done something terrible, Megan."

Jennifer sniffed and Cody heard Landon approach. She waved him off and stepped farther away.

"It's about you and Ryan. I found the article in the paper about the mistaken kidnapping. I helped them find you."

Cody lost her breath. What was Jennifer saying? The plastic edges bit into her fingers as she gripped the phone.

"I didn't know they'd find you. I hoped they wouldn't. I swear, I did. I never meant to hurt you."

It was all bullshit, Cody thought as another call beeped through. Cody hung up on the message and answered the phone. "Megan Riggs," she said, for the first time in almost seven years. It sounded unbelievably foreign to her own ears.

"Megan, oh, my God. It's Jen. Oh, thank God. Are you okay?"

"What do they know?" she said, refusing to waste even a moment catching up on lost time.

"I only gave them the article."

"Goddamn it, Jennifer. What do they know?"

There were racking sobs from the other end of the phone.

"Jennifer. Where is Ryan?"

"I don't know, Megan. I swear to God I don't know."

"What do you know? Do they know where he is?"

Jen continued to sob so that only small grunts and groans came out in the place of words.

"Do they know?"

"Yes," she finally choked out. "They know. Dmitri was drunk and mumbling about it. He told me that his father paid the kidnapper six hundred thousand for Ryan." She gasped and started to sob again. "I thought they'd come after you." She gasped. "Oh, God. Poor Ryan."

Cody bent to the ground and lifted up again. The muscles in her entire body tensed and she felt like she might explode. She did her best to keep moving. Don't hang up. Find out everything she knows. "What did Dmitri say? Anything about where they were?"

"No. He said that his father had wasted six hundred thousand dollars on the boy."

"Where is Dmitri now?"

"He's here."

"Ask him, Jennifer. Ask him where Ryan is."

"I can't."

"Ask him, Jennifer. Fucking ask him now!"

Jennifer began to sob again.

"Calm down, Jennifer. I can't understand you."

"He's dead, Megan. I killed him. He's dead and I killed him. Oh, God."

Cody froze, her chest tight, everything suddenly hot and cramped. "Who, Jennifer? Who did you kill?"

"Dmitri. I shot him. He's dead."

Cody exhaled. She wished she could have shot him herself. "It's okay, Jen. It's going to be okay. Tell me more about Ryan. Where is he? How did they find his kidnapper?"

"They tracked him through some guys in Vegas. The kidnapper owes some money. Oskar found him and offered money for the kid."

"That was it? He didn't say who was coming for Ryan? Or where they were going?"

"Oskar's coming. I don't know who else. A camp in California. That's all they said."

"Call Mei, Jennifer. Call Mei and tell her what's happened. They can help you." You don't deserve it, she thought. "I have to go. I have to find Ryan."

"I'm so sorry," Jennifer cried.

Cody hung up without responding. She spun around and pocketed the phone. The Russians were on their way to get Ryan.

She found the sheriff at the edge of the woods. "I need help and I need it fast."

She turned to the colonel. "Get the map of the cross location of the moths."

The colonel started for the car.

"What moths?" Travis asked.

Cody ignored him. "Get in touch with the Chicago office of the FBI," she told the sheriff. "Ask for Mei Ling and tell her that Ryan Riggs has been kidnapped by Oskar Kirov."

The sheriff looked at Landon and then back again.

"Do you want me to write the names and number down?" she pressed.

The sheriff drew his pen and pad and started scratching notes.

"What moths?" Travis asked again.

The colonel returned with the map. She spread it open on the hood of the car, noticing how poorly her fingers worked in the freezing cold. "I need a list of all the camps within five square miles of the marked area."

"Who the hell are you?"

The question came from Landon, but the sheriff had the same one on his face.

Cody didn't look at either of them. Instead she focused on the colonel. She thought about what was left to lose. Her face was plastered on the news. The police would find her, the Russians would find her, the FBI would find her. It didn't matter. Only Ryan mattered. And she needed to figure out how to get to him as fast as possible. She took a deep breath and spoke slowly. "My name is Megan Riggs. I'm an agent with the Federal Bureau of Investigation. I was in the Federal Witness Protection Program after the Russian mob killed my husband and threatened me and my son, Ryan. Now they may have him. We've got about three minutes to get the hell on the road. I'll answer more questions later. Is there anything else that needs to be addressed now?"

No one spoke for a moment. Finally the sheriff said, "What was that number in Chicago again?"

Cody recited it and gave him her cell number to call with the list of camps. Then she turned to the car and handed the keys to the colonel. "Can you drive?"

"Absolutely."

He took the keys as Cody got into the passenger seat, pulled her laptop out of the backseat, and pushed the power.

Travis came to the window. "Wait—"

"Go home, Travis," she said as she shut the door in his face.

She linked her laptop to her cell phone and powered it up to check the Web site one more time. Kirov had to get there from Chicago. That gave her the advantage of time. She wouldn't consider how fast a chartered or direct flight would be or when he'd actually left. She would reach Ryan in time. She had to.

She knew she was hoping for a miracle.

But damn it, she was due.

Chapter 29

Mei was still in her office at three A.M. She, Steve, Allen, and Andy were trying to retrace everything Jennifer had requested from research over the past four months. Each request was then cross-referenced with their current caseload to see whether it related to a legitimate case or not. Most did not. It was almost unbelievable the quantity of requests she had made using closed or stale case reference numbers.

Two local Chicago police had been sent to Jennifer's apartment, but she hadn't answered the door and they'd finally left to obtain a warrant. Mei couldn't imagine where she was. The task force assigned to the local mob had confirmed that Oskar Kirov had left town with three of his men. There was no record of him flying out of O'Hare or Midway, though, and the police were trying to locate him. Neither of his sons had been located either.

Andy had contacted the San Francisco field office and they had roused two agents from sleep and sent them to the address where Megan Riggs now lived under the name Cody O'Brien. They had called back less than twenty minutes ago to say that the house was vacant and clean.

"Someone's cleaned it very recently. We have some prints, but no personal information," Andy reported, his expression glum. The Russian mob wasn't known for its cleanliness, but Megan's absence had everyone thinking the worst.

When Mei's pager began to vibrate across her desk at quarter to four, the room jolted alive. Mei looked at the local number. "It's Jennifer at home."

Andy pulled the phone toward her and leaned against the desk as she dialed. She sank into her chair and listened to the phone ring. At this late hour, with his shirt unbuttoned and his sleeves rolled up, Andy looked even better than he had in the café.

Their eyes met and Mei turned away when there was a click on the other end of the phone line.

"Jennifer? It's Mei."

The line was silent except for a ragged breath.

"Jennifer? Are you there? What's going on? Push a button if you can't talk."

Nothing happened.

Mei covered the phone. "She's not responding, but someone's there."

Andy pulled his cell phone off his belt. "Keep her on the line. I'm going to get someone there as fast as I can."

She nodded. "Jennifer, it's Mei. Let's talk. Tell me what's going on."

There was the slightest moan, and it was the first indication Mei had that Jennifer was on the other end of the phone. At least, it sounded female.

Allen pressed the button for the speakerphone and they all listened to the silence.

Steve rolled his hand for her to continue as Mei searched for things to say.

"Jennifer, I know you're scared. I am, too. But I can help you. I know what you were doing. I know you were looking for Megan for those men. I know they were hurting you. But they won't anymore. I swear. We can stop them. I can help you. He won't hurt you again."

"I know," Jennifer said. She made a sound like a giggle, and for a moment, Mei thought this might have been another of Jennifer's cruel jokes. But as Jennifer spoke again, Mei knew it wasn't funny.

"I killed him, Mei."

Allen made a low whistling sound and they all exchanged glances. Mei looked back at the phone. Stay calm, talk her down. "It's okay, Jennifer. Tell me what happened."

"It doesn't matter. It's over. But Oskar's going to get Ryan."

"Ryan?"

"Ryan Riggs." Jennifer sounded breathless, like she'd just run a marathon.

Mei waited impatiently.

"He's been kidnapped, but Oskar is paying the kidnapper." There was another long pause. "Oskar's going to California to get him. This is the revenge for Viktor. From all those years ago, Mei, he still wants revenge."

"Where in California?"

She didn't answer immediately. Finally she said, "I've been thinking and thinking and I can't remember. A camp. I told Megan that, too. It was a camp. That's all I know."

"A camp?" Mei repeated, thinking how many places in California would have fit that description.

Andy came back in. "Five minutes and they'll be there," he whispered.

Mei nodded. "Can you remember anything else about the camp?"

"You can't let them die, Mei. You can't. It's my fault."

"They won't die," Mei said. "Help me find them, Jennifer. We need your help. Who was going out there? Oskar and who else?"

"I don't know. I know he's going to kill them. She hates me, Mei. Megan hates me just like them. They all hate me. And they should. I never thought they should, but now I know it. I know I deserve it. Tiffany was the good one. They knew it but I didn't."

Mei felt Jennifer slipping from her. She tried to focus, to get Jennifer back, like she'd learned in Bureau training. "Jennifer, stay with me. Talk to me. Tell me who they are. How did you find out about Ryan? Who told you?"

Jennifer whimpered. "It was always Tiffany. They knew. It took me all this time to see it."

Who's Tiffany? Andy mouthed.

Mei shrugged as Jennifer continued. "Dad always said she was the good one and I couldn't see why. Now I know. Tiffany never killed anyone, Mei, but I did. I killed them. I killed them all."

"Jennifer, listen to me. You didn't kill them. It wasn't your fault." She was lying, but she didn't stop. Jennifer would suffer consequences later, but they needed answers first. "Ryan and Megan aren't dead yet. We can help—you and me. Help me help them. Come on, Jennifer."

Mei felt the pressure of Andy's hand on her back and tears welled in her eyes. She blinked hard, cursing her reaction. So American, her mother would say. American women always cried. And it wasn't sadness for Jennifer. Pity, maybe, but mostly fear for Megan and Ryan.

"I can't."

"Yes, you can. You can help them. What else did he say about California? What kind of camp?" Jennifer paused for so long, Mei finally said, "Do you remember, Jennifer? Is there anything else you can tell us?"

"God, I don't know. He said standard camp or snow camp," Jennifer said.

They all exchanged looks. "Standard camp?" Mei repeated.

Jennifer mumbled and Mei shook her head. "She's not making sense."

"Ask simpler questions," Andy directed. "Northern or southern California?"

"Jennifer, was he going to San Francisco? Or Los Angeles?" she asked.

It was silent.

Every passing moment made Mei feel tighter, more ready to explode. She'd never dealt with this sort of situation. She measured her breaths and kept trying. "Jennifer, do you remember where they were going?"

"I don't know. I'm so sorry. Please tell Tiffany I'm sorry. She was right. I was wrong." Jennifer's voice grew softer.

"Where the hell are the police?" Allen whispered.

Mei felt herself stiffen. "Jennifer, you can tell Tiffany yourself. You tell her. I'm going to come there. I'm going to stay with you until this is over, okay? Can you hang in there for a minute?"

Jennifer let out a low moan and they could hear knocking behind her.

"It's the police," Andy said. "Tell her."

"Oh, God. They're here."

"It's us, Jennifer. We're there. We're there to help you."

"No, it's them. He came for his snow boots; he was only coming for a few minutes. He wasn't supposed to be gone for so long. They know he's gone. They know I killed him."

"Oh, Jesus," Steve muttered.

The room seemed to spin around her and Mei tried to steel herself against the panic. "Jennifer, it's us. We're there to help you. It's not them. It's us. Can you let us in?"

"Oh, God. No. No. I can't." She was screaming.

Everyone started whispering suggestions to Mei at once.

She couldn't think straight. Just keep talking, she told herself. "It's okay, Jennifer. Just wait. Hang in there."

There was no response.

"Damn," Steve whispered.

"I hope she doesn't have a weapon," Allen said.

Andy snapped at Allen to shut up.

"Where are you?" Mei said into the line. "Jennifer, are you there?"

"I'm dead, Mei. They're going to kill me."

There were voices in the background. The cops were yelling out to her.

Jennifer screamed. *"On umer. On umer!"*

"What? What did you say?" Mei asked, trying to hear Jennifer for the background noise.

"I think it's almost over. I took a bottle of pills, Mei. I took them all."

"What did you take, Jennifer?" Mei asked.

"I took them all." Her voice slurred.

Andy reached out, but Mei registered the change in Jennifer's voice. "Hang in there, Jennifer."

"I feel better now," she said, her words slowing. "Much better . . ."

"Jennifer. Stay with me," Mei yelled.

There was no answer.

"Jennifer!"

"'Bye, Mei."

In hazy focus, Mei could see the mouths moving around her, but the only sound she heard was the whisper of Jennifer saying good-bye over and over.

Chapter 30

The pain in his gut had grown worse since they'd left the airport. He remained doubled over as the Jeep floundered its way along the lake, the chains on the tires crunching against the ice. The snow was high and the road not plowed, and each tiny chunk of ice on the frozen path tossed him up and down.

He closed his eyes and leaned his face out the open window. The cold air reminded him of home.

The men in the back complained about the bitter cold, but he called them sissies and told them to be silent.

He glanced at his watch and then back outside, trying to remember the last time he'd taken a Dronabinol. The nausea was growing unbearable again. The medications weren't working, and he couldn't remember the last time he'd eaten. Everything made him sick.

Even his vodka had lost its appeal, though he still carried a flask with him for times when the pain medication alone didn't help.

He was almost done. This was his last battle. After this, it was all up to Dmitri.

"We're not far now," the driver said.

Oskar nodded, the closest he'd come to a smile in weeks. He pulled out the flask and swallowed two pills with a swig of vodka. The smell made him nauseous again, so he leaned his head back out the window.

He must have dozed momentarily because when he woke, the car was parked in front of a cabin.

Ivan, Pyotr, and Sasha were out of the car, pulling their bags from the back. He'd brought Pyotr since Mikhail was dead, but he was not sufficient replacement. It would take time to find another like Mikhail. Probably Oskar would be gone before then. The driver was still in his seat.

Oskar handed him a wad of cash and waved him off. The Jeep pulled out as soon as Oskar had closed his door, the driver seeming more than happy to be gone.

Ivan unzipped his bag and was pulling out a gun when Oskar snapped at him. "Not here, moron," he said in Russian. Ivan looked up, his expression blank.

Oskar couldn't believe how dumb he was. He had been too hard on Dmitri. Dmitri, at least, had some sense. Ivan had been born with none.

"Wait until we are not in the open," he explained.

Ivan seemed to finally understand and gave a low grunt in response.

His hand pressed into his thigh for balance, Oskar checked the address of the house. This was it.

He motioned to Pyotr and told him to go around the back of the house and be ready to move in. The kidnapper had promised Oskar that he would be alone with the child, but Oskar didn't trust him. He trusted no one.

He wasn't going to lose the money and the kid. In fact, he didn't intend to lose either.

He let Pyotr head around the side of the house and then told Ivan to stick with him. Oskar took the .38 special out of his bag and tucked it in his belt. It was the gun his father had given him when he'd turned sixteen and he'd never missed with it. He couldn't remember the last time he'd fired it, but that didn't matter. That was why he had his men.

Ivan carried the bag with the money and his own guns and Sasha followed behind. Ivan had two semiautomatics and an Uzi in the bag. Sasha carried a semiautomatic and a Browning rifle. It was too much gun power, but better too much than too little when money was involved. Not that Ivan had six hundred thousand dollars in his bag—not even close to that.

Oskar was still trying to recoup the damage that Feliks and Gary had done, and at the moment he wasn't worth six hundred thousand. The thought made him cough. If he were younger, he would worry. But he'd be dead within weeks. Some days death was coming faster than he would have liked, but most days it wasn't coming fast enough.

The bag Ivan carried contained around fifty thousand dollars—stacks of clean fives with hundreds on top. To an amateur, it looked like a ton of money. To a pro, it wasn't nearly enough. The extra gun power was in case they ran into a pro. The kidnapper, a man named David Murphy, certainly hadn't seemed the part.

He reached the door and raised his arm to knock. The drugs had fogged the pain and he was able to lift his arm without more than an uncomfortable tug at his middle.

He knocked and then licked his fingers and used them to smooth his balding hair across his scalp.

"Who's there?" came a voice from inside.

Oskar nodded back to Ivan. "It is Oskar Krov," he said, pronouncing his name like the word for "blood" and knowing the irony was lost on whoever stood behind the door.

He could hear the click then slide of Ivan's gun chambering a round. Ivan tucked it back into a holster under his jacket. The sound was followed by a second slide and click of the door being unlocked.

A man about Dmitri's age opened the door with a worried smile.

"Mr. Murphy?"

He nodded, looking at the three of them. "You're Krov?"

Oskar smiled. "Yes."

Murphy waved them in and Oskar took stock of the room. Unlike Mr. Murphy, the place reeked of money, and he wondered how Murphy had come upon it. Or who he had borrowed it from. If Murphy were dead inside it, Kirov needed to know who was going to find him.

"This is a nice place."

"Thank you," he answered as though he owned it.

"Where is Ryan?"

Murphy frowned.

"The boy," Oskar said. "Where is the boy?"

Murphy glanced toward the back of the house, and Oskar assumed the boy was still there—in a back room or the basement. "Where's the money?"

Oskar smiled and waved Ivan forward. "It is here. Six hundred thousand, just as promised."

Murphy kept an eye on Ivan as he opened the bag.

Murphy stared inside, his expression like a kid's at Disneyland.

As he reached in to grab a stack, though, Ivan smacked his hand hard.

Murphy complained, shaking his hand.

Oskar frowned at Ivan. "I apologize for him," he said to Murphy. "But we need to see the boy first. You understand."

Murphy nodded. "What about the gambling debts? With Kinzhalov?"

Kirov had promised to settle Murphy's gambling debts with Grigor Kinzhalov. His name translated to "of daggers," and there was trust between them—as much as anywhere within the Russian community. "Settled."

"What proof do I have?"

Kirov tightened his lips. "You have my word. Or if it is not enough, you may call him."

Murphy looked at him and then gave a brief nod. "I think I'll call." He turned his back to go to the phone when Kirov nodded to Ivan.

Ivan went to check the other rooms while Sasha stayed with him. Oskar crossed through the entryway into a living room with skylights and an open dining area. His instincts told him it was clear.

Murphy came back with the phone in his hand. "Where's the other guy?"

"He went outside to relieve himself."

Murphy glanced around again and, after a small hesitation, he placed the phone to his ear. "Kinzhalov's not answering."

Kirov nodded. "We will wait until you reach him," he lied. "But I would like to see the kid."

Murphy nodded and turned around.

Kirov could feel the excitement in his gut.

When Murphy returned, he had Ryan by the collar. "Here. Take him." Murphy headed right for the bag of money just as Ivan returned to the room. He looked at Ivan, and Oskar could see his brain working. He lifted the bag and started to back up.

"Keep him here," Oskar directed in Russian.

Murphy turned and ran, but Ivan was there. Murphy called out. Oskar didn't respond. Instead he ordered his men to keep Murphy quiet.

He reached out for the boy, waving his fingers. "Come here, Ryan."

The boy didn't move.

Oskar had seen Ryan Riggs only one time, and Ryan had been hardly three, but Oskar had a picture of the couple—Megan and Mark Riggs—that he had looked at almost daily since his Viktor's death. And this little boy had his father's nose and mouth.

"Don't you remember me?" he asked.

The boy shook his head.

"I'm a friend of your mommy and daddy's. From Chicago."

The boy's gaze narrowed, suspicious.

Oskar smiled. He had some of his mama, too, right there in the eyes. What a pleasure this was going to be. He only wished he'd get to see the expression on Megan Riggs's face.

"What the hell is going on here?" Murphy screamed.

The boy turned around.

Murphy was kicking and clawing at Ivan and Sasha, who held him between them. "We had a deal."

The boy was watching Oskar now, those eyes staring. He looked so tough, so brave, just like his mother had. Oskar wondered how long that façade would last. Not much longer, he guessed.

"What do you want?" Murphy screamed. He lashed out at Pyotr and caught him in the jaw. Pyotr dropped his grip and Murphy reached out for Ryan. Sasha pulled out his gun but Oskar yelled at him to stop.

Oskar motioned Sasha toward the stairs. "Take care of him. Downstairs," he said in Russian.

His men stepped forward and Murphy began to backpedal. "We had a deal," he repeated.

"I'm afraid it didn't work out," Oskar said.

Murphy struggled as Ivan took hold of him again and dragged him toward the basement stairs, Sasha following.

Ryan watched them go before turning back to look at Oskar.

"We've come to take you back to your mother. She's been worried." Breathless, Oskar sat down in a chair and waited for the men to return. If Ryan tried to run, he could get his men fast enough. But now Oskar needed to sit.

The pain started to crystallize again. He pushed it away. He wanted to savor this moment, take his time with it. There was no hurry. Dmitri hadn't shown up with the boots in time to come to California with Oskar, but he was handling his part of the deal. Jennifer Townsend. The end of it. He had promised Dmitri. He would still send someone for Megan, but he couldn't wait for her himself. It was time they moved on. Oskar knew he didn't have much time left, and he ought to spend it with Dmitri. There was a lot to pass on before he was gone.

The boy stood motionless. Oskar watched him,

and the boy returned the stare as though it were some sort of contest.

Oskar conceded the first round and motioned to the couch. "Come sit. I'm going to call your mother now."

The boy began to rock from foot to foot but remained rooted to the same spot.

Oskar pulled his phone from his pocket and checked for messages. Dmitri hadn't called yet. He was surprised it had taken so long, but perhaps his son had wanted one last night before he took care of his friend. It wouldn't have been Oskar's way. He had always taken care of business first, but things were different now. Times were easier, and so his son didn't take the work as seriously. Dmitri had always been that way. Viktor less so, but still, he had played the risks. And in the end he'd lost for it.

Oskar didn't allow himself to focus on Viktor's death. Today was a day to celebrate his life. It was the final celebration. And then the past would be buried. And soon, he alongside it.

He dialed Dmitri's line and listened to it ring. Even busy, Dmitri knew to answer it.

Oskar sat up and glanced at the boy, who was still standing with his hands behind his back, rocking left to right, left to right. The motion made Oskar sick, and he leaned forward against the pain. Cool sweat beaded along his brow, but he ignored it and dialed the familiar number.

He answered on the first ring. "*Allo.*"

"*Eta Kirov,*" he said, his head down. "You've heard from Dmitri?"

"*Nyet.*"

"No? Well, have you checked on him?"

There was a substantial pause, and for a moment

Oskar thought the connection was lost. "*Allo,*" he snapped, irritated. He looked up to make sure Ryan was still there.

"Yes. I am here."

"Have you seen Dmitri?"

"Yes."

"He didn't answer his phone. Tell him he must keep it on him at all times," Oskar scolded. "We need to be in touch. Now let me talk to him."

"He can't talk now, Oskar Ivanovich."

Oskar was surprised by the formal way he was addressed, using Oskar's father's name. "Why not?"

He did not answer, and Oskar reared his head back in fear as pain severed him front to back. He roared. "What has happened?"

His voice was almost a whisper, soft and lethal. "He's dead, sir. I think she shot him."

The phone slipped from his hand as he yelled out for his son. "*Bozje!*" he cried, pleading to God. All three of his sons. They were all dead. He flattened his hands across his chest, the pain a throbbing surge. "*Nyet.*" His dead sons.

Dead from his own hand, sure as if he'd shot them himself. He squeezed his eyes tight, dug the knuckle of his thumb into the pain in an attempt to drive it away. It burned in confirmation.

Oh, God. It was true. He'd caused their deaths. His Viktor, Dmitri, even weak Feliks. He should have saved them. He should have saved them all.

He pushed himself from the chair and felt a grip on his arm. He looked up, praying to see one of his boys. Instead, Ivan's empty stare returned his. He pushed Ivan away and then dropped to his knees. He moaned and the silent sobs racked him until the pain was so wrenching that he had to stop.

He lay on the floor for a moment and then pushed himself slowly up. His men stood motionless above him. "Help me, damn you," he screamed.

The men lifted him to his feet as he fought to keep his balance. He strained to catch his breath and pressed his fingers against the throbbing between his ribs. "Where is Murphy?"

"Below, as you said."

"Somewhere that they will find him?"

"Visible, yes."

Oskar nodded, working to pull himself together. Damn it all. He shouldn't have been last. He should have been first. He was the leader, the man. And now he was left to die alone.

"Should we hide him?"

"No," he said, feeling the anger harden. He would show them. He wanted them to find him. Find him and worry about what was happening to Ryan. Oskar clenched his fists.

He couldn't wait to deal with Ryan. Ryan would pay for all three of his boys. One little child. It was hardly enough to make up for his loss, but at least Ryan Riggs would be a last reminder of who Kirov was. His last mark on the world. He should have gone out bigger. He had so little energy left, but he would take his time with Ryan.

Oskar felt a bit refreshed at the thought of what misery little Ryan would endure before he succumbed. He licked his fingers and ran them through his hair.

He turned to see the boy's face, but he was no longer standing in the same spot. Oskar looked around. "Where is the boy?"

The men exchanged glances.

"Find him now," Oskar roared. "He hasn't gotten far in this snow."

The men ran off, and Oskar pushed himself toward the back of the house. Out the back window, he saw a Ford Expedition that must have been Murphy's. Beside it were two matching red Yamaha snowmobiles.

He scanned the kitchen counters until he spotted three sets of keys on a counter by the back door.

He staggered to them. Two of the key chains were marked Yamaha. Gripping one tight in his fist, he headed out the back door.

He found his men, tromping in the snow. "Forget it," he told them. "Stay and guard the house."

His men were worthless. He would find Ryan Riggs himself. And then he would see how much agony one small body could withstand. Oskar would work until Ryan had suffered the way his own sons had.

He would avenge their deaths once and for all. And then he would join them. He looked most forward to that.

He pulled himself onto the machine and felt the invigorating cold rip through his fur-lined leather coat. He turned the key in the engine and felt his own heart rev with it.

For one last moment, he was young and dangerous.

And he was on the hunt.

Chapter 31

Cody was trying to get her wireless modem connection to work as the colonel headed toward the mountains. They had no idea where they were going. Only another bug or a more descriptive picture could give them any guidance. That or something more from Jennifer Townsend. Cody hated the thought of depending on her even in the least, but right now she'd take whatever she could get. She'd launched the wireless icon when the cell phone rang again.

"Hello," she answered.

The colonel focused on the road with the kind of attention that made her feel he wasn't listening, even though he undoubtedly caught every word. Florence was still asleep in the backseat, so Cody kept her voice low. "Hello," she repeated.

"Megan?"

"Who is this?"

"It's Mei Ling."

Cody didn't answer.

"From the CIS."

The Computer Intrusion Squad. How long ago that life had been. Three short letters brought it all swimming back. She remembered seeing a yellow truck with those letters painted in red on its side when she was living in New Orleans. It had been some computer company's truck, but just the acronym had stopped her in her tracks and left tears streaming down her face. There were no tears now. She was over the FBI. She was alone. Ryan was hers to find, and hers alone.

"Megan, are you there?"

"I'm here, Mei."

"I left you a message earlier. I wasn't sure if you got—"

"I got it."

Cody wanted to hang up the phone, but she didn't dare. She would not ask for anything, but if the FBI had something about Ryan to offer, she wasn't about to refuse them.

"Oskar Kirov has left town," Mei said. "Agent Townsend indicated he'd left by plane, but we can't locate his flight origin."

Cody heard Jennifer referred to as Agent Townsend. What a joke. Agent Townsend was a goddamn traitor. "Who's interviewing Agent Townsend? Because she knows where they are. She sent them here."

There were a series of hushed whispers in the background.

"Mei," Cody said, her tone significantly softer.

"I'm here."

"Let's cut the crap, okay?"

Mei didn't answer.

"Jennifer sold our whereabouts to the Russians. Who the hell knows what she got for it, but she did. Now, she knows where they are going. And that's where my son is. So send some agents over there and shake it out of her."

There was more whispering.

"Damn it, Mei. Take some fucking action. Interview her. Find out what she knows."

"Jennifer's on her way to Cook County Hospital. They don't know if she'll make it. She took a bunch of pills."

Cody felt the prickling of hot needles behind her eyes. She refused to offer them any condolences. She and Jennifer had been close friends once. But that wasn't why she felt sick now. Jennifer was her link to Ryan. Without her, all Cody had to work with was some nameless camp.

"Megan?"

She cleared her throat. "I'm here." She forced Jennifer's condition from her mind and focused on Ryan. "There's a camp. She said something about a camp."

"To us, too. We're running a search now. Will you be at this number?"

"Leave a message if you hear the voice mail."

"I will."

Cody started to shut off the phone when she heard Mei's voice call her name. "Yeah?"

"We'll find him."

Cody bit back a harsh retort. She hung up without answering.

As the colonel drove toward the Sierras, Cody plugged the phone connection into her laptop. She waited through the series of beeps and clicks that told her she was there. It was so dark it was almost impossible to see anything outside the car. She let the colonel do the driving and focused on the small screen in front of her.

A small gray box appeared, confirming her connection, and she launched Microsoft Internet Explorer and chose the first bookmark: www. ivegotpeter.com.

The picture loaded slowly, one tiny row after another, but she knew instantly that it was a new one. She gasped at the promise of new information.

"Tell me what you see," the colonel said, keeping his eyes on the road.

"Not much yet. Mostly white walls again. A tiny bit of ceiling." She waited, her pulse making double time with the *whoosh* of the windshield wipers pushing the snow off the glass.

As the room slowly appeared, Cody searched left and right for Ryan. Finally the small round top of his head appeared. "He's there—lying on the floor, it looks like."

"Anything new?"

She knew the colonel meant bugs, and she scanned Ryan's clothing and the area around him. "I can't tell. It's too dark."

The colonel punched the button overhead for her reading light.

"It'll be too hard for you to see the road."

He shook his head. "I can drive. You find us something new."

She brought her legs up and crossed them under her, pulling the screen closer to her nose. Ryan was lying on his belly with a magazine open in front of him. "It's a new one." She couldn't tell what the magazine was, although from the small portion of his face she could see, he seemed interested. She wished he were looking at her.

Unlike the pictures before it, this one was taken at a distance. He was wearing the same clothes, but that was almost all she could confirm. From the small side view, there was no way to be sure he was truly okay. She imagined a huge laceration bleeding out on the other side of his face and forced the image away. He was fine. He looked fine.

She studied his surroundings but found nothing else to add any value. The carpet beneath him was short and gray with flecks of other colors. It looked very generic, and she was certain it would offer them no clues. There was a small metal mixing bowl in front of him, and she imagined at home it might be filled with microwave popcorn. The scene was peaceful, and from his posture, Ryan could just as easily have been lying on a friend's floor.

"You're awfully quiet."

"I can't find anything distinctive yet."

"Describe what you see."

"White walls. No visible texture. Gray Berber-like carpet. Ryan's lying on his belly, horizontally across the picture. The left side of his face is visible. He's looking at a magazine or something. I can't tell what it is. There's a small metal mixing bowl." She exhaled. "Damn it. That's all. Nothing else. No lights, no furniture."

"It look like the same place?"

"Maybe. There's nothing to suggest it is. And nothing to suggest it isn't."

"What about insects?"

She shook her head, inspecting the picture again. "Nothing."

"You're sure?"

"No. I can't be sure. It's too dark."

The colonel turned on his blinker and shifted lanes.

Cody looked up to see Landon's Porsche still in the left lane. "What are you doing?"

The colonel met her gaze for the first time since they'd left the dead boy's crime scene. "I'm pulling over so we can take a good look at that picture."

Cody felt her stomach drop. "But we need to get to—"

The colonel touched her hand and she stopped talking. "We don't know where we need to get to. Let's take five minutes and find out what's in that picture."

She shook her head. "I don't know."

"Trust me."

She looked down at the image of Ryan, sprawled on the carpet. Without a word, she nodded.

The colonel pulled off the next exit and she could see Landon slow down and move to follow. They stopped at a well-lit gas station and the colonel pulled to the pump.

He got out and started to fill the gas tank.

Cody turned the screen into the light and examined the picture again. There was nothing else there.

Landon's Porsche pulled up beside them, and a flash of his headlights hit the inside of the car. Cody spotted something near Ryan's head. But Landon's headlights flipped off and it was gone.

She blinked and searched for the impression again but it was gone. Opening the door, she stood from the car, the laptop in her arms. She shifted the screen up and down and right and left, aiming the light at it from different angles in hopes of finding something.

Landon appeared beside her.

"What are you looking for?"

"It's a new image," she said quickly, still wondering what it was that she'd seen in the light of his headlights. Landon crossed in front of the light, and as it shone on the screen again, she caught sight of a tiny reflection in the surface of the metal bowl. She squinted but couldn't make it out. She would have liked to save the image to disk and work with a photo editor to blow it up, but she didn't have the right software on her laptop.

Landon peered over her shoulder, his breath warm in her ear against the cold night. He leaned into the screen and his breathing sounded erratic. "See anything?"

She didn't respond. Her own pulse was racing as she tried to make out the distorted reflection in the bowl. It was probably nothing, she told herself. And yet, as she stared at it, willing it to turn into something worthwhile, she couldn't help but feel some excitement. It was a mistake, something the kidnapper had overlooked. It had to be.

She shifted the screen back into the light, wishing he would be quiet. "Do you have a flashlight?"

"Sure. In the car," he said without moving.

"Can you get it?"

"What for?"

She looked up at him, fury in her eyes.

Landon paused and then turned toward his car, saying something she didn't hear.

Cody focused on the gray-brown reflection, trying to make it out. It was a distorted semicircle, but she couldn't get the image to crystallize.

Landon returned with a flashlight and handed it to her. She took it and pushed it on but it was dead.

The colonel screwed on the gas cap and walked to her.

"I need a flashlight," she told him.

He took the one from her hand and gave it a hard smack. "Probably dead."

"It's been in the car forever," he said quickly. "I don't know the last time I used it."

The colonel opened the flashlight's chamber. "I'll get batteries inside."

Landon remained over her shoulder, staring at the screen.

"Do you see something?"

He coughed and made a sound that indicated he didn't.

She glanced up at his face and she could tell something was wrong. "What?"

He shook his head. "I don't know."

She looked back at the screen and then up at him again. "Landon, spit it out."

"It looks familiar."

She stared back at the screen.

Just then the colonel came back with batteries and loaded them into the flashlight. He flipped it on and handed the bright light to Cody.

Landon stared at the screen and then seemed to collapse. "Oh, Jesus."

Ignoring Travis, she centered her full attention on the screen. "See the metal bowl?"

"Something reflected in it," the colonel said.

"Can you tell what?"

The colonel ran the beam of the flashlight back and forth on the image.

Landon pulled himself up. His voice was weak when he spoke. "I know what it is. I know where they are."

Cody opened her mouth to ask him what he was talking about when the colonel pointed to the reflection and said, "It's a fireplace."

Cody gasped.

The colonel ran his finger along the screen in a small half circle. "Do you see it? Big reddish brown stones."

Cody saw it and then immediately lost focus, fury swimming across her vision. When she regained it, she saw exactly what the colonel was pointing out. Reflected in the metal bowl was a large reddish brown stone fireplace with a heavy oak mantel.

She could see it perfectly because she'd seen it in a photo before—a photo at Landon's house.

Cody met his eyes.

"It's mine."

The colonel gave a sideways glance to Landon as he grabbed Cody's arm. "You okay? You look like you need to sit." He took the computer from her hand and set it down in the car.

She didn't answer. She couldn't. Her gaze was somewhere else, picturing that same fireplace as it looked in a photograph of Landon and his son that she saw in his house.

"Cody?" the colonel repeated. "What is it?"

She didn't respond to the colonel but met Travis's gaze.

Landon shook his head. "I didn't know," he said. "I swear, not until just now."

She saw the fear there. Words boiled to the surface but none were strong enough for what she felt. Her control dissolved and she moved like a robot, detaching herself from the colonel and launching herself at Travis Landon.

Chapter 32

Jennifer heard the voices around her. They were yelling. Everyone was yelling. Her father was there, yelling, and her mother. Tiffany. No, Tiffany wasn't yelling. Tiffany was crying.

"Fault." "Blame." The words chased each other like little yellow and pink Pac-Men around a strange electric-blue maze.

There were other voices, too. "BP's seventy over fifty and dropping," a woman said.

"Damn," said a man's voice.

"She's going to code," said another.

A series of beeps played in the background of the game. A long bleat, then a short one, long then short. The big yellow Pac-Man chased the other.

"This is your fault," the yellow one shouted. She saw her father's face. "Your fault," he told Tiffany.

Finally something was Tiffany's fault, she thought.

"You're going to have to leave," someone said, and Jennifer heard her mother make a high-pitched sound.

"You're not allowed in here."

They were there. They had all come. She wasn't alone.

She felt cold and woozy, and the voices grew more distant, less clear. She shivered.

"Get them out of here," a male voice said.

"We're losing her," someone, a woman, shouted.

Jennifer thought about loss. She could see the perfect picture of her parents and Tiffany, the one framed on the mantel in the living room. Tiffany, perfect and blond, in her little gray dress and white pinafore.

"Draw up the epinephrine for an intracardiac injection," a man's voice said.

Intracardiac. The letters tumbled apart and drifted across her mind. N-A-R-C, D-A-N-C, T-R-A-I-N, they danced into different forms.

"At least Jennifer had some ambition. She did something with her life," her father shouted.

"Out," a woman yelled. "You're going to have to leave now."

Jennifer smiled at the image of her father's yellow Pac-Man face. "You can't tell me to leave. That's my daughter."

She tried to shake her head. She didn't want them to leave. She wanted them to yell, to scream and cry right there, right in front of her. Her perfect family, dissolved.

"Then you'll have to be quiet. We're trying—"

The bleating noise changed into a long, low whine. *Beep beep*, she thought. *Beep beep*. She was cold. Cold and tired. Suddenly she just wanted to rest. Yes, tell them to all go away.

"What's happening?" her mother screeched.

"She's fibrillating. Get the paddles."

"Set it at two hundred," someone called.

Jennifer felt pressure on her chest. "Step back," a man's voice called from above her.

The room grew silent and Jennifer felt a jolt run through her. Her body jumped sharply but she felt only a little rise, like driving over a speed bump.

"Increase to three hundred."

Jennifer watched someone turn a dial on a machine. Three hundred volts, she thought, staring down at her own body from the ceiling. The sounds grew softer, quieter. It was nice up there.

"Clear." She watched her own body jump and felt a distant, uncomfortable kick. Her loose hair tossed around her face. It was time to have it cut, she thought. Especially the ends. They looked ragged and unhealthy.

"Three-sixty," the man said.

She saw the paddles on her chest again.

Her body jumped. This time she felt nothing.

"No change," a woman reported.

"Jesus. What's happening? What's going on?" her father shouted.

Her mother dropped to the floor.

Her father pushed toward her.

I'm up here, she thought to her father. Still, he pushed toward her limp body.

"Damn. One more time," the man called. "Hold him back," he yelled as her father reached for her.

There was a surge of activity. More paddles, someone at her head, someone on her arm, holding her still. She wasn't moving anyway. Her father was crying, sobbing, ignoring Tiffany, who wept by herself. Her mother was on the floor. She watched as the man drove a long needle into her chest. She felt nothing.

Suddenly she was surrounded by heat. Like a

warm bath, it enveloped her. She sank her head back, let herself relax. They weren't perfect. They weren't perfect either, and they did care.

She heard a long, piercing screech and everything went dark.

Chapter 33

Travis stepped back from Cody's angry gaze.

She lunged at him like a cat, every move as though she were ready to pounce.

Heat pooled in his gut.

"What's going on?" the colonel asked.

Cody moved closer. "Why don't you tell him, Travis? Tell him what's going on."

He shook his head. "I don't understand it either, Cody. It's my cabin, but I had nothing to do with it. I don't know who did this."

"The picture was taken at your cabin."

He nodded. "I know."

"You didn't recognize it before?" Cody screamed.

"What do you mean, his cabin?" the colonel shouted.

"I mean Landon knows where Ryan is. It's the same fireplace I saw in a photo at his house. The one you see reflected in the bowl."

Travis rubbed his face. "Jesus Christ, I have no idea what they're doing there."

The colonel grabbed his shirtsleeve. "What the hell's going on here?"

Travis approached Cody. "I don't know. I just rec-ognized the fireplace myself."

She gave him a glare. "You self-serving bastard."

He shook his head. It didn't make any sense. How the hell had this happened? And how could she blame him? His child had almost been kidnapped, too.

"You had something to do with this; I know you did."

"That's crazy. Why would I kidnap a child? It's horrible, and what would it gain?"

"I don't know, Landon. But you'd better not be in-volved in this. And if he's missing a single hair on his head—" She halted. "We need to get to him. We have to reach him before Kirov does."

"Let's go, then," the colonel said.

"Get in the back," Cody said to Landon.

He nodded, his mind still spinning at the possibil-ities. "Let me just move the Porsche."

"Get in the damn car, boy," the colonel yelled.

Landon looked at his car parked at the pump. "Fine." He patted his pocket to be sure he had his cell phone and wallet. Turning his back on the car, he climbed into the Jeep beside the colonel's wife, who was still asleep.

Cody was behind the wheel again and the car was moving almost before Travis could shut the door. "What's the fastest way?" she said.

His heart was pounding in his temples. "Continue on Fifty. We're about ten or fifteen minutes." His voice was breathy as he searched for something to tell her.

She pulled out onto the two-lane freeway and swerved as she straightened the wheel. Travis grabbed hold of the back of his seat but stayed silent.

The colonel picked up Cody's cell phone. "I'm going to call my contact up here. What's the name of this place?"

Travis licked his lips. "The cabin is at Fallen Leaf Lake. It's 118 Fallen Oak Road." But he knew the police up here were rangers and it would take them time to get there, especially since they didn't plow the roads in the winter. Most likely they'd arrive before the police did. He didn't say that out loud.

When the colonel began to dial, Landon lifted his own cell phone and dialed McCue. Cody glared at him in the rearview mirror, and he did his best to deflect the guilt he felt. He hadn't done anything wrong.

He explained the situation to McCue and asked him to call the FBI and get someone to his address. Then he gave directions on Cody's cell phone to the police. He wanted to call his lawyer too, but he didn't dare. Instead he leaned forward between the seats after the calls were made. "I know you don't believe this, but I have no idea how this happened."

Cody didn't take her gaze off the road.

"What about that damn table?" the colonel said after a few minutes of silence.

"What table?" Travis asked.

Cody nodded. "That corner was distinctive. I'd have known it in my house."

He felt the guilt rise in his throat. He'd known something was wrong about that picture. But he hadn't realized it was his own cabin. He swallowed hard. Had he?

He shook his head. "I didn't know. I never imagined it could be mine. I swear it. I had nothing to do with this."

Cody didn't answer.

The colonel turned back and looked at him with little more than a grunt.

He leaned back and watched out the window as they got closer. "Turn right here," he directed when they reached the turnoff.

Cody turned and immediately he saw the fresh tracks. Someone had been there before them. His chest was tight and he thought about the corner of that table. Had he recognized it? Had he somehow subconsciously shut out the possibility that the kidnapper had gone to his own cabin?

And what if Kirov reached R.J. before them because of his oversight? Suddenly he felt a wave of terrible carsickness.

Chapter 34

Mei rested her head on the window and tried to sleep. It was six-thirty in the morning, Chicago time, and she had yet to doze at all. They had gone straight from the office to the airport. The engine purred beneath her and below, through the thick white clouds and orange light of dawn, was Nevada.

They were expected to arrive at the Lake Tahoe airport at five California time, so in roughly a half hour. After that, she knew she wouldn't be able to sleep. But she wasn't having much success now either.

Each time she drifted to the edge of consciousness, she heard Jennifer's last words, her final apology, and she was jolted awake. An image of Jennifer, stumbling across their office, played through her mind like the disjointed memories of movies she'd seen as a kid.

The hospital was reporting Jennifer critical, and everyone said it didn't look good. She had taken two dozen Percocet, and the doctors said the damage would be permanent, if she even survived. Mei had been the last person to speak to her. That thought kept driving through her brain. She could have done something to stop it. There had to have been something she could have done.

Mei shuddered and she felt Andy turn and tuck the small red blanket back over her shoulders. She didn't want him to know she was awake. She didn't want to talk. She wished she were at home, at her mother's home, even. The red egg and ginger party was today, and she was going to miss it. Her mother would never understand. She'd probably already left a half dozen messages at her house, asking her to come over early to help.

Mei should have been there. She wasn't supposed to be involved in this. The Russian mob, a witness from the Federal Witness Protection Program. She wasn't a field agent. She was barely an agent. She was a computer analyst.

This job was something for the Office of Professional Responsibility and field agents, people trained to fight. But they wanted her there because she was the only one in the group who knew Megan Riggs from her time at the Bureau.

Andy shifted beside her, punched another number into her cell phone, and started to talk again. They'd left the office so quickly, he'd forgotten his own phone, so she'd given him hers. Unlike commercial flights, the Bureau plane had no rules against the use of cellular phones except on takeoff and landing. So Andy was making arrangements for someone to pick them up.

They hadn't heard from Megan again. Mei hoped she was okay. The Bureau had finally found Kirov's flight records, and the last report had confirmed that Kirov and three of his men were headed for California. They'd caught a commercial flight on Delta from Cincinnati, Ohio, to Sacramento via Salt Lake City. And their flight was due to arrive at eleven the night before. A whole six hours before the FBI. That was the worst news of all. Mei didn't even want to imagine what damage the mob could do in six hours.

A phone rang and she tried once again to shut out all the brutal images. She remembered the games she used to play as a child when she was trying to fall asleep over the sounds of her sisters snoring in the cramped room they shared. She pictured the noise as a running stream and then the wind billowing through a tree. A bird made the chirping sound of her phone, and she was picturing a vast green field with a tree in its center when Andy began to speak in Cantonese.

"Yes. My name is Andy Chang," he said.

Mei started to sit up, but the next words halted her.

"Hello, Ling Tai Tai." Andy addressed her mother with the proper formality.

Mei considered what she would say to her mother. Oh, God. Was it worse to try to talk to her now in front of Andy? Or to let him explain what was going on? She paused, torn.

Andy laughed at something her mother said. She was being her most charming, Mei was sure. "Yes, I work for the FBI as well."

There was a pause, and Mei wished she'd taken the call when it first came through. What was she telling him?

"No, I'm not her boss. I work in a different department."

Another pause. Mei wished Andy would do more of the talking. She was sure her mother was running off at the mouth. She felt the red rush to her cheeks and she held herself still. Pretend to be asleep. That was the best she could do now.

"No, I'm not married."

Oh, this was too much. She had to rescue him. She shifted and pretended to start to wake up.

"Yes, I do think she's very nice."

She halted. He thought she was nice. What did that mean? Now that her mother was drilling him, she hoped she asked him something better than that.

"She doesn't have a boyfriend? You're sure?"

Mei wanted to crawl under her seat. This was torture. She rubbed her face and sat up, blinking as though she might have been asleep for the past few minutes. She didn't want him to think she was eavesdropping, even if it was her own mother on the phone.

Andy met her gaze and smiled. "Well, I'm glad to hear that," he told her mother.

Mei frowned. She wondered what he was glad to hear. She prayed her mother wasn't telling him about all the children her sisters had and how fertile they were. It would be just like her mother to try to sell Mei off for her fertility.

"Yes, I do." He smiled and added, "I think she's very beautiful." *Keuih hou leng*, he'd said. He thought she was beautiful?

Mei felt her face flush and looked away, but Andy tapped her shoulder and pointed to the phone, mouthing, *Your mother.*

She widened her eyes as though she were surprised and then shook her head to indicate she didn't want to talk.

He gave her a wink. "No, Ling Tai Tai, this is just a business trip. We'll be back tomorrow or the next day. Good luck with the party. I know Mei will be sorry to miss it."

He paused again.

"No, she said so on the way to the airport." He winked at her again and Mei rolled her eyes at her mother. "Yes, she was very upset not to be there. She knew how important it was to you and Lai Ching."

Mei wished she could grab the phone and hang up on her mother. Stop babbling, she wanted to scream.

"I love salted fish with minced pork." He nodded. "Yeah." Nod. "It's her favorite, too?"

Mei shook her head, wishing her mother would shut up.

Andy just grinned at her as though this conversation would cost her something later.

She blushed again, thinking what it might be. Had he really called her beautiful? Maybe they were talking about someone else.

"I will look forward to it. I'm sure you're a wonderful cook."

The ultimate praise. Mei watched Andy, wondering if he had any idea what he'd just committed himself to. If he wasn't interested in her, she was going to have to kill him, because her mother would never get over him.

"I'll have her call you as soon as she wakes up." With that Andy Chang hung up the phone and smiled at her. "Your mother is very nice," he said to her in English.

"Do you have any idea what trouble you've caused?" she answered in Cantonese to exclude the three other agents on board from understanding her.

Andy looked hurt. "What do you mean?"

His pathetic expression made her smile. "I mean,

you know she's going to expect you to be at dinner now."

His face relaxed. "I'd love to have dinner at your mother's."

"But she thinks we'll be together."

"Well, I'm not going to your mother's house without you," he said in English.

"I mean, she thinks we'll be a couple," she said in Cantonese.

That made him laugh.

"I'm serious. She will. You don't know my mother."

"I'm not laughing at your mother. I'm laughing at you," he answered in Cantonese.

She switched to English. "Why?"

"Because I know you heard the whole conversation."

Her cheeks burst into little heat pockets. "So?" That was the best she could come up with.

He shrugged. "So, I meant what I said."

"About going to dinner?"

"Everything."

"Everything?" She felt like a schoolgirl, but she didn't care. She wanted to hear him say it, to hear confirmation from him.

"Yes."

She watched him and then looked away.

"I meant it when I said I thought you were beautiful," he said in Cantonese.

It was about the nicest-sounding thing she'd ever heard. She savored the words in her head before turning to him. *"Do jeh,"* she thanked him.

"I didn't say it to get a thank-you."

She shifted her gaze across his face until it settled

on his lips. She forced herself to turn away. "Why, then?"

"So you would know. So you'd know this wasn't a joke for me. The meeting, us. It's about work, I know," he said, and for the first time she sensed he was nervous, too.

"But I hope when the work is over that there might be something else." He paused and shook his head, laughing at himself. "I'm not making any sense, I know." He turned away, but she touched his hand.

"No. You do—you are making sense. And I'd like that, too."

Just then another agent appeared at their aisle.

Mei pulled her hand off Andy's arm and turned to the window.

"You two are going to have to cut out all that Chinese shit," Kyler Wisenor said. Kyler was tall, lean, with blue eyes and light brown hair. Women in the Bureau thought he was gorgeous. The Bureau's own Brad Pitt. "Bernadini's back there getting jealous, and I'm wondering if you two aren't about to start making out up here."

"What?" Andy laughed.

"That's ridiculous," Mei added.

Kyler leaned down and winked at Mei, giving Andy a conspiring elbow. "Hey, the words might be different but love sounds the same no matter what the language."

Mei could hear the other guys from the Office of Professional Responsibility let out a series of whoops and whistles from the back of the plane. She didn't answer.

"Get the hell out of here, Wisenor," Andy said, but Mei could see him blushing, too.

Kyler Wisenor made a kissing face and smacked his lips before sauntering down the aisle to the back of the plane.

Mei tucked the small paper-thin pillow back under her head and closed her eyes.

"Sure," Andy whispered. "Sleep and leave me to take all the abuse."

Mei smiled but didn't open her eyes. "Pretending to sleep seems to have worked for me so far."

She opened one eye and caught him looking at her. He opened his mouth to talk when the cell phone rang.

"If it's your mother, you want to talk to her this time?"

Mei laughed. "She probably called back to ask you if you want to join us for Chinese New Year next year."

"Oh, good, I didn't have plans yet." He winked. "Chang," he answered.

His face dropped immediately.

Mei closed her hands over the armrests.

"When?" He nodded at her response. "Okay. Thanks for the news."

He shut the phone and looked over. "Jennifer didn't make it."

Mei nodded and felt the slightest hint of relief. Jennifer's life was a loss, but Mei's focus was on Megan now. Megan and Ryan. "Jennifer didn't but Megan and Ryan have to," she whispered, more for her own benefit than anyone else's.

Andy squeezed her hand as she thought about the reason they were together. The playful spirit was gone, but Mei knew this was much more important.

"We'll be on the ground in twenty minutes," the

captain announced from the cockpit. "Make sure everyone's belted in."

"You hear that, lovebirds," Kyler Wisenor shouted. "Break it up so you don't lose any teeth in the landing."

Mei and Andy ignored them. "We'll find them," Andy said.

"We have to," Mei agreed. "Megan Riggs deserves that much from us." Mei thought she deserved a hell of a lot more after what Jennifer had done to jeopardize her life and the life of her son. But keeping Oskar Kirov away from her and putting him behind bars would certainly be a good start.

As the plane started to bump lower into the sky, Mei focused her thoughts on Megan and Ryan, praying that they would be there in time to help.

Chapter 35

Cody watched as the end of Fallen Leaf Lake came into view. The FBI and the local authorities were on their way, but she was pretty sure she was the first to arrive. None of them had said much since they had left the gas station. The trip had taken them seven hours with the stop. It was normally a four-hour drive.

Cody pointed to a sign that directed people to Stanford Camp, and for the briefest moment in her mind, she could imagine being in a car with Ryan and Mark on their way to drop Ryan at camp. A normal family, a normal life. The ones like her sisters Alison and Amy and Nicole had.

Ryan had never been to camp, of course. She wouldn't let him. She would now. She bargained with whoever might be listening. Just bring Ryan home to her and she'd swear to let him live a more normal life.

As they rounded the last bend, she switched the headlights off. Florence had started to make a breathy snoring sound, and Cody was thankful for the way it broke the otherwise steely silence.

"It's that one." Travis pointed to a shingled house

that looked to be almost as large as the one he had back in the Bay Area. It was dark except for one light toward the back of the house. But there was a car out front.

"You recognize the cars?"

"No."

Cody ignored the fact that he sounded almost relieved.

She imagined most of the houses were locked up this time of year. There wasn't any skiing close by, so the lake's inhabitants came mostly for summer vacations. Though the main road hadn't been plowed recently, there were tire tracks, and she could see that they led right up to that one house.

"Cody?"

She nodded without taking her eyes off the house. "Okay." The scent of fire filled her nostrils and she realized it was from her memories. She had not been this close to Oskar Kirov or his people since that day three years ago.

"What do we do from here?" Travis asked.

She pointed to a dark parking lot off to their right. "We go there and you wait with Florence."

She pulled the car ahead slowly, using the emergency brake to slow down to avoid the bright red of the brake lights.

When they were stopped, Cody opened the glove compartment and pulled out her 9mm SIG Sauer, cleaned and loaded, and checked the magazine. She set it in her lap, then pulled her Model 66 .357 Magnum out from under the seat and checked to make sure all six chambers held rounds. She left the motor running, and Cody zipped her jacket to her chin and pulled on a pair of thin black wool gloves. She knew she hadn't brought nearly enough to protect her against the weather, but her adrenaline would more than keep out the cold.

The colonel closed his own jacket and turned the collar up toward his ears.

"You guys leave the car running. If you don't hear from me in ten minutes, head back to town and get help."

"No way I'm letting you go in there by yourself," the colonel said.

She noticed Travis was silent.

Cody shook her head. "It's too dangerous. And you should be here with Florence."

He looked back at his wife and his eyes softened as he gave her a sad smile. "She'll be fine. She sleeps like a baby, and someone will arrive shortly. Plus, Travis'll watch her."

"Sure," he said quickly.

Cody paused. She didn't want the colonel to get hurt, but she knew she could use the help.

His mouth made a flat line. "She'd want me to do this, Cody. I won't let her down."

Cody shook her head. "I can do this alone. At least let me check it out. I can signal if I need you."

"Give me that Magnum. It was always my favorite anyway." He reached for the gun.

"You don't—"

"Let's go get Ryan."

She met his gaze and nodded. "Thank you."

"Don't thank me until we're all safely on our way home."

Landon explained the layout of the house and Cody took it in, focusing on each detail as she committed it to memory. Then Cody handed the colonel a gun and he weighed it in his grip as though getting the feel of it before snapping it open, rolling the barrel, and clicking it shut again.

"Ready?"

She picked up the SIG Sauer and put her hand on the door handle.

"No use waiting, then," he said, and before she could respond, he was out in the cold.

Without another word to Landon, Cody opened the door and latched it softly behind her. She saw only the thin gray exhaust coming out the back, and even that became quickly invisible as they moved toward the house.

The night was silent in the way a city never was. She heard the crunch of snow beneath their feet and the occasional *swish* of snow dropping from the trees. The wind had picked up, and it made a low whistling sound off the water as if it were warning them of something.

Cody listened with her eyes half-shut, hearing the sounds and adjusting her eyes to the blackness. The moon was a sliver on the far end of the lake, and it offered little light for them to go by.

She heard the low groan of a motor revving in the distance and halted.

The colonel was beside her. He pointed. "There."

"It's a snowmobile," she said.

"Can you tell who's on it?"

She squinted, but it was too dark to make out anything but the shape of the vehicle. "Not from here."

"What now?" he asked.

"The house, I think."

"Right," the colonel agreed, continuing up the hill.

They plodded on in silence for a few minutes, and Cody felt her lungs burn from the altitude. She pushed herself on despite it.

Two-thirds of the way up the hill to the house, Cody heard the colonel slip. He made a low grunting sound, and before she could react, he had slid by her.

She turned to try to find him, suddenly panicked that he might be injured and she might be alone. She opened her mouth to whisper his name when someone coughed loudly from beyond them. She knelt in the snow, ducking down behind a short pine tree and holding the gun pointed outward.

In the light of the cabin's back porch, she caught the reflection of a thick patch of smoke, and at first she thought it was her own breath. But something moved and she was able to make out a man on the porch, smoking a cigarette. It wasn't Oskar Kirov. He was too young and too agile to be Kirov, but she immediately sensed he didn't belong there either.

She swung around at the sound of steps beside her.

"It's just me," the colonel whispered.

She exhaled, pressing her palm to her chest.

"You okay?"

"You scared me. Are you okay? Did you fall far?"

"I'm fine," he said, then motioned with his chin to the porch. "That our kidnapper?"

She shrugged.

"You think that's a Russian?"

She looked at him, working her bottom lip between her teeth. "I don't have any good reason for thinking it's him."

"Just your gut?"

"Right."

"Sometimes that's the truest warning."

"How are we going to get up there?" she said, watching the man pace back and forth across the deck. His hands were bare, and she tried to determine what to make of that. Was he from up here and used to the cold? He shivered and threw his cigarette off the porch. Then he turned his back and disappeared back into the house. "I know how to be sure who it is," she said.

"How?"

"I'll show you." Keeping her head low, she moved in a low crouch toward the house. The wind stopped momentarily, and besides their own steps, the only sound she could hear was that of the colonel's breath behind her. She was pushing him, she knew, and she tried to get herself to slow down.

They reached a patch of tall pine trees less than twenty yards from the porch when Cody stopped. The colonel was behind her, his breathing fast and heavy. Her own heart was pounding and the cold burned her throat.

Under the porch, she crouched in the white snow. Squinting, she searched the uneven surface until she found what she was looking for. Picking up the discarded butt of a lone cigarette, she moved back into the shadow of the porch.

It was a hand-rolled cigarette, only half-smoked, the acrid scent of the tobacco definitely Russian. They were already there.

She felt her legs give beneath her, and suddenly she was palms-down against the freezing ground.

At the crunch of footsteps she forced herself off her hands and knees.

"It's me," the colonel whispered. "What'd you find?"

She opened her mouth to answer and held the cigarette butt out dumbly.

"They're here."

"We need a plan, a way to get in," she said.

The colonel lifted his gun and checked their backs. "How many do you think there are?"

"I'm guessing Kirov would bring at least two others, so at least three."

"We can do three."

She didn't dare contradict him. They had to. She took a quick look around and motioned them toward the side of the house, away from the front door. They moved slowly, Cody leading. Her vision was better and she was in better shape, but the colonel stayed right behind her, only the ragged hiss of his breath indicating he was there.

They edged along the side of the house until they reached a lighted window. She motioned for him to stop and she ducked low, moving past the window and then lifting herself to peer in the far corner.

The living room was bright, the familiar fireplace in the center, two large brown leather sofas forming an "L" in front of it. An ornate carved table looked strangely out of place between the two casual couches. She recognized the table, though. It was like the one that had been in the edge of the first photo. This was the right place. But there was no one in sight.

A door somewhere slammed and Cody dropped. She heard no voices, only the low thud of boots on the deck above them. The colonel swung back around the corner to take a look and she waited, pressed against the house. Where was Ryan?

The colonel came back and motioned her toward him. It was obvious he'd found something, and she half ran, half slid down toward the back of the house to catch up.

When she reached him, she saw that he'd found

access to the basement. She moved toward the open door in near silence, the sound of boots still echoing from above.

As she followed the colonel into the darkness, she had to hold herself back from calling Ryan's name. Oh, please. Please let this be him.

The colonel was moving in front of her and she watched his shadow cross the room. Then there was a thud and he tripped. Something clattered and the colonel groaned.

The steps above halted in a hard thunk and then the deck door squeaked open.

"He's coming," she whispered. "Colonel?"

"I'm here. There's something here, on the ground."

Suddenly they were flooded in light. Stunned, Cody was thrown off balance. She caught herself and blinked hard.

Boots were clattering across the floor, getting closer.

Her pulse was speeding. Her vision cleared and she found the colonel, who was staring at the ground.

"Come on—" she started to say as she focused in on the object in front of him.

At first all she saw was a denim leg, and she immediately thought it was Ryan. The image knocked the wind from her, and her stomach convulsed as she made a panicked scan up the leg to the rest of the body. He was too big. She focused on an unfamiliar face. A man.

He'd been shot in the head twice. "Oh, God," she whispered.

The colonel had her arm and was pulling her back toward the door.

"Wait." She tried to pull herself free, scanning the room for others. "I have to see. Is he here?"

"No. It's only him. Only the man." He gave her a firmer pull until her feet loosened and she moved toward the door.

The sound of boots came thundering down the stairs.

Cody was out the door when her jacket caught. She was jerked backward but the colonel tore her free. He had her hand and he was pulling her toward the trees, away from the house. Her mind was spinning like a top, but only one thought came out: Where was Ryan?

They reached the trees and the colonel pulled her behind one. Together they listened as the basement door swung open. Someone cursed in Russian and the sound made her knees tremble beneath her.

They didn't move. It was too far to run for the hillside. They'd never make it back to the car without at least one of them getting hit.

She listened, her heart a deafening drumbeat. Behind it, though, every sound was perfectly clear.

The Russian's boots crunched in the snow, his breath had a wheezing tick, and she heard the click of the safety releasing on his gun. Change jingled in his pocket, the sound getting closer.

She pulled herself away from the colonel and turned toward the sound. Her own gun raised, she waited until the clinking and clicking were almost on top of them. Then, sucking in as much air as her lungs could hold, she swung her weapon out and shot, moving in an arc of bullets from left to right.

One bullet fired back and then she heard the distinct thump of a body hitting the frozen ground.

The colonel looked out, and then he touched her

back the way a father would his daughter. "Nice shot."

She didn't answer. Instead she released the empty magazine into the snow and pulled a full one from her pocket, sliding it into place. She held the gun in front of her as she moved toward the Russian. She'd gotten him square in the chest and the wound was still pumping blood when she pried his gun from his hand and, ignoring his open eyes, moved past him to the house. She hesitated at the perimeter, knowing the others would be coming soon.

The colonel followed. They'd only gotten past the edge of the basement toward the side of the house when she felt a rush of cold air behind her. Something was wrong, she thought as the cold sliced through her thin jacket.

She spun back, the gun in front of her. But she knew immediately that the weapon would do her no good.

The colonel's expression was sheer terror. Behind him, one of Oskar Kirov's thugs had what Cody recognized immediately to be a Glock pressed to his head. She thought about what the chances were that she could fire over the colonel's head, but she knew they were less than slim.

"Megan Riggs, I suppose," he said in an accent that Cody heard in her worst dreams. She didn't answer.

"You drop your gun if you want your friend to have another breath."

Cody ignored the colonel's shaking head. She had a chance to get out of there with the colonel and Florence. She owed him that.

"Don't—" he started, but the Russian butted him with the gun.

Her mind flashed to Travis Landon sitting in the car, but he wasn't coming to help them. She knew that much.

Cody tossed her gun out into the snow by the dead Russian, watching it land. She memorized its location in hopes that she'd have a chance to come back for it later.

Chapter 36

The colonel shook his head. Cody had made a mistake. She should have gone on. "Forget about me," he whispered, his eyes watching Cody.

"Move, old man," the rough accent barked from behind.

The colonel looked in the snow where Cody's gun had landed and tried to nod at her to go for it. Once they were inside, their chances would be nil. But Cody had already conceded.

He thought about Florence in the car and wondered if he'd have a chance to see her again. She slept soundly, but if she woke, she might panic at Landon. God, he hoped that jackass didn't leave her. If she got out of the car and wandered, she'd freeze to death before anyone could find her.

Roni crossed his mind. All this time he'd never called her, and when he was finally set to see her, he'd gotten himself ready to be killed.

As the Russian motioned Cody toward the basement, he knocked the colonel on the back of the head. Before he could touch the spot, though, the man knocked him again and snarled something in Russian. The colonel didn't speak a word of Russian, but he knew a derogatory term when he heard one. And he'd been hearing those for all of his sixty years.

The Russian pushed him again and the colonel upped his pace, remembering his first drill sergeant in the Marine Corps. It had been the 1960s and the sergeant hadn't liked black folks much. Hadn't called them black folks though. He'd been called a nigger back then, probably more than not. The colonel had survived Sergeant Bennick and he would survive this asshole, too. Damn if he was going to give up before he had a chance to make things right with Roni.

As they headed up the basement stairs, the colonel leaned forward and whispered to Cody, "Hope you got a plan."

"Shut up," the Russian shouted, ramming his gun into the colonel's back.

The jab hit him square in the kidney and the colonel lost his footing with pain. But he forced himself to pretend he'd just tripped, and as he lifted himself up the last few steps, he blinked away the agony in his back. He was definitely too old for combat. Where the hell were the police or the FBI?

They passed through the doorway to the main level. The colonel watched Cody touch her back. At first he thought maybe she was in pain, too, but the gesture caused a strange bump to form in the back of her shirt. She quickly straightened it and moved into the main room.

She glanced over her shoulder and he met her gaze and knew immediately that she had another weapon. He suppressed a smile and hoped he got the chance to blow off the head of one of these mobsters, then reminded himself to stay calm until he had the chance.

From the small lump he saw in the back of her shirt, he guessed it was something without much firepower. But it was something nonetheless. And that was something more than he had.

Cody crossed the room and called for Ryan.

"He's not here," the Russian said. "Sasha," he yelled, adding something in Russian that the colonel assumed informed his colleague that he'd caught them.

Cody launched herself at the Russian, and the colonel saw her reach for the gun. "Where is he?"

The colonel grabbed her arm and held her from drawing the gun until the other man arrived. He didn't want her giving up their trump card too soon.

Cody clawed at the colonel to get to the Russian. "Where's my son?"

The Russian smiled and the colonel had to hold himself back almost as hard as he did Cody.

"Where is he?"

"Gone."

"Gone where?"

The Russian shrugged.

The colonel saw that Cody had reached the breaking point. In a rush of anger and certainly fear, she tore through his grip and reached for her back.

He screamed to her to stop, to wait, but he couldn't hold back the torrent. The colonel fell backward, unable to hold on to her.

As she broke his hold, the Russian laughed at them. He pointed to the colonel, who was trying to pull himself off the floor, and then looked back at Cody. His head thrown back, he almost missed her drawing her gun.

His smile faltered at the sight, but his own weapon was close at hand. He raised it.

The colonel was barely back on his feet. He took a running jump and launched himself at the end of the barrel, driving it toward the floor.

The next few seconds were a blur of ringing shots and curses. He heard his own voice in the mix as though he were trying to speak in very slow motion. But what came out wasn't words at all. It was a groan as he felt the searing heat of what felt like a dagger piercing his thigh.

As he collapsed, he caught sight of the Russian falling back. The man reached for his neck, which spurted blood like water from a fountain. It was a bright red that looked too fantastic to be real.

Cody sank beside the colonel, the gun still outstretched in her hands. "Oh, God. Ryan. Ryan," she whispered.

The colonel put an arm around her and pulled her toward him. He glanced at his leg and was amazed to find there was no knife sticking out from his skin. He realized he must have been shot. "Cody. There's another one around here."

She gripped the gun and stared at the dead Russian. "Where the hell is Kirov? Jesus, where is he?"

He knew what she was thinking. She'd killed her source to Ryan. She straightened her back and shifted her gaze off the dead man. She kept her back to the colonel and scanned the room, the gun in front of her.

The colonel looked up at the empty room and wondered where the other Russian was. Surely he'd heard the noise. At that moment, he caught a flash of motion through the window to the deck.

He pulled Cody down just as the window exploded toward them. Shots rang out and he heard one ping against the stone fireplace they'd seen in the picture of Ryan. Another made a dull thud as it sank into the Sheetrock wall. The Russian's Glock was within reach, and the colonel shifted himself onto his belly to grab it.

As soon as he did, he was back in Vietnam. He saw the thick, lush grass and smelled the heavy scent of burning opium. The bugs covered his face like dirt, and he no longer even tried to swat them away.

He forced himself to take aim on the dark spot in the distance. He fired once, then twice, then three times. He heard the rattle of fire back and then it was silent.

When he moved, Cody was pulling herself up beside him, silent tears streaming down her cheeks. The gun was tucked under his arm. On the deck, he could see the body of another Russian. The gun burned in his hand and he pushed it away.

"Cody," he begged.

She shook her head. "I'm okay."

"He's not dead, Cody."

She didn't respond.

"He's not. He can't be. Not yet."

She looked up and nodded, the tears on her cheeks like tiny stripes.

He'd never seen anyone look so vulnerable.

"The snowmobile," she whispered, her eyes wide with hope.

The colonel nodded. "It had to be him."

She put her hand on his leg and he winced at the rush of misery that followed. She looked down. "You're shot."

"I'll be okay. Go. Search the house."

Without a backward glance, she got up and ran. He closed his eyes and took measured breaths, waiting for her to return. He focused on every sound. It was too quiet. When he opened his eyes, she was standing before him.

He didn't need to ask. He knew she hadn't found Ryan.

As she knelt beside him, he watched as the tough agent took over again. Leaving the gun, she pushed herself to her feet and pulled a flannel shirt off a nearby chair. Using the sleeves as a tourniquet, she bound his leg and put two pillows under his knee to keep him from losing too much blood. As she looked over her work, the colonel grabbed her hand.

"Go find that boy."

"I don't want you bleeding out on me."

He pushed her hand away. "I saw another snowmobile out there. You take that and find Ryan. And then you get back here."

She looked around the room and handed him the Russian's Glock.

He took her hand and gave it a tug so her eyes met his. "I want you to get the hell out of here. Now!"

She held his gaze and then nodded. Then, tucking her weapon at the back of her pants, she was off in a sprint.

He heard the back door slam closed and he fought off a wave of panic. Using his hands, he dragged himself backward, stopping to pull the Glock along, until his back was flat against the fireplace. Then, setting the gun in his lap, he shifted the pillows under his knee, checked the bleeding, which seemed to have stopped for the moment, and sat back to wait.

He hadn't been much of a praying man, but he'd done it in the last war and he'd gotten out of that one alive. Maybe he was pressing his luck, but he figured it was worth a try.

Lord, Jesus. Watch over Miss Cody. Find her Ryan and get them back here so I can go get my Florence and take her to see her baby. She's been sick, Lord, but she never did anything to deserve that. Maybe you're punishing me, and I surely deserve it. But don't punish Florence. And Roni.

And as he pressed his back into the cold stone and felt the warm thick, blood ooze across the wound, one thought crossed his mind: Goddamn it, I am going to die.

Just then he heard the stomping of feet on the stairs. He hoisted the gun up off the ground and waited for the war to begin anew.

Chapter 37

The snowmobile bounced through the hard- and soft-packed snow like a Jet Ski in the ocean, and Cody could feel her nausea rising over the crest of her gut and crashing up into her throat. It was almost pitch-black, and it was all she could do to focus on the tracks of the other snowmobile. The moon came in slices of light, which mostly served to make the headlight less effective against the bright snow.

Each time she ran into a patch of moonlight, she had to pause to let her eyes adjust to the new brightness before she could find the other trail again. The wind had picked up, and the path, which had been relatively clear in the untracked snow, was starting to be covered by the fresh snow the wind blew across the snowmobile's tracks. Panic nipped at her chest, and she drove it back and kept moving.

The snowmobile was a new sensation, too. Her life used to be filled with new experiences. In the past five years, she'd done very little that was new to her. Keeping Ryan safe, guarded had been her primary activity. She'd become soft, she realized. After what she guessed was a half mile, she had finally mastered the pressure on the throttle. Still, each time the machine buffeted against a hard pack of snow, Cody bumped halfway off, sometimes even losing hold before righting herself.

She concentrated on Ryan, trying to will him to stay strong. If he'd been on the snowmobile she'd heard, then she figured he'd been out here twenty, maybe twenty-five minutes at the least. But without the proper clothes, that could be forever.

A million questions flashed across her mind. How many had him? Where was Kirov? She saw Ryan's tiny body sandwiched between two giant Russians and thought that at least he wouldn't be cold. The wind whipped through the thin fleece she wore and she had to alternately open and close her fists to prevent them from cramping. Mostly, though, she was just feeling numb. She understood how people decided that freezing to death would be better than going by fire. She thought of the irony of Kirov's first attempt. Maybe he would get her by ice.

Her chest tightened and she felt the tears cloud her eyes. She allowed herself to think no further.

She swiped her face with the back of her hand, the scratch of the frozen wool against her cheeks a welcome distraction from the self-pity. Her focus needed to be somewhere else. The colonel and Florence crossed her mind, and she prayed someone from the police or the Bureau was there by now.

She could be the only one left up here before too long, and she wasn't sure she could handle the number of deaths. No, it wasn't going to be that way.

She pushed the throttle down with a solid grip and the mobile jolted forward. She clutched the handles as the machine bumped along the road. As she started to make a turn, she caught sight of a small set of tracks in the snow. At first she assumed they were animal tracks, but as she slid by one, she realized it was too long and narrow to be any animal she could think of. She stopped and leaned down, setting her own foot beside one.

It was smaller than her own print, but the same basic shape. That would be about right for Ryan. She felt her heart dance. She looked at the next and then the next, searching for a bit of tread that hadn't been erased by the wind. The search was futile, and Cody knew that even if she saw a tread, she wouldn't know if it was Ryan's. But the shoe size was right, and she couldn't help but be encouraged.

She looked around and felt her chest tighten. Where was he? Had he been let go here in the dark to freeze to death? Oh, Jesus.

"Ryan," she screamed.

She paused, listening to the silence. She got off the snowmobile, following the footprints. There were only ten or twelve steps before the snowmobile track crossed them again. She pulled herself up and turned full circle. Had he dropped something, given her some clue?

On her knees, she pushed the snow left and right. "Ryan," she screamed again.

The silence was even louder than what she'd heard before. Was he somewhere nearby, hearing her, but unable to call back?

As she got to her feet, she heard something.

She halted, staying as quiet as she could.

The sound was gone. She turned toward the other snowmobile's path. It had come from that way, hadn't it? Was she hallucinating?

She shook her head and brushed her knees off, running back to the snowmobile and getting on. No.

She had heard something. She was sure of it. Someone was out there.

It had to be Ryan. She revved the engine high and bent forward over the handles. "Ryan," she screamed again.

As she pushed the throttle down harder, she thought she heard another response. She pressed on, ignoring the lashing her pelvic bone took as she was tossed across the seat.

In the distance, the edge of the lake appeared, and she caught the tracks leading that way in her headlight. She squinted at the snow up ahead, hoping for a sign of the other machine or machines. She wondered if she was even following the right track. She shook the thought free. Kirov would want her to think that way. She would not give in to him.

She rode the accelerator as she neared the lake. Surely it would be easier to see him in the more open landscape. She ignored the tracks momentarily and pressed the accelerator as far as it went. Large white flecks had just started to fall again.

She glanced back down to check the tracks and caught sight of a log in her path. The other snowmobile had gone right, so she braked and turned right hard.

She was too slow and the machine caught the edge of the log, making a loud crack. Cody flew off and felt the log smack her in the ear. She rolled over, breathless.

Her vision blurred and there was a clanging in her ear. She struggled onto all fours and let out a choking sob.

She pushed herself to her feet and stumbled to the snowmobile. The left front of the machine was lodged against the end of the log, and Cody fumbled to turn off the engine.

Her feet braced against the log, she tried to push the snowmobile free. It was stubborn and weighed a ton. With her face to the machine, she squinted in the dark to see if there was a reverse mode. The seconds ticked by and her pulse grew faster with each one. Leveraging herself off the log again, she gave the snowmobile three hard shoves until it finally came loose. Jumping back on, she revved the engine and hit the accelerator. She drove recklessly, trying to make up for lost time and having no idea how far behind she even was.

At the edge of the lake, she forced herself to slow to scan the far side of the lake. Be calm. She had to believe that if there were others, they would be using their headlights. But it was nearly pitch-black and she might not see them in the distance. Along the right side of the lake, she could make out the homes that they had passed on their way in, but they were all darkened. There was no sign of anything.

She sped up. The pain on the side of her head had dulled, but she felt the sensation of warm moisture there. She touched the finger of her glove to her head and then brought it in front of her face.

Catching the reddish tint in the light, she knew was bleeding. She ran her whole hand across the wounded area and looked at her glove again. The entire surface of it was red. She wondered how long she would last out here. As she wiped her hand on a patch of snow that had formed on the side of the snowmobile, she caught a flash of light in the distance.

She looked up, slowing down as she tried to focus on its origin.

She caught it again and realized it was a headlight cutting through the trees on the far side of the lake. She shut off her own headlight and pushed forward, using just the light of the moon as she tried to see how many there were.

The headlight pointed straight at her, and Cody hunched behind the machine as she watched. For a moment all she could see was the round light of the headlight. Then the machine turned away from the lake and she saw the side of it. The driver was a man, she was sure, and he had something in front of him. It could have been a satchel or an animal, but she dared to hope it was Ryan. In another second, the snowmobile cut behind a tree and was gone.

Wind picked up bursts of snow and tossed it in her eyes. It was gritty and dry and felt more like sand than snow. She brushed it off her face and ignored the burn it left.

She moved forward, still without her headlight. The tracks she followed edged the lake now, and she felt herself tremble at the thought of the frozen water, how fast hypothermia would hit. Ryan was a strong swimmer, she told herself. He loved it like his father always had.

She kept an eye on how far she was from the pebbled shore while also watching for the headlight in the distance.

She cut her engine and listened to the silence. Only the wind and the water broke the stillness. Panic tightening in her chest, she started the engine and moved on again. She drew her gun from the edge of her pants and tucked it between her legs.

She circled a small group of trees and studied the

darkness for shadows. She had the sensation of being followed and yet she saw no evidence of anyone else. She crossed her own path and made another circle and still she saw nothing.

No one was behind her, she told herself. She pressed on and moved more quickly, bouncing along at a pace that she knew would be impossible for someone on foot. When she reached the far corner of the lake, she made the turn and looked up ahead. She was within one hundred yards or so of where she had seen the other snowmobile. But now, looking into the distance, she saw nothing.

She scanned the hills, searching for a sign of where the other vehicle had gone. The tracks, though somewhat scattered by the wind, were still in front of her. She followed them, then halted, seeing the trail turn and then what looked like more tracks crossing back on themselves.

She turned back to look for an alternate trail in the other direction but saw none. She continued along, noticing how there appeared to be two sets of tracks together. Although they continued, she couldn't tell if the two sets were from two different vehicles or the same one crossing back on itself.

"Damn," she cursed.

The path turned a corner and then disappeared. She searched for a new set of tracks, but the snow in front of her looked untouched.

She shut the engine off again and screamed at the top of her lungs, "Ryan!"

Breathless, she stood in the dark, panting and on the verge of tears.

"Mommy!" The voice came from behind her, but she recognized it. It was Ryan.

She almost ran toward it. "Ryan, Mommy's coming," she screamed, not caring who heard her. "I'm coming." Ecstatic, she actually choked out a laugh. He was alive; her baby was alive!

She twisted the key and hit the accelerator as fast as her frozen fingers would move. She ran the snowmobile in a tight circle and pointed it back toward the cabin.

"Ryan!" she screamed again.

And as she waited for the response, the dark night was filled with the unmistakable crack of a gunshot and the almost simultaneous scream of an eight-year-old boy.

Chapter 38

His blood was like brilliant rubies against the whiteness of the snow. It caught a reflection off the headlight, and he could see the sparkle of the snow beneath the red. Even in the dark, the color was vibrant. All the colors were. The light glowed amber against the brown of the tree trunks. The green of the pines was as rich as he imagined an Irish field would be. She was there. He'd heard her yell and she was close. He would have them both.

He felt like an ox and a lion and a tiger all mixed together. He was strong and fierce and cunning. He'd done it all on his own.

He slapped his thigh and felt his belly shake as he laughed. What amazed him most was that he didn't ache. For the first time in months, he could sit up straight and not hurt. He wasn't nauseous. He felt magnificent. What a perfect way to go. He was ready.

Only one thing left to do. And that was entirely within his power. There were things he would have changed. There were always things that one would change. But overall, he had it good. He'd had strong blood—fierce blood—and he'd never let it be jeopardized. He would go to the grave with his power and his dignity. He would not soon be forgotten.

Oskar thought about blood—his own. It seeped down his hand. But he was used to spilled blood. He had lived that way. And he knew he would die that way. His blood had been spilled through Viktor, then Feliks, and finally Dmitri. Now his time had come. But Megan and the boy had to be first.

He watched the outline of her snowmobile make its way closer. He had nothing to lose. Let her get close. Let her get close enough to watch.

Oskar lifted the gun and aimed it again, just for practice. The first shot had only been for show. He'd wanted Megan Riggs to know the danger. And he'd wanted the boy to be scared. He'd succeeded at both.

His wound wasn't lethal. He'd caught his hand on a tree limb. The blood was like borscht, the thick beet soup his mother had made, and he savored the texture of it on his fingers. When he'd been young, he had eaten the soup with his fingers. But only when his mother wasn't watching.

Still, the blood was exciting. He imagined himself a great warrior, coming to the final battle. And then it would be off to heaven. His father had always told him he would go to heaven. "Why, Papa?" he'd asked.

"Because even God wouldn't put a Kirov in hell," his father had answered with the slur of vodka on his tongue. Kirov took another swig of his own supply. He tipped the flask back and felt the liquid burn against the back of his tongue and smolder a path to his gut.

He pressed the accelerator and moved the snowmobile toward the boy, who had only made it ten steps before sinking into the snow. When he was close, he reached down and pulled him up by the back of his collar.

The boy swung his hands and Kirov drew his gun and smacked it hard against the boy's head. "Stop it or I'll shoot you here."

The boy sobbed louder, collapsing into the snow. His limp body was even harder to lift than when he was struggling, and Kirov considered for a moment that it had been a mistake not to go for the woman. At least her, he could have enjoyed. The kid was like killing a puppy. It wouldn't feel good until it was over and he could admire his handiwork.

"Get on," Kirov commanded when the boy's face finally emerged from the snow.

The boy hesitated but Kirov lifted the gun as though to smack him again.

"You getting on?"

The boy nodded, his eyes crumpled, his bottom lip pushed out. Leaning forward, the boy moved close, keeping his head low as though searching for something in the snow.

Kirov reached out and smacked him. "Keep your head up," he yelled in Russian.

The boy began to sob again.

The urge to strike had reminded him momentarily of his boys, and Oskar scolded himself for getting soft. He reached around with his bloodied hand and grabbed the boy's face. "Stop crying," he screamed.

The boy saw the blood and began to shake, fighting not to cry despite the fright.

Then, reaching for the boy's hand, he jerked him back and forced him onto the machine. Cutting his headlight, Kirov listened in the dark for the hum of the other machine.

The boy made a high-pitched whimpering noise and Kirov warned him to shut up. Over the boy's struggles to be quiet, Kirov could hear Megan Riggs's snowmobile approach.

"That's your mommy," Kirov whispered. "She's coming to save you."

The boy met his gaze, his expression fierce.

Kirov laughed until the pain was too much. "Shall we go and meet her?" He restarted his engine softly and pulled forward without turning on his headlight.

"Mommy, it's a trap," the boy yelled.

Kirov slapped the butt of the gun into the boy's head and started toward the far end of the lake.

"I'm coming," he heard Megan yell for Ryan.

But the boy was sobbing too hard to respond.

"Oh, yes, Ryan. Mommy's coming, but she's not going to be able to help you. By the time she sees you, it'll be too late."

The boy put his head down in the space between the handlebars and was coughing in choked attempts to stop his crying. Oskar watched up ahead and tried to decide how best to do it. The end should be dramatic—clean and final but dramatic.

He heard Megan Riggs call again and started to veer toward the lake. But he had second thoughts. Maybe he'd try something else first—just a little more play before the end.

He saw a thick tree about a hundred yards up. In the darkness, he couldn't tell clearly if there were obstacles in his path or not.

Megan Riggs was getting closer. He could hear her calling out.

"Keep quiet, if you want to live," he warned the boy. Though, of course, he would not live. He paused, moving slowly until he was sure Megan was close enough to see them.

Then he revved the throttle and pointed the snow-mobile toward the tree. With a deep laugh that shot agony through him, he pushed the accelerator as far as it would go and swayed backward as the snow-mobile headed straight for the tree.

Ryan's head popped up and he let out a piercing scream as the tree drew close.

Oskar hadn't felt this good in months.

Chapter 39

All that mattered was Ryan. His scream punctured her like a sharp blade, and she pressed the accelerator flat to the handlebar and felt the machine jolt forward beneath her.

She saw Kirov's snowmobile veer sideways, and for a moment she thought they were headed into the lake. She hunkered down over her own machine and kept her eyes straight ahead, squinting in the dark. She thought she heard the wail of sirens in the distance, but couldn't be sure. Get there. Get to him. She could overtake Oskar Kirov, but she needed to get close enough. And she wouldn't aim a gun until Ryan was out of the way.

She was gaining on them. The moon reflected on the lake and from her angle, the light made them momentarily visible. She called out to Ryan and he peered back at her. He started to lift his arm to wave, but Oskar smacked him.

His face crumpled in fear as he sank back out of her sight.

Anger rose like hot air until she could have taken off like a rocket. She tightened her legs around the snowmobile, steeling herself to go as fast as it could.

Oskar and Ryan were less than ten yards ahead, but Oskar was picking up the pace. He made a sharp left turn around a tree and headed straight up the hill.

Cody had to brake hard to keep from missing the turn herself. The snowmobile skidded right. She punched the gas and it slipped left. She let out a tiny gasp as she slid toward the water. It was still a few feet away, but she hated the thought of it.

She flashed her headlight back on for a moment and sped up the hill after them. What could she tell Oskar to stop him? There was nothing. If he didn't already know that Jennifer had killed Dmitri, she didn't want to bring it up now. She had no leverage. According to what she knew about him, Oskar Kirov had nothing to live for but revenge. And he probably thought he was about to get it. Her fists clenched with impatience.

She drew a deep icy breath and blew it out in a rush of white steam. All she could do now was keep up.

Even after less than a half hour, Cody's back ached from hovering down to block off the cold. Oskar had to be uncomfortable, too, she told herself.

"Come on," she whispered. Her thoughts shifted to Ryan's light shirt and jeans. He had to be freezing. She crossed it from her mind. He had body heat. He'd be fine. "Just hang in there, buddy."

Oskar spun the snowmobile around a bush and she heard it scrape as it hit something. The engine made a choking noise and something else crunched. But it picked back up again. He turned hard and Ryan let out a scream.

"Stay strong," she whispered, willing him to keep quiet.

Oskar laughed and the urge to ram him sprinted through her. A red light caught her eye and she scanned the dashboard on her snowmobile. She squinted at the red shape, but she knew what it was even before she made out a small flaming gas tank.

"Shit."

She tried not to press down on the gas so much, but she knew her time was growing short. She had to push Oskar to make a move.

She willed herself to stay calm though she felt the prick of tears against her eyelids. She could do this. She had to. Ryan was counting on her. And she was not going to let him down.

She punched the gas and moved up on Kirov until she was almost beside him.

He spun right and stopped. Before she could stop, she'd sped by. She looped a bigger circle and came up behind him again.

She could make out the details on Ryan's face. He was almost close enough to touch.

"Finally, Megan Riggs wants to play," Kirov said, gaining speed.

"Mommy," Ryan called.

Cody's voice caught in her throat.

Ryan reached out to her.

Cody reached back. "It's okay, baby."

Oskar hit his brakes and Cody flew by them again. She turned hard, skidding in the snow as she did. Tears fell down her cheeks, burning against her frozen face.

Cody came up beside them again, but Oskar was moving faster and she could see his dashboard. His red light wasn't on. She would be out of gas first.

She reached for Ryan again.

Oskar snaked his arm around Ryan's waist. "Get too close and I'll throw him into a tree," he warned.

Ryan whimpered.

Cody pulled her hand back. "This won't do you any good, Kirov."

He didn't respond. He kept moving in circles, and she realized they were actually making their way back toward the cabin.

She scanned the darkness for signs of someone else, but saw nothing. What was he doing? What was his plan?

He curved left and she lost him again. She hit her brakes and turned hard, slipping across a patch of ice as she started up again.

Her engine sputtered and died.

"Mommy!" Ryan called.

She jammed the key in the ignition and felt the engine vibrate below her. She pushed the gas and moved forward. The trees blocked the moonlight and all she saw was a patch of blackness.

"Ryan," she screamed. "Call to me."

"Mom!" he called back, but his voice was muffled and she couldn't be certain if it was because Kirov was holding him or if they'd already gotten that far away.

She felt panic seize her and she pushed the gas harder, calling again.

There was no response.

"Ryan!" she screamed, her throat burning.

"Mommy." His voice was right in front of her. She switched the headlight on and spotted them immediately. They were down the hill, and Kirov moved in a straight path.

She sped up.

Kirov had stopped. He was completely still. Ryan

appeared to be struggling, but he couldn't seem to free himself.

Cody thought maybe something had happened. Maybe Kirov had suffered a heart attack. She prayed it was that.

She was within ten feet of him when she saw Kirov's face light up. There was a log between them and Kirov had a clear path. If she went for Ryan, she was sure he'd get away.

She saw the red light glaring up from her machine. How much longer could she go?

"Say good-bye," he said.

She scanned the area for another person, but there was no one. She looked at his hands for a weapon of some sort, but one hand held Ryan's chest and the other was planted firmly on the handlebar.

She looked out in the darkness again.

What was she missing?

"Kirov, there's no one here. No one can help you."

"That's true," he agreed.

She frowned.

His smile grew. "But no one can help you, either." His accent seemed thicker and she watched him pull something silver from his jacket.

She reached for her gun, but Kirov laughed. "You won't shoot little Ryan, would you?"

Ryan's eyes widened.

"You're fine, baby," she said.

Kirov pulled out a flask and put it to his mouth.

She pulled her gun up and aimed it at him. She could make this shot. She would not hit Ryan. She could free them both right now.

"Mommy," Ryan said, watching her.

"It's okay," she whispered. "Don't move." She cocked her gun.

In a lash of his arm, Kirov threw the flask at her. Startled, Cody ducked.

She heard the rev of an engine.

Ryan screamed.

Kirov's snowmobile gunned straight ahead. She pressed on the gas but the engine was dead. She turned the ignition off and then cranked the key. Nothing happened.

"Come on." She cursed, trying it again.

The engine made a sputtering noise, then died.

Kirov's engine whined louder.

She turned her headlight off and tried again. Still, the engine didn't turn over. She was out of gas. Panic clogged her throat. Think. Flipping on the headlight again, she squinted into the night.

Her heart racing, she jumped off the snowmobile and ran toward them, tucking the gun down the front of her pants. Gravity helped propel her. She fought to keep up.

Ryan screamed out again.

Oskar paused as though to tease her.

Cody sprinted toward them, the snow thick and heavy like weights around her ankles.

"I think we're even now—a son for a son. Goodbye, Megan Riggs."

She pumped her arms and ran toward them. "Ryan!" she screamed, her legs moving faster than she could control them.

Kirov revved his engine again and she could see Ryan's arm reaching for her.

"I'm coming."

"Too late," Kirov said when she was almost ten yards from them.

He hit the accelerator and the snowmobile took off.

Cody kept running, trying to focus on what was in front of them.

The form took shape slowly as the light from the moon reflected on its shimmering surface. Water.

The lake! They were heading toward the lake.

Cody gasped. "No. Ryan, no!"

She heard Ryan scream and then all she heard was the heavy splash of the machine hitting the water, her son with it.

Chapter 40

Water. It burned through her brain like fire. Still, she hesitated for only a brief moment before she threw her gloves in the snow and then her jacket, tearing it from her chest as she sprinted.

"Ryan," she screamed.

There was no answer. She strained to hear the sounds of water thrashing, but it was silent.

She reached the water's edge and searched for movement. Oh, God.

"Ryan!" she screamed again. She heard a gasp in the darkness. "Ryan, where are you?"

Her throat burned and the cold shot through her thin top. And yet, as she scanned the water, sweat began to line her brow.

She didn't let herself think. With a running jump, she plunged into the water.

The cold stole her breath. She came to the surface, every part of her body shrieking in pain. She felt herself struggle to stay afloat. She was going to drown. She had no air. There was no air.

Ryan. She focused on her son. Her breath came back and it was all she could do to remain above the surface. There wasn't time to rest. "Ryan," she called again.

From behind her, she heard the slightest whimper. She splashed toward the sound. Each time her arm hit the water, she felt a new wave of icy chill.

"Ryan!"

Something moved behind her and she spun around to reach for it.

A heavy hand reached back.

"It's too late," Kirov said. "He's been under too long."

Cody spun around in a tight circle, searching the darkness for Ryan. The moon cast a yellow glow on the water's surface, but there was no sign of him. "No," she screamed, lashing out at the water.

When she turned back to Kirov, he launched himself at her. His hands pressed on her shoulders. He dragged her down.

Her head went under. She struggled to surface. She found a small patch of air and sucked it in before he pushed her down again.

She kicked out, but he was gone. She drove her arms down and buoyed to the surface. She felt a stirring in the water and tried to move away, but Kirov grabbed her again.

Her hair in his fist, he pulled her down. Her eyes were open as she tried to twist and escape from Kirov's grasp. She spun, arms flailing, in search of Ryan. He couldn't be gone. She shouted his name under water.

Her skin was numb, and even the sharp pain on her scalp eased. She pulled a leg up and kicked out as hard as she could. She hit something and the weight on her loosened. She pushed herself away and struggled to the surface. Gasping and choking, she inhaled water and flailed to clear her chest.

"Mom."

She heard the soft whisper in the dark and shot toward it. "Ryan, where are you?"

There was no answer.

Then a short cough.

"Ryan!" she called again.

She felt a current behind her and kicked her foot out, but hit nothing. Kirov was lurking somewhere and she spun around to look for him. "Ryan. I'm here, baby." She felt her chest heave. She was exhausted, her lungs burning and her arms aching. She wanted desperately to stop moving, but knew she couldn't. She had to find Ryan.

"Here, Mom."

Sobs choked her as she made out the shape of Ryan in the distance. "Stay there, baby. I'm coming."

As she took in a breath and pushed herself forward, she felt something loop around her neck. The air spit from her lungs as she was yanked backward.

She pulled at the chokehold, trying to loosen it.

Kirov was talking behind her, but she couldn't make out his words. They were foreign, or maybe it was her head. She wrapped her fingers beneath what felt like a belt and tried to loosen it.

It yanked tighter and the sky brightened as her oxygen wore out.

Ryan appeared in her view and she could see him coming closer. "No!" she choked out.

Kirov pulled the belt tighter, and Cody kicked herself under the surface to try to force him under, too. There was a rush of heat in her chest as she struggled to breathe and still no slack in the noose.

Cody felt her arms weaken and the belt cut tighter. She shook her head, battling for the energy to fight back. The belt slackened slightly and she heard Kirov groan.

Cody was able to twist free. She hit the surface and saw Ryan on Kirov's back.

Kirov lashed out and struck Ryan across the face.

Ryan fell into the water and Kirov reached out for him.

Cody pulled her fist back and slammed it hard into his head just above his ear. The water slowed the impact but his head was rocked back on his neck, and he disappeared under the water. He caught her leg and tried to pull her down with him.

She kicked herself free. On the surface, she filled her lungs with air. "Ryan," she screamed.

Just as the word was out, she felt Kirov's grasp again. He pressed her shoulder down. She struggled against his weight when she felt his foot in her stomach.

She lost her air and doubled over, letting herself sink lower into the water before swimming away. Even at the surface, she couldn't breathe.

She gasped and choked, sputtering out water as her teeth chattered and she fought to stay afloat. Everything ached, and the weight of her clothing dragged her down. She wanted to quit. God, no. Not yet.

Fighting, she took a stroke toward the middle of the lake when she felt Kirov grab her shirt. He yanked her backward and down under the water.

Just as she surfaced, she saw Ryan swim past. He grabbed at Kirov's hair, trying to get him to let go of her.

Kirov struck backward and pushed Ryan off.

Cody tried to wave him away, but Ryan came back. Her arm slid across her front and her shirt came free from her pants. The metal gun was icy against her belly.

She pulled the gun and tried to remember what she'd once learned about which guns worked underwater. She prayed this was one of them. It was rounded; the bullet should be chambered.

She saw Ryan in front of her and she grabbed his arm and wrenched him away from Kirov.

Kirov was still gripping her, and she lost hold of Ryan. She lifted the gun above the water and pointed it at Kirov's head. The trigger was stiff, but finally released.

She felt the shot's recoil. No pain.

The grip on her disappeared. She gulped fresh air and saw Kirov's body sink below her in the water. She didn't stop to see if he was dead. She searched for Ryan. He couldn't be far. She spun in circles, scanning for his face.

"Ryan," she called softly. He'd been right there. It had been only a moment ago.

There was no answer. In the distance, she could still see the spot where Kirov had gone down. She kept moving, swimming in a circle.

Each second that ticked by made her chest tighter. Her pulse shifted into higher gear until she felt like her torso might explode.

"Ryan!" she screamed to the sky. Sobs loosened and she let them shake her warm. Tears streamed down her cheeks, creating paths of heat on her frozen face.

She saw a glimmer a few feet away. Something moving. She made broad strokes toward it.

She recognized the head, the back of his shirt. It was Ryan. Facedown.

"Oh, God. No!"

She reached out and grabbed his hair, yanking his head back. The sight of his pale face made her scream.

She put her right arm across his chest and under his arm and used the other to drag herself toward shore. She was sobbing and her vision blurred.

She fought to hold herself together, but it was too much. Ryan wasn't moving.

It seemed like forever before she could feel the lake's rocky bottom beneath her feet. The cold battered her, but she ignored it. She dragged Ryan to the shore and sat in the cold snow, pulling him across her lap.

She dipped his head back and opened his airway. Choking back her own sobs, she took a deep breath and forced it into his lungs.

She waited for his response, counting in her head. Nothing. She pushed on his chest with her free hand and then moved her mouth down to give him more air.

The three seconds took forever. And still he didn't move. She laid him on his back on the snow and leaned over him to try again. There was still no response.

She gave him three hard thrusts on his chest.

He lay lifeless.

The water was still.

"No." She sobbed. She was completely alone.

Kirov was dead, but she had never felt so terrified.

She tried another breath and then applied the pressure on Ryan's chest.

His diaphram constricted and his chest jumped.

"Ryan," she shouted. "I'm here, baby. Mommy's here." They were the same words she always said to him every night when she left his room. His whole life.

She studied his body for the slightest flinch and saw nothing further.

Sobbing, she shook him. "Ryan! You come back here." She turned to the sky and cried out. "Goddamn it. You give him back."

She turned her face back to Ryan's and gave him a long, hard breath and then three fast, strong jolts just below his breastbone.

Ryan made a short choking sound and then started to throw up.

Cody let out a startled laugh and turned him on his side, pulling him toward her as he emptied the water from his lungs and stomach.

She felt him breathing and cradled him in her arms. His breath was warm on her cheek.

"Ryan," she whispered. "Please, honey. Can you hear me?"

In the distance, she could hear the sounds of motors getting closer. She didn't look up. All her focus was on Ryan.

"Ryan, it's Mommy. Can you hear me?"

Ryan's eyes flashed open and closed and she felt him shiver in her arms.

He blinked again and she smiled, squeezing him and kissing his neck and head and throat.

"Ryan. Ryan, baby. Can you say something to Mommy?" She paused, waiting. "Please."

Ryan opened his eyes and frowned. He licked his lips and looked around before settling his gaze on her.

"Can you say something, sweetie?" she repeated.

He swallowed and blinked hard before whispering, "It's cold."

Cody laughed and pulled him tighter into her arms. "Oh, thank God. Thank you, God," she said, crying harder than she ever had.

Chapter 41

Mei felt the pressure in her head rising as they curved around the small alpine lake. The voices of the other agents faded in and out like a radio as she concentrated on the slice of moon that reflected on the dark water.

Behind them was a caravan of FBI. Two other cars carried local field agents—one car from Sacramento and another from the San Francisco office. They'd borrowed whoever the offices could lend. They had no idea how many Russians or who else might be in the cabin when they got there, or what the body count might look like. She tried to focus on something else.

"They shot that bodyguard movie here," someone up front said.

"What bodyguard movie?"

"Yeah, the Kevin Costner one," Jack Bernadini said.

"I heard they actually put some big hot tub under the water for when he jumped in."

"Wimp," Kyler Wisenor cracked.

"Hell, no. You know how cold it is out there?" someone else countered. "Freeze your nuts off!"

Mei felt Andy tap on her shoulder. "You okay?"

She glanced over at him without turning her head away from the water. "Just thinking."

"About Jennifer?"

She thought about the news that Jennifer hadn't made it. Her parents and sister had arrived, but she'd never regained consciousness. She hadn't really been thinking about Jennifer. Her death was sad, but Mei was clinging to the hope that something good would come of this trip.

"Mei?"

She turned to Andy. "I'm sorry. I was thinking."

"Maybe we shouldn't have brought you," he whispered.

She shook her head. "Don't say that. I'm fine. I'm tired, but I want to be here. I need it. I just need a little time to think while we're getting there." She spoke firmly, hoping he would understand her plea for silence.

In the darkness of the car, he leaned forward and wrapped his fingers in hers. He didn't say anything else to her. Instead, he leaned forward to block the view of their hand-holding and continued to join in on the conversation, which had now turned to a comparison between the characters Kevin Costner played in *Bull Durham* and *Tin Cup*.

She let his hand cover hers, feeling the chill dissipate. She still watched the lake, anxious to be there, to know. And equally anxious to go right back to the airport and get on the plane home.

Her thoughts drifted to how things would be at the office without Jennifer. She'd go through some mandatory counseling for the loss of a partner; then she'd get someone new for a while, probably more tenured, just to make sure she was doing okay.

Andy squeezed her hand. And Andy would be there, she hoped. That would be different.

The next time she surfaced from her own thoughts, the road had become rougher and the car's headlights were off. Andy let go of her hand and everyone in the car seemed to be shifting about.

"We're there?"

"We think so. The house Travis Landon owns is that one there." Jack Bernadini pointed to a large, shingled cabin with dark trim up on the hillside. It was the only house in the area with any lights on.

Mei pulled her holster off the floor and strapped it across her shoulders. She checked the gun and unsnapped the leather hold on it. "Looks like someone's home."

"Looks can be deceiving," Wisenor cracked.

Mei didn't answer but listened as the agent in charge of the Sacramento team gave directions. He and the two other field agents were going to lead the way.

"You and I are going to bring up the back," Andy said. He tapped her gun. "Just because you've got this, don't get any ideas. We're only here for support for Megan and Ryan and for the paperwork on Kirov. Once these guys call it clear, then we go in."

"Fine by me."

The field agents dressed themselves in full raid gear with black Kevlar vests and helmets. Mei shivered at the thought of an eight-year-old boy facing whatever it was that prompted eight men to dress like they were going to war. She prayed Ryan still had a chance.

The men continued to huddle and she found herself growing weary of waiting. She wanted them to move. Now.

The men split after another minute and crept across the parking lot as they went in twos to approach from different sides.

Andy stood watching their approach, but Mei couldn't stop pacing. She needed to walk it out, to stretch her legs. She wished she'd had some coffee on the plane. Her stomach was nauseous from exhaustion and adrenaline and it was a sensation she hadn't felt since staying up all night in college. She hated it.

As she turned to pace back toward Andy, she heard a loud pop.

Andy reached for her and together they dropped to the ground. Her pulse was trampling across her ribs. "It came from there," she whispered, pointing into the darkness.

They didn't move, and the only sounds Mei could hear were Andy's breathing in her ear and the gravelly crunch of feet moving steadily closer. Mei studied the darkness until she saw a form take shape. It moved slowly in an unstable shuffle.

"Is it someone wounded?" he asked.

"I don't know. It looks like someone older."

"Kirov?"

Mei hesitated, watching the form catch a foot and fall.

"Oh, dear," a woman's voice said.

Mei started to get up. "It's an old woman, Andy."

"What if there's someone else?"

"Using an old woman as a front?"

"Maybe."

Mei considered the possibility. "Then cover me while I find out."

Andy reached to stop her, but she was already gone. She moved slowly into the darkness toward the woman. "Are you okay?" she called out when she thought she was close.

"Oh, is someone there? It's so dark and I seem to be lost."

Mei found the woman and helped her to her feet. She was wearing house slippers and a sweat suit with a jacket over them. "You must be freezing."

"I don't remember the last time it's ever been this cold in Memphis."

Mei wondered where the woman could possibly have come from. She certainly was a long way from Memphis. "Are you here alone?"

"Oh, no," she said, and Mei could see her bright smile even in the dark. "I'm here with the colonel."

"The colonel?" Mei repeated, wondering if that was a name for Oskar Kirov. But this was an older black woman, and having grown up with prejudices herself, Mei couldn't imagine Oskar Kirov bringing along this woman as a travel companion unless he'd meant to dump her along the way.

"Colonel Walter Turner of the U.S. Marine Corps."

"Does he have a house up here?"

"We certainly do. We've lived in the same spot for more than thirty years. Our baby, Roni, was born in that house. All sorts have come and gone, but we've been there since three years after the house was built. That first couple found something fancier, but not us. We love that house."

Mei looked around and thought there was no way this woman was from around here. Mei had read that this area had been developed over the last twenty years or so, but certainly not thirty. One way or another, the woman was confused.

The woman did not seem at all comfortable on the slippery snow, and so Mei held her arm tightly and took cautious steps. They reached the spot where Andy was waiting. "They've called down. It's clear," he announced.

Mei tightened her grip on the woman. "Megan?"

At that moment, they heard sirens blaring through the quiet dark. One of the agents came running toward them. He was from the Sacramento office, Mei thought, but in her exhaustion, she wasn't certain. And she realized she didn't really care.

Three squad cars came streaming into the lot, their sirens piercing the darkness. Behind each car was a trailer pulling a snowmobile.

The agent looked back at her and Andy. "It's all clear. Four dead, one injured."

Mei let go of the old woman, who immediately slipped.

Andy caught her.

Mei turned back and took her arm again, but she moved closer to the agent at the same time. "Megan Riggs? Is Megan there?"

"No. The dead men are all young—thirty to forty, I'd guess, so I don't think we've got either Ryan Riggs or Oskar Kirov."

"The injured man, who is he?"

"He says his name is Walter Turner. Colonel Walter Turner. He's lost a lot of blood, but he was worried about his wife, Florence. Said she was in a car out here." The agent motioned to the older woman. "Looks like you guys have that under control."

Andy and Mei exchanged glances but neither said a word.

"Does the colonel know where Megan Riggs is?" Andy asked.

The police were out of their cars as the other FBI agents came back. Two of them were carrying Walter

Turner on the bench from a picnic table as though it were a stretcher.

"Oh, thank God, Walter." The woman stepped toward him. "Where on earth have you been?"

Walter took the woman's hand. "Sorry, Florence. Didn't mean to scare you." He looked up at Mei and Andy. "Oskar Kirov had a snowmobile. Cody took off after him."

"Cody?" Wisenor asked.

"The name Megan Riggs has been using," Mei said.

The colonel nodded.

"Any idea where they went?"

The colonel frowned as though he'd caught a wave of pain. "None."

Just then a man came running up. "They're on the other side of the lake. I was trying to get through but the snow's too thick."

Mei looked at him. "Who are you?"

"I'm Travis Landon. It was my son who was supposed to have been kidnapped." He looked over at the colonel, who turned away. "It was a media ploy by a firm some of my investors hired." He frowned. "It wasn't supposed to turn out this way."

"You did know about it!" the colonel yelled.

Landon shook his head. "Not until I finally got through to our director of marketing on my cell phone. When the kidnapper was using my house, I figured someone I knew had something to do with it. I just finished making some calls."

The colonel grunted, but Mei ignored him. She'd obviously missed something earlier on, but she didn't care right now.

"Tell us where Megan and the boy are."

"The lake wraps around," he said, pointing into

the softening light. "They've been gone almost forty minutes or so. If you follow the lake, I think you'll find them. Without a snowmobile, I couldn't keep up." He looked at the colonel. "Plus, I couldn't leave Florence long enough to keep going."

The police and the other Bureau members huddled over three snowmobiles that the police cruisers had towed in.

"How do you want to handle this?" Bernadini asked Andy.

"Those are two-seaters?"

One of the local law nodded.

"Take six, then," Andy determined. "Three who know the area and three of our guys."

"I want to go," Mei said.

The men all started shaking their heads and talking at once.

Mei started to drum up ways to explain it to them.

"Cody doesn't trust anyone," the colonel said above the other voices. "You're not going to be able to help her without a face she knows."

"It's too dangerous," Andy said, but when he met her gaze he shook his head. "Maybe."

"No way," Wisenor said. "You're not letting her go."

"There's only one other snowmobile out there besides Megan's. Even if you don't want to count me, you'll have plenty of manpower with five," Mei said.

"At least we'll have someone who will stop to ask directions," Bernadini cracked.

"I need to be there. No matter what's happened, I'm the closest thing Megan and Ryan have to family right now," Mei said.

"And she's going to need family," the colonel

agreed. "That's the most important thing," he added in a raspy whisper.

The two officers loaded him into the back of a cruiser and one went to help his wife into the car with him.

"You tell her to call me when she and Ryan are home safe," the colonel said. He looked at Travis and added, "And I hope those assholes who did this end up rotting in jail."

Landon nodded. "Me, too, Colonel. Me, too."

Mei looked straight at Andy and watched him concede with a short nod.

"She goes," Andy said. "Bernadini and Wisenor, you go, too." He met her gaze and said softly, "Please be careful."

She was waved to the back of one of the snowmobiles and she pulled on the helmet and gloves she'd borrowed from one of the locals. It was all too big but at least it buffeted off the freezing wind.

The snowmobile lurched forward and Mei was forced to tighten her grip around the middle of the officer in front of her. She wondered how much dare-deviling he would do to try to convince her she should have stayed back.

She blinked hard and told herself she didn't care. She could handle it. And she was going to be there when they got Ryan and Megan back. That was all that mattered.

With Landon's directions, it only took ten minutes to get around the side of the lake on the snowmobiles. About a quarter mile down, they found one abandoned snowmobile. Mei and two others jumped off in search of bodies, but there was nothing.

"I've got blood," one said.

Mei squeezed her eyes shut to keep from crying.

Just then she heard something.

"Move on up?" Bernadini said.

"Shh," she hushed him, straining to hear.

She heard it again.

"Someone's there."

"Hello?" she called.

Several of the men shot her glares for calling out, but the response she got was all she needed.

"Here," a woman's voice called out. "We're down by the water."

Mei didn't bother to get back on the snowmobile. Instead she turned and ran down the frozen bank toward the water's edge. "Bring blankets and supplies. They might need them."

As she cleared the trees, she saw Megan Riggs sitting on the bank. At first she didn't see Ryan, but then she noticed another pair of legs sticking out from Megan's lap.

"It's me, Mei."

Megan Riggs smiled at her and Mei was sure it was genuine. She reached Megan and Ryan and dropped to her knees. "Are you okay?"

Megan was crying and that was all Mei needed for her own tears to start. "We're okay. I think we're going to be okay."

Mei looked around as the other agents arrived, pulling heating blankets and first aid from a pack one carried. "And Kirov?"

Megan's eyes shone. "He's gone, Mei. He's gone forever."

Mei stood back as Megan held her son. Both of them wrapped in blankets, Megan whispered softly to him and he smiled. Mei thought again of Jennifer and wondered if her parents had ever held her the way Megan held Ryan.

Mei thought probably not, but she bet that it might have made all the difference.

Epilogue

Ten Days Later

Cody watched through the living room window as Ryan and Peter Landon and the colonel's grandson, Michael James, ran back and forth across the grass in their small yard, chasing after a bright orange soccer ball. She cupped the hot tea in her hands and pulled the blanket over her legs again. Ryan had managed to bounce back from his time in the freezing lake as only an eight-year-old could. In the meantime, Cody had suffered the worst cold she'd had in a decade.

But they were there. They had survived.

The colonel shifted back in the chair he'd started to claim as his. "You let me drift off again."

She looked over at him, his bandaged leg propped on a pillow. "You need your rest."

From the kitchen, she could hear Roni and Florence talking. They were making sugar cookies in the shapes of footballs for the boys. Roni had come down to take care of Florence while the colonel was in the hospital. He'd been out three days now and she'd made no mention of going home. They had a lot of issues to work through. Roni's marriage had

had its rough spots, but her husband, Doug James, was a good father and husband, and after all these years, they'd worked through the worst stuff.

The colonel supported her fully, he said, and Cody was pretty sure he was dead serious about it. Doug had been down a few times, and he was trying to get to know the colonel and Florence as though courting their daughter for the first time rather than having been married to her. It wasn't easy for any of them, but they were muddling through. That was what family was about, and Cody was happy to watch it.

Cody hoped Roni stayed awhile. It was nice for all of them. And she was taking notes of her own. She'd called her family and told them her story. She'd been on the phone at least four times a day with them since her return. She and Ryan were booked to go to Chicago in a month, and in some ways Cody felt as nervous as poor Doug looked. She still didn't know who had pointed the Russians to New Orleans. Mei Ling had volunteered to head a team to look into it. Cody thought maybe it was Jennifer, maybe someone else. The important thing was that everyone thought she was no longer at risk.

Still, since she and Ryan had returned home, she'd hardly had a day without the colonel, Roni, and Florence spending a few hours at her house. The colonel swore it was because his oven needed repair, but Cody knew they were taking care of her. And she was starting to like it.

Florence seemed to be doing better. The Alzheimer's wasn't improving, of course. The disease didn't work that way, but having her daughter around seemed to make her lucid moments all the more enjoyable.

And the colonel was all but bursting with joy at

having his grandson around. The boy and Ryan had become fast friends, and they'd even had two sleep-overs in less than a week.

"He's quite an athlete," the colonel said.

Cody looked at Michael and smiled. "Must get it from his granddad."

The colonel grinned. "I was thinking he gets it from his mother."

Cody watched Ryan dribbling the ball, as Florence and Roni entered the room with cookies. Roni went to round up the boys for treats, and Florence sat in the chair beside the colonel. Cody envied them each other, but as Ryan bounded into the room and took a cookie in each hand, she knew she had all she needed.

Roni reappeared, wearing a frown.

"What's wrong?" the colonel asked.

"Travis Landon's at the front door. He wants to talk to you," she said to Cody.

"Tell him to get lost," the colonel said.

"Not in front of the children, Walter," Florence whispered.

"It's okay," Cody said. "I'll go." She pushed the blanket aside and set down her mug. As she passed the boys, huddled in front of the television, she leaned down and gave Ryan a kiss on the forehead.

The other kids laughed as Ryan's face grew rosy.

"Aw, Mom," he complained.

"Sorry. You're just going to have to live with the kisses." She passed them and went to the entryway.

Travis Landon stood at the door. He wore a dark gray suit and a navy tie. But despite the attire, he looked disheveled and uncomfortable.

"Peter's fine playing, if he wants to stay for a while."

He nodded and clasped his hands together and stared at them. "Thanks. I appreciate it." He stopped and looked up. "That's not why I'm here, though." He shook his head. "I mean, of course, I'll take Peter home if it's time, but I wanted to talk about everything else."

She paused and then waved him into the dining room, away from the crowd. She knew they'd have to have this discussion, but she wanted it to be quick and then over. She'd heard the confessions of those who were responsible for the ridiculous media plan that had led to Ryan's almost-fatal disappearance. Still, she couldn't help but think somehow Travis had let it happen. He wasn't to blame criminally, of course. He had scapegoats for that. But how could he not have recognized that table? How could he not have had some clue from those first pictures? She just didn't buy it.

She sat in one of the chairs belonging to the modest dining room set she'd bought to fill the room. She and Ryan had eaten in that room only a half dozen times. Sometimes they did on Christmas or Thanksgiving, to make the occasion feel more special, but it never did. Instead the room felt strangely fancy and overly large for just the two of them. Usually they preferred the comfort of the small kitchen table. Thinking what the struggle for TecLan had done to Travis and Peter, she'd keep her cozy kitchen table any day.

Travis sat across from her. "So what now?"

She frowned. "You wanted to talk."

"About what happens from here, what you're going to do."

She shook her head and leaned back in her chair, giving him time to sweat. "I don't know yet." She considered what she would do. She'd thought about the offer the FBI had made, but she wasn't sure she could go back to Chicago without Mark there. There was always the San Francisco office, they'd said. She wasn't sure about that either. She liked it here, for sure. And Ryan had friends. She thought about the colonel and Florence and even Roni. And maybe she had friends, too.

"I hope you know those people are being punished."

"I noticed the company has taken a hit with the news, too."

He watched her face. "Hopefully people will realize it wasn't the company's fault and give us the benefit of the doubt. I assume the media has contacted you as well."

Cody had to smile. Travis was still thinking about how this would affect his company.

"What's so funny?"

She shook her head. "Nothing."

"I think it's fair to ask. I mean, I'd like to prepare myself—" He halted. "And Peter for whatever reaction you will have for them."

She laughed, standing from the table.

He stood, too. "What?"

"Nothing," she said again. "I'm not going to say a thing, Travis. I don't want anything to do with the media, and the police will make a statement on whatever they discover. That's good enough for me."

"But what about the police and the FBI? They've come by the house twice to talk to me. They must have asked you about my involvement."

She shrugged. "They asked, but I told them I honestly don't know if you were involved." She met his gaze. "And I don't. You say you weren't, and I'd like to believe that. I want Ryan and Peter to stay friends."

She thought about that weekend. "I gave the police Oskar Kirov. That was enough for me." Actually, it had taken a water search crew twelve hours to find his body in the lake. But they had him, all the same. The loss of life had been staggering. The three Russians, plus Kirov, and the hired kidnapper. Jennifer Townsend. Dmitri Kirov. Mei had even related the story about Feliks Kirov and his boyfriend. All of them dead.

She shook her head and looked back at Travis, who was watching her. "But one rule from now on . . ."

"What?"

She smiled. "Absolutely no more overnights at your house."

Travis laughed.

And so did she.

With that, she showed him to the door, and he promised to be back for Peter later in the afternoon. As she watched him walk to his car, she genuinely hoped the police found no evidence of his involvement in the kidnapping. She wanted to believe there were good people in the world, and she thought maybe he had potential.

That night after the house had cleared out, she and Ryan had their last root party. They'd had hot dogs for dinner after insisting Roni and the colonel go home for a change. After all the good food they'd been eating, she was amazed at how wonderful hot dogs tasted.

She made root-beer floats, and Ryan found a sack

of hard root-beer candies that had probably been in the cupboard for a year. He put two on top of each of their floats like cherries. They quickly sank to the bottom and Ryan shrugged.

They sat on the bathroom floor and drank their floats as Cody cut two half circles out of the bottoms of plastic bags to act as smocks. She thought about how she used to wrap up all the evidence of their dyeing and take it to a different dump site. This time she'd shove it in her own trash. It was almost surreal not to be running anymore.

Ryan slurped the last of his float and then set down the glass, picking up the box of hair dye and looking at it.

"Is it going to be weird to be blond again?" she asked.

"I think I'm going to like it," he said.

She smiled. "Oh, yeah?"

"I heard blondes have more fun."

Cody choked on her float until she felt it tickle her nose. "Where'd you hear that?"

He shrugged, wearing a shy smile. "Someone at school."

Cody pulled one plastic bag over her head and handed the other to Ryan.

"Can I ask you something, Mom?"

"Of course."

"What's my name going to be?"

"What do you mean?"

"I mean, people are calling me Ryan O'Brien." He scrunched his nose.

"You don't like it?"

"It sounds dumb."

She watched him for a moment, wondering what

was going through his mind. "I guess we should probably use Riggs."

His eyes widened. "Can we?"

She nodded.

"Ryan Riggs," he said as though testing it out.

"You like it?"

He nodded, smiling. A moment later, his smile disappeared and his brow furrowed. "What about you?"

"I'll go by Riggs, too. You want us to have the same name, don't you?"

"Yeah, but what about your first name?"

She pondered. She hadn't thought about her name in a long time. She'd always just taken for granted that it would occasionally change over the rest of her life. "I don't know. What do you think? Megan Riggs?"

"I kind of like Cody."

"Cody Riggs?"

He hesitated and focused before nodding slowly. "I think so."

"Cody Riggs," she repeated.

"Yeah, Cody Riggs."

She shrugged her shoulders. "Okay. Cody Riggs, it is." She picked up her root-beer float and took a long draw on the straw.

Ryan rolled onto his back and giggled.

She reached out and tickled him. "What on earth is so funny?"

"I'll bet I'm the first kid who ever got to name his mom."

She winked. "I'll bet that's true."

Ryan leaned back, clearly impressed with himself. He pulled the plastic bag over his head as Cody snapped on the plastic gloves that came with the kit. "That's so cool. Wait until I tell the kids at school."

And for the first time, she thought how nice it must be for him to be *able* to tell.

How nice it would be for them both.